A COLORADO HIGH COUNTRY NOVEL

PAMELA
CLARE

Holding On
A Colorado High Country Novel

Published by Pamela Clare, 2018
Cover Design by © Carrie Divine/Seductive Designs
Image: Petr Joura/Depositphotos

Copyright © 2018 by Pamela Clare

ISBN-10: 0-9987491-8-4

ISBN-13: 978-0-9987491-8-1

This book is dedicated to the all of hard-working dogs—search-and-rescue dogs, service dogs, military dogs, law-enforcement dogs—who save lives and make life better for all of us. It's also dedicated to the wonderful people who train them.

Acknlowledgements

This book would not have been possible without the insights and support of Cathy Bryarly, whose work training SAR and HRD dogs has saved lives. She is a hero.

Many thanks to Michelle White, Benjamin Alexander, Jackie Turner, Shell Ryan, and Pat Egan Fordyce for holding my hand and encouraging me. For me, every book feels like Mt. Everest.

Thanks, too, to my father, Robert White, for answering questions and instilling in me at an early age a love of the outdoors and the mountains. Additional thanks to my brother, Robert White Jr., for his insights into big-peak climbing. He has touched the sky.

Last but not least, a big thank you to my loyal readers. You make it all worthwhile.

Prologue

Fifteen months ago
Mt. Everest
6:10 a.m.

HARRISON CONRAD TOOK A BELAY STANCE, watching while Felix and Luka Stenger, twin brothers from Switzerland, made their way across the ladder spanning the crevasse. One at a time, they stepped out over a seemingly bottomless fissure in the ice, their crampons making their steps on the ladder's rungs awkward.

Felix went first, showing no hesitation, and Luka followed, pausing for just a moment before he took his first step.

"Don't worry, mate!" Bruce called from the other side near the base of a massive serac, a grin on his face. "If you fall and your harness fails, it will only kill you."

"Nice." Conrad grinned, feeding Luka more slack.

He kept both hands on the rope, even though the stubble on his jaw itched from the barley flour that had been thrown at them during the Puja—the prayer cere-

1

mony—at Base Camp. He wasn't religious, Buddhist or otherwise, but given the dangers of this mountain, he didn't object to a bit of intercession on their behalf.

They'd hit the ice at 4 a.m. It was a perfect day on Everest, the sunrise in their eyes as they headed east up Khumbu Icefall, Everest and Lhotse before them. Today was their second day on the mountain. Yesterday, they'd gone up the Icefall to Camp One then come back down to sleep at Base Camp to give their bodies time to acclimate to the extreme altitude. Tonight, they would sleep at Camp One.

It was Conrad's third time climbing Everest. He and Bruce had climbed the Seven Summits—the highest mountains on the seven continents. They'd also climbed the rest of the 8000-meter peaks, including K2, Annapurna, Nanga Parbat, and Makalu. But it was Felix and Luka's first time up an 8,000-meter peak. The brothers had made a name for themselves climbing all over Europe, in North America, and in the Andes. Anyone who could climb the Eiger in winter without ropes could handle Everest.

Luka made it to the other side, stepped off the ladder, then turned to belay Conrad over the abyss.

Conrad waited for Luka to take up the slack, finally scratching his jaw.

"On belay!" Luka called.

"Climbing!" Conrad stepped out onto the ladder. It was actually two ladders lashed together, their ends overlapping in the middle. Beneath their rungs lay nothing but air, the void disappearing into a monotone blue of glacial ice. He took one step and another and another, enjoying the buzz of adrenaline.

A groan. A cracking sound.

The ground shook, pitching him to his knees, the ladder rocking beneath him.

He heard the others cry out and looked up to see the serac falling, tons of ice collapsing onto Bruce and the others.

"Fuck!"

It couldn't end like this.

Something struck Conrad's helmet, and he fell, the world around him going black.

Scarlet Springs, Colorado
Just after 7 p.m.

KENZIE MORGAN KNELT down beside Gizmo, stroked the golden retriever's silky chest to focus him, then unclipped him from his lead. "Okay, Gizmo. Search!"

Gizmo took off at a run, slowing to sniff some fallen timbers then moving on, his powerful canine nose leading him across the site of Scarlet Springs' old landfill. The place had become an illegal dumpsite, but that made it a perfect location to test the skill of search-and-rescue dogs. Gizmo had forty-five minutes to find the hidden human remains to stay certified in HRD—human remains detection.

Kenzie followed after him, hustling to keep up. She knew that he was more than equal to the task. He was five years old now and had been working as an HRD and SAR dog for four years.

"Wouldn't it be funny if he found an actual dead body?" JoAnne hurried alongside Kenzie, a clipboard in her left hand.

"Yeah, that would be hilarious." Kenzie watched

3

Gizmo, who skirted around a rusted box spring and headed toward a pile of discarded lumber.

A mountain cottontail darted out of the pile, catching Gizmo's attention.

"Leave it!" Kenzie called.

The dog stopped to watch but didn't give chase.

Good boy.

"Back to work!" Kenzie called.

Gizmo let the rabbit go, dismissing the lumber and heading toward a jumbled pile of broken concrete blocks. He stopped, pawed at the rock, climbed to the top of the mound, then ran down again, circling to the other side. He pawed, sniffed—and sat.

Kenzie glanced at her watch. "That didn't even take him five minutes."

She hurried over to him, drew a bag of doggy sausages out of her pocket, and fed him a few pieces, petting and praising him. "Good boy! Good boy! You found it."

The "it" in this case was a bit of donated cadaver—a section of humerus with decomposing muscle, adipose tissue, and skin still attached. Kenzie kept it in a steel container in the freezer in her garage, taking it out early enough so that it could thaw and release its god-awful stench for the dogs. Fortunately, she wasn't a dog. Unless she was right on top of it, she couldn't smell it at all.

JoAnne knelt down beside Gizmo, her gray hair fluttering in the warm evening breeze. "Good job, Gizmo. I guess you passed HRD—again."

"You hear that, buddy?" Kenzie pulled Gizmo's favorite toy out of her pocket and played tug-of-war with him for a minute before letting him have it. "Who's up next?"

Back down at the road, several other handlers waited beside covered pickups and SUVs, dogs crated inside, each waiting its turn to be tested. Most had driven long distances from homes across Colorado to be here today. It wasn't a bad day to hang out in the mountains. The sky was cloudless, the sunshine warm, the breeze fresh.

JoAnne was busy filling out Gizmo's certificate. "Cathy's here with Sam. She has to get to the airport to pick up her brother, but she wants Sam to have a shot."

Sam was a young bloodhound, barely a year old. Today would be good practice for both Cathy and Sam. A handler had to relearn search-and-rescue with each dog, as each dog's body language was different. That had been true for Kenzie when she'd started training Gizmo, and she was a professional dog trainer.

JoAnne handed her the certificate. "Are you going to stay, or do you have to get back to the kennel?"

Kenzie glanced at her watch. "I might hang around to see how Sam does."

Kenzie wasn't in any particular hurry. It was Friday, so she didn't have any classes to teach this evening. She trusted her staff to close up her pet supply store and manage the kennel while she was out.

She bent down, clipped the leash to Gizmo's collar, and was about to take him back to her truck to give him water and crate him when her Team buzzer went off.

Kenzie had been a primary member of the all-volunteer Rocky Mountain Search and Rescue Team, called the Team by locals, for five years now. She wasn't a climber like most of its members, but provided canine help.

She drew the pager out of her pocket, glanced at the message—and the breath left her lungs.

DISASTER ON EVEREST. LISTENING IN TO BASE CAMP.

Harrison.

Gizmo whined, always sensitive to her mood.

"Uh-oh." JoAnne looked up from her clipboard. "Something happened."

"I have to go." Kenzie jammed the pager back into the pocket of her jeans and ran toward her truck, heart thrumming, Gizmo bounding along beside her.

"What do you want me to do with the human remains?" JoAnne shouted after her.

"Stick them in your freezer!" Kenzie was barely aware of what she was saying. "I'll pick them up later!"

Had Conrad's team been hit by a blizzard? Had someone fallen?

Please don't let it be Harrison! Not Harrison.

Harrison Conrad was a world-renowned climber and the Team's lead alpinist. More than that, he was a good friend. He'd left Colorado a couple of months ago, hoping to summit Everest again with his Aussie friend Bruce Jones and those Swiss climbing twins. Kenzie couldn't understand what drove him to risk his life like this, and she'd told him as much. He had already climbed Everest twice. Why take his chances with the mountain again?

He'd grinned, his tanned face so damned handsome. "I promise I'll come back in one piece."

He'd better not have broken that promise, or she would kill him.

Damn it, Harrison!

A sick feeling in her stomach, she fumbled with her keys as she unlocked the topper, dropped the tailgate, and opened Gizmo's crate. "Hop up. Time to go."

Gizmo jumped up, stepped into the crate, and plopped down, tongue lolling. She would have to give him water at The Cave—Team headquarters.

She shut the crate, the tailgate, and the topper, then

ran around to the front of her truck and climbed into the driver's seat. The drive down to Scarlet Springs took only ten minutes, but it seemed like an eternity. She parked outside The Cave's big bay doors, opened the topper to give Gizmo air, then hurried inside, dread like lead in her stomach.

She hurried through the bay doors, past Rescue 1 and Rescue 2—the Team's big SAR vehicles—and walked through the entrance to the Ops Room.

Most of the Team was already there, gathered near the table that held the radios and computer. Eric Hawke stood in his turnout pants and a navy-blue T-shirt next to Austin Taylor, who wore his hunter-green park ranger uniform. Chaska was there, too, with his younger sister, Winona, a wildlife vet. Sasha Dillon, the Team's other celebrity climber, sat beside Megs Hill, the Team's co-founder and director, and her partner, Mitch Ahearn. Jesse Moretti and Creed Herrera stood toward the rear, tatted arms crossed over their chests. Gabe Rossiter, whom Kenzie hadn't seen in ages, stood off to one side with Malachi O'Brien, who was still dressed in scrubs from his shift in the ER.

The grave expressions on their faces told her that something terrible had happened.

She hugged her arms around herself and went to stand beside Hawke, who met her gaze and shook his head.

God! What did that mean?

"What happened?" Kenzie whispered.

"A serac collapsed on Conrad's team on the Khumbu Icefall. Someone who was watching through binoculars from Base Camp witnessed it. He says it buried them all."

Kenzie's knees gave. She sank into a chair, her throat tight. "No."

Harrison couldn't be gone. He couldn't be.

Even as her heart told her this was impossible, she knew no one could survive being buried under tons of ice.

Hawke rested a reassuring hand on her shoulder but said no more.

A burst of static came from the computer, its browser open to one of the adventure climbing sites that monitored Everest expeditions every spring. Then came the sound of a woman's voice.

"They're starting up the Icefall now."

Megs glanced over her shoulder at the rest of them. "It's going to take the rescue team a few hours to reach the site."

"A few *hours*?" The words were out before Kenzie realized she'd spoken.

"The Icefall is a death trap," Gabe explained. "They have to be careful."

"Right. Okay." Kenzie knew that.

The Khumbu Icefall was where climbers began their ascent of Mt. Everest. An enormous, near-vertical river of ice, the glacier was prone to avalanches. It also had deep crevasses and towering walls of unstable ice, called seracs, that could collapse without warning.

Please, not Harrison.

Images played through her mind. Harrison carrying a lost little boy on his shoulders after Gizmo had found the child. Harrison teasing Kenzie about her thirtieth birthday. Harrison flying up the climbing wall at Knockers, the town's brewpub and social hub. Harrison washing mud off Rescue 1 wearing nothing but shorts, his body all lean muscle.

He couldn't just be … *gone.*

The minutes ticked by with agonizing slowness, the woman who was operating the radio at Base Camp giving them periodic updates. Other Team members drifted through the door, sitting or standing in silence. Isaac Rogers. Dave Hatfield. Nicole Turner. Bahir Acharya, the new guy.

Kenzie couldn't just sit here. She went out to her truck, leashed Gizmo, and brought him inside. She filled his water bowl in the kitchen and brought it to her seat beside Hawke. Gizmo drank thirstily before curling up at her feet to nap.

A burst of static.

A woman's voice came through the computer's speakers, her message breaking up. "I'm getting a report … popped up out of nowhere … Looks like … Waiting to get confirm…"

Kenzie's pulse skipped, everyone in the room seeming to hold their breath.

"Still waiting for confirmation," the woman's voice said.

Another burst of static.

This time the excitement in the woman's voice was unmistakable. "… Conrad… It's definitely him… must've fallen into the crevasse or something … He's alive!"

The Ops Room exploded in cheers.

Boneless with relief, Kenzie found herself blinking back tears.

Chapter 1

Tengboche, Nepal
August 26

HARRISON CONRAD SAT in the lotus position in the back corner of the Dokhang—the prayer hall—at the Tengboche Monastery, his eyes closed, his back pressed against the wooden planks of the wall.

"Om muni muni maha muni shakyamuni soha."

He chanted along with the monks, focusing his awareness on the words and music. The monks' deep voices filled the space around him, drums, cymbals, and horns punctuating the chant. The spice of incense mingled with the warm scent of butter lamps and the musky odor of so many human bodies together.

The last of the season's tourists were there, too, watching, sneaking illegal videos with cellphones, coughing from the altitude, but Conrad had forgotten about them. Everything around him was light. It penetrated him, raised him up, driving out the darkness that lived inside him.

"*Om muni muni maha muni shakyamuni soha. Om muni muni maha muni shakyamuni soha.*"

Om, wise one, wise one, greatly wise one, wise one of the Shakyans, Hail!

Time lost all meaning, the mantra spinning itself over and over again, weaving through Conrad's consciousness until his mind was blank, the emptiness bringing with it a sense of peace. No pain. No regret. No guilt.

Then it was over.

The monks shuffled out, but Conrad stayed as he was, sitting, waiting for the tourists to leave, his eyes closed. Any trekker or climber who came to this region likely knew who he was. Some would stare. Others would try to get his autograph. Some would ask questions, and those questions would bring the darkness rushing back.

He willed himself to focus on the feeling of emptiness, trying not to hear the shuffling and whispering around him.

"Is that Harrison Conrad?"

"Yeah, man."

A hand touched his shoulder. "Hey, dude, can I get an autogra—"

A familiar voice silenced the first. "If he wanted to hand out autographs, he wouldn't be meditating, would he? Let him be."

Megs.

Conrad's eyes flew open. What the hell was she doing here?

"You're Megs Hill!" said a guy in a Peruvian ski hat.

"You win the prize. Want me to sign that?" Megs took a notebook and a pen from him and scribbled her signature across the page. "Okay. Show's over. It's time to go. This is a prayer hall, not a party."

Megs walked over to Conrad, waiting until they were

alone to speak. "It's time to knock this shit off and come home. Do you think you're the only climber who's ever lost a partner?"

Conrad's temper surged, but the exhaustion on Megs' face broke his fury. He knew only too well that she had lost friends, too. "What are you doing here?"

Tengboche was high in the Himalayas on the route to Everest Base Camp, but it was the end of August now. Climbing season was long over.

"I came to bring you home."

Conrad got to his feet, staring down at her, too astonished at first to say anything. Getting here from Kathmandu involved a flight to Lukla, followed by a tough hike of a few days over gorges and mountain terrain. "You wasted a lot of time and money. I'm not going back."

"So, you're converting to Buddhism and plan to spend the rest of your life drinking yak butter tea, chanting mantras, and enjoying celibacy."

When she put it like that…

"No." He ran a hand through his hair, suddenly self-conscious about the fact that it now reached his shoulders. And his beard … Well, he hadn't shaved or gotten a haircut in more than a year. "I just need some time."

"It's been *fifteen* months."

"Did my agent put you up to this?" His agent had been contacting the monastery almost weekly for most of a year now, probably worried that her gravy train would dry up if Conrad didn't do something to appease his sponsors soon.

"Do you think I'd come all this way for your agent's sake?"

Conrad thought about that for a half second. "Probably not."

Conrad walked out of the Dokhang and down the

empty hallway, Megs keeping up with him as he made his way to the front entrance of the main building.

"Rain just had a baby girl with Joe," she said, as if they'd been talking about Scarlet Springs all this time.

"Wow." Everyone knew that Rain and Joe had a thing for each other—except for the two of them. It seemed they had finally figured that out. "They had a baby?"

"They got married at Knockers last Christmas. You should have seen Rain's gown. Rumor is it cost a fortune."

Conrad had all but forgotten about Knockers. Scarlet Springs felt so far away—like part of another time, another life.

Megs went on. "Vicki had her baby the day I landed in Kathmandu."

"Wow. Hawke's a father? How did that happen?"

"A lot of unprotected sex. That's my guess."

Megs had always been a smartass.

Hearing his friends' names brought their faces to Conrad's mind, an unexpected pang seizing his chest. He missed them.

Joe. Rain. Hawke. Victoria. The rest of the Team.

"The town is in the middle of a baby boom. We had a blizzard that dumped seven feet last December. I don't think I've ever seen more pregnant bellies at Food Mart than I have this past summer."

"Wow," he said for the third time.

Clearly, it had been a while since he'd had a real conversation with another human being. His vocabulary had shrunk.

"Kenzie is still single." Megs let that hang in the air.

"Huh." He tried to sound indifferent to this news, even as an image of Kenzie with her long dark hair, big blue eyes, and sweet smile lodged itself in his mind.

If there had ever been a woman who tempted him to settle down …

Kenzie was everything a man could want, but Conrad's father had taught him not to shit where he ate. He hadn't asked her out because she was on the Team, too, and he didn't want to risk a professional association for sex. Besides, Megs frowned on casual hookups between Team members. It wasn't against the rules exactly, but no one wanted to get on Megs' bad side.

More than that, Kenzie wasn't into his crazy lifestyle. If Conrad had learned anything growing up, it was that two people had to want the same things in life to make a relationship work, and Kenzie didn't climb.

Neither do you. Not anymore.

"Does she still have Gizmo?"

"Of course."

Conrad opened the heavy, wooden door for Megs, following her outside and down the steep front steps. Prayer flags in red, yellow, blue, green, and white snapped in a chilly wind, storm clouds obscuring the views of Everest and Ama Dablam, the air sharp with the promise of rain.

"Is Ahearn here?"

Legends of the climbing world, Megs and her husband did most things together. They had met in Yosemite in the Seventies and then come to Colorado to tackle its fourteen-ers. They'd started the Team after a friend of theirs had died of hypothermia waiting for a rescue.

"Mitch is holding down the fort in Scarlet."

"You came all this way by yourself?"

"Hell, no." Megs looked up at him as if he were nuts. "I hired a nice man with a couple of yaks. I brought a bunch of ghee for the monastery—a thank you to the Lama for hosting you."

That stopped Conrad in his tracks. "Why are you doing this?"

This trip, the Sherpa and yaks, the ghee, the permits— it must have cost her close to ten grand.

"You're one of mine. I can't just leave you here."

Her words washed over him, made his throat go tight. He drew her into a hug, her head barely reaching his chest. "It's good to see you, Megs."

She hugged him back. "That's what you say now."

———

CONRAD HAD dinner with Megs at her lodge. Most nights he cooked for himself on his camp stove, so this felt like a luxury. Tonight, the lodge's dining room— which consisted of three rough-hewn communal tables and a wood stove—was all but empty. A row of windows looked out toward the obscured mountains, fat raindrops pelting dirty glass, the fire barely enough to warm the space.

"What have you been doing—besides meditating and growing facial hair?" Megs took a sip of her black tea, still wearing her down parka and woolen hat.

Conrad stirred his *thukpa*—a thick noodle soup of chicken broth and vegetables flavored with turmeric and cumin—waiting for it to cool. "I've done a lot of handyman work for the monks, repairing buildings and walkways. I helped them erect a new stupa for a shrine up the trail."

"You put your homesteading skills to work."

Conrad had grown up in Alaska with parents who lived off the land—until his mother had given birth to a still-born baby and gotten sick of roughing it. She'd taken him to Anchorage, where they'd lived in a little apartment.

He'd only seen his father and the homestead during the summer after that. "I didn't want to be a burden."

Their host arrived at the table, setting down two mugs of *tongba*, a hot millet beer drunk through a straw, and a basket of *momos*—steamed dumplings with vegetables. He gave them a broad smile and a polite bow.

Conrad thanked him in the Sherpa tongue. "*Thuche.*"

For a while, neither he nor Megs spoke, the two of them eating in companionable silence. That was one thing Conrad liked about Megs. She didn't do small talk.

"What happened up there, Conrad?"

Then again, small talk wasn't all bad.

Some part of Conrad wanted to ignore her question. He hadn't spoken about that day with anyone other than the monks since leaving Base Camp and then only vaguely. Besides, Megs had surely read the story in a climbing magazine or online somewhere. But Megs was a good friend, a fellow climber, and she'd come a long way for his sake.

Unable to meet her gaze, he looked out the window. "Bruce wanted to lead. Luka and Felix were in the middle. I brought up the rear."

"That makes sense. This was Luka and Felix's first attempt at an eight-thousand-meter peak, wasn't it?"

Conrad nodded, doing his best not to feel. "I was crossing a ladder over a new crevasse that had opened up that season. There was a crack and a rumble. Before any of us could react, the serac collapsed, crushing the others and knocking me off the ladder. I must have been hit by a chunk of ice because I was unconscious for a time."

"Jesus."

"I opened my eyes to find myself dangling upside down over the crevasse, still roped to the others. The ladder was gone. It took me forever to climb the ice to get out. Other than my rope, which trailed away beneath the ice, there was no sign anyone had ever been there. I tried to follow the rope to dig them out, but my ice tools weren't enough. Then the rescue team came."

If Megs had tried to comfort him or showed him sympathy, Conrad might have broken, but she kept it technical. "Thank God your harness held."

"Yeah." His life would have been shorter—and a lot simpler—if it hadn't, but he couldn't think about that. Not now. "What else is going on?"

"The Team helped rescue a woman who'd been attacked by a couple of escaped cons. Remember Winona's wolf, Shota? He found her. Chaska married her."

Conrad stared open-mouthed. "Belcourt is married now, too?"

"That's what I said." Megs sipped her *tongba* through the straw. "Naomi, his wife, is Lakota, too. She's an artist. She opened a gift store on Main Street. It's a nice place— lots of beautiful things. She and Chaska are starting a summer camp for kids from the reservation. They'll bring them to Scarlet for a couple of weeks, read Lakota stories and history for literacy, and do outdoor adventure stuff to boost their confidence. A lot of the Team wants to be involved."

"Huh." Chaska had never seemed like the paternal type to Conrad, but what the hell did he know? "What did Rain and Joe name their baby?"

This was going to be good.

"Angel."

All things considered, that was a disappointingly ordinary name for Rain. After all, she'd named her first daughter, who was now in her early twenties, Lark.

"How about Hawke and Vicki's son?"

"They named him Caden after an ancestor of Eric's

who was murdered by Joe's great-great-great-grandfather, Silas Moffat."

"I never heard that story."

"Neither had most of us. Moffat Street was named in honor of Silas, remember? Right before I left, the Town Council voted to rename it in honor of Joe instead."

"Moffat Street became … Moffat Street?" Conrad couldn't help but laugh.

Only in Scarlet.

Megs shared other news with him, mostly about the Team, telling him about some of the high-profile rescues they'd done over the past year. "We've had a good year for fundraising, but I need my lead alpinist."

He'd known she'd get back to this sooner rather than later. "I'm done with climbing. Even if I come back, I'm off the Team."

"Fine. Leave the Team if you want. Just quit hiding and come home."

His anger flashed hot. "I'm *not* hiding."

"Right. You're just hanging out in one of the most inaccessible places on the planet for the fun of it."

Conrad drew a deep breath, unwilling to shatter the small amount of peace he'd found by yelling at someone he respected. "I don't want to deal with the media shit storm. I don't want reporters ambushing me and asking for details. I don't want every person I meet to ask me what happened like you just did."

"People are going to ask questions. Ignore them. As for the media, no one but Mitch knows I'm here. There won't be any media—not when we arrive, at any rate. Of course, someone could always mistake you for the Yeti and call the tabloids."

Conrad glared at her, rubbed his beard. "I'm not *that* hairy."

Megs arched an eyebrow in challenge, then let it go. "There are people in Scarlet who love you, Conrad—or who at least miss you."

For some reason, Kenzie popped into his mind again. "I'll think about it."

"Think fast. We leave the day after tomorrow."

CONRAD SAT in the small room he rented from the monks, a row of butter lamps flickering against the saffron-colored walls. He'd tried meditating, but he couldn't let go. A part of him wanted to go home, to return to his old life, to see Hawke and Taylor and Kenzie and the other Team members, but it would never be the same.

Bruce had been his best climbing buddy, the man who'd tackled the Seven Summits with him, who'd fought his way up K2 beside him, who'd climbed Ama Dablam with him for the hell of it after their last Everest expedition. He was gone, leaving his wife and two sons without a husband and father.

God, how Conrad missed him.

Luka and Felix had been in their late twenties—so young to die. Their mother and father had lost both sons in an instant. Conrad had called them from Base Camp to give them the news along with his condolences, their mother's cries shattering what had been left of Conrad's heart. He had promised to watch over them.

What an idiot he'd been to make that promise! On Everest, a man had enough to contend with trying to keep himself alive.

Conrad would never make that mistake again. He would never be responsible for any life but his own. He was done with climbing.

If he went back, he would have to deal with his agent and his sponsors, who would drop him soon if he didn't climb again. He would have to get a job doing … *something*. Without a degree, he had no idea what that would be.

He would also have to contend with the media. Once they found out he was back, they would stalk him, at least for a while.

A knock came at his door.

He opened it to find himself staring into the smiling face of the Nawang Tenzing Gulu, the Incarnate Lama of Tengboche, who stood together with a few of the monks.

Conrad stepped back to allow the men to enter, then pressed his palms together in front of his forehead and bowed deeply.

Tenzing sat in the only chair in the room, motioning to the bed. "Please sit."

Conrad sat cross-legged, careful not to point the soles of his feet at these venerated men—a sign of disrespect. The Lama had never visited him in his room before, though he had spoken to him elsewhere in the monastery and shared tea and meals with him a few times.

A monk entered with tea and served a cup first to the Lama and then to Conrad.

"You have a guest," the Lama said at last.

"Yes. Megs Hill. She's a good friend."

"She said she has come to take you home. I came to talk with you about this, to see where your heart lies."

"I don't know how I feel." Even if Conrad had wanted to, he couldn't have lied to this man. Besides, the old monk would probably see right through him. He carried the unmistakable energy of one who had devoted his life to enlightenment. "It is probably time for me to return home, but…"

The old man watched him patiently, waiting for him to finish.

"I don't know how to face the world again."

The Lama gave a slow nod, nothing but compassion on his weathered face. "You still blame yourself."

"I know in my rational mind that there was nothing I could have done to save them, but some part of me can't accept that I'm here … and that they are all gone. Survival guilt, I guess."

The Lama sipped his tea, expectant silence filling the small room.

"Such tragedies are difficult to understand," he said at last. "It is no wonder that your mind is troubled. But consider this: If you did not bring about their deaths, why should you feel guilty to be alive? Is your survival not a gift, a cause for gratitude?"

"Yes." Conrad gave the Lama the expected answer— but he didn't *feel* it.

The Lama smiled, not fooled in the least. "We have been happy to have you as our guest. We are grateful for your help with our repairs and especially the new stupa. You are always welcome here. But I fear the answers you seek cannot be found within these walls. If your truth were here, you would already have found it."

They talked of other things after that, finishing their tea in amicable conversation, but the Lama had delivered his message.

It was time for Conrad to leave Tengboche.

⊏⊐

CONRAD SPENT the next day fixing a leaky roof for the monks, buying what supplies he and Megs would need, and packing his things together. He also borrowed a razor from the monks and shaved off his beard.

"Oh, thank God," Megs said when she saw him. Then her gaze landed on his expedition backpack. "That's all you've got?"

"I left most of my gear at Base Camp." He'd taken only what had fit in this backpack, leaving thousands of dollars of junk behind.

"Someone at Base Camp must have thought they'd won the lottery. Harrison Conrad's gear for the taking."

Conrad couldn't care less.

They had dinner at the lodge again, and Conrad spent his last night at the monastery in the little room that had been his refuge these past months, joining the monks in the Dokhang for two hours of prayer and meditation. Even so, he found it hard to sleep, worries rolling through his mind like pounding surf.

What the hell was he going to do with his life now?

He gave up trying to sleep at 4 a.m. and joined the monks again for morning prayers and meditation, then walked through the rain to Megs' lodge for breakfast.

"Did you have to come for me in monsoon season?" He wiped the rain out of his eyes.

She grinned. "Poor baby. How will you cope?"

After breakfast, they worked with Tenzing Dorje Sherpa to load supplies onto the yaks. Most of it was firewood the Sherpa was bringing back to his family, but the yaks were also able to bear their backpacks.

"This is going to be a walk in the park." Conrad was used to carrying sixty to eighty pounds on his back.

Then it was time to leave.

"I want to say goodbye."

Megs nodded. "We'll meet you in the camping area."

He started toward the monastery building, stopping when he rounded the corner.

There on the front steps stood the Lama and all sixty monks with umbrellas.

Conrad drew a breath, fighting to control his emotions, and walked to the base of the stairs. "I came to say thank you—and goodbye."

The monk who'd served the tea last night stepped out, white scarf in his hand. He offered it to Conrad, then stepped back.

Conrad presented the scarf to the Lama, bowing low.

The Lama took the scarf and draped it around his neck. "Have a safe journey, Harrison Conrad. May you find peace."

Conrad stood upright again. "Thank you—for everything."

The Lama gave him a gentle smile, then turned and walked back up the stairs.

Conrad watched while the monks retreated to the shelter of the monastery, then joined Megs, who stood nearby.

"For a moment, I thought I might get a tear in my eye." Megs watched him. "Ready to go?"

Conrad turned to look at Everest, emotions tangling in his chest. Sixteen months ago, he'd passed through Tengboche with Bruce, Luka, and Felix. The summit of Everest had been hidden then, too, crowned in clouds. The two younger men hadn't been able to talk about anything but the mountain. Now it was their tomb—and Bruce's, too.

Conrad was going home alone.

Nearby, one of the yaks grunted.

No, not alone.

He turned his back to the mountain. "Let's go."

Chapter 2

Scarlet Springs, Colorado
September 6

KENZIE MORGAN HURRIED through the dairy section of Food Mart, trying to remember what she'd written on her shopping list. Naturally, she'd left the list at home on her table where it would do her no good. This was her second trip to the store in as many days because she'd forgotten the list yesterday, too.

Eggs and toothpaste.

What else had she forgotten?

Mustard. Salt! God, yes, salt.

She made her way through the aisles, tossing things into her shopping cart, aware that she needed to get home. Gabby, her eight-week-old golden retriever puppy, was at home in her crate and would need to go potty soon.

Kenzie had gotten the puppy just yesterday from the same breeder who'd sold her Gizmo. This breeder was the only one in Colorado who bred dogs specifically with SAR skills in mind, selecting dogs for their health, curiosity, and fearlessness. Though Gizmo probably had a few good working years left, it usually took a couple of years to get a dog fully trained and certified. Kenzie was doing her best to be prepared so there wouldn't be any break in the availability of an SAR dog here in Scarlet.

That's what she told herself.

The truth was that she'd gotten one look at little Gabby, with her fluffy, cream-colored fur and big brown eyes, and hadn't been able to walk away without her.

If only puppies weren't so damned cute.

She set a box of salt in her cart, added a bag of chocolate chips for eating in front of the TV, then rounded the aisle, nearly running into someone. "Oh, sorry."

She glanced up—and froze, her pulse tripping. "*Harrison?*"

Without thinking, she left her cart and jumped up to wrap her arms around him. "Oh, my God! It's *so* good to see you!"

He hugged her back. "It's good to see you, too."

She stepped away, embarrassed, and took a good look at him. His brown hair now hung down to his shoulders and had a little wave to it. But he had the same ridiculously handsome face—square jaw, firm mouth, proud nose, dark brows, gorgeous gray eyes. But something was different, something in his eyes …

She cleared her throat. "When did you get back?"

"Yesterday."

"You must be jet lagged. That's a long trip."

He nodded. "Yeah. I'll be turned around for a while."

"I've been really worried about you."

"You have?"

Was he surprised?

"Of course. We all have. We were all there in the Ops Room listening when it happened. I don't think I've ever been more afraid for anyone in my life." The tension on his face told Kenzie not to say more—or to ask questions about that terrible day. "Where are you staying?"

"Remember the old English teacher?"

"Mrs. Beech? Yes. She passed on in January."

"Her son is trying to sell her old place. I'm renting it while I sort things out."

"Oh. Good. You're here in town, then?"

"For now." He changed the subject. "How's Gizmo?"

"He's great. He's still healthy and working. You should stop by and see him sometime. I'm sure he'll remember you." When Harrison gave no sign that the idea appealed to him, she added, "You'll run into us at The Cave sooner or later."

He shook his head. "I left the Team. I'm done climbing."

That news made her stare. "Truly?"

"Yeah. I'm looking for a job. If you hear of something…"

She started to object, to remind him that he lived to climb, but stopped herself. The tragedy on Everest had changed him.

Of course, it had. How could it not?

She didn't want to hurt him by saying something stupid. "Well, the invitation to stop by the house or the kennel is open-ended. I'm so glad you're home."

He smiled, but it wasn't the megawatt smile she remembered, the smile that had left her weak in the knees. "It's good to see you, too, Kenzie."

Then he walked away, leaving Kenzie to stare after him.

CONRAD DROVE home from Food Mart, groceries in the back seat. He'd picked up his 4Runner from Megs and Ahearn's place yesterday when they'd gotten back to Scarlet. It felt strange to be behind the wheel again. He parked in the garage, carried his groceries inside, and put them away, sticking dry goods in cupboards and perishable items in the mint-green 1950s fridge.

Mrs. Beech clearly hadn't wasted a dime modernizing. Her son had left most of her furniture in place. An old red Formica table with chrome accents and matching red-and-white vinyl chairs. A big console TV that still worked but couldn't handle broadband. An end table with a built-in lamp. A mint-green stove that matched the fridge.

This shit was probably worth a fortune to someone.

Conrad folded the paper bags and tucked them between the fridge and the counter to use again on his next trip to the store. Then he made himself a sandwich for lunch, and sat at the table to eat, trying not to think about her—and failing.

Kenzie looked just like he'd remembered her—lush in the right places, her blue eyes bright, her face beautiful. His heart had given a hard knock the moment he'd seen her, and he'd been hit by an overpowering jolt of lust, probably setting a world record for going hard.

How long has it been since you've gotten laid, man?

He hadn't hooked up with anyone in Nepal, and he hadn't been in a relationship before he'd left. That meant it had been almost … *two years?*

What the *hell?*

The realization left him stunned—and a little depressed. Then again, he'd spent most of those two years in a monastery.

He finished his sandwich, put the plate in the kitchen sink next to his cereal bowl, and stretched out on the sofa.

Well, here he was, back in Scarlet.

He stared at the ceiling. What the hell was he supposed to do now?

He needed to call his agent. That wouldn't be fun.

He should get his stuff out of storage. He had packed it away in the attic at The Cave. Going to get it would mean running into his fellow Team members, and he wasn't sure he was ready for that.

He also needed to look for a place to live long term. Before that, he had to find out how much he still had in the bank—he'd had almost two million in assets when he'd headed off to Nepal—and start applying for jobs.

Did he need to make a resume, too? *Shit.* What would that say?

Profession: Climber.

Education: School of Hard Knocks.

Career goals: Just a paycheck, thanks.

Yeah, he could see that going well.

His mind drifted back to Kenzie. She had invited him to stop by her house or the kennel. It was the only idea that held any appeal. He'd be able to see her again and Gizmo, too.

I've been really worried about you.

He'd been able to see in her eyes that she'd meant what she'd said, and it touched him to know she cared about him. Now that he wasn't on the Team, that barrier between them was gone. But it didn't change the fact that the two of them had little in common. She had a college education, a couple of successful businesses, and a life here in Scarlet. Conrad was unemployed with a high school diploma, a climbing resume, a good chunk of money in savings—but no idea what to do with his future.

Outside of the climbing world, what was he good for? He could be a handyman. His father had taught him how to do most anything. Or he could work in a climbing gym or a gear shop selling shit to climbers who would look at him and see a has-been.

Despair settled in his chest like a lead weight, and for a time, he didn't budge.

Get off your ass, man.

He couldn't rebuild his life like this.

He glanced at his watch. It was almost midnight in Tengboche.

It seemed to take every ounce of will he possessed just to get up and go in search of his cellphone. He found it, dialed Candace's number, and drew a breath.

She wasn't going to like what he had to say.

She answered on the second ring. "Oh, my God. You're back!"

"I got back to Colorado last night."

"Finally! Do you have any idea how hard I've been trying to hold things together for you? Fifteen months is a long time to go AWOL." Then she got down to business, seeming not to take a breath as she brought him up to speed. "You lost your sponsorship with Earth Bars, but the big gear companies have been patient. I've got interest from a couple New York publishers if you want to write a book about what happened. I think that's a great idea, by the way. Write a book, do a tour, get back on your feet. There might even be film interest. People are going to want to know what happened up—"

"Candace, stop." Had she always rattled on like this? "I'm *not* writing a book. I don't care about the sponsor-ships. I'm done climbing."

There. He'd said it.

Silence.

She cleared her throat. "You don't really mean that."

He'd known she'd say that. To be fair, this represented

30

a significant loss of income for her. "I'm done. Finished. No more climbing. No more sponsorships. You should drop me from your client list."

"But you're the best alpine climber in the world."

"I *was* the best alpine climber in the world. That was a long time ago. Now I'm just some fucking guy."

———

Thursday, September 20

KENZIE SAT in the Ops Room, Gizmo curled up at her feet, Gabby exploring as far as her leash allowed her. Kenzie had been talking with Megs about Harrison when Esri had walked in to see Megs about something else. Now Megs and Kenzie had pulled Esri into their conversation.

"I ran into Harrison two weeks ago at Food Mart," Kenzie told her. "He didn't seem like himself. No one has seen him leave his house since. He hasn't been to Knockers even once—or the climbing gym. Something is wrong."

Megs nodded. "He barely said a word on the flights home. He just stared out the window or slept. He seemed like himself in Tengboche, but once we got to the airport in Kathmandu, he shut down."

Esri Tsering, who volunteered for the Team by offering free therapy to Team members, seemed to consider what they'd told her, pausing before she spoke. "I hear that you're worried, and I get that. But unless he calls me and asks for my help, there's really nothing I can do. I don't feel comfortable talking about him behind his back like this. I know you want to help him but—"

Gabby latched onto Esri's handbag and started to drag it, puppy-growling.

"Leave it!" Kenzie picked the puppy up. "Sorry."

Esri smiled. "That's okay. She's adorable."

Megs reached over to pet Gabby. "We're not asking you to violate Conrad's privacy or break any ethics rules—or we don't mean to. We'd just like to have some idea what we can do to help."

"Give him space. Give him time."

Kenzie gaped at Esri. "But it's been *fifteen* months."

Esri nodded. "Fifteen months might seem like a long time to you and me, but for him, it probably feels like his friends died yesterday. He's back home for the first time since then, and that means he has to process what happened all over again."

Kenzie could understand that. As long as he'd stayed in Nepal, he was isolated. Now that he'd come back to Scarlet, he had to face what had happened in the context of the rest of his life. "There has to be something we can do."

Gabby squirmed, insisting that Kenzie put her down. She climbed onto Gizmo, who patiently endured her playful attention, thumping his tail on the floor.

"He'd gotten into a routine with the monks." Megs smiled at the puppy's antics. "He joined them for meditation and prayers, shared some of their meals, and did handyman work for them. He talked and ate with the Lama sometimes, too."

"Wow." Esri seemed impressed. "I've always wanted to visit Tengboche. Maybe Conrad would be willing to tell me about it. My father was Tibetan. Some of his ancestors were monks there."

Kenzie hadn't known this. "I thought you were Jewish and Japanese or something."

"Or something." Esri didn't seem offended. "My mother is Jewish, so according to Jewish law, I'm Jewish. My father was on the staff of the Rinpoche who helped start the Mahayana Buddhist school in Denver. That's where he met my mom. I call myself a Jewdhist."

Megs grinned. "I bet you have interesting holidays."

"Oh, yes." Esri got them back on topic. "A regular routine probably gave Conrad something solid to hold onto without making too many demands on his emotions or his time. It wouldn't hurt him to build some kind of routine here, even if it's just getting up at the same time every day and going for a hike."

"If he refuses to leave his house, how can he build a routine?" Kenzie reached down to untangle the leash from around Gabby's hind legs.

"She's a real ball of energy, isn't she?" Esri picked Gabby up and cuddled her. "It's a good thing you're cute."

"She definitely keeps me on my toes. If something awful happened in my life, I would still have to get up and feed these two, take them outside to go potty, and…" Kenzie's voice trailed off, a crazy idea coming to her.

She met Esri's gaze. "Pets can be therapeutic, right?"

Esri was caught up in Gabby, who had worn herself out and curled up on Esri's lap for a nap. "Yes, very much so. They offer connection and affection, lower blood pressure, give people something to focus on besides themselves."

Megs looked up at Kenzie. "What are you thinking?"

Esri looked up, startled. "You can't get a pet for Conrad."

Kenzie smiled. "Of course, not. But I can ask him to babysit Gabby for a while, can't I? He can always say no."

She just had to find a compelling enough reason, one he couldn't refuse.

Friday, September 21

CONRAD WAS asleep when the knock came at his door. Who the hell would bother him so early in the morning? He raised his head, looked at the clock.

It was almost noon. "Shit."

He shoved the blankets aside, stepped into the pair of jeans that lay on the floor, and strode out to the living room to open the door. "Kenzie."

"Hey." She stood on his porch looking beautiful in a peach V-neck T-shirt and jeans that made the most of her curves, her long hair drawn back in a ponytail. In her arms was a tiny, squirming puppy. "I hope I'm not bothering you."

"Not at all. I was just … uh… " He ran a hand through the tangled mess of hair on his head, wondering when he'd last had a shower and hoping he didn't stink. "I was just about to jump in the shower. Come in."

He glanced around at the mess—pizza boxes, beer bottles, piles of unopened mail from his PO box. "Sorry. I need to clean this place up."

She stepped inside, set the puppy on the floor. It bounded over to a pizza box and sniffed. "I came to ask you a really big favor."

It was then Conrad noticed the worry on her face. He gestured toward the sofa. "Have a seat. What's wrong?"

Kenzie sat on the sofa. "It's the puppy. Her name is Gabby."

Conrad glanced down at the little thing. "Hey, Gabby."

The puppy pawed at the pizza box, her little tail wagging.

"Gizmo is six now—that's about forty-two in golden retriever years. He's still healthy, but it takes a while to train a dog for SAR work. So, I got little Gabby here. She's ten weeks old—the perfect age to start training—but Gizmo doesn't want her around. She's got so much energy. She's always hopping on him and trying to play with him. She gets on his nerves."

Gizmo had always seemed like a friendly dog to Conrad, one that got along well with dogs and people. But what did Conrad know?

Kenzie went on. "I think he'll have an easier time dealing with her when she's a little older. I was really hoping you could foster her for me—just for a month or so. It's essential that she begin her training now if she's going to get certified, but the situation with Gizmo is making that hard for me. He's jealous."

Conrad must have misunderstood. "You want *me* to foster the puppy?"

"Yes, please. Just for a little while. I'll tell you everything you need to know. She's a really good little girl."

"Isn't there someone else?" The last thing Conrad needed in his life right now was some little creature depending on him.

Hadn't he vowed never to take responsibility for another life again?

Kenzie shook her head. "Most of the people I know work all day or have new babies or dogs. There really isn't anyone else I would trust with her."

Well, shit.

"I don't know how my landlord would feel about my having a pet. She might pee on the carpet or something. He's trying to sell the place."

Kenzie glanced down at the worn green shag carpeting. "Anyone who buys this house is going to want to replace this carpet before they move in anyway."

Yeah, that was probably true.

Conrad was running out of excuses.

"Besides," Kenzie added, "there are ways to prevent accidents. Puppies aren't rocket science."

"I'm not really in a great space now." He hated having to admit that.

"Neither is Gabby."

Damn.

The puppy had wandered over to Conrad's feet. She sniffed, looked up at him through big, brown eyes, a creamy ball of complete innocence.

Fuck.

He was screwed.

He bent down, picked up the furball, and held her. She was small enough that he could hold her in one hand.

She licked his face, her little tail wagging.

Kenzie smiled. "I think she likes you."

"She probably likes everyone." Conrad reluctantly set her down again. "I'd like to help, but I have to find a job."

"How's the job search going?"

What could he say? It wasn't going. He hadn't filled out a single application.

"I'm still trying to figure out what I want to do."

Kenzie nodded as if this made sense. "How about this? If you have a job interview, you can always drop her by the kennel."

He supposed that would work. "What about training her? I don't want her to be an SAR dropout because of me."

Kenzie laughed. "Training a puppy this age isn't very involved, and Gabby is super smart. I'll help."

Conrad watched the puppy bound around his living room, stumbling over a pile of mail and sending letters scattering around the floor.

"Please, Conrad. It would be such a huge help to me."

Conrad met Kenzie's gaze, about to tell her that he wasn't the man for this job, but the pleading look in those blue eyes stopped him. "Okay, but don't hold it against me if she flunks out of rescue school."

Kenzie jumped up, threw her arms around his neck, and kissed his cheek. "Thanks so much, Harrison! You're a life-saver."

No. No, he wasn't. But he could at least help Kenzie with this.

"Can you help me carry her stuff inside?"

"Yeah, okay." How much stuff could a little puppy have?

Chapter 3

KENZIE HATED LYING TO HARRISON. Not that this was a bad lie. She was trying to help him. Still, what she'd told him wasn't true.

She carried a box of puppy toys and the bag of puppy food inside and set them down in the kitchen. Then she went out to grab the bag of groceries she'd bought for him and put the salad veggies, meat, seafood, cheese, milk, and eggs in the prehistoric mint-green fridge. "Does this thing even work?"

Harrison saw what she was doing. He glanced into the bag from Food Mart, a frown on his face. "What's all this?"

"It's called 'food.' Most people keep it around."

"You didn't need to do that."

"I can't have you eating Gabby's kibble."

"Funny." Harrison glanced around, the sight of him without a shirt almost enough to make Kenzie drool. "I had no idea a puppy needed so many things."

Those hairless pecs. That six-pack. His shoulders and biceps. Silky, tanned skin.

She swallowed. "You think that's a lot?"

There wasn't that much—just Gabby's crate, her car carrier, her training harnesses and leads, her grooming supplies, her food and water bowls, her toys, her treats, her favorite blanket.

He grinned. "You don't?"

It was the first real smile she'd gotten from him since he'd come back, and it put a flutter in her belly. "I guess I'm used to it."

She'd written down instructions for Gabby's care to make things easier for him. She pulled the pages out of the bag of puppy food and was about to go over them with Harrison when he decided it was time to gather up the pizza boxes and take them out to his recycling bin. He disappeared outside, a stack of pizza boxes in his arms, returning a minute later.

"That's better." He scooped Gabby up and sat at the table with her in his lap. "Okay, go ahead."

But Kenzie was in the middle of a hormonal meltdown, the sight of little Gabby against Harrison's bare chest making her ovaries squeal.

How was she supposed to get through this?

She forced her gaze onto the page and read the sections about feeding and crate training first, fighting to stay focused. "Give her a treat every time she goes into the crate. She'll sleep there at night. She might cry a bit, but she's okay. Don't take her out and put her in your bed. That will only make the problem worse."

"Got it."

"When you let her out of her crate, always take her straight outside to go potty. That way, she'll come to associate leaving the crate with going outside to do her thing."

"Won't she just go potty in the crate?"

Kenzie shook her head. "She'll try very hard not to.

That's why you have to pay attention. Little puppies can't hold it very long. I've been taking her out right before I go to bed at night and then putting her in her crate with a treat and her toy afterward. She usually wakes me up at about four in the morning needing to go out again, and then she lets me sleep until about six or seven."

"Six or seven? So, she's your alarm clock."

Kenzie laughed. "A furry clock that doesn't come with a snooze button."

Harrison gave a slight frown, clearly not certain how to feel about the fact that he'd be getting up early for the foreseeable future.

"It's important never to use the crate to punish her. Also, no hitting or kicking her or… " She stopped at the horrified look on Harrison's face. "You would never do that anyway, I know."

"Never." He kissed the top of Gabby's head.

This time, it was Kenzie's heart that squealed. She had a soft spot for men who loved animals. "Do you want to learn how to train her to follow?"

"Sure." Harrison set the puppy down.

Kenzie took hold of Gabby's leash and grabbed a few treats. "I hold her leash in one hand, and I hold a treat in the other and bend down like this so that I'm keeping the treat at her face-level next to my leg while I walk. She wants the treat, so she goes right where I want her. Use the command 'Follow.' It's a little awkward to walk like this, but they learn quickly." Kenzie took a few steps. "Gabby, follow."

Gabby trotted along at her heel, taking the treat from her fingers.

"Then you praise her." Kenzie knelt. "You're a good girl, Gabby. Yes, you're just so smart."

"How often do you want me to do that?"

"I'd say a few times a day. She already knows how to sit." Kenzie grabbed another treat. "Gabby, sit."

Gabby looked up at her, then plopped her little bottom onto the floor.

Kenzie gave her the treat. "Make sure to praise her. Good puppy! What a good puppy you are!"

"I thought dog trainers use those clicker things."

"I've taught clicker training in classes, but I don't any longer. Whether you use a clicker or not, it's all about rewarding desired behavior. If I'm consistent, my pups will learn to be consistent."

"So be consistent. Got it."

He looked so serious that Kenzie had to smile. "Exactly. I wrote it all down in case you forget something."

She glanced at her watch, saw that it was just before noon. "The last thing I should show you is puppy runaways. That's the first step in training her for SAR work."

"Puppy runaways? You want her to run away?"

"No, I want *you* to run away."

"Me?" A dark eyebrow arched.

Kenzie knew she was taking a chance here, but things had already gone far better than she'd imagined. She gave Gabby credit for that. Harrison had always been fond of Gizmo, and it was clear that he'd fallen in love with the puppy at first sight. Kenzie couldn't blame him. So had she. "Why don't we put her in her car carrier and drive to that new park near the library?"

"Scarlet Springs has a *library*?"

Oh, God. He didn't know.

"Joe Moffat built a library and donated Silas Moffat's journals and a bunch of historic photographs. The town had a big book drive. Now we have our own library. They built it on the site of the old schoolhouse. The school became part of the library, and the playground became a pocket park."

"Cool. Okay." He glanced down at his bare chest. "I guess I'd better get dressed."

Bummer.

Well, all good things must come to an end.

CONRAD STRUGGLED to get the squirming puppy into her tiny harness. "Okay, that's too cute to be legal."

Kenzie laughed, the sound melodic and sweet. She reached over to help, her arm brushing against Conrad's, contact sending a jolt through him. "All that cuteness—it's a survival strategy."

What were they talking about? Survival strategy?

The puppy.

"Okay, let's talk about puppy runaways." Kenzie knelt down in the grass. "I'm going to love her up a bit, and then I'm going to run a short distance away—probably to that little pine tree over there—and hide. Then you let her go and say, 'Go find!' Hopefully, she'll follow me."

"What if she doesn't?"

"I'll take her favorite toy with me and give it a few squeaks to give her some incentive. Follow her, and when she finds me, we both praise her and give her a treat."

"Okay." That didn't sound too complicated.

Kenzie tousled Gabby's floppy ears and kissed her. "Who's my sweet puppy? Are you my sweet puppy? You are too cute."

Then Kenzie looked up at Conrad. "Don't let go of her until I'm hidden."

She hopped up and ran to hide behind a pine tree, her ass doing amazing things for her jeans as she moved.

Head out of the gutter, man.

The moment she was hidden, Conrad released the puppy. "Gabby, go find!"

Gabby stood still for a second and cocked her head as if wondering what Kenzie was doing. Then she heard her toy squeak and ran toward the sound. It was only a distance of about twenty feet, so it didn't take long before Gabby rounded the pine tree and gave an excited bark.

"Good girl! Good girl!" Kenzie gave Gabby a treat and let her have the little squeak toy. "That went well. Let's do it again. This time, you run and hide."

Conrad played with Gabby, then he took some treats and the toy and bolted for the next pine tree, crouching down behind it.

"Go find!" Kenzie commanded.

Conrad peeked through the branches to see the little ball of fluff bounding his way. Halfway there, Gabby sat on the grass. Remembering what Kenzie had done, he gave the squeak toy a squeeze. Gabby jumped to her feet again and ran toward him, rounding the tree and hopping into his arms.

"Good girl! What a smart doggy!" He gave her a treat then squeaked the toy again before letting her have it.

Kenzie stood over them, watching, arms crossed. "You're a pro."

"How often should we do this?" He chuckled at the sight of Gabby tumbling through the grass with the squeak toy in her jaws.

"Every couple of days is good enough, but it shouldn't always be the two of us. We don't want to train her to track only us. We need her to get used to following scent trails, so that means using different people."

That made sense. "How do I do that?"

"Give someone a call, meet them somewhere, and tell

them what to do. She needs to get used to different distractions and surfaces, so it would be great if you could use a variety of locations—here, your yard, a trail in the mountains, your driveway. Different surfaces interact differently to scent and feel different to her paws."

This was a little more responsibility than Conrad had expected. Then again, what the hell else was he doing? Nothing.

Kenzie seemed to study him. "Am I overwhelming you?"

He *did* feel a little overwhelmed, but he couldn't admit that. "I've got this."

"Let's do a couple more."

Kenzie ran and hid behind a nearby bench, which forced Gabby to run through the sandbox. The puppy stopped to sniff, apparently intrigued by the texture of the sand, but a few squeaks from her favorite toy got her back on task.

Then it was Conrad's turn to hide. He crouched down behind a garbage can some distance down the sidewalk, his heart melting at the sight of Gabby bounding toward him, tongue out, ears flopping. "Good girl!"

He gave her a treat, let her have the toy.

She played a bit, shaking the toy furiously, then walked off into the grass and plopped down, dropping the toy near her front paws.

"I think she's all tired out." Kenzie knelt down beside Gabby. "She still little enough that she can only work for a short time before she needs a nap."

"I know how she feels." In truth, Conrad had barely left his house since coming home, and it felt good to be outside again. The sun was shining. The aspens had turned, clothing the mountains in gold. The high peaks were topped with snow.

Kenzie glanced at her watch. "I need to get going. I've got—"

"Kenzie? Conrad?" A man's voice came from behind them.

"Hey, Jesse!" Kenzie waved.

Conrad turned to see Jesse Moretti walking his way with his twins, Daisy and Daniel, who had grown a lot while Conrad had been away. They didn't look like babies now. They looked like, well, kids. How old were they? Four?

Conrad got to his feet. "Hey, Moretti."

Moretti drew him into a bear hug, grinning from behind mirrored sunglasses. "You son of a… "

He stopped, glanced down at his kids, cleared his throat, and started over. "It's great to see you. I'd heard you were back in town."

Moretti was a former Army Ranger who'd come to Colorado to cope with war trauma and had fallen in love with climbing. He'd stayed, perfected his skill, and become a primary Team member in just a year.

"Oooh! A puppy!" Daisy shrieked with delight and hurried over to Gabby, her brother turning to follow her.

Conrad tensed, ready to intervene if the kids were too rough, but Kenzie had it under control.

"Be careful. She's just a baby. Pet her gently." She took first Daisy's hand and then Daniel's and showed them how it was done. "Like this."

"She's just a baby, Danny," Daisy admonished her brother. "Be nice."

"I like the puppy, too, Day," Daniel was especially careful.

"You're looking good," Moretti said.

"You, too."

Moretti had married Ellie Meeks, a war widow and the

twins' mother, shortly after Conrad had left for Everest. Conrad had gotten an invitation before he'd flown to Nepal. "Being a married man and a father seems to be working for you."

"More than I ever could have imagined."

Conrad could see that Moretti meant what he said. The man exuded happiness. "You still working up at Ski Scarlet?"

"Yep. We're hiring for Ski Patrol if you're interested. It doesn't pay much, but money is money. Megs says you're looking for a job."

Ski Patrol.

Conrad might be able to do that. "How do I apply?"

"Go to the website. I'll put in a word with my boss, if you like."

"Sure—if you think that will help."

Moretti laughed. "It won't hurt if that's what worries you. Once he hears you're interested, he'll want to hire you. Are you kidding? You would give him someone to brag about. Harrison Conrad, a member of Ski Scarlet's Ski Patrol."

Conrad wasn't sure how he felt about that.

⊏⊐

KENZIE SWALLOWED the lump in her throat as she drove away from Harrison's house. She missed Gabby already. Puppies grew up so quickly, and Kenzie didn't want to miss any of that precious time. But she'd seen the way Harrison's gaze had gone soft the moment he'd seen Gabby. He had perked up, put a shirt on, gone down to the park. He'd laughed. He'd gotten some sunshine. He'd even talked about a job with Moretti.

All because of a puppy.

He *needed* Gabby right now.

She turned left off West Pine onto Highway 119, which bisected the town, an image of Harrison holding Gabby against his bare chest coming into her mind. It was wrong to be jealous of her own puppy, but, *damn*, she would have loved to trade places with Gabby, to have Harrison look at her with the same adoration.

Stop torturing yourself.

She wasn't the kind of woman who would interest Harrison Conrad. She didn't climb and wasn't a fitness geek. She had zero interest in slogging her way up a four-teener. She'd climbed a mountain once, tackling Mt. Evans with some fellow Team members. The best part about the experience had been when the climb was over.

She would rather stay home, putter in her garden, take her dogs for a hike, read a book. Although she liked the outdoors, she didn't need to go to Kamchatka or Nepal or the Arctic to hike or camp. She got her fill of adventure volunteering with the Team.

Besides, Kenzie had already done the climber thing. Her first boyfriend had broken up with her after college graduation to work as an adventure guide in Alaska. He'd died in a helicopter accident six months later. Her second boyfriend, who had also loved to climb and ski, had gone to Austria to ski in the alps and had met a woman there, a tall, blonde, extreme skier. He'd broken up with Kenzie via email.

Harrison was another one of these ripped, sexy men who turned her on—but who would never stick around to build a life with her. He said he was done with climbing and off the Team, but she didn't believe that. Once he'd had time to heal, he'd start planning his next trip and head off to climb the unclimbed, risking his life again.

Well, she was done with that.

She was a homebody. She loved her little garden with its tulips and daffodils in the spring and roses in the summer. She enjoyed her work with dogs. She loved Scarlet Springs. Her grandparents had lived here when she'd been a little girl growing up in Boulder. Living in their house—an old Victorian—reminded her of those good days.

Harrison was probably lousy in bed anyway.

Wouldn't you just love to test that theory?

She was so lost in thought that she missed her turn. Only when Bear waved to her from the roundabout, where he typically preached in the afternoons, did she realize that she'd gone too far She had a two o'clock appointment with Lexi Taylor to go over her third-quarter financials. "Shoot."

Kenzie waved at Bear and saw him laugh as she used the roundabout to make a U-turn and head back the way she'd come. Bear had lived in the mountains west of town for as long as anyone could remember, and he hadn't changed much through the years. He preached the Gospel and blessed passersby from the roundabout in exchange for spare change or a meal. Though he had the heart and mind of a child, he was big like his namesake, with a bushy beard and buckskin clothes he'd probably made himself. No one knew why he was the way he was, but they all did their part to make sure he had enough to eat and shelter during the cold months of winter.

Her mind off Harrison, Kenzie made a left onto East First Street, parking in front of the purple Victorian cottage with the white trim. It was one of the few houses to have survived the big fire that had destroyed most of the town in 1878. Out front was a sign that read, "Jewell and Associates."

Kenzie grabbed her handbag, stepped out of her truck,

and walked through the iron gate, rose bushes laden with late-summer blooms on both sides.

Lexi opened the screen door, looking both gorgeous and casual in a long, Bohemian sundress in navy blue and white, her long red hair swept up in a twist. "Hey! Come on in. Can I get you something to drink?"

"Water would be great." Kenzie stepped inside.

"Make yourself at home. I'll be right back."

"Thanks." Kenzie sat in a plush wingback chair in what had once been a front sitting room but was now Lexi's office.

Lexi's family—the Jewells—had lived in Scarlet from the beginning. Her father owned the Forest Creek Inn just down the street, an enormous Victorian house that had been in their family and served visitors to Scarlet since the 1860s.

Kenzie glanced at the photos on the walls. A wedding photo of Lexi and Austin, her park ranger husband who volunteered for the Team as one of its lead rock climbers. A photo of Lexi and Austin soaking wet and laughing in a river raft. A new photo of their baby girl, Emily, who was eighteen months old—and asleep in a crib in the next room.

"Ice or no ice?" Lexi called from the kitchen.

"Ice, please."

Lexi was a year older than Kenzie and had everything —a successful career, a man who was crazy about her, a sweet baby, a well-behaved dog. Kenzie had the successful career, too, and two amazing canines, but the man…

Mr. Right wasn't even on her horizon.

Then again, Scarlet Springs was a tiny town with a small pool of eligible men her age. Most of the single guys she knew were into extreme sports, which put them off limits. Since she refused to venture into online dating or go anywhere near Tinder, her prospects for finding someone before her ovaries gave up weren't promising.

Lexi returned with her water and sat at her desk, her feet bare. "Where's the puppy? I was hoping you'd bring her."

Kenzie didn't know how to answer. She decided to tell Lexi the truth. "I told Harrison that Gizmo and Gabby weren't getting along and asked him to foster her for me for a while."

Lexi looked confused. "But Gizmo loves Gabby."

"Yes, but Harrison doesn't know that. I had to do something. He's been shut inside that house for two weeks. He hasn't spoken to anyone—at least until today. He and I went to the park to do some puppy training."

Lexi gaped at her, laughing. "Oh, you are a genius—devious, but a genius. That's perfect."

"Don't tell anyone. If Harrison were to find out, it would ruin everything."

"We won't breathe a word of it to him."

"*We?*"

Oh, right. Kenzie had forgotten that secrecy was a relative thing on the Team. By tonight, everyone but Harrison would know.

Chapter 4

CONRAD TOOK a shower and shaved while Gabby napped in her crate. He rinsed off the shaving cream and met his gaze in the mirror.

What the hell have you gotten yourself into?

If it had been anyone but Kenzie, he would have refused, but he was a sucker for her big, blue eyes, for that smile. Okay, he was a sucker for dogs, too, but could he truly handle a puppy? Since he'd gotten back to Scarlet, he'd barely been able to handle himself.

I guess it's time to get your shit together.

Hadn't he been trying?

Apparently, not hard enough.

He walked back to the bedroom to get dressed. He had only the clothes he'd brought home from the monastery. He hadn't washed any of it yet. He grabbed the same pair of jeans he'd been wearing for two weeks off the floor, pulled them on, then gathered everything up, and started a load of laundry. Thank God Mrs. Beech had at least bought a modern washer and dryer.

Once he'd gotten the washing machine going, he went

out to the kitchen and was embarrassed at what he saw. Kenzie had seen this, too. The sink was filled with two weeks' worth of dishes. The trash was overflowing—and it stank. The floor hadn't been swept since he'd moved in.

If you don't want her to think you live like a slob, then don't live like a slob.

There was no dishwasher, so he washed the dishes by hand and then swept the floor and carried the trash out to the bin.

When he came back in, he heard Gabby crying in her crate.

The sound went straight to his heart.

He went into his bedroom, where Kenzie had told him to keep the crate, and opened the little door. "Hey, little girl."

Gabby bounded out, her entire body wagging.

Remembering what Kenzie had told him, Conrad picked the puppy up, grabbed a few treats, and put her down just outside the back door so that she could do her business.

Gabby sniffed her way around the overgrown lawn, barking at dandelion fluff when her curiosity sent the little seeds dancing in the wind.

Conrad couldn't help but laugh. What must it be like to be new in the world, to be fascinated by everything?

Gabby made her way to the edge of the yard, where, finally, she peed. She finished and then bounded over to him, taking the treat he offered, her tail wagging.

Conrad praised her. "Good girl!"

Maybe this wouldn't be so difficult after all.

He sat in an old lawn chair, giving Gabby some time to explore, trying to figure out what to do with the rest of his day.

He needed to get to The Cave, load his shit into his

4Runner, bring it here, and unpack it, or he'd be wearing these jeans forever. But the thought of going to The Cave put a knot in his chest.

It had once been his home away from home, part of the trinity of his social life—The Cave, Knockers, the rock gym. Now even his home didn't feel like home. It's not that he didn't want to see his friends. He had enjoyed catching up with Moretti and his kids more than he could have imagined. But his fellow Team members might ask questions he didn't want to answer and offer him compassion he couldn't accept.

You're weak, pathetic.

Disgusted, he willed himself to his feet and called Gabby over, giving the puppy another treat when she came. He carried her indoors and set her down, then walked into the bedroom to put on a shirt.

He couldn't run away from this forever. His shit wasn't going to drive itself here. Once he had retrieved it, he wouldn't have to go to The Cave again. If anyone pressed him with questions, he could just refuse to answer.

He went in search of his shoes and then had to search for Gabby.

He found her near the back door, where she stood sniffing…

"Oh, man. Shit."

The little thing had pooped on the floor.

———

KENZIE LIVED next door to her business, so she drove home, parked, and walked to the kennel to find the place quiet. With the peak months of summer behind them, they had only six dogs boarding now, and they were all out in the play yard with Quinn, her manager, who was also looking after Gizmo and her own dog, Sheba, a black lab.

That was one of the perks of working at the kennel. Every day was Bring Your Dog to Work Day—provided the dog was well-trained and got along with other pooches.

Kenzie made her way to her office and filed the Q3 tax documents Lexi had given her, making her Q3 payment online. Then she read through her email—a couple of inquiries about reserving space for the Thanksgiving and Christmas holidays, a shipping confirmation for an order of hypoallergenic pet shampoo, and an email from a woman who wanted to know how to keep her new puppy from tearing up her couch cushions.

Kenzie answered the woman with a few suggestions and attached a couple of flyers—one about crate training and the other a schedule of upcoming puppy kindergarten classes—and immediately got an angry reply.

"You think I want to spend more money on this animal? I just need you to tell me what to do!"

Kenzie's heart hurt for that puppy. Why did people bring companion animals into their homes without learning how to care for them? The failure wasn't the puppy's, but the owner's.

Kenzie decided it was probably a bad idea to reply with the words that had come to mind, so she simply deleted the woman's email.

She left her office and walked out front to the store, fighting the urge to text Harrison to find out how things were going.

She found Dree, who'd worked for her for about a year now, getting ready to close up the shop.

"Where's Gabby?" Dree asked.

"I left her with a friend."

The store wasn't as profitable as the kennel or her

obedience training classes, which both got clientele from across Forest and Boulder counties. Scarlet Springs was a small town, after all. Still, Kenzie had been able to stay in the black so far, while offering the residents of the area the best in natural pet food and other supplies.

No one, including Kenzie, wanted to make the trip down the canyon to Boulder just for good pet food.

"How did the day go?" Kenzie sorted the mail.

Junk mail. Bills. Catalogs.

"It was pretty busy, actually."

Fridays were often busy. The store was open only from 10 to 3 on Saturdays and was closed on Sundays to give Kenzie and her staff a day off.

"People are trying to get what they need before the weekend."

Kenzie cashed out the register, leaving Dree to mop the floor and do a quick restock of the shelves before locking up. She carried the cash to her office and had just filled out a bank deposit slip when her cell phone buzzed.

A message from Rose Ellery, the town's psychic and leading gossip.

I forgot that Gandalf needs more dry food. I'm in the middle of a chakra realignment and won't make it before you close. Can you leave a bag of the silky coat formula outside the door? I'll drop a check through your mail slot.

Kenzie texted her back.

Sure thing. It will be waiting in the cooler outside the door.

She went back to the store, where Dree had just finished mopping, and grabbed the bag of cat food Rose wanted. Kenzie rang it up and carried the cat food outside to the large cooler that sat by the store's front door, shutting the food inside with the bill.

She wouldn't have been able to do something like this in Boulder or Denver because someone would steal the cooler, not to mention the cat food. In Scarlet, all she had to worry about were the bears that sometimes wandered into town looking for a meal.

She locked the door, turned the sign on the door to CLOSED. "Have a good night, Dree. Thanks for your hard work today."

She left Dree to turn out the lights and went out to the play yard to get Gizmo, who whined and ran over to her, tail wagging. "How's my big boy?"

She hugged him, tousled his ears, and petted his chest.

Quinn held the door open. "I was about to take them inside to feed them."

"I'll help." Kenzie's Team pager went off. "Or maybe not."

She drew the pager out of her pocket, scrolled through the message.

K9 NEEDED AT FOURTH OF JULY TRAILHEAD.

"It's time to go to work, Gizmo."

⸻

EVERYTHING at The Cave was just the way Conrad remembered it. Litters and enormous bags that held ropes hung from one wall, together with skis and snowshoes, while a fortune in climbing gear hung from the other. Medical kits sat on shelves, their sides marked plainly with red crosses. In the far corner lay a naked crash-test dummy.

Fred had lost his britches again—the poor bastard.

No one was there besides Megs and Ahearn, which was both a relief and a little disappointing. It might have been nice to see the others.

Megs' gaze fixed on the puppy. "Are you babysitting or something?"

"Kenzie asked me to foster Gabby for a few weeks. She said Gizmo hasn't taken to the puppy very well."

Ahearn looked confused. "I thought Gizmo loved Gabby."

Megs looked over her shoulder at Ahearn, whose expression changed abruptly.

Ahearn cleared his throat. "But I don't know a thing about dogs—not a thing."

Megs turned back to Conrad. "How's it going?"

"So far, so good, I guess. She had an accident, but we're putting that behind us."

Why this made Megs smile, Conrad couldn't say. She reached over to pet Gabby, speaking in the silly voice people used when talking to cute animals. "Did you go potty on Conrad's messy floor? You just don't know better, do you?"

While Megs watched Gabby, Conrad carried dusty boxes down from the attic and loaded them into his vehicle. With the puppy's carrier, he didn't have as much room as he might otherwise. But there was no harm in an extra trip or two. When his vehicle was full, he grabbed the puppy, drove back to the house, and unloaded.

On his third trip, he arrived at The Cave to find Rescue 1 gone.

Something had happened.

He got Gabby from her carrier, clipped on her leash, and led her into Ops, where he found Megs and Ahearn at the radio.

"Eight sixty-five." That was Sheriff's Deputy Julia Marcs.

"Eight sixty-five, go ahead."

"The mother arrived with a scent article. K9 is just down the road."

Kenzie was on her way to the scene.

"Eighteen forty-five."

Conrad lifted Gabby into his lap, listened to the radio traffic. How strange it was not to be part of the action, to sit on the sidelines like this.

Megs turned to face him, filling him in. "A woman reported her adult son missing last week. Marcs found his vehicle up near Fourth of July Trailhead. He parked it near some aspens, and judging from the leaf litter, Marcs thinks it has been there for a while."

"Shit." That didn't sound good.

A burst of static, and then Kenzie's voice. "Sixteen eighty-eight, arrival."

Dispatch replied with the time. "Eighteen forty-six."

Megs turned back to the radio.

Feeling out of place, Conrad left Ops and went up the back stairs to the attic, carrying Gabby, who was just too little to manage stairs as steep as these. He set her down on the wooden floor and fixed her leash to one of the support posts. He sorted through the remaining boxes, making quick trips to his SUV to load them, Gabby whining when he disappeared and greeting him with tail wags when he reappeared.

When he had everything he needed, he scooped the puppy into his arms and headed back to Ops. He still had climbing gear here, as well as furniture. He would leave it until he bought a place. There was no reason to move all of it twice.

Megs and Ahearn were still sitting at the radio.

Conrad waited for a second to be sure he wasn't interrupting radio traffic. "I'm heading out. I've got some furniture and gear up there still."

Megs said nothing, her brow furrowed.

Ahearn glanced over at him and nodded.

A burst of static, and then Kenzie again. "Sixteen eighty-eight, victim has been located. Code black. We're going to need a DBT."

A dead body transfer.

A tightness crept into Conrad's chest.

"Son of a bitch." Megs closed her eyes, exhaled. "So much for a happy ending."

"Sixteen eighty-eight, copy on the DBT. Nineteen twenty-eight."

"Sixteen twenty-seven, on site. We'll handle the DBT. Tone out the ME." That was Hawke, who, in addition to being a primary Team member and a new father, served as the town's fire chief.

Dispatch replied again with the time. "Toning out the ME. Nineteen twenty-nine."

Conrad had been a part of rescues like this—kids who'd been washed away by swift mountain streams, suicides, people who'd gone hiking alone, gotten lost, and been killed by hypothermia, falls, rock slides. Hawke and his crew would put what was left of the guy in a body bag and drive him to the medical examiner's lab in Boulder. Someone would have to tell this guy's parents that he was gone, breaking their hearts forever.

Conrad's pulse picked up, the sensation of tightness rising into his throat, making it hard to breathe. He stood and, without saying goodbye, left Ops, climbed into his SUV, and drove home.

What the hell was wrong with him?

It was only when he pulled into his driveway that he

realized he hadn't put Gabby in her carrier. He was still holding her.

KENZIE DROVE HOME, feeling sick. She hated searches that ended with a dead body. Those poor parents. Though Kenzie wasn't an ME, it looked to her like the guy had slipped from the cliff above and broken his neck.

She brushed Gizmo, settled him with his supper, then took a quick shower to wash away the feeling of death. She put on a sundress and walked to Knockers, where she knew the rest of the Team would gather. It was a tradition to let off steam together at the brewpub after a rescue, regardless of the outcome. Caribou Joe—Joe Moffat, the pub's owner—always had a table waiting for them.

She stepped inside, the strains of bluegrass music coming from the stage, the tables full. It was Friday night, after all, and this was the only brewpub in town.

Cheyenne Taylor, Austin's younger sister, met her just inside the front door. Tall and blond, Cheyenne had taken on the job of host when Rain was promoted to general manager. With Rain on maternity leave, Cheyenne was more or less doing both jobs now. She didn't have Rain's cheerful disposition, but she had mastered the caustic comment.

Everyone missed Rain.

"Sorry about today. I guess you can't win them all." Cheyenne handed Kenzie a menu and pointed. "They're all back at the usual table."

Kenzie threaded her way to the corner, where Megs and Ahearn sat together with Julia Marcs and most of the primary members and some spouses—Austin and Lexi with little Emily, Eric and Victoria with their new baby,

Creed Herrera, Sasha Dillon, Nicole Turner, Malachi O'Brien, Isaac Rogers, Jesse Moretti with his wife Ellie and the twins, and Chaska Belcourt and his wife Naomi and sister Winona.

"Hey, Kenz." Lexi waved.

Eric gave her a nod. "There you are."

"How you holding up, Kenzie?" Austin asked.

"I'm fine." She walked over to Vicki Hawke, peered down at the tiny baby boy in her arms. "Congratulations! This must be little Caden. Welcome to the world, little guy. God, he's precious!"

He was sleeping now, two little fists clutched to his face, his dark hair mostly hidden beneath a blue knitted cap.

Kenzie wanted to kiss his chubby cheeks. "How are you feeling?"

Vicki had had an emergency C-section. "I'm healing."

Eric put his arm around his wife's shoulder and looked down at his infant son, love shining on his face. He kissed Vicki's cheek. "She'd be doing better if this little dude would let her sleep more than two hours at a time."

Kenzie would give almost anything to have a man look at her like that.

Vicki smiled. "He's finally nursing well. Eric stayed home for the first two weeks, but he has the firehouse to run. Robin has been a godsend. I don't know what I would do without her."

Robin was Eric's mother. She lived down the mountain from Eric and Vicki.

"I'm glad she's been able to help." Kenzie watched the baby sleep. "He really is perfect."

Vicki kissed his forehead. "Thanks. We think so."

Kenzie glanced around the almost-full table, looking for a seat.

"Sit by me." Winona, a wildlife vet, scooted to make

room for Kenzie, patting the bench beside her. The two had bonded over their love of animals when Winona had moved to Scarlet Springs with her wolf, Shota, to start her wildlife rehabilitation clinic. "How are you really?"

Kenzie had learned that the Belcourts didn't waste words on unimportant things. Born and raised on the Pine Ridge Indian Reservation, they were Oglala Lakota. If they asked you how you were doing, they truly wanted to know.

"I'm okay, I guess." It wasn't the first time Kenzie and Gizmo had gone searching for a live person and found a corpse. "I wish we'd had a different outcome. I always feel so bad when parents lose a child, even an adult child."

Winona's brow bent in a thoughtful frown. "You and Gizmo brought those parents closure. You enabled them to bring their son home. That's something at least."

"Yes. True." Worse than finding a corpse was finding *nothing* and leaving a family with unanswered questions and the agony of false hope.

"Good work today," Megs called from across the table.

"Thanks, but Gizmo deserves the praise."

Megs gave her a sarcastic look. "Right—because he taught himself how to find bodies. What a smart dog."

Their server came—a young woman Kenzie had seen walking down the street with a crash pad on her back. New to Scarlet, she was obviously here for the climbing. "I'm Sam. I'm new here. Can I get you something to drink—a brew, wine, one of Marcia's concoctions?"

"I'll have a Sex in the Spotlight." It was Kenzie's favorite drink, although she'd never participated in the activity after which it had been named.

Sam took the rest of her order. "I'll get that drink over here as soon as I can. I heard what happened today. Thanks for what you do."

Megs waited for the server to leave. "Conrad came by The Cave today. He had Gabby with him."

Creed looked surprised at this news. "Conrad is back?"

"Seriously, man, do you pay attention to your Team emails at all?" Malachi asked. "Megs went to Nepal and brought him back two weeks ago. He left the Team, and he's lying low for now. I don't think he wants company."

"Well, shit. I should give him a call," Creed reached into his pocket for his phone.

Megs turned to Creed. "What you need to give him is space."

Kenzie needed to know. "How was he? Did he seem like he was managing?"

Megs nodded. "He said Gabby had had an accident, but he kept that puppy close. You're a genius. I think he's in love."

The words "in love" made Kenzie's pulse skip.

If only Harrison loved her as much as he loved her puppy.

―――

CONRAD TURNED OVER, put a pillow over his head, trying to sleep. But it was no good. Gabby cried and whimpered in her crate.

He'd just taken her outside to go potty, so it couldn't be that.

He threw back the sheet, climbed out of bed, and walked naked to the kitchen to read through Kenzie's instructions again.

It's not unusual for a small puppy to whine or cry at night. It's important that she gets used to sleeping in her crate. As long as she's gone potty recently and has her blanket and a toy, she is fine. It will pass.

DON'T TAKE THE PUPPY OUT OF HER CRATE AND BRING HER INTO YOUR BED. It will just make the problem worse.

Well, it was after midnight, and Gabby was still crying.

It broke his heart, but then he wasn't a dog trainer. Kenzie knew what she was doing—didn't she?

He took a leak, washed his hands, and went back to bed, doing his best to ignore the whimpers. Five minutes. Ten. Twenty.

It felt so mean to ignore the puppy.

Thirty minutes.

"Damn it." Why, exactly, had he agreed to do this?

You want to get inside Kenzie's pants. That's why.

He sat up, looked over at the crate, a shaft of moonlight shining through the frilly curtains to reveal Gabby looking pleadingly up at him.

That was it.

He got out of bed, opened the crate, and lifted Gabby into his arms.

She wagged her tail, licked his face, clearly happy to have contact with another living creature.

He got back into bed, settling Gabby beside him. "Don't tell your mommy you slept with me, okay, little girl?"

That didn't sound pervy at all.

Gabby curled up, closed her eyes, and fell asleep, allowing Conrad finally to do the same.

Chapter 5

CONRAD SWUNG like a pendulum in mid-air, dangling above an abyss, ice all around him, enclosing him like a tomb. Heart thudding, he glanced around, tried to figure out where he was and what the hell had happened. He reached for the rope that was tied into his harness, but something frozen in the ice caught his gaze.

"Bruce!" Conrad stared in horror, his shout echoing along the crevasse.

God, was Bruce dead?

He must be. He was blue and encased in the ice, like a fish in a frozen sea.

"No!" Conrad's throat constricted. "*No.*"

The rope supporting Conrad's weight moved slowly in a circle, turning him away from Bruce to reveal more shapes in the ice, blue on ghostly blue.

Luka. Felix.

God, no.

One was arching backward as if caught in a backflip, a look of terror on his face, the other curled in a fetal position. Both frozen. Both dead.

The serac.

Conrad remembered now. It had collapsed. It must have knocked him into the crevasse—and buried the others.

Refusing to accept this, Conrad caught the rope in a fist and began to climb it, hand over hand, trying to free himself. Then he noticed what he hadn't before.

His blood went cold.

The ice was moving. It was closing in around him.

Then something licked his face and whined.

Conrad woke with a gasp to find Gabby sitting on his chest, licking him and whimpering. Confused, he fought to rein in his adrenaline, to figure out what the hell was going on.

A nightmare.

He'd been having a nightmare, and Gabby had woken him. He held the puppy close, accepting her kisses, his throat going tight.

The dream had felt *so damned real.*

He was here in his bed in Scarlet, but Bruce, Luka, and Felix—they were gone, buried beneath the ice forever.

I'm sorry. I'm so sorry.

The torrent of his emotions seemed to catch in his throat, bringing him to a sitting position, a rush of rage and despair making him want to *do* something. But there was nothing he could do.

Nothing at all.

It was a damned miracle he'd gotten out of there alive.

Gabby pranced on the bed beside him, wagging her tail.

Conrad glanced at the clock. It was almost five. "You have to pee, don't you?"

He scooped her up, carried her to the back door, and

stepped outside with her, not caring that he was naked. Who would see him at this hour?

Okay, so it was a bit cold, close to freezing.

He stood next to the back door, freezing his nuts off and watching while Gabby walked a short distance away from the door and squatted down to pee. He hoped she would be quick about it and do her business before his testicles sought refuge in his throat.

Whose fault is it that you're standing out here naked?

It sure as hell wasn't the puppy's fault.

From somewhere nearby, he heard the hoot of a great horned owl. He glanced around, saw its dark outline high in the branches of a nearby tree.

He loved owls. Beautiful birds.

It hooted again and then took to the sky, gliding toward the house on silent wings.

Gabby.

Shit.

She had finished piddling and had wandered over to the fence line where she was busy sniffing God only knew what.

Conrad ran, bare feet against the frosty grass, his gaze searching for the owl. A dark slash of wings against the sky. Talons reaching.

"Get out of here!" He waved his arm and shouted at the owl to frighten and distract it, sending it skyward again. He scooped the puppy into his arms.

The owl soared back into the tree.

Conrad looked at Gabby, his pulse still pounding. "You were almost breakfast. You understand that you're snack-sized, don't you?"

Gabby wagged her tail, clearly not getting it.

"That owl could have carried you off and eaten you."

He headed toward the back door, his feet freezing. "I need to be more careful when I let you outside."

How would he have been able to explain that to Kenzie?

Sorry, but an owl swooped down and carried Gabby away.

He'd gotten lucky.

"Hey, mister!" An older woman's voice came from next door. "Get some pants on! What kind of neighborhood do you think this is?"

Conrad glanced around and saw a woman's head sticking out of one of her back windows, curlers in her hair. "Sorry, ma'am. I had to save my puppy from an owl."

She wasn't appeased. "I look outside to see what all the noise is about, and I see you running around with your frank and beans hanging out!"

Frank and beans?

Conrad fought not to laugh. "It won't happen again."

The woman slammed the window shut.

He stepped through the back door into the warmth of the kitchen and carried Gabby back to the bedroom, determined to get a few more hours of sleep.

━━━

GIZMO WOKE Kenzie two minutes before her alarm was set to go off. She unlocked the doggy door so he could go outside and then opened the blinds in the kitchen. The weather had changed overnight, leaving frost on the grass. Clouds hung low over the mountains, hiding the high peaks from view.

Kenzie went back upstairs and threw on a pair of jeans and a sweater. She had an impulse to text Harrison to see how his first night with Gabby had gone, but she didn't want to risk waking him. She knew only too well how a puppy could disrupt sleep.

When Gizmo came back inside, she fed him, then put on her rubber boots and led him over to the kennel, where her boarders were anxiously waiting for their own trip outdoors—and breakfast.

She stepped inside to excited yaps, barks, and wagging tails.

"Good morning to you, too." She opened the kennels with the press of a button, and the dogs dashed out, or trundled, as in the case of Miss Piggy, a plump Chihuahua. Most headed out the dog doors to the play yard, but Crank, the pit bull, rolled onto his back, demanding belly rubs. "You're just a big lover boy, aren't you?"

Tongue lolling, paws bent in front of his chest, he seemed to grin at her.

By the time Inéz, her weekend manager, arrived at seven, Kenzie had fed the dogs, given Miss Piggy her medication, and poop-scooped the play yard, something she and her staff did several times a day depending on the number of dogs boarding with them. That was the reason for her rubber boots. They cleaned easily if she happened to step in dog poo—a hazard of the job.

Yes, her life was glamorous.

"I'll take it from here." Inéz scratched Bentley, a spoiled Goldendoodle, behind the ears. "What a sweet doggy you are."

"Thanks." Kenzie left Gizmo with Inéz, hurried home for a quick shower, then made a quick trip to Food Mart for a box of donuts.

Saturdays were Puppy Kindergarten days.

The training room back at the kennel was an ice box. Kenzie set the donuts on the table, turned on the heat, and made a big pot of coffee. This was the second week for this class. Last week, they'd done the human-only orientation. Training puppies to become happy, manageable dogs was largely about training people. She'd gone over crate training and how to deal with some challenges they might face at home, like puppies that nipped people or damaged furniture, and conflicts between the new puppy and other pets.

This week, the fun began.

She set out supplies for the class—lots of puppy treats, flyers about puppy training, and spare leashes for anyone who'd forgotten theirs. Then she arranged chairs in a wide circle and took out the items they would use for puppy playtime—a rolled-up square of artificial turf, a small set of stairs, a crinkly tunnel to run through, a shiny metal trash can, an exam table like one might find at the vet, and lots of balls.

Puppy Kindergarten involved teaching puppies a few basic commands, but it was mostly about socialization—giving puppies a chance to play together so they would learn that other dogs were their friends. It also involved handling their paws and touching their tummies so they would be more cooperative during vet visits, and exposing them to strangers and different kinds of sounds and objects so they wouldn't be afraid.

Dogs that feared the world could become aggressive.

She finished with a little time to spare. She poured herself a cup of coffee, stirred in creamer, and sat outside in her parka. The scent of fall was in the air, summer now in full retreat. It was her favorite time of year.

Her cellphone buzzed.

Harrison.

Holy mother of hotness.

He'd sent her a photo of himself cuddling Gabby

against his bare chest. His hair was tangled, and there were circles beneath his gray eyes, but he was smiling.

Then came the text message.

Proof of life.

Kenzie laughed, typed out a reply.

Did she let you sleep?

Conrad responded immediately.

A little.

Kenzie wished she were with the two of them rather than about to teach a class. On impulse, she made an offer.

Want to come to my puppy kindergarten class? There are donuts.

She waited for an answer, hoping that Harrison would say yes. It would be good for him and for Gabby.

Admit it. You just want to spend time with him.

Okay, sure. She did want to spend time with him. That wasn't illegal, was it?

No, it wasn't illegal. It was delusional.

He'll never be interested in you.

Her phone buzzed with his reply.

Donuts with sprinkles???

Kenzie laughed, tapping out a response.

Lots of sprinkles.

A moment later, her phone buzzed again.

On our way.

Oh, gosh!

Kenzie jumped to her feet and dashed home. She brushed her hair, letting it hang loose, then put on a little mascara and tinted lip gloss.

Why are you doing this? He won't notice. He's not interested in you.

She ignored that voice and hurried back to the training room, where her first client was just walking through the front door.

"Good to see you, Marge. Who's this?" Kenzie knelt down to pet a tiny cinnamon-colored toy poodle puppy.

"Snickerdoodle," Marge answered.

The puppy was trembling from head to foot, clearly terrified.

"Hi, there, Snickerdoodle. It's okay, sweetie. You're going to have lots of fun today." Kenzie stood again. "Feel free to pour yourself a cup of coffee and grab a donut while we wait."

━━

CONRAD COULDN'T TAKE his gaze off Kenzie. She was at the center of her world, the calm amid the chaos, and, God, she was beautiful. She usually kept her dark hair in a ponytail, but today it hung loose, making his fingers itch to run through it. Her cheeks were flushed from playing with puppies, a happy smile on her sweet face. She wore a blue sweater that hugged the curves of her breasts and jeans that did the same for her ass.

He shouldn't be thinking any of this.

Pay attention, idiot.

Seven puppies—a mutt, two black Labradors, a Great Dane, an Akita, a beagle, and Gabby—played and gamboled together in the center of the room, with Kenzie acting as referee. She intervened when the play got out of control and rewarded puppies who played well together, all the while answering questions from the puppies' owners.

Conrad had known that Kenzie was an expert with dogs. He'd watched her act as Gizmo's handler at the scene of dozens of rescues. But there was so much more to know about canines than he'd realized.

"The fastest way to housetrain your puppy is to be consistent with the crate." She reached down, pulled the Akita off the Great Dane, and held the puppy, effectively putting it in time-out. "When your puppy isn't in her crate, you'll need to watch her, just like you'd watch over a human toddler. If you give her the run of the house and don't keep an eye on her, she's going to have accidents."

D'oh.

Hear that, dumbshit?

"How do you know when they need to go to the bathroom?"

Kenzie put the Akita down. "When you see your puppy trying to sneak behind the couch or walk off into a corner, pick her up and carry her outside right away."

"That means I have to keep a constant eye on him."

Kenzie smiled. "That's life with a puppy."

Gabby jumped and rolled with the two black Lab puppies. Kenzie scooped her up, leashed her, and carried her over to a toy poodle that stood behind a slatted, folding divider. Kenzie had put up the little divider to make the poodle feel sheltered and safe, giving it its own little space.

She knelt down on the other side of the divider and set Gabby on the floor, holding her, giving the little poodle time to decide whether he wanted to meet Gabby or not. "It's okay, Snickerdoodle. This is Gabby. She's just a puppy, too."

Snickerdoodle stretched out his little neck, leaning forward on trembling legs to sniff Gabby through the slats of the divider. Then he wagged his tail.

Gabby gave a little yip and wagged her tail, too.

Kenzie gave Gabby a little slack, allowing her to poke her head around the divider. The poodle seemed afraid at first, but stretched out to sniff Gabby again. Slowly, Kenzie allowed Gabby to enter the little poodle's space, until the two of them stood together, sniffing each other, their tails wagging. She gave both puppies a treat. "You're such a brave boy, Snickerdoodle."

Kenzie glanced over her shoulder at Conrad. "Can you come hold Gabby's leash and keep an eye on her? I need to get back to the class. Don't let her jump on Snickerdoodle or do anything to scare him."

"Right." Conrad got to his feet, crossed the room, and took the leash from her, sitting on the floor to the side of the divider. "Hey, Snickerdoodle."

Who would saddle a tiny dog with a name like that?

"I'm Marge." The poodle's owner smiled at him—and blushed.

What the hell was that about?

Come to think of it, he'd been getting a lot of female attention today. The woman who owned the Akita had asked him if he wanted to walk their puppies together and had given him her phone number. The one with a black Lab had asked him if his girlfriend liked dogs—after looking at his finger and seeing no ring. The owner of the beagle had smiled a lot and told him fifteen times how cute Gabby was.

He'd heard that a puppy was the best way for a man to pick up women. Maybe there was something to that.

"What's your puppy's name?" Marge had to be thirty years older than Conrad.

"Her name is Gabby, but she's not my puppy. I'm watching her for Kenzie."

Marge's face fell. "Oh. The two of you are together. I've seen you watching her."

Conrad started to say they were just friends but decided it was really none of Marge's business. Some part of him wished he and Kenzie *were* together, so it didn't bother him in the least that Marge had made that assumption.

He glanced over at Kenzie and saw that she was watching him. She met his gaze, then looked away. Had she overheard?

Conrad watched while Gabby and Snickerdoodle slowly became friends, eventually rolling and playing together like the other puppies.

"Look at him!" Marge smiled. "Snickerdoodle's not afraid now."

Kenzie walked over to them. "He just needs to move at his own pace."

Conrad felt a sense of pride in Gabby—which was stupid because she wasn't his puppy. He had done nothing to mold her behavior. In fact, he was teaching her to be a juvenile delinquent, letting her sleep in his bed and poop on his floor.

Playtime ended. The puppies were leashed and led around the room to experience all the stuff that Kenzie had set out for them. Some tried to avoid the artificial turf, probably because it poked their paws. Some struggled with the stairs. The Great Dane knocked over the metal trash can, yelped, and ran. Most hesitated to enter the tunnel—but not Gabby.

Gabby wasn't afraid of anything. She darted around on the artificial grass, made her way up and down the stairs, ran inside the metal trash can, and made a game of darting through the tunnel.

Kenzie walked up to Conrad, that sweet smile on her face. "How's she doing?"

"She's fearless."

Kenzie nodded. "That's one of the qualities we look for when picking a puppy to train for SAR and HRD work."

That made sense to Conrad.

They worked on Sit and Follow after that. Gabby was a pro, doing what he told her to do, taking the treats from his fingers. As far as he was concerned, she was the valedictorian of her class.

Then it was over.

"Remember to practice throughout the week," Kenzie called to her clients as they carried tired puppies out the door. "Consistency is the key."

Ms. Akita came up to Conrad, tilted her head, and looked at him from beneath sooty lashes, puppy in her arms. "Do you want to take the dogs to the park now? The puppies can play, and we can get acquainted."

She was pretty—tall, blond, athletic. He should have been attracted to her, but he wasn't. The woman who interested him stood nearby watching this exchange through narrowed eyes.

Uh-oh.

Conrad took a chance. "Sorry. I can't. Kenzie and I have a brunch date." He looked over at Kenzie. "Are you ready?"

"Um … oh, yes." Kenzie struggled to cover her surprise. "Let me lock up, and we can go."

Ms. Akita's face fell, but she quickly covered her disappointment with a smile. "Maybe some other time."

Kenzie walked up to him, arms crossed over her chest, waiting to speak until the others had gone. "You're welcome."

"For what?"

"For being your excuse not to hang out with that woman."

"I wasn't just making an excuse. Want to have brunch with me?"

She blinked, staring up at him through wide blue eyes. "But I already ate."

"So what? Eat again."

Chapter 6

HARRISON HAD CALLED it a brunch date, but Kenzie didn't think he'd meant it that way. They were just sharing a meal at the New Moon. It wasn't a *date* date.

Don't you just wish?

Kenzie had watched her clients fall all over him today and had wanted to kick them all out of class. But she had absolutely no right to feel jealous. She had no claim on him. If he wanted to hang out with Hannah and her Akita, that was his business. Besides, she wasn't into climbers.

Keep telling yourself that.

Harrison attacked his home fries and scrambled eggs as if he hadn't eaten in a week. "How did you end up working with dogs?"

How could he eat so much and stay in such great shape?

"I've always loved animals." She picked at her soggy fruit salad. "I wanted to be a vet when I was younger, so I got a biology degree from CU. I got a job working for a vet after graduation. One of the vet's regular clients was a woman who trained SAR dogs. She invited me to a training one day, and that was it. I knew I wanted to train dogs. I started learning, and my businesses grew out of that."

"And you're how old—thirty-three?—and you own two businesses. That's impressive."

"I had help. I inherited my grandparents' old dime store and their house. I moved into the house, and the dime store became the kennel and the shop. My parents gave me an interest-free loan to remodel the store and the house, and I paid that off last year. If I'd had to buy the property and start from scratch, I'm not sure I could have done it."

He nodded as if this made sense. "I bet your parents are proud."

"I suppose. I don't see them all that often. They retired to Belize."

"How do you balance your businesses with dog training and SAR work?"

"The store is closed on Sundays, but the kennel is open every day year round. I have a staff of ten who run both operations, plus a vet tech and a groomer. If I get sick or toned out for a rescue, my managers can handle everything. I teach classes on Tuesday, Wednesday, and Thursday nights and Puppy Kindergarten on Saturdays, with some private lessons thrown in here and there. Once in a while I have to cancel class when I get toned out for a rescue, but it doesn't happen often."

He looked confused. "When do you find time to go on trips, take vacations?"

"Vacation?" Wouldn't that be nice? "I haven't taken a vacation since… I can't remember. Running a business makes that difficult."

"What if something happens with the dogs at night when no one's there?"

"I live next door, and I have a surveillance system inside the kennel. My app allows the owners to check on their dogs at any time to see how they're doing, and I'm able to see what's going on when I'm home or out on errands."

She drew out her smartphone, clicked on her own app. On the screen, Inéz was playing with Crank, while the other dogs romped in the play yard or dozed in their kennels. She turned her phone so that Conrad could see.

"An app?" He leaned in to look. "That's high tech."

"People feel better when they can see that their dogs are safe, and I have to stay competitive somehow. I have to persuade people to drive up the canyon from Boulder if I'm going to stay in business."

He grew quiet, glancing down at Gabby, who napped at his feet, his expression troubled. "She woke me up from a nightmare."

The abrupt change of topic took Kenzie by surprise. "You had a nightmare?"

He nodded, his gaze still on the puppy. "I was there, hanging over that crevasse again. Bruce, Luka, and Felix were frozen into the ice all around me, like fish frozen in a pond. Then I saw that the ice was moving. It was closing in on me."

Kenzie knew that he really had regained consciousness hanging above a crevasse. She couldn't imagine how terrifying that had been.

She reached out, took his big hand in hers. "What a horrible dream. I'm so sorry."

Awareness arced between them, startling her.

His gaze met hers, his fingers threading with hers, a muscle tensing in his jaw. "Gabby woke me up. One minute I was trying to get out of that crevasse, and the next, she was licking my face. Do you think…?"

His voice trailed off, his question unasked.

"Do I think what?" She wasn't thinking much of anything right now to be honest, his touch warm, mesmerizing, intoxicating.

Snap out of it!

She was an idiot to let this affect her. Even if Harrison were truly interested in her—and he wasn't—he was still the kind of man who would leave her for a pile of rocks one day. She was done with that. Wasn't she?

He shook his head. "I'm being stupid."

Kenzie tried to piece together his unasked question. "Are you asking whether Gabby knew something was wrong and woke you up on purpose?"

His gaze met hers, his lips quirking in a grin. "Stupid, right?"

She traced her thumb over his knuckles. "It's not stupid at all. Dogs can be very sensitive to the emotions of their humans. When I'm upset about something, Gizmo will whine, lick my hands, and try to get me to pet him. He wants to help, to cheer me up. I'm sure Gabby, as little as she is, realized something was wrong."

"You knew what you were doing when you chose her. She's special." Harrison returned the caress, sending shivers up Kenzie's arm.

Then it hit her.

She gaped at him open-mouthed. "You let Gabby sleep in your bed! Don't try to deny it. How else could she have licked your face when you were dreaming?"

Harrison's gaze met hers, guilt on his handsome face. "Busted."

─────

"IS it too late to plead the Fifth?"

Kenzie pinned him with her gaze. "You can't plead the Fifth *after* you confess. That's not how it works."

Conrad could tell from the gleam of humor in her eyes that she wasn't truly angry with him. She hadn't pulled her hand away, either. He liked that. Her touch was electric, her fingers delicate, her hand silky soft and so much smaller than his.

If this is how it felt to hold her hand, how would it feel to kiss her?

Don't go there.

Kenzie was saying something. "I know how hard the first several weeks with a new puppy can be, but if she doesn't learn good habits now, it will be tougher for her to learn them later."

"I know. Sorry." He looked down at the sleeping puppy again. "She was crying, and it seemed so heartless to leave her there."

"Did you have dogs growing up?"

"Oh, yeah—sled dogs. Thirty-five of them."

Kenzie gaped at him. "Thirty-five *sled* dogs?"

"Alaskan Huskies. I grew up there, remember?"

"Yeah, but … thirty-five Huskies? I guess you didn't have an HOA."

That made him laugh. "No, no HOA. No neighbors, either. My parents homesteaded along the Copper River. My dad built the house and the outbuildings from the ground up. We lived completely off the grid with a boat as our only motorized transportation. My dad trained sled dogs so that we could get around in the winter to get wood, forage, hunt."

"That's totally bananas!"

"Bananas?" Conrad laughed at her reaction. "I didn't know anyone lived any other way until I was five. My mom got sick of roughing it after the next baby was stillborn. She blamed my dad for not calling a bush pilot to get her to a hospital. My father helped her bundle me and one of the dogs into the boat and brought us downriver. He left us in Cordova and headed back to the homestead alone. My mom made her way with me in tow to Anchorage and got a job at a diner."

"God! How awful for your parents. It couldn't have been easy for you, either. It must have been a shock to find yourself in a modern town."

"When you're a kid, you just take it all as it comes, but I do remember how much I loved electric lights and warm running water. I drove my mom nuts flicking the light switches on and off and playing with faucets."

That made her smile, but the smile quickly faded. "It must have been hard for your dad to let the two of you go, especially after losing the baby, too."

Conrad nodded. "He loved my mom, and she loved him, but she couldn't take the subsistence lifestyle. He knew he couldn't live in the city, so he let her go. He was always the perfect gentleman to her, never even raised his voice."

"Did you see him again?"

Conrad nodded. "Every summer, he made the long journey to town to get me. Then he'd hire a bush pilot to fly us to the homestead with supplies. I spent summers with him, learning how to set up a fish wheel, how to smoke salmon, how to hunt ptarmigan, elk, and moose, how to build and fix things. I loved it."

"I guess the outdoors is in your DNA. What do he and your mother think of your climbing?"

"My mother hates what I do. Last time I saw her, she laid into me, told me I was just like my dad." She'd said a lot more than that, crying and shouting in his face that he would probably die in the wilderness one day just like his father.

Conrad had *almost* proved her right.

Kenzie caressed the sensitive inner surface of his fingers with her own. "What about your dad?"

"My father died when I was sixteen. He was supposed to pick me up for the summer, but he never came. My mom sent a pilot to check on him. They found him long dead on the floor of the house he'd built. An autopsy found that he'd died of sepsis from a ruptured appendix. If he had only radioed for help … I don't think my mother will ever forgive him. She sold off his dogs and buried him at the homestead next to the baby."

Kenzie's eyes filled with sympathy. "God, Harrison, that's terrible. I'm so sorry."

Behind him, the door to the café opened with a jingle.

Kenzie looked over, smiled. "Hey, Esri."

Conrad reflexively pulled his hand away, instantly regretting it, the loss of contact leaving emptiness. "Hey, Esri."

Esri walked to their table, her cheeks red from the chill and exertion, a Peruvian wool ski hat pulled over her short dark hair. "Hey, Kenzie. Hey, Conrad, welcome home. It's great to see you."

Conrad had known they'd run into someone he knew sooner or later. That was the price for walking out his front door. Scarlet was a small town, after all. It wasn't that he didn't want to see Esri. He just didn't want her pushing him to get therapy.

"It's good to see you, too." Remembering his manners, he pointed to one of the empty chairs at their table and stood. "Want to join us?"

"No, thanks. I'm just here to grab a chai. I've been out hiking, and it's cold out there this morning. It looks like fall is finally here." Esri looked straight at Conrad. "I heard you stayed for a while at the Tengboche Monastery."

Conrad sat again. "I was there for about fifteen months."

"I have ancestors on my father's side who were monks there."

Whatever he'd expected her to say, that wasn't it.

"Amazing. Small world. Do you have any relatives there now?" He might have met them or shared a meal with them.

Esri shook her head. "The last was my father's uncle. When you get some time, I would love to talk with you about that experience. I've never been there, but I've always wanted to visit. I'll treat you to coffee. How does that sound?"

Conrad didn't have an objection to that—provided Esri didn't use it as a pretext to psychoanalyze him. "Sure."

Esri's face lit up, and she pulled out her smartphone. "How is tomorrow at ten?"

"What's tomorrow?" *As if you have anything going on.*

"Sunday," Kenzie and Esri answered in unison.

"I'll have to bring Gabby. I'm fostering her for Kenzie for a while."

"That's fine with me." Esri bent down to pet the puppy. "She's a doll."

"She's the smartest puppy in her kindergarten," Conrad blurted, instantly feeling like an idiot.

"I bet she is." Esri stood again. "I should let you two get back to your conversation. It's great to see you, Conrad."

"It's good to see you, too."

As she walked away, Conrad could have sworn she winked at Kenzie.

KENZIE FOLLOWED Harrison through his front door, grateful to get out of the cold wind. She glanced around at the dozen or more dusty moving boxes that filled his living room. "This was all upstairs at The Cave?"

When he'd told her that he planned to spend his afternoon unpacking, she had offered to help.

"I've still got climbing gear and furniture there." Harrison unleashed Gabby, who bounded off to explore. "I brought mostly personal stuff. I figured I couldn't wear the same pair of jeans forever."

"Yeah, probably not." She slipped out of her parka, which he took and hung in an almost empty coat closet near the door. "Thanks. Where do you want to start?"

"Music." He ran a hand through his hair, glanced around. "I never do anything without tunes. One of these boxes has my sound system. I labeled it so I could set it up first. Now I just have to find it."

Kenzie walked among boxes, turning them to read their sides. "Here it is."

Harrison whipped out a pocket knife, walked over to the box, and sliced through the heavy tape to reveal a lot of bubble wrap.

He pulled out a black box that at first reminded Kenzie of an old-timey clock radio and carried it over to an end table. "I can connect my phone to this via Bluetooth or play CDs on it. It comes with wireless speakers for different rooms of the house, but I won't bother with those until I move into my new place."

"Fancy." Kenzie didn't have anything that sophisticated. She walked into the kitchen for a glass of water. "What kind of music do you like?"

"Classic rock, metal, adult alternative, post-grunge,

dubstep, country—pretty much everything but mindless pop," he called after her. "How about you?"

"Mindless pop." She smiled to herself when he laughed at her answer. "I'm not picky, as long as it's music and not just noise."

"Got it."

She opened a cupboard near the sink and found it full of hobnail glassware in turquoise blue. She took out a glass, felt its weight. "This is so cool."

Mrs. Beech's house was an antique shop.

She filled the glass with cold tap water and drank, setting it down on the counter just as the Lumineers' *Ophelia* began to play.

She found Harrison standing in the middle of the room, looking rugged and handsome, hands on his hips, a smile on his face.

"How's that?"

It took her a minute to realize he was talking about the music.

"It's perfect."

They got to work, Gabby supervising while Kenzie opened boxes and announced the contents so that Harrison could carry the boxes to the appropriate room— towels to the bathroom, clothes and sheets to the bedroom, cooking stuff and cleaning supplies to the kitchen.

He looked into a box that held flatware and utensils. "I'm not sure I need any of this. The house came with almost everything."

Kenzie opened another box. "Files and magazines— and, oh! Your old high school yearbooks. You kept them."

She reached in, took one out. "West High School Eagles."

She walked to the sofa, sat, and started thumbing through it. "What grade were you in back in 2000?"

He stepped out of the kitchen. "A junior. What are you doing?"

"Trying to find you." She turned to the juniors' section.

"Oh, God." He scooped the puppy up and sat beside her. He turned a few pages and pointed. "That's me."

She stared at the kid in the photo. He was a younger, less muscular version of the man who sat beside her, but his smile was the same. "You were hot even back then."

Her heart gave a knock when she realized what she'd just said, her gaze jerking to his, heat rushing into her cheeks.

A grin tugged at his lips, the warmth in his eyes making her pulse skip. "You think I'm hot?"

She stammered. "Well, I didn't say … I only meant … Can I plead the Fifth?"

Could the world please swallow her now?

His grin grew into a broad smile that put flutters in her belly. "I'll let you off easy—this time."

They worked through the afternoon, Kenzie asking him questions about growing up in Alaska—and secretly ducking into the bathroom once or twice to refresh her lip gloss and check her hair.

You are hopeless, girl.

They took a break so that Gabby could have some outdoor playtime, practicing puppy runaways until it started to rain. Then, with the puppy worn out and asleep in her crate, they went back to unpacking.

Most of what Conrad had brought from The Cave was basic household stuff, tools, and personal belongings like clothes, towels, and sheets. Much of it needed to be washed and dried after spending more than a year in storage. But there were strange odds and ends, too—old albums, pieces of rock that Harrison had brought back from mountains all over the world, a box of old phone chargers and electronics.

"Where do you want me to put these?" Kenzie held up a shoebox of rocks.

Harrison glanced up from the drawer he was stuffing with socks. "You can stick that on a shelf in the closet."

She stepped into the closet to find the lower shelf already crammed full. The upper shelf was almost empty, but it was beyond her reach. She glanced around for something to stand on—all she needed was another couple of feet—and spotted an old wooden step ladder in the back of the closet. Mrs. Beech had probably used it, too. She hadn't been much taller than Kenzie.

Box tucked under one arm, Kenzie moved the step ladder into position. She didn't like heights, but she would only be a few feet up. She stepped onto the first rung, the second, and then the third, only to feel the top step give way. She toppled sideways with a shriek, rocks scattering.

Harrison caught her in mid-air. "Going somewhere?"

He didn't set her on her feet, but held her in strong arms, his face inches from hers, his body hard.

Kenzie could barely breathe, being close to him like this sending her pulse into overdrive. Somehow, she managed to speak. "How did you get to me so quickly?"

"I was already on my way to help you. You don't need a ladder when I'm here."

Then his gaze dropped to her lips—and he kissed her.

Chapter 7

AT THE FIRST brush of his lips against Kenzie's, Conrad knew he was in trouble. She was perfect. Everything about her was soft and sweet—her lips, her skin, her scent, the feminine feel of her body.

Hell, yes.

He kissed her again, deeper this time, and she came alive in his arms, wrapping her legs around his waist, curling her fingers in his hair.

The heat that had simmered inside him all afternoon, that hungry spark of desire he felt for her, burst into open flame. Blood rushed to his groin, his cock straining against his jeans, lust pounding in his veins like a pulse.

It hit Conrad that he could fuck her *just like this*. She was small and light in his arms. Yeah, he could fuck her like this—standing, holding her, her body clinging to his.

An image of her, naked and grinding against him while he held her filled his mind—and then he remembered where they were.

Not in the damned closet.

He turned, walked with her to his bed, and lowered her

to the mattress amid piles of laundry, following her down, his hips cradled between her thighs. He looked into her eyes, saw what he thought was longing.

He needed to be sure. "Do you want this?"

She nodded. "*Yes.*"

He took her mouth with his again, and this time he didn't hold back. Neither did she, answering his need with her own, her tongue meeting his.

He'd fantasized about kissing her, touching her, fucking her. Before this last trip, he'd fantasized almost every night. At the monastery, too.

Kenzie, always Kenzie.

But the reality of kissing her beat any fantasy. Her fingers fisted in his hair, and her body moved beneath his. She didn't wait for him to make the next move, but slid one hand beneath his shirt, moaning as she took in the feel of him, her palms spreading fire over his skin.

Why hadn't they done this before now?

He tore his lips from hers and returned the favor, raising himself up on one elbow to cup one of her breasts through her sweater and bra.

She moaned, arched into his hand, her nipple a hard pebble beneath the fabric.

He rucked up her sweater, moaned at the sight of her —the soft swells of her breasts, creamy skin, wine-red nipples peeking through black lace. He kissed her breast-bone, then pushed the cup of her bra aside, and licked her nipple.

"*Oh.*" She gave a gasp, her areola drawing tight.

Then he lowered his mouth to her breast and suckled her.

A knock.

"Is anyone home?"

Kenzie's eyes flew open. "*Rose?*"

"What the hell?" Conrad levered himself up. "Stay here. I'll be right back."

"I'm not going to hide." Kenzie stood, adjusted her bra, pulled down her sweater.

"Hello?" Rose called again, clearly *inside* his house now.

Kenzie looked like she was trying not to laugh, but Conrad didn't find it funny at all. He adjusted himself, made sure his shirt covered the ridge of his erection, and walked out to the living room, Kenzie one step behind him.

Rose stood there, snooping through boxes, her back to him.

Conrad fought not to lose his temper. "Looking for something?"

Rose jumped, turned to face him, a magazine in her hand. "The door was unlocked—"

"So you just walked right in?" Conrad reached for the magazine.

Rose held it up so that the cover faced him. "The good old days, huh?"

On its cover was a photo of him and Bruce standing on the summit of Everest in 2008, both half frozen, both smiling. The sight of it hit him like a fist.

He jerked the magazine away from her. "Why are you here?"

Rose ignored the question, her lips curving in a knowing smile. "I thought that was your truck out front, Kenzie."

"Hey, Rose," Kenzie answered.

"We're unpacking," Not that it was any of Rose's business, but Conrad didn't want to expose Kenzie to gossip.

"You were being very quiet about it."

Conrad opened his mouth to tell her to mind her own

damned business, but Kenzie spoke first. "Gabby, my puppy, is asleep."

From Rose's smile, Conrad could tell she wasn't buying it.

"I brought you a little housewarming present, a gift to welcome you back." She held out a green-and-white striped paper gift bag that read "Rose's New Age Emporium" on one side. "I heard you stayed at a Buddhist monastery. Did you convert?"

"No—not that it's your business." Conrad took the bag, opened it, and found a large crystal on a silver chain.

He held it up. "Thanks. What do I do with this?"

"It's a Feng Shui crystal. Hang it in a window. It will activate positive energy and break up old, dark energy in your home. This place *needs* new energy." She glanced around as if this energy of which she spoke were as visible to her as the breadcrumbs on the countertop.

But Conrad wasn't fooled by her caring neighbor routine. He suspected she'd invited herself in so that she could check out Mrs. Beech's house—and perhaps find something about him she could share with her network of gossipy friends.

"Thanks for stopping by, and thanks for the gift. Next time, please wait for me to open the door before you come in. Some folks in Scarlet might not mind when neighbors walk in unannounced, but I'm not one of those people."

Rose didn't seem offended by this. "Fine. We all have our boundaries."

"Yes, and you crossed mine."

There was a moment of awkward silence.

"Well, I'll just let you get back to … unpacking." The way she said it left no doubt that she didn't think they'd been unpacking at all.

"I'll walk you to the door," Kenzie offered.

"You don't need to do that." Rose passed Conrad, a smug smile on her face.

Conrad followed her and locked the door behind her. "Why does she think she can just walk into my house?"

Kenzie shrugged. "I have no idea. The whole town is going to hear that you and I were kissing before tomorrow morning. I hope that doesn't upset you."

"No, not at all. I don't give a damn what people think. Besides, how can she be sure what we were doing? She didn't come into the bedroom."

Kenzie looked up at him, seeming to hesitate, a smile tugging at her lips. "You're, um, wearing my lip gloss."

Conrad ran the back of his hand over his mouth.

It came away rosy and sparkling.

———

KENZIE TOOK Gabby outside to do her business, a cold wind blowing down from the mountains. She wrapped her arms around herself to ward off the chill—and the sinking feeling in her chest.

She had hoped she and Harrison would pick up where they'd left off before Rose had intruded. They'd barely touched second base, and her body still ached for him. But Harrison had gone back to unpacking as if nothing had happened between them.

He was pulling away from her. They'd spent a perfect day together. They had kissed—and more. But now he was pulling away.

At first, Kenzie had thought Rose was to blame for his abrupt change of mood. That was undoubtedly part of it. But when he'd refused to make eye contact with her moments ago, she'd known there was more to it than that.

She watched Gabby sniff her way along the fence,

watching the skies and nearby trees for the owl Harrison had warned her about.

What should she do?

She could pretend like nothing had happened and go home, but she hated it when people brushed important things under the rug. They were adults, for God's sake. And, yes, this *had* been important—to her, at least, but maybe not to him.

She could ask him what was going on, try to get him to talk about it, but she had no idea how he'd react. He might push her away, and that would be it.

Tell him how you feel.

Right.

Hey, Harrison, I'm super attracted to you and think you kiss like a dream, so please stop brooding, get naked, and pound me.

He *did* kiss like a dream, using just enough strength and force to make her feel swept away and enough skill and gentleness to keep it pleasurable.

It was time for her to head home anyway. She needed to put together a bank deposit, pick up something for supper, and retrieve Gizmo from the kennel.

Gabby finished and bounded across the lawn back to Kenzie, probably as eager to get out of the cold as Kenzie was.

"Good girl." Kenzie gave her a treat and then went back inside with her to find Conrad sorting through a box he'd set on the kitchen table—the box Rose had been poking her nose into. "She did what she was supposed to do."

Conrad nodded, his expression softening when Gabby trotted up to him. He bent down, petted her. "Who's a good puppy? You are. That's right."

Gabby pranced and wagged, delighted to be the center of his attention.

And once again, Kenzie was jealous of her puppy.

She glanced inside the box and saw a stack of magazines, all of them with Harrison's face on the cover. "Cool!"

She took one out, opened it.

"They're just old interviews. I'm tossing them in the recycling."

She shook her head. "You can't do that. You're on the cover."

"I don't want them." There was an edge to his voice.

"Can I take them?"

He faced her, apparently not happy with that idea. "What would you do with them? You're not into climbing, and you don't need to read them because you can ask me anything you want."

Okay, fine. "Why are you all tense and angry?"

He frowned. "I'm not angry."

"Right." She scooped up the magazines and carried them out of the kitchen and toward the front door. "I'll donate these to the Scarlet Springs Library."

He followed. "The library isn't going to want this shit."

"Not true. You're local, and you're kind of a big deal."

"That's in the past."

"Well, Silas Moffat is dead, so he's a *lot* more in the past than you are. Joe still donated his journals to the library."

"That's different."

"You're right. Silas was a murdering jerk, and you're a hero to a lot of people." Kenzie dropped the stack of magazines next to her handbag.

"I'm *not* a hero."

She opened the closet door to get her coat. "Thanks for a fun day. I really did enjoy myself."

He shut the door. "What's going on, Kenzie?"

"That's what I tried to ask you." She crossed her arms over her chest. Okay, so she would have to go first. "I'm angry because you won't be honest with me."

He narrowed his eyes, shook his head, as if he wasn't quite keeping up with her. "I won't … *what?*"

She took the plunge. "You're sorry you kissed me, aren't you?"

He gaped at her, then laughed as if she'd said something hilarious. He drew her into his arms, kissed the top of her head. "No, I'm not sorry—not for that. But that doesn't mean it was the right thing to do."

"I was right. You're sorry."

He let her go. "My life—it's fucked up right now. I can't seem to get my act together. I don't have a job. I don't have my own home. I'm not even sure I'm going to stay in Colorado. I don't want to drag you into my mess. It wouldn't be fair to you."

Did he mean this, or was he just trying to let her down easy?

"Let me decide what's fair to me, okay?" Wait. What had he just said? "You're thinking of leaving Scarlet?"

"Yeah. Maybe. I don't know." He let out a breath, ran a hand over the stubble on his jaw, his gaze falling on the magazine on the top of her pile, the one with a photo of him with his climbing buddy, Bruce, who'd died on Everest.

A muscle in his jaw tightened.

The good old days.

That's what Rose had said to him while holding up that exact magazine.

For someone who claimed to be a psychic, a therapist, a witch, a healer, an energy worker, and God only knew what else, Rose could be an insensitive ass at times.

You're not much better.

Kenzie was thinking about herself, while Harrison struggled with his grief.

Heart aching for him, she reached out, took his hand. "Give yourself time. You'll get through this. You have friends here, people who care about you. I'm one of them."

"Thanks for your help today." He released her hand, took her coat out of the closet, and held it up for her.

"You're welcome." She slipped her arms into the sleeves and turned to face him. "Can I come by to check on Gabby tomorrow?"

She'd be checking on him, too, but he didn't need to know that.

"Sure. Come any time." He drew her close, ducked down, pressed a soft kiss to her lips. "See? I can't help myself."

She liked hearing that. "Then don't. Don't help yourself."

He drew away again, ran his thumb down her cheek, his expression troubled. "You're beautiful, Kenzie. You're smart and fun. But I don't think I'd be good for you."

She heard the despair in his voice and was sure now that he wasn't just saying this to spare her feelings. He truly believed it. "How about this? Kiss me whenever you want, and we'll take it a day at a time."

CONRAD ROLLED OVER, drew a pillow over his head, but it was no good. He'd been a bastard and had made Gabby sleep in her crate, which meant that her crying had kept him awake. Now she was waking him up.

He sat up, glanced at the clock. Six a.m. "Don't you sleep?"

Gabby wagged her tail, nose pressed through the front bars of her crate.

"It's a good thing you're cute."

To be fair, the puppy wasn't the only thing that had kept him awake. Kissing Kenzie had left him so horny that he'd had to beat off to get to sleep. Even then, he hadn't been able to get her out of his mind. He'd tried to blame two years of celibacy, but he knew that wasn't it.

He wanted Kenzie.

"Kiss me whenever you want," she'd said, her words following him into sleep.

Yeah, well, that would certainly keep them both busy.

He grabbed his jeans and pulled them on. He didn't want to freak out the neighbor lady again. Then he lifted Gabby out of her crate and carried her to the back door, grabbing his parka along the way. Outside, the first snow of the season lay on the ground. Just a dusting, it barely covered the grass.

"I'm not sure you're going to like this, but you still have to do your business outside. Got that?"

Gabby looked up at him, tail wagging.

He opened the screen door, laughing when she darted outside—and came to an abrupt halt. "Yep. Snow. You live in the mountains. Get used to it."

The puppy sniffed the snow, barked at it.

Yeah, that was the cutest thing he'd ever seen. "It's okay. It's just snow."

Kenzie hadn't told Conrad what to do in case of snow, and he wasn't going to call her at this hour on a Sunday to ask.

He spotted a shovel leaning against the wall near the back door to the garage. "I have an idea. Hang on, Gabby."

He grabbed the shovel and cleared the snow off a few

square feet of grass, then watched while Gabby took a few tentative steps, sniffed, and finally did her thing. He gave her a treat, praised her. "Good job, Gabby. Good girl."

The puppy couldn't get back inside fast enough.

"I suppose you're hungry, too."

She looked up at him expectantly, little tail wagging.

"Okay. How do eggs Benedict and coffee sound? No? Okay, kibble it is then."

He mixed kibble with warm water and set the bowl on the floor, wondering whether he should try to get more sleep or whether he should suck it up and make coffee. He looked down at Gabby. "Are you ready to go back to bed?"

She picked up her favorite squeak toy.

"Okay, fine. Let's play. Who needs sleep?"

He played with the puppy and took her out into the snow again, both for a potty break and so that she could start getting used to it. When she was worn out, he made himself a big pot of coffee and got to work breaking down cardboard boxes and straightening up the place. Kenzie would be dropping by later, and he didn't want her to think he was a lazy slob—even if that's precisely what he was.

If it weren't for the puppy, he would still be in bed.

He got a text message from Kenzie just after nine asking him how the night had gone and how Gabby had handled the snow. He answered, sending her another photo of the puppy, curled up and sound asleep.

See you at 2?
Sure.

Conrad crashed for a while, getting a little sleep, and then it was time to meet Esri. He packed the puppy's crate, grabbed his laptop with his photographs of Tengboche, and drove with Gabby to the café. Snow had transformed the Indian Peaks, which rose like white titans against a blue sky.

He would never get tired of that view.

He found Esri waiting for them at a table near a sunny window.

She stood, gave Conrad a hug. "I thought the puppy might like some sunshine."

"She didn't know what to make of the snow this morning." Conrad settled Gabby and then ordered himself more coffee—*yes, God, please*—and the eggs Benedict he'd been thinking about all morning.

Esri ordered fruit and a chai. "I'm sure you've got some mixed memories of Tengboche, but I'd love to hear whatever you care to share with me about life there."

Conrad showed her photos and told her how the monks had taken him in and let him have a small room so that he didn't have to live year-round in his tent. He told her about the monks' daily routine and his conversations with the Lama. He told her about the work he'd done for them and for some of the villagers.

As he spoke, he could almost smell the incense, hear the monks chanting, and feel the cold wind on his face.

"The view from the monastery—Ama Dablam, Lhotse, Everest…" A rush of emotion, unexpected and unwelcome, made his throat go tight. "I looked up at Everest every day, knowing they were still there. Somehow, being nearby made it seem like I hadn't left them behind. But now…"

He swallowed—hard. "I think some part of me kept waiting for them to walk into Tengboche and ask me why I'd gone on without them. That probably sounds stupid."

Keep it together, idiot.

Esri shook her head. "No, it doesn't."

He cleared his throat, fought to rein in his emotions.

He was *not* going to break down in front of Esri. "Sorry. This wasn't supposed to turn into a therapy session."

Esri gave his hand a squeeze. "No worries. We're just two friends talking. I really appreciate everything you've told me. I've always wanted to visit Tengboche, and now I have through your eyes. Thank you."

"Is that invitation to join you for meditation still open?" Meditation was the only way he'd been able to escape his emotions when he'd been at the monastery.

Esri smiled. "Always."

Chapter 8

KENZIE CLEANED her house and then went grocery shopping, as she always did on Sunday morning. When she'd gotten everything on her list—thank goodness she'd remembered it this time—she made her way back to the pharmacy to get condoms.

Do you truly need them, or are you trying to create the illusion that something exciting is happening with your love life?

Hey, Harrison had kissed her. She hadn't imagined that.

Yes, but will he do it again?

He'd said he couldn't help himself, and that right there was reason to hope—and reason enough to buy condoms.

She looked at all the different kinds of condoms, wondering what kind he might prefer and what size he'd need. He was *not* a small guy. She'd been able to feel that through his jeans.

Ribbed. Extra lubrication. Twisted. Flavored. Extra thin. Tingles.

Warmth spread between her thighs at the idea of Harrison sheathed in one of these and thrusting into her.

Stop. Just stop.

Uncomfortably horny now, she grabbed a package that claimed to be extra thin and had an XL label and dropped it into her shopping cart.

In the checkout lane, she found herself standing behind Kendra Jewell, Lexi's stepmother. Kendra turned, glanced into her cart, and smiled. "I hear you and that sexy bastard Harrison Conrad are an item. Extra-large? I'm not surprised."

With the condoms sitting right there in plain sight, Kenzie didn't try to explain. Denials would only make things worse.

Sometimes living in a small town sucked.

"Rose has been busy, hasn't she?"

Kendra laughed. "Always."

After Kenzie had gotten everything home and put away, she dropped Gizmo off with Inéz at the kennel and made the short drive to Harrison's house, a couple of condoms in her handbag. Better safe than sorry.

He answered the door in a pair of low-slung jeans and a black, cable-knit sweater, his long, dark hair and the stubble on his jaw giving him a bad-boy look that all but made her knees go weak. "Hey."

He smiled, but there were shadows in his eyes. "Hey."

Kenzie stepped into the warmth to see Gabby bounding across the carpet toward her. She scooped up the excited fluffball, accepting puppy kisses. "How's my baby girl?"

"She misses you."

"I miss her, too. Are you behaving for Uncle Harrison?"

Lips that had kissed her senseless curved in a grin. "No accidents today. She slept in her crate last night, which means I didn't sleep much at all. She's been out in the snow a few times to go potty. I shoveled off a bit of grass for her because she didn't want to walk on it."

"Great idea. See, Harrison? You're a natural at this." Kenzie snuggled the puppy close. "Snow is new to you, isn't it, Gabby?"

"She slept for most of the time I was at New Moon with Esri."

Kenzie was relieved to know he'd spoken with Esri today. "How did that go?"

"We talked about life at the monastery. That's about it." His tone of voice made it clear that he didn't want to say more.

"Can I help with anything?" The moving boxes were gone, and the place looked clean and organized.

He shook his head. "I'm good. I got a lot done last night and this morning."

"Maybe we can take Gabby outside and play in the snow a bit. If she's going to do avalanche work, she needs to feel comfortable in snow."

Charlie, an avy dog Kenzie had trained, had saved a man's life a couple winters past. Kenzie wanted Gabby to have the same abilities.

Kenzie waited with the puppy by the back door while Harrison put on his parka and grabbed Gabby's squeak toy.

Once outside, Kenzie walked far out into the yard, away from Gabby's shoveled potty spot, and set the puppy down in the snow.

Gabby sniffed the snow and then picked up one front paw, looking up at Kenzie as if pleading to be picked up again.

"It's just snow. Snow is fun."

Harrison knelt down a few feet away and gave the squeak toy a few squeezes. "Come here, Gabby, girl."

Gabby took a few tentative steps in his direction, churning up snow as she moved. She seemed to notice the flying snow—and then she went bonkers.

She ran to Harrison, got down into a "let's play" stance, and barked. Then she took off running around the yard as fast as her little legs would carry her, a furry torpedo, kicking up snow as she ran.

Harrison chuckled. "That's the cutest damned thing I've ever seen."

He took a little bit of snow, turned it into a tiny snowball, and tossed it into Gabby's path. The puppy tried to catch it with her jaws, but the snow crumbled. She barked, growling as she danced around biting at the snow, trying to find her new toy.

Harrison laughed, tossed another.

Gabby bit it and jumped about, tail wagging, snow sticking to her muzzle.

The game went on, Kenzie laughing along with Harrison, her heart lifting to see him enjoying the moment, whatever had been troubling him forgotten—at least for now. But this was hard work for Gabby, and soon, she trotted over to Harrison and put a paw on his thigh, asking to be picked up.

"I think we wore her out."

He scooped her up, brushed her off. "You know what, Gabby? You're a badass."

The neighbor's back door opened, and an older woman Kenzie vaguely recognized stepped outside and headed toward her wood pile. She glared at Harrison, then looked sharply at Kenzie.

"I knew your grandparents, Miss Morgan. I don't think they would approve of you spending time with a man of this sort." With that, she filled her arms with firewood and disappeared indoors.

Kenzie looked over at Harrison. "What was that about? What have you been doing to that poor woman?"

"I came outside naked once when Gabby had to go, and the old lady opened her curtains and saw me."

Kenzie gaped at him. "You were outside naked? As in *buck* naked? That's bananas. Why would you do that?"

"Gabby couldn't wait, and it was five in the morning. I had no idea she was an early bird. Honestly, she must have craned her head to see me." Harrison chuckled, heading for the back door, Gabby in his arms. "She called my junk frank and beans."

"Frank and beans?" Okay, that *was* funny.

But now Kenzie was jealous of that old lady, too.

CONRAD LOOKED INTO HIS PANTRY, in search of something decent to make for lunch. "I could open a couple of cans of soup."

That's how you impress a woman—canned soup.

Kenzie stood and walked to his fridge. "I got you shrimp, pasta, and stuff to make marinara sauce."

"You did?"

"Didn't you look?" She opened the freezer door and pulled out a bag of cooked, frozen shrimp. "If you haven't used the crushed tomatoes and the pasta, we should be good. I'll need an onion and some garlic, too."

He turned back to the pantry, found the crushed tomatoes and the pasta.

She set the frozen shrimp down on the kitchen counter, then walked back to the fridge. "Put those in a colander and run cold water over them, and I'll start the sauce."

Instead of doing what she asked, he stood there like an idiot, watching while she bent over and searched the vegetable crispers for the other ingredients. No, he wasn't watching *her*. He was watching her *ass*.

Way to make your mama proud, man.

He tore his gaze off her, set the pasta and tomatoes on the counter, and went in search of a colander, looking through Mrs. Beech's cupboards. Pots and pans. Mixing bowls. Glassware. "How many pie plates does one person need?"

"Maybe Mrs. Beech—" Kenzie's Team pager went off. "Damn."

She drew it out of her pocket, scrolled through the message. "Sorry, but I have to go. You can thaw the shrimp under cold water, pat them dry, and sauté them in butter and garlic. Then just sauté the onion, and—"

"I'll go with you."

She stared up at him, clearly surprised. "Other Team members will be there, probably Scarlet Fire and the sheriff's department, too. Are you sure you're up for meeting everyone?"

He wasn't, not really, but he couldn't stay cooped up in this house forever. Besides, he didn't want to say goodbye to her—not yet. "Don't worry about me."

"Okay. You can put Gabby's crate in the back of my vehicle. I have to stop by the kennel to pick up Gizmo, and I need to put on some warmer clothes."

"Same here." Jeans wouldn't cut it on a cold-weather rescue that might go on all night. "How about I meet you at your place in ten?"

"That sounds good." She pulled her coat out of the closet, grabbed her handbag, found her keys. "I'll see you there."

The moment she was gone, Conrad stripped out of his jeans and sweater and got into a pair of long underwear and some old summit pants. If they were good enough for the Himalayas, they could handle whatever the Rockies threw his way. He slipped into a T-shirt and a wool sweater and zipped himself into a down-filled summit jacket. Then he went for his Team gear.

It had been almost a year and a half since he'd touched his Team backpack. He had always kept it ready to go so that he wouldn't have to wonder what was in it before each rescue. He didn't have time to unpack it and check his gear now. He wasn't really on the Team anyway. He was just going to support Kenzie.

You just want to be close to her.

Was that such a bad thing?

When he'd loaded his gear into his SUV, he put Gabby inside her crate, settling her with treats and kibble. "You ready to go on an adventure, kid?"

Gabby curled up, closed her eyes, and fell asleep.

"That's how you have enough energy to keep me awake at night."

He shut the liftgate, climbed into the driver's seat, and drove to Kenzie's house— a modest two-story Victorian with a wrap-around porch. No sooner had he parked, then she stepped out of the front door, wearing ski pants and a blue down parka, a backpack on her back, Gizmo leashed and following at her heel.

Conrad got out of his vehicle and greeted Gizmo, who *did* remember him, judging from the whimpers, licks, and wagging tail. "Hey, buddy. It's good to see you, too."

"I told you he'd remember you," Kenzie stopped at her tailgate. "Let's put Gabby in the back of my truck. It will be easier than moving all my stuff over to your vehicle."

Conrad moved Gabby, together with his own gear, then climbed into the passenger seat. "Are we sure it's okay for Gabby to be with Gizmo back there?"

Kenzie took the wheel. "They're in separate crates, so it should be fine."

"Where are we headed?"

Kenzie turned on her police radio. "Indian Peaks Trailhead. A married couple went hiking yesterday morning and never came back. A sheriff's deputy found their vehicle parked near the trailhead."

"Not good."

This couple's survival depended entirely on how well equipped they'd been to spend the night in snow and freezing temperatures.

Kenzie raised the mic, waited for a break in radio traffic. "Sixteen eighty-eight, K9 en route."

There was a burst of static as Dispatch answered with the time. "K9 en route, sixteen twenty-three."

As Kenzie backed out of the driveway, Conrad relaxed into his seat.

It felt good to be *doing* something.

KENZIE PARKED next to Rescue 1 in the parking lot at the Indian Peaks Trailhead. A couple of sheriff's vehicles were already there, along with a rescue truck from the Scarlet Springs Fire Department. Team members stood together with sheriff's deputies waiting for her—or, really, Gizmo.

She reached over, took Conrad's hand. "Just remember that everyone here is your friend and cares about you."

His eyes were hiding behind sunglasses, but he nodded. "Let's do this."

She climbed out of the vehicle, got Gizmo out of his crate. "Are you ready to get to work, buddy?"

He wagged his tail, standing patiently while she put him in his harness. Gizmo loved working. To him, it was all a fun game. He found the people and then got treats and playtime with his favorite toy.

But this was about saving lives.

Deputy Julia Marcs walked over to her, then stopped—and stared. "Oh, my God, Conrad!"

"Hey, Julia."

Julia hurried over to him and gave him a hug. "I'm so glad you're back."

"Holy shit. Look who's here." Eric grinned and started their way. He pulled Conrad into a bear hug. "God, it's good to see you."

"It's good to see you, too. I hear you're a father now. What the hell was Vicki thinking?"

Eric chuckled. "I'm a lucky man. I can't wait for you to meet our little guy."

Kenzie's throat went tight.

She wasn't the only one who had missed him.

Austin hugged him, too, slapping him on the back. "I wasn't sure we'd ever see you again. Damn, it's good to have you home."

"I bet Lexi and Emily are keeping you busy."

Austin grinned. "You know it."

Chaska shook Harrison's hand, slapped him on the shoulder. "Welcome home. You've been on quite a journey."

"And you went and got yourself married."

Chaska laughed. "No one was more surprised about that than I was."

A shrill squeal. "Conrad!"

Sasha Dillon ran across the snowy parking lot and jumped into Harrison's arms. "Oh, my God! I can't believe you're really here! You scared the shit out of me!"

He kissed her cheek. "It's good to see you, too, kiddo."

The top-ranked female sports climber in the country,

Sasha was the other A-list climbing celebrity on the Team. At only twenty-five, she'd won more championships than any woman in the history of sports climbing. Athletic, sunny, and blond, she had always seemed to Kenzie like the sort of woman Harrison would want.

Are you jealous?

No, she wasn't. Okay, maybe a little.

Everyone adored Sasha, including Kenzie. She was always so bright and cheerful that it was impossible *not* to like her.

Ahearn walked up to them. "Hey, Kenzie. Conrad. Can we do the reunion at Knockers after we're done here? We've got some people out there who might be in a world of hurt right now."

Julia took over, bringing Kenzie up to speed. "We got a call this morning from a woman who said her son and daughter-in-law were supposed to have come to dinner after going for a hike on the Indian Peaks Trail. They never showed up, and they haven't answered her calls. Cell service is patchy up here, of course, so that doesn't necessarily mean anything. That Subaru Outback over there is theirs."

"Can we get inside the vehicle, find some scent articles for Gizmo?" Kenzie had trained Gizmo to be a trailing dog, not an air-scent dog. He needed a way to scent the person or people he was supposed to find.

Julia nodded. "They didn't lock the door."

Which meant they probably hadn't intended to be gone for long and likely weren't prepared to be out overnight.

"Will you be staying here in the parking lot, Julia? I need someone to keep an eye on Gabby." Kenzie had left the window open just a crack, but she didn't want someone to come along and take the puppy.

Julia nodded. "I'm Incident Command, so I'll be right here."

"Perfect. Thanks."

Julia, as the sheriff's deputy, opened the door, and Kenzie let Gizmo hop inside, where he could pick up their scent. She bent down and looked in, relieved to find a pair of gloves in the back seat.

Kenzie took the gloves, drew Gizmo out of the vehicle and down to the trailhead, and then let him sniff the gloves. "Gizmo, go find!"

Gizmo took off, heading up the trail, Kenzie walking as fast as she could to keep up, Harrison beside her, the others following behind so as not to mess up the scent trail.

"It's amazing to me that he can pick up a scent that's more than twenty-four hours old and buried under three inches of snow."

"The snow actually helps, especially if not many people passed by here after our couple. From the look of things, the storm kept most people away."

They continued up the trail for a good half hour until Gizmo stopped. Kenzie watched his body language for negatives—a sign that he'd lost the scent. He searched an outcropping of rocks just off the trail, sniffing his way toward the edge.

"Careful, buddy." She didn't want him to slip.

Harrison looked to the west. "They might have stopped here to look at that view."

It was a beautiful spot. Across the valley, Navajo, Apache, and Shoshoni peaks rose white against the sky.

Kenzie waited for Gizmo to give her some sense of what was going on, wondering whether she should back-track with him and try this stretch of the trail again. Then he stepped off-trail and led her to a steep hillside.

From below came a cry. "Help! Help us! We're

down here!"

She let Gizmo go, following him down the hillside toward his quarry.

"Be careful." Harrison walked beside her with long, sure strides. "It's steeper here than it looks, and there are a lot of buried rocks. You might slip—"

"Oh!" Kenzie stepped on a hidden rock, which flipped beneath her boot.

"—and fall." Harrison caught her, his gaze meeting hers.

Her pulse skipped. "Thanks."

Nearby, she heard Gizmo bark, and she knew he'd found the hikers. They were huddled together in the shelter of a few boulders, wearing nothing but jeans, T-shirts, and light jackets.

Kenzie got on her radio. "Sixteen eighty-eight to Indian Peaks Command. The missing party has been located."

"Oh, thank God, you're here. My wife fell from the top of those rocks up there and broke her leg. I think she has a concussion, too. I tried to keep her warm, but…"

The woman lay still and pale, her head resting against her husband's chest.

Kenzie wasn't a paramedic, but she could tell the woman was in urgent need of medical help.

Harrison opened his pack, drew out some hand warmers, and activated them. "Tuck these inside her jacket. Paramedics are right behind us."

"I'm Kenzie Morgan from the Rocky Mountain Search and Rescue Team, and this is Gizmo." She petted Gizmo, praising him and giving him treats. "Good boy, Gizmo. You did it."

Gizmo had earned his paycheck.

Now it was time for the rest of the Team to take over.

Chapter 9

WHILE KENZIE WALKED BACK to the parking lot with Gizmo, Conrad worked with Belcourt to create the anchor that would enable the Team to bear the two victims in litters up the steep, snowy slope. He hadn't tied a knot or worked with a piece of climbing gear since that awful day on the Icefall, but his fingers hadn't forgotten.

It surprised him that the others had let him be involved. He was no longer a member of the Team, after all, and Megs, who was staffing the radio back at The Cave, was a hard-ass about protocol. Team rules demanded that all rescue participants be Team members or first responders. The rules also required any Team member who'd been through any kind of trauma be cleared by Esri before working a call. But apparently, Megs hadn't voiced an objection.

Conrad double-checked the belay he'd rigged around a large ponderosa pine. "Do you want to look at this?"

Belcourt shook his head. "You've been at this a lot longer than I have. Maybe you should check *my* knots."

Conrad grinned. "Nah. I trust you."

"Likewise." Belcourt was an engineer and a genius. He'd come to Colorado from the Pine Ridge reservation to study engineering and had fallen in love with climbing, mastering it in a year and becoming a primary Team member as fast as Moretti. For him, rescues were interesting physics problems that had to be worked out on the fly. He spent his free time engineering gadgets to make rescues more efficient and safer.

This rescue was pretty straightforward. They had two adults to get up the slope in two separate litters, and the anchor had to be strong enough to support their weight, plus the weight of the six Team members who would carry each litter. The Team members would be walking, but to minimize the risk of them slipping and dropping the litter, they would also be on belay. That meant the anchor had to hold about two thousand pounds.

Once the litter reached the top of the slope, they would remove the ropes and attach big ATV wheels to the bottom —one of Belcourt's innovations—and roll the litters quickly down the trail to the parking lot, where two ambulances waited. Taylor and Hawke, who were both paramedics, said the woman had a fractured femur and that both she and her husband were hypothermic.

They were both damned lucky to be alive. Conrad had seen more than one fractured femur sever the femoral artery, causing the victim to bleed out in minutes.

Conrad and Belcourt finished the anchor, then attached ropes to the first litter while six Team members— Ahearn, Taylor, Sasha, Nicole, Herrera, and Moretti— roped themselves in.

Apart from the fact that he didn't have a radio and wasn't listening in to the radio traffic, it felt like old times. The first litter up the slope carried the wife, who was much worse off than her husband.

Conrad and Belcourt detached the ropes, then crawled beneath the litter and affixed the big ATV wheel, and six Team members headed off down the trail with the unconscious woman. Then they repeated the entire process with the husband's litter. Now that his wife was safe and the adrenaline gone, he had lapsed into semi-consciousness, though he kept insisting he could walk.

"Let us handle it from here, okay, buddy?" Hawke's voice was reassuring.

It was a quick rescue as rescues went, with both parties off to the hospital within an hour of being located. There were high-fives in the parking lot, where Kenzie was waiting for Conrad by her truck.

"Good work, folks," Ahearn called. "We'll debrief this at The Cave and then head to Knockers."

Kenzie reached for Conrad, hugged him. "Thanks for being here."

"I didn't do much."

"You helped solve the anchor problem, leaving another Team member free to carry a litter."

Okay, that was true.

Inside her truck, Kenzie turned to him. "Are you sure you want to go to Knockers? It's Sunday, so it probably won't be too busy."

Knockers, named for the legendary tommyknockers that supposedly lived in the abandoned mines around Scarlet Springs, was the place where locals came to unwind, eat, drink great beer, play pool, and show off their moves on the climbing wall. Conrad had been avoiding the place, but now…

"I'm fine with it. Are you hungry?"

Kenzie backed out of her parking space and followed Rescue 1 back toward the highway. "Starving."

Back at The Cave, Megs had hot coffee waiting for

them. Conrad helped unload equipment. Every rope would be washed, dried, and inspected, every piece of gear examined for wear or damage. Nothing would be loaded back onto Rescue 1 until they were certain it was safe to use again. Unloading took longer than the debriefing itself, which was over in ten quick minutes.

"Good job, everyone. We saved two lives today." Megs bent down to run her hands through Gizmo's fur. "You are a rock star, buddy."

Conrad held Gabby to keep her away from Gizmo. "Thanks for letting me be a part of it, even though I'm not a member."

Megs looked confused. "It's against standard operating procedure for anyone who isn't a member to participate, so of course you're a member. You're tenured."

"I'm … what?"

Tenured members were those with the most experience and the greatest privileges. They were free from having to attend routine meetings and trainings and could do pretty much whatever the hell they wanted on-site at a rescue—lead climb, fix anchors, render first aid, clean climbing routes afterward, act as Incident Command.

"We made you a tenured member during your prolonged absence."

"But I resigned from the Team."

Megs looked over at Ahearn. "Did you get a resignation letter from Conrad?"

Quiet snickers passed through the room.

Ahearn shook his head. "I haven't seen anything."

So that's how they were going to play this.

They didn't have a letter because Conrad hadn't sent one. He'd told Megs in person that he was off the Team—and she had ignored him.

Conrad couldn't help but smile. "Okay, fine. I'm a tenured member."

Megs pressed a pager into his palm. "Congratulations. We're lucky to have you."

Cheers.

———

KENZIE DROPPED Gabby and Gizmo off with her staff at the kennel, then climbed into Conrad's vehicle. It was six when they arrived—the start of the dinner rush. The stage area off to the right was dark. Instead of a live band, music from the jukebox played Eighties hits over a sound system.

Conrad leaned down. "This is like stepping back in time."

"In a good way, I hope?"

He took her hand, nodded, his smile giving her belly flutters again.

Cheyenne greeted them with menus, her long blond hair piled on her head. "Welcome back, Conrad. It's good to see you. What the hell took you so long?"

Kenzie and Conrad made their way toward the Team table in the back, but were stopped by Bear, who got up from a nearby table and stepped into Conrad's path, his eyes wide with surprise.

"Harrison Conrad." Bear held up his hands. "My heart rejoices in the Lord, for I delight in your deliverance!"

It was one of the things about Bear. He was able to express himself better when he quoted the Bible, which he knew inside and out, so he expressed himself mostly in Bible verses. It wasn't easy for him to come up with words himself.

But Bear had gotten people's attention, and the restaurant fell quiet. Then came the whispers and hushed exclamations.

"Oh, my God! That's Harrison Conrad. He's finally back from Nepal."

"Is that Conrad?"

"Look who's back."

Kenzie knew Conrad must have heard, too.

He ignored it, releasing her hand to shake Bear's. "Thanks, Bear."

But Bear pulled him into a hug. Bear was one of the few men around who matched Conrad in height, but when he spoke, his voice was soft and shy, deep and yet somehow childlike. "I didn't think I would see you again."

Kenzie's throat went tight.

Conrad clapped him on the back. "I wasn't sure about that myself, friend."

Kenzie motioned toward the table where Bear had been sitting. "It looks like you've got a nice meal."

Bear gave a nod. "Whoever is generous to the poor lends to the Lord, and He will repay him for his deed."

She reached out, squeezed his hand. "Enjoy your supper."

The Team table was packed. Most of the primary members had turned out, probably because word had spread that Harrison would be there. Megs and Ahearn. Austin, Lexi, and little Emily. Eric, Victoria, and baby Caden. Chaska, Naomi, and Winona. Bahir. Malachi. Sasha. Isaac. Nicole. Creed. Jesse, Ellie and the twins. Dave Hatfield and his new girlfriend.

Was her name Amy? Kenzie couldn't keep up.

There were many hugs and handshakes and a few introductions, as Harrison had never met Bahir or Naomi. Kenzie used the distraction to slip away and find Joe.

"Hey, Joe." She lowered her voice. "Harrison's here."

Joe's face split in a wide grin. "That son of a bitch. It's about damned time."

"Please don't make a big deal out of it. No toasts or speeches. The attention makes him uncomfortable."

Joe nodded. "Okay. Got it. But I am calling Rain."

Kenzie started back toward the table, only to find herself waylaid by Cheyenne.

She lowered her voice to a whisper, a knowing smile on her face. "I hear you and Conrad got together. Is he as well hung as I've always imagined he was?"

Kenzie gaped at Cheyenne, heat rushing into her face. "I'm not sure where you heard that, but it's not true. As for your question, I have no idea."

That wasn't exactly true. She'd been able to feel his erection through his jeans and knew he was well endowed. But *no way* was she going to talk about the private details of Harrison's anatomy with Cheyenne or anyone else.

"Bummer." Cheyenne gave Kenzie a disappointed frown and walked away.

Kenzie arrived back at the table to find Harrison perusing his menu. She didn't really need to look. "I think I've eaten everything on this menu a thousand times."

"It all feels new to me. I haven't eaten any of this for a long time. Oh, man, they're doing a Philly cheesesteak sandwich now?"

"Philly cheesesteak a la Colorado." Joe's voice came from behind them. "It's got jalapeños and pepper jack."

Harrison grinned, got to his feet. "Hey, Joe."

The two men embraced.

"Welcome home. We missed you."

"Thanks. I hear you and Rain finally figured out that you belong together."

Joe laughed. "Yeah. It only took us twenty years. She's

on her way into town. She wants to see you, and she's bringing Angel, our baby girl."

Harrison opened his mouth to respond but was cut off by a shriek.

"Oh, my God. Conrad!" Marcia, the bartender, stood a few feet away from the table, staring wide-eyed at Harrison. She dashed up to him, planted a kiss on his cheek. "Whatever you want to drink—it's on me. I'm so glad you're back."

Harrison's gaze met Kenzie's. "So am I."

CONRAD FINISHED the best Philly cheesesteak sandwich he'd ever eaten while Rain, who sat beside him, logged into a website on her smartphone to show him photos of her and Joe's wedding. It wasn't really Conrad's thing, but he wasn't about to say that.

He'd told Kenzie that stepping into Knockers was like stepping back in time, but really it was like taking a jump forward. This place was the same, but his friends' lives had moved on. Who said nothing ever changed in Scarlet?

Rain held out her phone. "This is Knockers all decorated."

Conrad was impressed. "Wow."

That seemed to be his go-to word these days, but what else could he say? Pine garlands. Red roses. A zillion white lights. In these photos, Knockers had been transformed from brewpub to Christmas romance fairyland.

"This is Joe in his tux."

"He cleans up well."

Joe had always been a loner, an eccentric millionaire who didn't share details about his life with anyone. Getting together with Rain had changed something in him, and it was there on his face.

What was it like to a love a woman so much that just being with her transformed everything?

Conrad would probably never know.

He glanced over at Kenzie, got a hitch in his chest. She sat on his other side, holding little Angel, a look of adoration on her face, the baby's tiny fist wrapped tightly around her pinky finger.

Rain scrolled to the next photo. "Here I am with Lark."

Conrad turned his attention back to Rain. Although she looked stunning in her silvery white wedding gown, it was the image of Kenzie that knocked him flat. She stood off to one side in a beaded dress in bright, screaming red, the cloth clinging to her body like a shimmering second skin.

His mouth watered. "Holy shit."

Kenzie apparently thought he was reacting to the image of Rain in her gown. "She was the most beautiful bride, wasn't she?"

All Conrad could see was Kenzie. "Beautiful."

"Hey, Conrad! Get over here!" Herrera stood beside the climbing wall, where Sasha was on belay for Nicole, who was crushing the crux move on a 5.11 route.

Conrad shook his head. "Not tonight."

Rain scrolled to the next photo. "This is the ceremony. Chaska's grandfather officiated. He got stuck in Scarlet, thanks to the snow. He was wonderful."

Conrad leaned in, saw an image of Joe and Rain standing together in front of Old Man Belcourt. Kenzie was there, too, this time from behind, the back of her dress dipping down toward the luscious curves of her ass. "It looks like a happy day."

Rain smiled, her gaze on the photo. "It was the happiest day of my life."

"Conrad, come on, man!" Herrera called. "Rope up. I'll be your belay slave."

Herrera was a damned good climber and utterly fearless, but sometimes he could be a pain in the ass.

"I'm trying to have a conversation here!" Conrad called back, then apologized to Rain. "Sorry for the interruption."

"That's it, really. I won't bore you with the rest of the photos."

"A wedding and a baby. When Megs told me in Nepal, I thought, 'It's about damned time.' I'm really happy for the two of you."

"You done talking yet?" Creed walked up beside him.

"I don't feel like climbing."

"What?" Creed laughed as if he'd said something insane. "That's loco, man."

From across the table, Hawke met Conrad's gaze, silent understanding passing between them. Hawke got to his feet. "I'll hit the wall with you, Herrera. Come on."

Herrera nodded. "Let's go."

"He's not trying to be a jerk," Kenzie whispered. "He missed you. Every time we all got together, he was the first one to ask about you."

"We did a lot of good climbing together before …" Conrad didn't want to think about that. "You looked pretty good in those wedding photos, too, you know. Don't think I didn't notice."

Kenzie gave him that sweet smile he loved so much. "Thanks."

Suddenly, Conrad needed to get her alone. "You ready to go? I'll get the check."

Rain put a hand on his arm. "Your money is no good here, Conrad."

Conrad was touched. "Thanks, Rain, but you don't have to do that."

"We came close to losing you, and I'm just so glad to have you back." Tears filled Rain's eyes. "Sorry. Postpartum hormones."

She sniffed, wiped her eyes with her fingertips. "Your dinner is on us. Yours, too, Kenzie. I heard Gizmo saved a couple of lives today."

"Thanks, Rain." Kenzie got to her feet and carried Angel back to her mother, carefully placing the baby in Rain's arms. "Thanks for letting me hold her. She's absolutely precious."

Conrad didn't want to drag out the goodbyes, so he stood and glanced down the length of the table. "See you all around."

"Take care."

"See you soon."

"Thanks for your help today."

He walked with Kenzie out to the vehicle, his hand resting against the small of her back, his mind fixed on the image of her wearing that bright red dress. "How about we go to your place?"

Her gaze shot to his. "What do you have in mind?"

"Oh, I can think of a few things."

———

WHAT DID Harrison mean by that? Board games? Netflix? Conversation?

Kenzie hoped he meant hot, screaming sex.

An image of him fucking her up against the wall darted through her mind. Then again, she'd hiked for an hour or so today and had gotten all sweaty. She needed a shower—and she had responsibilities.

She glanced at her watch. "I need to stop by the kennel and pick up the pups."

"Right." Harrison drove the two of them to her house and went with her to the kennel, where April, one of her part-time staff, was getting ready to close up and go home. Kenzie helped settle the dogs for the night, while Harrison played with Gabby, who had come bounding over to him the moment they'd stepped through the door. Then they brought the dogs back to Kenzie's place.

Harrison carried Gabby in one hand and her crate in another. "I don't want Gizmo to hurt her."

"Oh, Gizmo would never do that." Then Kenzie remembered her lie. "I mean, he wouldn't *hurt* her. He just gets, you know, grumpy with her."

The day had been colder than she'd anticipated. She left her heat on low all day, so her house was chilly.

"Will Gabby be safe if I put her down?" Harrison asked.

Kenzie nodded. "I'm going to put her in her crate soon anyway."

Harrison set Gabby on the floor and watched her bound after Gizmo, concern on his face. When Gizmo dropped into his dog bed and allowed Gabby to curl up with him, Harrison seemed to relax. "I'll get a fire going in your wood stove."

"Thanks." Kenzie wasn't used to having help, and there was something about seeing a big, handsome man carrying firewood that she liked.

By the time she got Gizmo and Gabby settled, Harrison had a blazing fire going, its warmth spreading through the house.

And then it was just the two of them.

Anticipation twined with nervousness in Kenzie's stomach. "Can I make you some coffee or get you a beer or a glass of—"

"I'm not thirsty." He drew her against him. "Do you know what really kept me awake last night? It wasn't just Gabby. I couldn't stop thinking about you, about all the things I want to do to you."

Kenzie's pulse skipped. "I … I need a shower. The rescue. Hiking. I got sweaty."

He bent down, nuzzled her throat. "You smell delicious to me, but if you really want a shower, I'd be happy to help."

Part of Kenzie was delighted by this, but she hadn't forgotten what he'd said to her yesterday. "What changed? Yesterday, you said this would be a mistake, that you wouldn't be good for me, and tonight …"

Tonight, he was talking about getting naked with her.

What about your *objections?*

Did she have any?

Oh, yeah. No climbers.

Well, to hell with that.

He drew back, looked down into her eyes, his expression serious. "I've got nothing to offer you and no idea where my life is going or what the next few months will bring. I can't promise you much, but I'll never mistreat you or disrespect you. You're the only part of my life that makes sense right now, Kenzie. I want you, and if that's a mistake, then it's the best mistake I've made in a long damned time."

Kenzie's heart all but melted. "*Kiss me.*"

Harrison backed her up against the wall, tilted her face upward, and took her mouth with his.

Chapter 10

AT HIS FIRST taste of her, Conrad forgot that he'd meant to go slowly, days of suppressed desire for her igniting in his veins like a backdraft. He'd meant to be gentle, but he wasn't. He pressed his lips hard to hers, claimed her mouth with his tongue, his fingers fisting in her hair. Some part of him wondered whether he was being too rough, but then she bit his lower lip, giving as good as she got, meeting his tongue with her own, stroking his erection through the fabric of his jeans.

Ah, Kenzie.

Why had he waited *so long* to do this?

He was about to scoop her into his arms and carry her upstairs to her bedroom or the bathroom when he remembered.

Condoms.

Fuck.

He dragged his lips from hers. "I need to drive to the store and get condoms."

How could he forget something like that? He knew

better than most people that success depended on having the right gear.

"Food Mart closed fifteen minutes ago." She pressed her hand harder against his erection, the sensation almost painfully arousing.

He was about to let loose a string of profanity.

She cut him off with a laugh. "Don't worry. I bought some this morning. They're upstairs in my bedroom."

A jolt of raw lust shot through him to know she'd been thinking of having sex with him, planning for it, preparing for it.

"God, woman, I adore you. What the hell are we doing down here?"

They kicked off their shoes, then she took his hand and led him upstairs.

"I'll meet you in the shower." She turned away to her bedroom, probably to get the condoms, leaving him to get acquainted with her bathroom.

There was an antique claw-foot tub in front of the window and a narrow walk-in shower stall in the corner. The walls were painted a cool shade of white, pale stone tiles on the floor. He found a couple of fluffy white towels, hung them on the rack outside the shower, and then peeled off his shirt just as she walked in behind him.

He turned, stopped, and stared, blood rushing to his groin.

She had stripped out of her clothes and slipped into a white silk robe, her dark hair hanging free around her shoulders, the thin fabric outlining her body in tantalizing detail, her nipples dark and pebbled, the skin of one thigh exposed.

"I hope these work." She handed him a box.

Condoms. Extra thin *and* extra large.

He grinned. "What if I need Tom Thumb size?"

She laughed, her gaze locked with his as she unzipped his jeans, took his erection in hand, and circled her thumb over the straining head. "I don't think so."

He sucked in a breath, the muscles of his belly jerking tight. "*Kenzie.*"

They worked together to strip away his jeans, Conrad catching his socks with his thumbs as he pulled the denim free. Hell if he would get caught in the sock gap—that awkward moment when a man stood there wearing nothing but a stiff dick and socks.

Definitely *not* sexy.

He tossed his jeans aside and then stood there, letting Kenzie explore him.

She ran her hands over his pecs and down his abdomen to his obliques. "God, you're gorgeous. I could stare at you all day."

He'd never been called gorgeous before. Ripped. Hot. But never gorgeous. Then again, most of the women he'd been with had been climbing groupies who only wanted his dick—and maybe bragging rights. "I hope not all day. I had other things in mind."

"Oh, yeah? Like what?" Kenzie took his cock in hand again and stroked his length, her touch making his breath catch.

Damn. "Like that."

He willed himself to hold still, fought the urge to thrust into her hand, knowing he had to stop her sooner rather than later. It had been so long since a woman had touched him, and he didn't want this to end before it began. Besides, it was *his* turn.

He reached out, tugged on the tie that held her bathrobe in place and pushed it from her shoulders. It fell in a puddle of white at her ankles, leaving her bared to him.

He sucked in a breath, his heart hitting his breastbone at the sight of her. "You are … *beautiful*."

A dusky nipple peaked through silky strands of dark hair, her breasts full enough to fill his hands. Her narrow waist drew attention to the curves of her hips. Her belly wasn't flat, but gently rounded, a triangle of thick, dark curls between her thighs.

He wanted to touch every inch of her, taste every inch of her.

She was nervous too, her breathing fast and shallow.

Or maybe that was arousal.

He took the weight of her breasts into his hands and stroked their dark tips with his thumbs, watching as her body tensed and her eyes drifted shut. "You like that."

"*Yes.*"

He moved his hands over her skin, savoring the feel of her as she had done with him—the fullness of her breasts, the flare of her hips, the silk of her skin. Everything about her was soft and sensual and feminine. Then he reached down and cupped her, giving his fingers free rein, seeking out her hidden places, stroking her clit.

She grabbed onto his free arm as if to steady herself, her nails biting into his skin.

He kept it up, watched the effect his touch had on her, her breathing faster now, her head falling back. But hadn't she said something about a shower?

He withdrew his hand, pressed his forehead to hers, lust pounding in his veins. "If you don't start your shower, I'm going to fuck you right here."

———

PULSE POUNDING, Kenzie took a few unsteady steps to the shower, opened the door, and reached inside to start the water. She fumbled with the faucet, the ache Harrison had conjured between her thighs making it almost impossible to think.

Focus!

Turning on the water shouldn't be a challenge.

Then again, she'd never expected to take a shower with Harrison. She had fantasized about him so many times, wanted him for so long, but she'd never imagined that he was attracted to her, too.

Was this really happening?

She stepped under the spray and turned to face him, stepping back to make room for him. He joined her, towering over her in the small, enclosed space, his big, muscular body crowding hers without meaning to.

God almighty, he turned her on.

"Is the water okay?"

"Perfect." He reached past her to grab the soap, lathered his hands, and began to wash her. "I love the feel of you."

He lingered on her breasts, cupping them with soap-slick hands, teasing her nipples with his thumbs, plucking the pebbled tips with his fingers.

"*Oh, yes.*" Her head fell back, her hands grasping his hips for balance, warm water sluicing over her hair.

His touch was gentle and arousing and nothing short of torture, every caress making the ache inside her worse. When his hands finally left her breasts and moved down to her belly, she moaned in protest.

He chuckled, kneeling before her to spread soap over her legs, magic fingertips tickling her inner thighs and the backs of her knees, his gaze sliding over her body until it fixed on the most private part of her.

"God, Kenzie." His brow furrowed, as if the sight of

her were some kind of torment. Then he stood, rinsed her, and kissed her hard. "Are you feeling clean yet?"

"I think I'm feeling dirty, thanks to you."

That made him grin. "Good."

"Your turn." She traded places with him, took the soap, and washed him, lingering on the flat brown discs of his nipples, savoring the feel of his abs and obliques, squeezing the hard mounds of his ass.

Then she dropped to her knees as he'd done.

She soaped his legs then took him in hand, stroking his length, watching the tension on his face, his fingers sliding into her hair. She would have gone down on him right there—she *wanted* to taste him—but he was too tall.

He must have read her mind. "I appreciate the thought, honey, but that's not going to work in here."

Short girl problems. They were real.

They rinsed and stepped out of the shower one at a time to dry off, Kenzie's body humming with sexual urgency.

She grabbed the box of condoms and took a step toward the bathroom door, but Harrison scooped her into his arms.

"Oh!" Startled, she held on, not used to being carried like this.

"Don't worry. I won't drop you. I've had backpacks that weigh more than you do." He carried her to her bedroom, holding her against his chest, his gaze fixed on her face every step of the way, his eyes dark.

Good freaking heaven! Was he even real?

He lowered her to her bed and stretched out above her. "I want to make you feel good. Tell me what you like."

She started to say something about how he was doing fine on his own, when he lowered his mouth to one of her nipples and sucked, a rush of pleasure turning her words into a whimper. Her fingers found their way into his damp hair, desire burning through her until she *had* to have him inside her.

"Fuck me. *Now.*"

He grinned, shook his head. "Patience."

Without breaking eye contact, he kissed his way down her body.

Her pulse quickened. Was he going to—?

He got to his feet at the foot of the bed, took her by the ankles, and dragged her slowly toward him, kneeling on the floor and pushing her thighs wide apart.

"Oh, God."

He was.

She covered her face with her hands, the anticipation almost too much as he parted her, his gaze hot upon her.

Then he tasted her, a single slow lick.

She gasped, her hips bucking at the shock of it, her fingers flying down to catch in his hair.

He moaned. "I love the way you taste."

Another slow lick.

She whimpered.

Then he lowered his mouth to her—and suckled.

"Oh … my … *God.*"

The heat of his mouth. The sweet suction. The caress of his lips on her clit.

She fought to hold still. "That … feels … *so* … good."

No man had ever done it exactly like this before, the pleasure almost too intense to bear. She arched, wiggled her hips, twisting to get away, but she didn't want to escape —not really. He pressed his forearm across her hips to hold her still, his mouth relentless. There was nothing for her to do but give in. Then he slid a finger inside her, stroking her, stretching her, stoking that sweet ache.

She came with a cry, orgasm washing through her in a

surge of bliss, lifting her up and up and up and leaving her to float somewhere beyond the sky.

For a time, she lay there, her eyes closed, her body warm and languid.

When she felt Harrison's weight shift, she opened her eyes.

He had torn open a condom wrapper and was rolling the condom down the length of his erect cock. His gaze met hers. "Are you sure you want this?"

She reached for him. "Shut up, and fuck me."

⸻

CONRAD SETTLED himself between Kenzie's thighs, his heart thrumming, her musky scent filling his head, her taste still on his tongue.

She lay beneath him, looking beautiful, her dark hair fanned out against the pillow, her breasts flushed from her climax, her pupils wide. She took hold of his cock to guide him, moaning as he nudged himself inside her.

Even through the condom, she was heaven—slick, hot, tight. "Oh, God."

He pushed himself deeper until he was buried inside her and then held himself there, giving her time to adjust to the feel of him—and giving himself a chance to relax and get his body under control. He'd never been a minute man, and he sure as hell didn't want to start with Kenzie.

She gave an impatient whimper, lifted her hips, urging him on. "Please."

He ducked down, kissed her. "I love a woman who knows what she wants in bed—especially when she wants me."

She laughed, but her laugh became a moan as he drew his hips back and thrust into her again. "*Oh.*"

"More?"

"God, yes."

He got into a rhythm, keeping it slow, withdrawing almost all the way before thrusting deep again. It had been so damned long. Something swelled inside his chest to see the erotic bliss that unfolded on Kenzie's face each time he rocked into her, and somehow that made it easier for him to hold on.

Holding his weight off her, he kept an easy pace, her response as enthralling as it was arousing. Her parted lips. The little sounds of pleasure coming from her throat. Her half-closed eyes. The flush in her cheeks. The sweet bite of her fingernails where they dug into his biceps.

"*Harrison.*" She wrapped her legs around his waist, opening herself to him fully, her hands sliding up to his shoulders, her hips meeting his, thrust for thrust. Her every exhale was a little cry now, a look of sexual anguish on her face.

Faster, harder.

Orgasm began to build at the base of his spine, and for a moment he tried to think his way through tying a figure-eight retrace.

Tie a single eight in the rope two feet from its end, then pass the free end through the tie-in point. Retrace the original eight with the free… God, yeah.

Ah, hell.

He couldn't focus on knots when he was inside Kenzie.

He shifted his hips so the base of his cock grazed her clit, hoping to speed her up and slow himself down.

Her eyes flew open in surprise, all ten fingernails biting deeper into his skin at once. "What … are you …? *Ohh.*"

Her words unraveled, became a moan, her eyes drifting shut again.

He fought to keep his pace steady, willed his glutes to

relax, watching the pleasure on her face, the tension in her building, her body going taut.

Kenzie, sweet Kenzie.

She gasped, her breath catching for the briefest second before she cried out, the ecstasy that washed over her face a glimpse of paradise, her inner muscles clenching around him, driving him closer to that shimmering edge.

He stayed with her, eager to give her all the pleasure he could. Then he shifted his hips again, sliding deep inside her. This time, he didn't hold back, driving into her faster, harder, until pleasure crashed over him, carrying him home.

For a time, he lay there, still inside her, his body replete, nothing in his world but the two of them—the pounding of his heart, the soft feel of her beneath him, the tickle of her fingertips tracing lines along his spine. If it had been possible, he'd have stayed like this forever. But it couldn't be comfortable for her. He outweighed her by almost a hundred pounds.

The condom.

Shit.

He raised himself up, kissed her. "I wish I could sleep inside you."

"Mmm. So do I."

He took hold of the condom and withdrew from her, tossing it in the trash and wiping off with a tissue. Then he turned toward her again and drew her into his arms, a strange sense of tenderness settling behind his breastbone.

She rested her head on his chest. "Your heart is beating so fast."

He stroked her hair, kissed the top of her head, not sure what to say, afraid of what might come out if he opened his mouth. "That's your doing."

"Is it?" She sounded happy about that. "You're incredible, Harrison."

"Why do you always call me that?"

"Why do I call you *Harrison*? I don't know. Maybe because it's your name?"

"I've never liked it."

"Well, I like it."

"Are you a Star Wars fan like my mom?"

Kenzie laughed. "Is that where she got your name?"

"Yeah." It had always embarrassed him. "I shouldn't have told you."

She grew serious for a moment. "Do you want me to call you Conrad like everyone else does?"

He kissed her forehead. "You can call me whatever you want."

"How about Harry?"

"Except that." Never that.

"Harrison, then." She reached down to cup his balls—not what he'd expected, but that was fine. He could go with that kind of flow. "Cheyenne would be so happy if she could see you now."

Um… "What?"

"Someone—Rose, of course—told her you and I had gotten together. She pulled me aside at Knockers and asked me whether you were as hung as she'd always thought you were. I told her I had no idea."

Conrad lifted his head, looked down at Kenzie. "Are you serious? Cheyenne really said that?"

"She did." Kenzie was obviously amused by this.

"Are you telling me that the good women of Scarlet talk about men's dicks?"

"Yep—some of them anyway."

"Okay. Good to know." He settled his head against his pillow, chuckling. "What are you going to tell her?"

Kenzie lifted her head this time and stared up at him. "I'm not going to tell her anything. What's between us is private and … special. I wouldn't cheapen it by gossiping about your anatomy with anyone—even if you are hung like a horse."

Conrad couldn't help it. He burst into laughter, Kenzie laughing with him, the two of them rolling on the bed in a tangle of limbs.

The conversation took random turns after that—the mole on her right breast, the fact that he'd never been circumcised, the way their height difference all but disappeared when they were both lying down.

"I guess that means I need to keep you in bed," she said.

"That's fine by me." As he drifted off to sleep, Conrad felt a kind of peace he hadn't known in a very long time.

Chapter 11

IT TOOK Kenzie a moment to realize that the awful noise stabbing her ears was her alarm clock. She reached over to turn it off, but Harrison beat her to it, reaching over her with a big hand and giving the snooze button a hard smack.

"Ignore it." He wrapped an arm around her waist and drew her back against him, nuzzling the sensitive skin at her nape, that same big hand moving to cup her breast, his fingers lazily teasing her nipple.

She tried to think—not an easy thing when she was still half asleep and getting more turned on by the moment. "What day is it?"

"Hell if I know."

"Monday." *Damn.* "I have to get up."

He pressed his hips against her, his erection hot and hard against her bottom, his hand still playing with her breast. "Are you sure?"

"I have to open the kennel, and I've got a private lesson in Boulder at ten."

"I guess I'll have to make this quick."

Anticipation shivered through her. "Okay—but not too quick."

He chuckled, releasing her breast and reaching down to cup her. He'd just gotten started between her thighs when he stopped, lifted one of her legs, and drew it back to rest on his thigh. "You gotta let me in, honey."

He stroked her clit, teased it, flicked it. "Show me what you like."

She reached down to guide his fingers, increasing the pressure. He was a fast learner, and she soon left him on his own. "Just … like … *that*."

Then he slid two fingers deep inside her, moaned. "You're wet."

"That's your fault." She closed her eyes, lost in the magic of those sweet thrusts.

Then he withdrew his fingers from her and reached over her to pull a packet from the box of condoms on her nightstand. She heard the wrapper tear, felt him shifting behind her as he rolled the condom down his length.

It seemed to take forever. "Hurry."

"Is this what you want?" He nudged his cock into her, stretching her to delicious fullness with a single, deep thrust.

"Oh, *yes*."

He began to move, his fingers reaching down to stroke her clit again. "I love how you feel inside."

She might have told him she felt the same about him, but she was beyond words, the combined sensations almost too much to bear—the hard in-and-out of his cock, the silky glide of his fingers over her clit, the hard press of his body behind her.

In this position, there was nothing she could do but ride out the pleasure as he drove into her, hard and fast, each thrust carrying her closer to climax. And then she was there, hovering above that incandescent edge, pleasure drawing tight inside her.

She shattered, bliss scorching through her as sweet and bright as a sunrise, Harrison driving her climax home with powerful thrusts. His breath caught and then broke, his body shuddering as he joined her in paradise.

They lay together for a moment, him still inside her, the two of them catching their breath.

Kenzie found herself smiling. "If all Mondays began like that, the whole world would run around saying, 'TGIM—Thank God It's Monday.'"

He chuckled, kissed her temple, the hand that had brought her so much pleasure skimming its way up her belly. "I think we can work on that."

He withdrew from her, turning to drop the condom in the trash bin.

She rolled over to face him, reluctant to leave his side, tenderness for him filling her chest. "You're wonderful. You know that, right?"

He ran a thumb over her cheek, started to say something.

Behind her, the alarm clock went off again.

Had all of that happened in only five minutes?

Wow.

Harrison wasn't just good at climbing.

"I don't want to get up—not when you're in my bed." She gave him one last kiss, then rolled over, turned off the alarm, and sat up. She'd gotten up once in the middle of the night to let Gabby out, but the poor little thing couldn't hold her bladder for more than a few hours. "I need to let the dogs out."

"I can do that. You get ready for work." He got out of bed, standing there in his full, naked glory, glancing around. "Where are my jeans?"

"In the bathroom, I think."

"Right." He turned and left the bedroom, his bare ass a work of art, those muscular mounds shifting as he walked.

You're staring.

Hell, yes, she was staring.

She took a quick shower and dressed and then followed the delicious aroma of coffee downstairs to find Harrison making scrambled eggs, Gizmo and Gabby eating kibble side by side, tails wagging.

Uh-oh.

He pointed with a nod of his head. "Look how well they're getting along."

She hated deceiving him. "Great. That's progress."

Kenzie and Harrison ate together—scrambled eggs, toast, coffee. They talked about her day and then his.

"I guess I need to write some kind of resume. Moretti says Ski Scarlet is hiring for Ski Patrol for the season." He didn't seem excited by the idea.

"Is that something you would enjoy?"

He tossed back the last of his coffee. "It's a job."

No, not excited at all.

He helped her clear the dishes from the table, and then it was time for her to go.

"Thanks for breakfast—and for last night." She slipped into his arms, uncertainty niggling at her, taking the shine off the elation she'd carried with her through the night.

She had no idea how Harrison felt about her, whether this was a one-time hookup or whether he wanted more from her. She wasn't sure he knew.

I've got nothing to offer you and no idea where my life is going or what the next few months will bring. I can't promise you much, but I'll never mistreat you.

She kept her next words light. "Can I entice you to come over for dinner? I don't have any classes tonight."

He looked down at her, the hint of a smile on his lips. "What's on the menu?"

The tone of his voice left Kenzie no doubt that food was the furthest thing from his mind.

———

CONRAD OUGHT to have noticed the green Subaru Outback parked on the street in front of the house, but his mind was filled with Kenzie, her sweet scent still on his skin. A stupid grin on his face, he parked in his driveway, climbed out, and walked around to the rear of the vehicle to retrieve Gabby and her crate—only to find a kid in a baseball cap and red parka standing there waiting for him.

The kid held up his cellphone to take a photo. "Hey, Conrad, man, I heard you were back. When did you get into town?"

Conrad didn't recognize him. Was he a local? "A couple of weeks ago."

Conrad opened his vehicle and reached in for Gabby's crate, hoping the kid would leave now that he'd gotten his photo.

"That must have been one hell of an experience—almost dying on Everest, watching your entire team get crushed, waking up to find yourself hanging over that crevasse." The kid was *still* holding up his damned cellphone. "What really happened up there?"

The question hit Conrad in the gut.

Was the bastard *filming* him?

Conrad stopped still, dangerously close to losing his shit. "Are you media?"

Didn't reporters have a moral obligation to announce themselves?

The kid hesitated for a moment, then grinned. "I'm with Climber's High. It's a climbing webzine."

Conrad had never heard of it, but he didn't say so. He didn't tell the kid to fuck off either. He'd learned the hard way that it was best to try to get along with reporters. Still, he didn't have to put up with this. "I haven't agreed to an interview, and you're standing on private property. You need to go."

There.

That had been polite, hadn't it?

He shut his vehicle, locked it, and carried Gabby, still inside her carrier, toward the front door, angry at himself, angry at the kid. He'd known the media would catch up with him sooner rather than later. He'd gone to Knockers where a lot of people had seen him. Word had gotten out.

What the hell did you expect?

"Cute puppy."

"Thanks." He slid his key into the lock.

"Rumor is that you've given up climbing for good." The kid now stood shouting at him from the sidewalk where he had a legal right to be. "Is that true?"

Conrad opened his door and took a step inside, fully prepared to shut the door behind him and ignore the son of a bitch.

"One bad accident, and you're giving up? Man, I thought you were the greatest

alpine climber in the world, but you're just a pussy."

Rage punched through Conrad's chest. He set Gabby down on the floor just inside the front door, shut the door behind him, and then turned to face the little fucker, pulse pounding. "How many eight-thousand meter peaks have you climbed?"

The kid looked surprised by this question.

"Come on—answer me."

"I haven't climbed any yet. I—"

"That's what I thought." Conrad kept his feet rooted to the spot, afraid he'd put the kid in the hospital if he got too close. "How many friends have you watched die in climbing accidents?"

The kid's stammered. "Well, I … um…"

"Right. Have you done anything more dangerous than hang out with your bros at the rock gym?"

The reporter's face turned red.

"Let me get this straight. You've climbed nothing big, lost no one, and have done nothing more than jack off at the rock gym, and you're calling me a pussy?"

The cellphone went back into the kid's pocket, his face still red as he made his way around the front of his vehicle. "Asshole."

Conrad watched him drive away, opened the door, and stepped into the dark warmth of the house, shutting the door behind him and leaning back against it. "Shit."

What the hell had he been thinking? He ought to have come inside and ignored the kid, rather than allowing that asshole to provoke him. The fucker had recorded most of what he'd said. In a few minutes—an hour at most—it would be all over the Internet.

So the fuck what?

The bastard had staked him out and stepped onto private property without identifying himself as a reporter. Conrad had gone easy on him.

Inside her crate, Gabby whined.

Conrad had almost forgotten she was there.

"Hey, girl." He bent down, opened the crate, and scooped the puppy into his arms.

She rewarded him with kisses, the solid, warm feel of

her taking the worst edge off the surge of darkness the reporter's questions had stirred to life. He sank onto the sofa, taking a wriggling Gabby with him, trying to get his anger under control.

Why did the media think it had a right to his memories, his grief, his anguish? Did being a public figure mean that he wasn't entitled to private feelings? Did they want his bone marrow, too?

What really happened up there?

Conrad closed his eyes, trying to ward off the images that flashed through his mind, his rage giving way to grief and guilt.

Felix crossing the ladder. Luka hesitating. Bruce joking about death, not knowing those would be his last words.

If you fall and your harness fails, it will only kill you.

That terrible rumbling *crack* as the serac collapsed.

Falling. Unconsciousness. Ice.

Gabby whimpered, licking Conrad's chin.

His mind far away, he petted the puppy, stroking her soft fur, a dark chasm where his heart ought to have been.

━━━

AN HOUR LATER, Conrad was contemplating getting drunk when his cellphone rang. He hoped to hell it wasn't Candace.

Not Candace, but his mom.

He answered. "Hey, Mom."

"I didn't know you were back. Why didn't you call?"

"I guess I didn't want to hear the 'I told you so.'"

"You truly think I would have said that to you in these circumstances?"

"That's what you said, more or less, when Dad died."

"I was heartbroken and angry. God, Harrison, I've

spent a year and a half worried out of my mind about you. I tried to reach that monastery, but I could never seem to get a connection. I wrote to you. Did you get my letters?"

"A few."

"Why didn't you write back?"

"I didn't know what the hell to say."

"How are you?"

"I'm okay, I guess."

"The article I just read online said you've given up climbing."

"You read an article online?"

"It was more of a video—some twit of a reporter harassing you in front of that dump of a house where you're living. It reported that you'd given up climbing."

Great. That video was already online.

"Yeah. I'm done."

"I don't believe it. You'll go back to it. You just need some time. The wilderness is in your blood, just like it was in your father's."

"I don't want to get into that again."

"I'm not getting into anything. I'm just telling you I know you better than that."

Whatever.

"Are you seeing anyone?"

"Do you mean like hallucinations or—"

"I mean women."

"Kind of." He didn't want to talk with her about Kenzie. "But don't worry. I remember what you said. 'Never marry a woman who doesn't want the same life you want. You'll destroy each other.'"

For a moment, his mother said nothing, and he wondered whether the call had dropped. He glanced at his screen. She was still there.

At last she spoke, her voice quavering. "I was wrong,

Harrison. I never quit loving your father. You know that, right? But when your brother was stillborn, it broke my heart. I was grieving. I blamed your dad. But it wasn't only his fault. I could have called for a bush pilot myself and had someone fly me to the hospital. The truth is, I would trade every day since the day we left to go back in time and stay with him. He might still be alive."

Conrad didn't know what to say. All these years, his mother had raged about his father, telling Conrad how she'd lost a baby because of him and how the man hadn't loved her enough to come with his wife and only living child.

"If you find someone you love, don't walk away from her. Don't turn your back on her. Fight for her. Don't make my mistake."

Conrad didn't know what to think about this. "Are you okay?"

"I miss him."

So did Conrad.

———

KENZIE'S MIND was stuck on Harrison as she drove down the canyon into Boulder for her private lesson. Sex with him was so easy. The man knew what he was doing between a woman's legs. That much was certain. He'd actually *asked* her what she liked, responding to her, even when she couldn't do more than moan. And what he'd done with his mouth when he'd gone down on her …

Lord have mercy.

She had expected him to have a lot of energy in bed. He was a world-class athlete after all. What she hadn't known was that he would be sensitive, too.

She turned off the highway, her thoughts shifting away

from Conrad to the hour ahead. Over the past couple of months, she'd come to dread this lesson. Mari, her client, was perhaps the most selfish person she'd ever met.

She pulled up to the gate and punched in the access code, waiting while the iron gate opened. She drove onto the property, following the curved driveway past a marble colonnade and parking where she'd been instructed to park —in one of several spots reserved for staff.

Prince, the three-month-old Cavalier King Charles spaniel puppy she was here to train, met her at the front door, his little body wagging.

She knelt down to greet him, petting his silky fur. "Hey, buddy. How are you? I'm happy to see you, too."

"He's had two accidents this week." Irritation on her face, Mari walked up behind the puppy, wearing yoga pants and a cashmere sweater, her blond hair tied up in a perfect mess of a bun. "I try to keep an eye on him, but that doesn't leave much time for anything else. I can't give up my entire life for a dog."

Kenzie stood, Prince in her arms, and tried to say something encouraging. "It's a big investment of time in the beginning, I know, but it's *so* worth it in the end. How are you doing?"

Mari shook her head, looking as if the weight of the world were on her shoulders. "I've got something to do every day this week."

Kenzie didn't know what to say to that. Mari didn't have a job, and her kids were at school all day. How could it be so hard to spend a half hour each day playing with this precious puppy? "Should we get started?"

She carried Prince through the house, which could easily have held her home, yard, and the kennel, to Mari's yoga room, waiting while Mari rolled up her yoga mat.

Mari carried the mat to the corner. "I haven't had time

to practice with him. I refuse to give up my spa time. Then there's Pilates and the kids. If I'd had any idea how demanding it was to be a mother, I would never have had children."

Kenzie tried not to let her shock show. "It takes only about ten or fifteen minutes twice a day to train a puppy. If you don't have fifteen minutes, then try five. It's important to get training time with him every day. Ultimately, this is about your relationship with Prince. You're his guardian, and he needs to respond to you."

"I thought I was paying *you* to train him."

"I told you from the beginning that the real work would be yours. I can only show you how to do it. I don't live here." *Thank God.* "You, your husband, and your kids have to be consistent, or it will confuse Prince."

"Fine." Mari walked over, took Prince from her, and set him on the wooden floor. "I don't need a lecture from you."

Kenzie ignored Mari's condescending tone and got to work, running through the commands Prince had mastered so far and turning him over to Mari to practice those that were harder for him—Stay and Follow.

Kenzie pushed Mari as far as she could. "The more vigilant and consistent you are the faster he'll learn. He really is a wonderful puppy."

"Do you want him?" Mari gave a sarcastic laugh. "I'd be happy to send him off with you, but I think my kids would hate me."

Kenzie wouldn't blame them. "If you do ever decide you don't want to keep him, I would be happy to adopt him."

She'd never said that to any client before, but Prince was such a sweet boy and Mari was such a bitch. It was clear that Mari felt that the puppy, like her children, was little more than an annoyance. No doubt she had something much more important to do, like getting a manicure or Botox.

Some people shouldn't be allowed to own pets.

For the first time since Kenzie arrived, Mari smiled. "It's a deal."

Kenzie got back to the lesson, only too glad when the hour was up. She cuddled the puppy, her heart aching to think he might not be getting the love and training he deserved. "See you next week, sweetie."

Kenzie picked up some office supplies and headed back up the canyon to the kennel. Crank's family was due back from their trip and would be coming to pick him up this afternoon. There, at least, was a happy, cherished dog.

She gave Quinn a lunch break, played with Gizmo and the other dogs, and then went home for a turkey sandwich, her thoughts turning back to Harrison.

Was he thinking of her, too?

She hoped so.

What should she make for dinner tonight?

She rummaged through her refrigerator and freezer and decided that salmon fillets would be perfect for a guy from Alaska.

She sent him a text message.

What time will you be over? I'm making salmon.

For twenty long minutes, he didn't answer.

Kenzie was back at the kennel and in the middle of checking Crank out when her phone finally buzzed.

Can T sum Th Ing Com Upl.

Kenzie's stomach sank, disappointment like a dark

cloud blotting out the sun. Then she thought about the typos. They were beyond the help of spellcheck. Harrison was never sloppy like that.

Had something happened? Was something wrong?

She finished checking Crank out, giving him a few belly rubs to say goodbye. "We're going to miss you, buddy. You're so much fun."

Ross, one of Crank's two dads, clipped a leash to Crank's collar. "We hope to be traveling to my mother's house for Christmas this year, so he'll be back then."

Kenzie was happy to hear that. "Make sure to reserve your spot in October if you can. The holidays fill up quickly."

When Crank and his family had gone, she leashed Gizmo and turned to Quinn, who was heading out to the play yard with the pooper scooper. "I've got to run. Something has come up. If you need me, shoot me a text."

"Will do."

Kenzie hurried outside to her truck, put Gizmo in his crate, and got behind the wheel to drive the short distance to Harrison's place.

Chapter 12

CONRAD TOOK another drink of Jameson, shuddering as it burned its way down his throat. He'd found the unopened bottle in one of the boxes. He and Bruce had bought it to drink when they got back from Everest. But Bruce had never come back.

Bruce, whose family had moved to Australia from Ireland, had loved Jameson. Conrad wasn't much of a drinker and didn't care for it. It tasted like shit as far as he was concerned. But the more he drank, the less he cared how it tasted.

Now Conrad was sharing it with his buddy in the only way he could—in front of the TV while watching documentaries of the two of them climbing together.

He sat on the floor beside a sleeping Gabby, while, on the TV screen, he and Bruce battled their way up the Black Pyramid—a steep wasteland of jumbled gneiss on the Abruzzi Spur of K2's southeast ridge.

A rumble in the background.

"Hear that?" said the Conrad on the TV, grinning at the camera from behind mirrored sunglasses. "Avalanche."

A plume of snow rose from the unclimbed east face.

"Don't worry," Bruce called from above. "I won't let the scary snow hurt you."

Drunk Conrad on the floor chuckled. "Kiss my ass."

A knock at the door.

That reporter. He'd probably come back.

Well, fuck him.

Conrad fought his way to his feet, stumbled to the door, jerked it open. "What the fuck are … *Kenzie*?"

She stared up at him through wide blue eyes, Gizmo beside her. She broke eye contact only to catch Gabby, who shot out the door past his feet to greet her big brother. "Hey, there, squirrely girl."

She scooped Gabby into her arms. "Can I come in?"

"Yeah." He stepped back to let her and the dogs enter, almost tripping on his own feet, then closed the door behind them.

She set the puppy down. "How long has it been since she went out?"

"Not too long." He couldn't remember when exactly, his attention on Gizmo and Gabby, who seemed to be getting along just fine now.

She glanced over at the TV, where he and Bruce were boiling water for coffee in their tent at Camp II, her gaze landing on the whiskey bottle that sat on the coffee table. "You're drunk."

"Well … I … yeah. I think I'm shitfaced."

"Did something happen?"

"When I got home, a reporter was waitin' for me." Conrad's words sounded slurred even to his ears. "He didn't say he was a reporter. Oh, no, no, no, no. He just started throwin' questions in my face like he had a fuckin' right to know. 'What really happened up there?' He called me a pussy."

"What?" Kenzie gaped at Conrad.

"It's all online. My mom saw it. She called." He didn't want to talk about that.

While she searched for the video on her smartphone, he decided it was a good time to take a leak. After managing that and fighting a bit with his zipper, he washed his hands and splashed water on his face. When he returned to the living room, he found her sitting on the sofa looking pissed off.

Her gaze softened when she saw him. "I'm sorry, Harrison. That reporter was way out of line. He doesn't know what he's talking about. He had no right to be on your property or to say those things."

Conrad plonked down on the sofa beside her. "What an asshole."

"Bastard." Kenzie stood, picked up the half-empty whiskey bottle. "I'm going to take the dogs out for a quick potty break and get you a glass of water."

"Where are you taking that? That's the bottle Bruce and I were gonna split when we got home."

Kenzie glanced at it. "It looks like you drank your half."

She disappeared with whiskey and canines.

Conrad stared at the TV screen, where he and Bruce were listening to radio reports from another climbing team of a collapsed serac on The Bottleneck, the narrow and perilous couloir that led to the summit. The two of them debated whether to take that route or to rock climb the adjacent cliffs instead.

Kenzie returned, Gabby and Gizmo at her heels, two big glasses of water in her hands. She handed one to him. "Drink."

She sat down beside him just as he and Bruce left camp and set off for Camp III. He expected her to chew him out, but she didn't. "When's the last time you had something to eat?"

He had to think. "Your place."

"How about I make some supper—it's almost dinner time anyway—and we watch whatever you want to watch."

At the mention of dinner, Conrad's stomach rebelled. He lurched to his feet, staggered into the bathroom, and spent the next ten minutes throwing up. He didn't want Kenzie to see this, but she had followed him and stood beside him, holding a damp washcloth to his forehead, bringing him some relief.

"For what it's worth, your liver is eternally grateful," she said.

Conrad moaned, flushed the toilet, and bent over the sink, some thought in his addled brain about brushing the god-awful regurgitated whiskey taste out of his mouth.

"I've got aspirin in my truck. I'll go grab one."

By the time Kenzie returned, an aspirin and his glass of water in hand, his teeth were brushed and he was standing upright-ish—and feeling disgusted with himself. He'd never claimed to be an expert on impressing women, but he was pretty sure that getting drunk in the middle of the day and puking his guts out wouldn't do it.

"Here you go."

"Thanks." He popped the pill, drank.

She led him back to the sofa and sat beside him. "Feel better?"

He nodded. "Except for my pride. I warned you. I'm a fucking mess right now."

"Don't worry about that." She took his hand, looked over at the TV, where he and Bruce were slogging their way up The Bottleneck. "Let's forget about supper for a while. This is your K2 climb, right?"

"Yes. How do you know?"

She laughed at his expression. "I've watched all your climbing films. In case you hadn't noticed, I kind of have a thing for you."

He reached out, took her hand. "Say that again when I'm sober, okay? I don't know if I'll remember it later."

———

BRUCE LOOKED AT THE CAMERA, grinning, his Aussie accent charming. "Conrad here is my climbing wife. We've been together for twenty years now. It's a marriage made in heaven."

The Harrison on the screen laughed. "More like hell."

Kenzie sat beside Harrison while they watched another climbing film, this one about their Makalu expedition, her heart aching at the anguish in his eyes. "You and Bruce made a great team."

Harrison nodded. "He always had my back. I couldn't have done half the things I've done without him."

She didn't believe that, but she didn't say so. "Where did you two meet?"

"In a bar in Fairbanks. We tried to hook up with the same woman—a sexy brunette. I hit on her and got shot down. He said something about women loving Aussie accents and moved in. She shot him down, too, and left with another woman." Harrison chuckled at the memory. "He and I ended up drinking a beer together to commiserate and found out we had more things in common than our taste in women."

"Climbing."

Harrison didn't seem to hear her, his smile fading. "I thought we could do anything."

She reached over, took his hand. "Can you do me a favor?"

He nodded. "What?"

"Can you promise me that you'll try meditating with Esri?"

He frowned, then nodded. "Okay. I promise."

"Will you remember that you promised me?"

"I'm not that drunk—not now, anyway."

"Okay." She stood, walked over to the box that held his DVDs, and searched through it. "What would you like to watch now?"

She tried to steer him away from climbing films. "Oh, I love *The Maltese Falcon*. *The Godfather*, too. Do you want to watch one of these?"

He didn't answer.

She turned and saw that he'd fallen asleep right where he sat, his chin against his chest. She set the DVDs aside and helped him to lie down, lowering his head to the plush arm of the sofa and lifting his feet off the floor. Damn, his legs were long—and heavy. Then she grabbed a blanket from his bedroom closet—she knew where everything was because she'd helped unpack it—and covered him.

"Oh, Harrison." She pressed a kiss to his forehead.

He didn't budge, his breathing deep and even, his face relaxed in the forgetfulness of sleep, his lashes dark against his tanned skin.

Hungry, she left him in peace and went to the kitchen to make herself a can of chicken soup. When she went back to check on Harrison, she found Gabby curled up asleep at his feet, Gizmo on the floor beside him.

The dogs had the right idea.

"You don't want to leave him alone either, do you?" she whispered to Gizmo, scratching behind his ears.

She went out to her truck and took out the travel bag

she always kept in the back in case a search-and-rescue call required her to leave town. Inside, she had a T-shirt for sleeping, a change of clothes and toiletries, as well as stuff Gizmo would need—a spare harness, dog food, a collapsible water bowl, and such.

Back inside, she found Harrison and the dogs still sound asleep. She went to his bedroom, switched into her sleep shirt, and crawled into his bed with her book—the latest romantic suspense release from the awesome Kaylea Cross.

She told herself she'd stop at 10 p.m. At 10, she told herself just one more chapter. Finally, at midnight, she reluctantly closed the book and took Gizmo and Gabby out for a potty break. Then it was time to sleep. She had to be up in six hours. She checked on Harrison, found him still sound asleep. She put Gabby in her crate, set the alarm on her phone, and crawled into his bed alone.

At some point during the night, Harrison got into bed with her, his arms going around her, holding her close. "You stayed."

"I was worried about you." She snuggled against him and fell into a deep sleep.

Her phone alarm woke her, pulling her from strange dreams about Harrison and Gabby and Everest Base Camp, where she had never been. Trying not to wake Harrison, she made quick use of his shower and then slipped into jeans and a T-shirt.

"Son of a bitch!"

Harrison's shout from outside the bathroom door made her pulse skip.

She opened the door, found him sitting on the bed, his smartphone in hand, staring at something on the screen, a look of naked fury on his face. "What's wrong?"

"He's gone too far." He stood, handed her his phone, and yanked on his jeans.

She glanced at the screen—and saw herself.

The reporter who had harassed Harrison had posted photos of her on his website. The photos had been taken yesterday afternoon when she'd first arrived and then last night when she'd gone outside to get her overnight bag. The headline read, "Harrison Conrad hooks up with mystery chick."

She stared, stunned. "Why post photos of me?"

"I wouldn't give him an interview, so now he's harassing you. He's hiding out there somewhere. I'm going to find him and put an end to this." Harrison left the bedroom with long, angry strides.

It took Kenzie a moment to realize that he truly intended to confront the reporter. She ran after him, stepped in front of the door to block him. "Don't."

Harrison glared at her, his jaw tight, angry tension rolling off him. "It's one thing for him to come after me, but I refuse to let him near you."

"He's trying to provoke you. If you go out there, you'll be giving him exactly what he wants."

"He wants to get punched in the face?"

"He wants you on camera doing something that he can post to get clicks for his meaningless little website. Let someone else handle this."

"Who?"

"Your agent."

"I got rid of my agent." Or he'd tried to anyway.

"Okay, well, then why don't we call the sheriff? There must be some law about taking photographs of people and posting them online without their consent." Kenzie thought quickly. "I'll text Quinn and tell her I'm going to be late. Then we can call the sheriff and let them know what's going on. You're welcome to stay at my place until this jerk gets tired and goes away."

Harrison raised an eyebrow, clearly not impressed with her idea. "I'm not running away and hiding. Besides, I bet they have your license plate number, and if they have that, they can get your address from the DVM."

"They can?" Kenzie didn't like that. "Do you have a better idea?"

Harrison closed his eyes, drew in a breath. "Not at the moment. I still think punching the little fucker is my best option."

"Right. Because jail is so much fun."

———

CONRAD CALLED the sheriff's department, which promised to run a patrol down his street looking for the green Subaru. The blip of a siren down the street ten minutes later told him they'd found the bastard.

He and Kenzie watched from the window as Deputy Marcs contacted the reporter, who had been sleeping in his vehicle a few houses down. Marcs spoke with him for a few minutes before running his driver's license. The moment she turned away from the Subaru, the kid tossed something into a nearby bush.

"I wonder what that was." Kenzie craned her neck for a better view.

"Something he really doesn't want Marcs to find."

But Marcs must have seen out of the corner of her eye. When she was done running his license, she slipped on a nitrile glove and retrieved it, holding up a plastic bag of something white.

"Drugs." Conrad wasn't surprised.

"Well, that explains a few things."

Twenty minutes later, the son of a bitch was cuffed and sitting in the back of Marcs' vehicle on his way to the county lock-up, his Subaru impounded.

The knot of tension Conrad had carried in his chest loosened.

Kenzie slipped into his arms. "Aren't you glad you're not in the cell next to his?"

Conrad kissed her. "You were right. Is that what you want me to say?"

She laughed, the sound putting a hitch in his chest. "You don't have to say it when we both know it's true."

"Oh, listen to you." He gave her ribs a little tickle. "Ms. Know-It-All."

She squealed, twisting in his arms in a way that made him wish she didn't have to go to work. He could spend the entire day twisting with her—in bed.

"I need to go."

"I know."

She picked up her little duffle bag and her handbag and took Gizmo's leash. "I teach a class from seven to eight, but I'll be free after that. Want to come to dinner? I have the salmon fillets I bought for last night."

Last night.

Shit.

Until this moment, he'd tried hard not to think about the past twenty-four hours. He'd gotten shit-faced drunk in the middle of the day, puked his guts out, and worried Kenzie so much that she had stayed overnight.

Proud of yourself, asshole?

He wanted to do something for her. "How about I cook while you teach your class? When you finish, dinner will be waiting."

Kenzie stared at him. "That's the sexiest thing a man has ever said to me."

"Really? What kind of jerks have you dated?"

"Climbers. One left me to be an adventure guide in Alaska and died in a helicopter crash. The other one went skiing in Austria, where he met an athletic blonde. He broke up with me via email."

"They sound like assholes."

"Remember you promised to meditate with Esri."

He frowned. "When did I … Oh. Right."

Kenzie stood on her tiptoes and kissed him, Gizmo threatening to trip her with his leash. "See you later."

"Hey, about last night …" He pushed aside his shame. "Thank you."

She smiled, turning in circles to untangle herself from the leash. "You're welcome. It's like I told you last night—I kind of have a thing for you."

Out the door she went, Gizmo following at her heels.

Conrad scooped Gabby into his arms and watched Kenzie drive away, somehow missing her already.

What was that about?

He took Gabby outside for a quick potty break, ate breakfast, then looked up Esri's number and left her a message. She called back almost immediately and arranged to meet him at her office at noon. Then there was nothing to do but pick up where he'd left off yesterday when he'd opened that bottle.

He had just cleaned up the place and was about to head to the park to practice puppy runaways when Candace called.

"You should have called me."

"Good morning to you, too."

"You need to do an interview with one of the networks or a major publication if you want to get these little guys off your back."

"I already told you—I'm not interested."

"As long as you stay silent, every climbing rag in the world is going to want to come after you in the hopes of being the first to get your story."

Conrad closed his eyes, wrestled with his anger. None of this was Candace's fault. "They'll go away eventually."

"I think you underestimate your importance in the climbing world. My phone has been ringing all morning with reporters from the big climbing mags wanting the exclusive. They know you're back, and now they know where to find you. That reporter published your address. Those photos are just the beginning, my friend."

Well, fuck.

He hesitated, weighing Candace's advice against his unwillingness to speak publicly about what had happened that day.

"Extreme Exposure will pay you fifty grand to do an interview on the Good Day Show and another twenty if you do an interview with Altitude. It will be the easiest seventy thousand you've ever made."

Conrad wasn't so sure about that. He'd be exposing his grief for nothing more than money. In the back of his mind, he heard Bruce's voice.

Fuck, mate, I'd do it.

"I'm not interested."

"You know where to find me when you change your mind."

Chapter 13

CONRAD STEPPED out of the cold wind and into Esri's office and sat in the waiting room. Decorated in shades of green, tan, and soft blue, it had a little fountain in one corner, the tinkling of water relaxing. A serene golden Buddha sat on the coffee table, presiding over the room.

Esri stepped out of her office. "Hey. Perfect timing. Where's the puppy?"

"I left her at home in her crate." He would only be away for about an hour.

"Want to get started?"

He followed her into her office, where two meditation cushions sat on the floor in front of a sliding glass door that faced the mountains.

She lit some incense. "How is your day going?"

Conrad sat on one of the cushions. "A reporter ambushed me outside my house yesterday. I refused to answer his questions, and we had a confrontation."

He hadn't meant to bring this up, but now that he'd started, the words wouldn't stop. He told her what the reporter had said and how the bastard had filmed him.

"Then, last night, he took photos of Kenzie when she came over, and he put those on his website, too. She kept me from punching the bastard. We called the sheriff, and the kid is now in the county jail on drug charges."

Esri sat beside him. "I can't blame you for feeling angry. What he did must have felt like a violation to both you and Kenzie."

"She handled it better than I did."

"She might have less at stake here than you do. That reporter was asking you to share your private pain with his readers."

"Yeah." Conrad could see that. "My agent called. She says the media are going to keep coming until I give them what they want. Apparently, one of my gear sponsors is ready to dump a lot of money into my bank account if I go on TV and do an interview about what happened. She thinks I should do it."

"How do you feel about it?"

He shook his head. "I don't know why people need the details. A serac fell. It killed two young climbers and my best friend. Why do they need more?"

"If I could answer that question, I'd write a book and get rich." Esri gave him a gentle smile. "That said, I don't think you should do anything you're not ready to do, no matter how much money is involved. You need to take care of that part of yourself that is grieving."

Conrad realized he was dangerously close to falling down the rabbit hole. "Sorry. I don't want to waste your time."

"You're not wasting my time. If I were in your shoes, I would want to talk about what happened, too. For what it's worth, I think you did the right thing by calling the sheriff."

Conrad let the subject go. "So how do we do this? I've

only ever done meditation in the Dokhang with the monks leading."

"Tell me about that."

Conrad described the mantras, the chanting, the music, the scents. "I sat in the corner and chanted along with them."

"Why don't the two of us try chanting the Shakyamuni mantra together?"

"Okay." Conrad sat in a lotus position and closed his eyes.

"Relax and let your thoughts drift by like clouds. You wouldn't hold onto a cloud, so don't hold onto your thoughts." Then she started. "*Om muni muni maha muni shakyamuni soha.*"

Her voice was so different from the low, guttural voices of the monks that it made Conrad smile. He pulled himself together and joined in, ignoring the strangeness of attempting this in Esri's office. "*Om muni muni maha muni shakyamuni soha.*"

It took a few minutes, but slowly the familiar chant began to relax his mind, worry and grief lifting like a fog, his body floating. Emptiness. Peace.

All too soon, it was over.

"Thanks so much for coming, Conrad." Esri got to her feet, stretched. "It's really special for me to share some part of your experience at Tengboche."

Conrad opened his eyes. "Thanks for inviting me. Can we do this again?"

"I meditate at noon every day. You're always welcome."

Feeling lighter than he had when he'd arrived, he stood and picked up the cushions, setting them on top a stack of cushions in the corner.

"Thanks." She put out the incense. "Got any exciting

plans for the afternoon?"

"I'm meeting Kenzie at her place and making dinner. After yesterday, it's the least I can do."

"You mean because of the reporter and the photos?"

He shook his head. "When she came over, I was drunk. I don't usually drink hard liquor, but I found a bottle Bruce and I had bought to drink together and … Kenzie stayed with me."

"I'm sure she was worried and wanted to help. Did it make a difference to have her there with you?"

"Yeah." More than Conrad could say.

But again, he'd let his mouth start a conversation he didn't want to finish. "Thanks. I might see you tomorrow."

"I hope so."

He left Esri's office, the cold wind seeming to suck his breath away.

KENZIE SIGNED for a shipment of dog food. She pointed to the stock room. "Can you put them over there?"

"Sure thing." The delivery woman rolled her dolly to the back of the store.

"Thanks." Kenzie spent the next ten minutes opening and unpacking the boxes, while Dree helped Frank, who owned the town's only gas station and car repair place, pick dog food for his aging black Lab with a sensitive tummy. She was about to make a suggestion of her own when her Team pager went off.

SHERIFF TONING OUT ALL HRD K9 UNITS.

A search for human remains.

She left the stock room and waved to Dree, who recognized the sound of Kenzie's pager and knew what it meant. "I'll be back as soon as I can."

"No worries. I hope you find them—whoever they are."

So did Kenzie. "Thanks."

Kenzie hurried to the kennel, leashed Gizmo, and told Quinn she'd check in via text message. "Miss Piggy's family will be here soon to pick her up."

"They just called to say they're on the way." Quinn was on top of it, of course.

"See you later." Kenzie stepped outside, a cold wind hitting her in the face.

To the west, gray clouds promised snow.

She hurried home, changed into warm clothing, and led Gizmo out to the truck. "Time to go to work, buddy."

At The Cave, she found a squad car waiting for her.

Deputy Julia Marcs came out to meet her. "Good to see you're bundled up. It's cold out here, and this might take a while."

Inside, Julia brought her up to date. A woman and mother of three had gone missing from her home in Boulder a few weeks back, and police believed her husband had killed her and dumped her body somewhere in the mountains west of Scarlet.

"The husband told police his wife went out shopping but never came home. Then he changed his story and said that *he'd* been the one out shopping for a laptop when his wife had vanished and that police had twisted his words. He told police he hadn't left Boulder that day, but his phone pinged off our cell tower that afternoon."

So, the bastard was lying.

"West of Scarlet could be anywhere. Do you have any idea where to start?"

Julia nodded. "Detectives discovered a hiking guide to

Russey Ranch in his trash. There were aspen leaves in his vehicle and stuck in the mud on his tires as well."

Russey Ranch was a vast expanse of wilderness and one of the county's more remote parks with only a handful of accessible roads and trails.

"It will be like looking for a needle in the proverbial haystack."

Julia nodded, weariness on her face. "That's why we need Gizmo's nose."

"How many K9 units are searching?"

"You're the first one here. I'm not sure who else will make it."

Kenzie lived closer than any of the other HRD dog handlers. "I guess Gizmo and I are it for now."

"Megs has toned out the Team for technical support."

If they found a body, someone would have to bring it in.

Kenzie sent Harrison a quick text, telling him she'd been toned out, then climbed in her truck and followed Julia and Rescue 1, with Creed and Nicole inside, up to the Russey parking area. Malachi, Mitch, and Austin arrived just after they did, Austin still on duty in his ranger uniform.

Kenzie climbed out, clipped the mic from her pack set onto her parka, and slipped her backpack over her shoulders. She did a quick radio check, harnessed Gizmo, and joined the others.

Julia handed Kenzie a plastic bag that held a glove. "I'm not sure if you use a scent article for human remains, but here you go. I've got something of hers and his."

"The scent trail is three weeks old, but we can try." Kenzie opened the plastic bag, took out the scent articles, let Gizmo sniff his fill, and then tucked them away in the plastic bag. "Gizmo, search!"

Gizmo seemed confused at first. Kenzie walked him along the edges of the parking lot, hoping to pick up some kind of trail. Then abruptly he headed off to the north, leading her down a narrow side trail that ran along a little creek, Julia and the others following at a distance so as not to distract him. Every so often, he stopped, wandered off the trail, then moved on again.

After about an hour of chilly, uphill hiking, they came to a little wooden bridge and crossed the creek, coming to a glade of bare aspens, their leaves like a carpet of gold coins on the forest floor. Beyond the aspens grew a thick stand of conifers.

Gizmo made straight for it, tugging at his leash now.

Kenzie hurried after him, dread curling in her stomach. What kind of bastard could kill his wife, the mother of his children?

Gizmo sat—and she saw.

A woman's head, her eyes lifeless, her mouth open as if in a silent scream.

Kenzie fought to hold herself together, reaching down to pet Gizmo. "Good boy, Gizmo. Good boy."

⎯⎯

CONRAD HADN'T YET GOTTEN BACK into the habit of keeping his Team pager charged and in his pocket. He was at Food Mart when Kenzie texted to say she'd been toned out for an HRD call and didn't know when she'd be home.

He took the groceries back to his place and then drove with Gabby to The Cave to find out what was going on.

"Code black. They just found the victim's head," Megs said when he walked in with Gabby on her leash. "It looks like her husband did it. She had three kids with him—the sick son of a bitch."

"Holy shit." What kind of man could do something like that? "I'm going to head up there and see if I can help. Can you watch Gabby?"

Megs raised an eyebrow, but reached for Gabby's leash. "If she pees on my floor, you're cleaning it up."

"Fine. Thanks."

"And, hey, try turning on your pager."

"Right." He would have to find it first.

He grabbed a radio and drove up to Russey Ranch, parked, and hiked up the trail. He reached the scene just as the other Team members were strapping a half-empty body bag to a litter, Kenzie watching with Gizmo off to one side. The area was cordoned off with police barricade tape, detectives in forensic gear still hard at work.

Conrad walked over to Kenzie. "Hey. How are you holding up?"

She tried to act like nothing was wrong, but there was a shattered look in her eyes. "I'm okay. I'm fine."

"Liar." He knelt down, petted Gizmo. "Good job, buddy. You're a rock star."

"That poor woman has been out here for three weeks. It looks like a bear or cat got to her, but I think we found everything that was left of her body."

Conrad took Kenzie's free hand, gave it a squeeze.

Herrera spotted him, grinned. "Nice of you to show up, Conrad."

"I thought I'd time it for when most of the work was already done." Conrad walked over to the others and crawled beneath the litter to clip on the ATV tire that would enable them to roll it down the trail.

"We could use your help getting the litter down." Taylor took one of the litter's handles. "The trail has some steep spots."

"You got it."

He, Ahearn, Taylor, O'Brien, Nicole, and Herrera rolled the litter back toward the parking lot in silence, Kenzie following with Gizmo, the awfulness of the situation weighing on all of them. Tonight, a family that had feared the worst for three long weeks was about to have those fears realized.

Conrad hoped the bastard who'd done this rotted in hell.

They'd been hiking for about ten minutes when Kenzie dashed off the trail and threw up in the bushes.

The Team came to a halt, waiting for her.

"You guys got this?" Conrad asked.

Taylor nodded.

Conrad left them and walked over to Kenzie, who was still bent double, her hand resting against a ponderosa pine. He rubbed her back.

"I don't want you to see this."

"Hey, I owe you, remember?"

She handed him Gizmo's leash. "Give me just a second."

He gave her space, leading Gizmo back to the litter, where the others still waited.

"Is she going to be okay?" Nicole asked.

Conrad took hold of the litter again. "She's a bit shaken."

Creed watched her, a worried frown on his face. "I don't blame her. That was some rough shit."

Kenzie rejoined them, took Gizmo's leash from Conrad. "Thanks."

They started down the trail again.

Hawke was waiting with an ambulance at the parking lot to make the DBT—dead body transfer. Without a word, he and Brandon Silver, his B-shift captain, lifted the body bag onto a gurney, slid it into the ambulance, and started the long drive to the medical examiner's lab.

Ahearn turned to the group. "I don't think we need to debrief this one. Great work, everyone. Well done, Kenzie and Gizmo."

Kenzie glanced around. "Where's Gabby? You didn't leave her in your vehicle."

"Hell, no! Megs is babysitting."

Kenzie gaped at him. "Megs? *Babysitting*?"

That made everyone laugh, breaking some of the tension.

While the others made plans to meet at Knockers, Conrad walked with Kenzie to her truck. "Because of you two, she'll get justice now."

"I'm not sure there is any justice." Kenzie opened the topper and lowered the tailgate for Gizmo, who jumped up and plopped down in his crate. "Those kids will never see their mother again. For the rest of their lives, they'll have to live knowing their father killed her and left her body to be eaten by animals."

She poured water out of a bottle into a plastic bowl, set it inside with Gizmo, and closed the crate.

Conrad shut the tailgate and drew Kenzie into his arms, the tension in her body easing as he held her. "You're right. There is no justice in this."

Not for the victim or her children or her parents or anyone who loved her. There was only loss and grief and heartbreak.

"I need to get back. I've got a class that starts in a half hour."

"Can't you cancel it?"

She shook her head. "I try very hard not to do that."

He had to admire her dedication. "I promised you dinner afterward."

"I'm not sure I'll ever eat again."

Conrad could understand that. He wasn't sure how much of an appetite he'd have after seeing what she'd just seen. "How do you feel about ice cream?"

She tilted her head back to look up at him. "What flavor?"

"Any damned flavor you want."

A little smile tugged at her lips. "Yes, please."

———

KENZIE DROVE HOME, arriving at the kennel for the dog obedience class just in time. She did her best to be cheerful and professional and to focus on her clients. Still, she couldn't get the brutality of the crime scene out of her mind.

After class, she walked home and took a long, hot shower, letting the tears come at last, her heart breaking for the victim, her kids, her family. By the time Harrison got there, she felt more in control of her emotions. She met him at the door wearing her most comfortable, but decidedly unsexy, leggings and sweatshirt.

"Hey." He gave her a kiss and set the shopping bag down on the kitchen counter. "You've been crying."

"I'm fine."

"You don't have to play tough around me, Kenzie. You can always be honest about your feelings."

"I should say the same thing to you."

His brows drew together in a frown. "I'm fine."

"Right." She bent down to pet Gabby, who bounded over to her, tail wagging. "Hi, there, sweetie. Oh, I've missed you, too."

Then she noticed that Harrison had dropped a duffel bag just inside the doorway.

"Are you going somewhere?"

"I'm staying here for the next few nights—if that's okay. I don't like the idea that the assholes from that webzine might know where you live."

Her heart gave a little squish to think he was concerned about her and trying to protect her. "Of course, it's okay—and thanks."

He made a fire in the wood stove while she fed the dogs and dished out ice cream—cookie dough for her and rocky road for him. They ended up on the sofa, eating their dinner in front of the TV and watching back-to-back episodes of *The Simpsons*.

After the third episode, Kenzie reluctantly turned off the TV. "Bedtime. I have to be up at six."

She stood, carried their bowls to the kitchen sink and was about to take the dogs outside when Harrison beat her to it.

"It's cold out there. I'll handle it."

"Are you immune to cold or something?"

He grinned. "Spend a few days in sixty below. Nothing feels cold after that."

She tried to imagine that, decided she didn't want to. "I suppose not."

She went upstairs, washed her face, and brushed her teeth.

Harrison met her at the top of the stairs. "I put the dogs in their crates."

"Thanks." She walked into the bedroom. "I'm afraid that when I close my eyes I'm going to see her again."

Harrison dropped his duffel near the foot of her bed. "Come here."

She slipped into his arms, grateful for the shelter of his embrace.

He kissed the top of her head, spoke in a husky voice. "I could try to give you something else to think about."

"You can't possibly be turned on by me in this outfit." She drew back and glanced down at her shapeless sweatshirt.

"It has nothing to do with what you're wearing." He lifted the sweatshirt over her head and dropped it on the floor. "It's about what's beneath. I've seen you. Tasted you. Been inside you."

Good freaking grief! Was he trying to make her spontaneously combust?

He undressed her and then himself and followed her into bed. Then he made long, slow love to her, taking his time with her, pleasing her with lips, tongue, and fingers before burying himself inside her and leaving her satiated and exhausted.

She snuggled against him. "Best sleeping pill ever."

He chuckled, kissed her forehead. "Good."

As she drifted off, the only thing on Kenzie's mind was how amazing it felt to be held in his strong arms.

Chapter 14

"WHAT THE ...?" Conrad jolted awake to find Kenzie going down on him, her hand and mouth gliding in tandem up and down the length of his cock, her tongue swirling over the aching head, the first hint of orgasm making his balls draw tight. "*God.*"

He'd thought it was a dream.

She looked up at the sound of his voice, her gaze meeting his, the desire in those sultry blue eyes bringing him close to the edge.

He slid his fingers into the silk of her hair, watching her, her breasts bobbing, her nipples tight. He willed himself to hold his hips still, letting her have her way with him because—*God, yes*—she seemed to know what she was doing. Relentless, she devoured him, until he was going out of his mind, desperate to come and just as desperate not to.

Tighter. Faster.

And her tongue—what the hell was she doing?

He was breathing hard now, every exhale a moan, heat gathering in his groin, his body tense, on the brink. No woman had ever done this to him, stripping him so completely of control, getting him so worked up.

Orgasm hit him with the force of an avalanche, driving the breath from his lungs, engulfing him in pleasure. She pulled her mouth off him, finishing him with her fist, cum shooting thick and white against her breasts.

He lay there for a moment, eyes closed, too dazed to move, too stunned to speak, too content to think.

Hot lips kissed a path up his body. "Good morning."

"Yeah," he said, stupidly.

He opened his eyes, watched her reach for a tissue and wipe herself clean.

"You had a hard-on. I couldn't let it go to waste."

Conrad's brain began to reboot. "I like the way you think."

He was imagining all the things he would do to her when she kissed him on the mouth and climbed out of bed. He caught her hand. "Hey, get back here. I'm not finished with you."

She gave him an apologetic smile. "As much as I'd like to see what you have in mind, I need to take care of the dogs and get ready to work. Besides, I came three times last night. I was just helping you catch up."

He chuckled. "That's sweet of you."

"Not really. I love watching you come." She walked off toward the bathroom, tossing him a sexy look over her shoulder, dark hair hanging down her back, her ass delectable.

Damned if she wasn't every man's wet dream—or at least *his* wet dream.

He sat up, called after her. "I'll handle the dogs."

"Thanks!"

His body glowing, he got out of bed, pulled on the boxer briefs and jeans he'd tossed on the floor, then made his way downstairs. He let the dogs out and then fed them. They seemed to adore each other, wagging their tails, meeting nose to nose. He knelt down to pet them. "Let's not tell your mommy the two of you are friends now. She might take you back, Gabby, and I don't want you to go."

Gabby licked his hand, apparently agreeing with him.

By the time Kenzie came downstairs, he had omelets, toast, and coffee waiting.

"This is better than room service." She stood on her tiptoes and kissed him. "I like a man who's good in the kitchen, too."

"Yeah, I figured that one out."

They talked about their plans for the day. Kenzie had a scent-work class from seven to eight at the kennel. Conrad had no idea what that was.

"Scent classes teach people's pets—dogs who aren't trained for SAR or HRD—to search and find things based on odor. It's not meant to turn them into working dogs. It hones a dog's natural hunting skills, teaches their people more about them, and strengthens bonds. It's a lot of fun for both dogs and humans."

"Cool." Conrad still had that resume to write up and a job application to fill out for Ski Scarlet. "Barring either of us getting toned out, I will finally cook up those salmon fillets and have dinner waiting for you when you get home."

Ten minutes later, Kenzie was ready to go, Gizmo on his leash. "Thanks for being there for me last night."

"Hey, you've been there for me, too." He bent down, kissed her, and was surprised to realize he didn't want her to go.

"See you tonight." She opened the back door, then glanced back at him. "Don't punch any reporters while I'm at work, okay?"

He walked her to the door. "I make no promises."

He drove home feeling more like himself than he had in a while. It wasn't yesterday's meditation that had made the difference. It was Kenzie. Something about her made everything better. It didn't hurt that she gave head like a goddess and was every man's dream in bed. But it wasn't just the mind-blowing sex.

When he was around her, his world felt whole again.

What the hell was up with that?

He turned the corner onto his street—and almost slammed on the brakes. Sitting in front of his home were two news vans from Denver TV stations, reporters standing in a throng on the sidewalk and in his driveway.

"Son of a bitch." He thought for a moment of driving back to Kenzie's place, but he wasn't going to let the media chase him out of his home.

He turned into his driveway, going slowly enough not to hit anyone but fast enough to send the message that they'd better damned well get out of his way. He pressed the button for his garage door, drove inside, and closed it behind him.

Candace had been right. This wasn't over.

———

KENZIE FOUND herself in the middle of a frustrating day. Dree went home with a bad migraine, so Kenzie had to take over at the store. That was fine. It was her store, after all, and she just wanted Dree to feel better.

But then the distributor of her most popular brand of organic cat food notified her that they would no longer be carrying the product, leaving her to search for a new supplier. The couple who had reserved a spot for their boxer called at the last minute to say their trip had been canceled. Bentley, the Goldendoodle, had gone back to his people this morning, leaving the number of dogs in the kennel at three, which meant a crimp in cash flow.

Then Wendy Hall, a local who worked as a reporter for the tiny *Scarlet Gazette*, walked into the store.

"Hey, Wendy, can I help you find something?"

"I'm here to talk to you. Do you have a minute?"

Wary now, Kenzie hesitated. "If this is about Harrison Conrad…"

Wendy shook her head. "It's about yesterday's search and the work you do for the Team. My editor wants a feature about you and Gizmo."

"Seriously?" Kenzie had been doing SAR and HRD work for years. The paper had never taken an interest before. "Why? Slow news day?"

Wendy laughed. "Every day is a slow news day in Scarlet. She wants more features that showcase the talents and work of locals. There are a lot of special people who live in this town, so why not write about them?"

Kenzie had never thought of herself as doing something special. "Aren't you afraid of boring your readers into a coma?"

"My job is to make it interesting. I'll put in a fundraising pitch for the Team, too."

That sealed the deal. "Okay, I'll do it."

Wendy's face lit up. "Can I ask you questions now? I'll record the answers, so it will be like having a conversation. Then maybe I can get a photo of you and Gizmo together."

"Okay, but if someone comes in, I'll need to stop to help them."

Wendy set up her recorder and took out a pad of paper on which she'd written a long list of questions. What had drawn Kenzie to training SAR and HRD dogs? How exactly did one train a dog to find missing people or human remains? Which dog breeds were best for this kind of work? How many hours a week did she spend training Gizmo? Didn't it creep her out to keep a container with human remains in her freezer? What other kinds of work did she do with dogs?

Those were easy to answer.

But then the questions grew more personal.

What was the worst call she'd ever been on? How did she cope with searches like yesterday's that end with finding a dead body? What exactly had she seen out there?

Kenzie did her best to remain professional, images from yesterday flooding her mind. "The worst calls are those involving children or those where you find nothing. You know the person is out there, but you can't find a trace of them. You can't give the family closure. When that happens, I try to take a step back and tell myself that we did everything we could. It's not always easy. As for yesterday's call, that was tough, but it's part of an ongoing police investigation. I can't comment."

Wendy didn't push her but seemed satisfied with her answers. "Thanks so much. That's all great. If we can snap a photo, I'll get out of your hair."

Kenzie put a "Be Right Back" sign in the store's window—she could get away with that in Scarlet—then went next door to get Gizmo. She brushed him, put him in his work harness, and went out to her backyard. It didn't dawn on her until then that she might want to put on some makeup or brush her hair.

Wendy took out a big DSLR camera and pointed to the north side of the yard. "The light is perfect in front of those aspens, and they'll make a nice backdrop."

Kenzie led Gizmo over to the aspens. "Sit. Good boy."

She knelt down beside him, turned her face toward

Wendy.

Click. Click. Click. Click. Click.

Wendy took several shots then looked at the results. "Oh, that's perfect. You can tell how much you love Gizmo and how much he loves you."

Kenzie stood, looked at the little screen on the camera. "Those turned out really well. Thanks."

"Thank you." Wendy put the camera back in its bag. "I think people are going to love this. By the way, if you're concerned about Conrad, you might want to know that the media have staked out his place—TV production vans, print media, all of it."

"What? Why?"

"Everyone wants his story. I was there for a while, but I left. It's clear he doesn't want to talk. He won't answer his door or come out."

Good for Harrison.

"I wish they would leave him alone."

"I'm sorry." Wendy handed Kenzie her card. "If he wants to talk to a reporter who won't cross his boundaries, here's my card."

Kenzie's temper flared. "You didn't really want to do a story about SAR work. You're trying to get to Harrison through me."

Wendy looked genuinely taken aback. "No! Your story is running in tomorrow's paper. Sorry. I just thought I'd leave you with the card just in case. If you don't feel comfortable giving it to him, then don't. I came here to see you."

"Sorry if I misjudged you." The surprise on Wendy's face convinced Kenzie that Wendy hadn't been trying to manipulate her. "I'll give it to him when I see him again."

"I heard the two of you were involved. I'm jealous."

"No comment." Kenzie had never dated a celebrity

before, and it was strange to have to say that.

Wendy saw through her. "Don't worry. I don't do that kind of journalism."

Kenzie went back to the store, let Wendy out, and went back to searching for a new cat food supplier. Not a minute later, she got a text from Quinn.

Do you have a plunger? The toilet is clogged.

Wasn't that just what she needed?

———

CONRAD WENT out into the backyard with Gabby, got a rake from the garage, and started raking leaves. He needed to finish this before the first big snowfall, and anything was better than sitting in the house, curtains drawn, while reporters took turns knocking on his front door. Didn't they get the message?

Gabby bounded about the yard, barked at the rake, and ran through the piles of leaves, making it difficult to get anything done, but she was so damned cute that he didn't care. Soon it became a game. Conrad raked together a pile and hid her favorite toy beneath it, and she dove in and retrieved the toy, tail wagging.

He found himself laughing.

"What did you do to get the media so riled up?" The old woman next door stood on her back porch in a floral housedress, a broom in her hand.

"I didn't do anything."

"Don't try to pull the wool over these eyes, young man. They wouldn't be standing out there if you hadn't done something."

"Okay, fine." Conrad tossed Gabby's toy into another

pile of leaves, watched her dive in after it. "I survived when the rest of my team was killed climbing Mount Everest. The media wants the gory details."

"You must have had an angel watching out for you."

Yeah, right.

The pile of leaves rustled, shifted, and out popped Gabby, toy in her mouth.

"Mount Everest, huh? You ever make it to the top?" she asked.

"Yes, ma'am—twice."

"Only a damned fool does something like that. I guess that explains all those muscles—and why you run around outside naked as a jaybird. Not enough oxygen to your brain."

Conrad turned to face her, saw that she was smiling, and couldn't help but laugh. "That only happened once—and only because I thought everyone would be asleep. I didn't know you were watching."

She gave a noncommittal humph. "Why can't you just tell those reporters that you don't want to talk?"

"I tried that."

"Bloodsuckers." She turned and walked inside her house.

He went back to raking, only to hear her voice again a moment later, but this time it was coming from the front yard.

"What's the matter with you people? You're disturbing the whole neighborhood. This guy doesn't want to give any interviews, so why don't you move along? If you block my sidewalk or set one foot on my lawn, I'll call the sheriff."

Stunned, Conrad stared toward the sound of her voice.

Grumpy Mrs. Frank-and-Beans was standing up for him.

"Do you know Harrison Conrad?" one reporter asked.

"No, I don't know him. He just moved in."

"Could you please ask him to answer his door?"

"I told you I don't know him. But if he wanted to answer his door, I'm sure he'd do it. Now, stop making a racket, and move on."

Conrad was going to buy her a box of chocolates.

He finished raking and bagged all but one pile of leaves, leaving that for Gabby to enjoy. He'd brought her back inside and was making himself a quick sandwich before heading to Esri's, when someone pounded on the front door. "For fuck's sake."

He ignored it.

More pounding. "Conrad, it's Moretti!"

Conrad set his sandwich on a plate and walked to the front door, Gabby at his heels. He scooped her up to keep her from running outside and opened the door.

Moretti stepped inside, closing the door quickly behind him. "How long have they been out there?"

"Since the ass-crack of dawn."

"Shit. That's crazy, man." He held out a piece of paper. "I brought this."

Conrad took it, saw that it was a job application for Ski Scarlet. "Thanks."

"Matt, my supervisor, is holding a position for you. It's yours if you want it. You need to fill this out and come talk to him in the next couple of days, or he'll give the job to someone else."

Conrad's first thought was that the job *should* go to someone else, but opportunity had literally come knocking at his literal damned door with a job his teenage self would have loved. "Okay. I need a resume, right? I've never made one."

"Print out that page from your website that tells about all the mountains you've climbed and skied. You're

Harrison fucking Conrad, man. You just need to walk into that office and say you want the job."

"Yeah?"

"Hell, yeah."

Three hours later, Conrad found himself sitting in the office of Matt Mayes, the resort's Ski Patrol supervisor, wearing a sports jacket, clean shaven, his hair cut. He'd brought Gabby with him, not knowing how long he'd be gone.

Matt held out his hand, a broad smile on his tanned face. "It's a pleasure to meet you. I've read about some of your exploits. Who's this?"

"This is Gabby. Kenzie Morgan is training her for SAR and HRD work. I'm fostering her for a while."

"Fantastic. Kenzie does amazing work with dogs. She trained Charlie, one of our two avy dogs, along with my Boomer. She and Charlie saved a guy a couple winters back." Matt petted the puppy then sat and motioned to a chair. "Take a seat."

"Thanks." Conrad sat and held out the completed job application and the page he'd printed from his website.

Matt glanced down at the paperwork. "I know you're quite the alpinist—one of the best in the world. What about your skiing experience?"

"I've skied Shishapangma, Cho Oyu, the South Col of Everest…" Conrad stopped because Matt was staring at him.

Matt put the pages down, chuckled. "Okay, you can handle our slopes."

"Yes, sir, I can." Had there been any doubt?

"How about your EMT certification?"

"It's good for another six months. I need to bulk up on continuing-ed hours."

"That's fine." Matt's brows drew together in a frown.

"To be honest, I hesitate to offer you this job because I'm afraid you'll find a winter of patrolling slopes and dealing with idiots to be pretty damned boring. If you accept, I will expect you to stick with us through the end of the season in April."

"That seems fair."

"I won't lie. We pay shit. The mornings start early. It's cold. You'll spend the whole day on the mountain, apart from bathroom and lunch breaks."

As if a day on the slopes were a hardship. "Perfect."

"There are a lot of drunk and stoned idiots on the slopes. Tourists. People who get in over their heads. It's our job to keep everyone safe, even when they don't follow the rules. *Especially* when they don't follow the rules."

"I can handle idiots. A lot of the rescue work we do on the Team involves people who make bad choices."

"After what happened on Everest, how do you think you'd handle an avalanche? When someone's life is on the line, we can't afford to have anyone fall apart."

Conrad hadn't expected that question. "I've had avalanche training. I can't say exactly how I'd react, but I'd like to think I'd keep my shit together."

Matt laughed. "The job is yours if you want it."

Conrad hesitated. If he accepted, he wouldn't be able to leave Scarlet until the end of next April—if he decided to leave Scarlet. He thought of Kenzie and Gizmo and Gabby and decided that he was in no hurry to go anywhere. "I've got one condition."

"Yeah? Name it."

"No publicity. You can put my name on your website like you would any other member of Ski Patrol, but no publicity."

"You've got it."

"Thank you. I'll take the job."

Chapter 15

KENZIE STEPPED through her back door with Gizmo—
and was stopped dead in her tracks by the delicious aroma
that filled her kitchen. She glanced around, her frustrating
day forgotten. Her best dishes sat on the table, her grand-
mother's silver beside them on cloth napkins. Two long
white tapers burned in her old crystal candleholders at the
center of the table.

She slipped out of her parka and hung it on its hook by
the back door just as Harrison ducked in from the living
room, Gabby behind him.

"Hey."

She stared. "Your hair. You cut it."

It was short the way he'd always worn it, and, *damn*, did
he look good, a touch of gray at the temples, his cheek-
bones somehow more prominent, his jaw more chiseled. As
if that weren't enough, he wore jeans with a gray sports
jacket, a black turtleneck beneath.

Damn.

"You look … *hot.*"

As in ovary-exploding hot. Knees-turning-to-jelly hot. Fuck-me-now hot.

He rubbed his head. "I figured it was time."

She cleared her throat, tried to pull herself together. She motioned to the table. "You've had a busy afternoon."

He grinned. "I got a job."

"Harrison! Where?"

"You're looking at the newest member of Ski Patrol at Ski Scarlet."

She hurried over to him, wrapped her arms around him, the warm, masculine scent of him filling her head. "Congratulations!"

He held her, kissed her. "Thanks."

"I bet that was the easiest job interview ever. 'How well do you ski?' 'Ever heard of the Himalayas?'"

He chuckled. "Yeah, that was pretty much it."

She drew back, looked up at him. "When do you start?"

"I'll be taking an EMT refresher course next week. There's a ton of paperwork to fill out. Training starts in early November."

The oven timer began to beep.

He walked over to the oven. "I hope you're hungry."

"Starving. I need to run upstairs and clean up. I was just wiping up dog pee."

"I'll handle this. You do what you need to do."

She hurried upstairs, washed her face and hands, put on moisturizer and a little mascara, and then looked in her closet. She was about to put on a clean pair of jeans and a sweater when she saw the red beaded dress she'd worn to Rain and Joe's wedding.

No. No, she couldn't wear that for dinner in her own house.

Why not?

She stripped to her skin, put on the red silk bra and panties she'd worn with it, then took the dress from her hanger, unzipped it, and pulled it over her head. She tugged up the hidden side zipper, fixed her hair into a quick messy bun, put on a pair of pearl earrings, then looked in the mirror, smiling at her reflection.

"Just try to resist this, Harrison."

She bent down to fluff her boobs, tucked a condom inside her bra, and then made her way downstairs.

Harrison was pouring wine. He looked up, saw her, and stared, his eyes going dark. "Oh, *hell*, yes. I've been fantasizing about seeing you in this dress since I saw you in that photo."

She pointed at the wine glass, trying not to laugh. "It's overflowing."

"Shit." He stopped pouring. "See what you do to me?"

It thrilled her to know she turned him on. "It's no more than what you do to me."

When the spilled wine was cleaned up, they sat at the table. Harrison helped with her chair as if they were at a fancy restaurant and then served the meal he'd made—salmon fillets, jasmine rice, and green beans with almonds.

"It smells wonderful."

"It's a recipe my mom used to make—salmon fillets with sundried tomatoes, feta cheese, and kalamata olives." He lifted a fillet onto her plate and followed that with a scoop of rice and another of the green beans.

Kenzie took her first bite of the salmon, the bright taste of tomato combining with the saltiness of the cheese and olives and the fattiness of the fish. "Delicious."

"You like it?" There was a hint of vulnerability in his eyes.

He truly wanted to please her.

Her heart gave a little sigh. "I love it."

While they ate, she asked him about his job interview and the rest of his day and laughed when he told her about his conversation with his neighbor.

"The next thing I knew, she was standing on her front porch yelling at them to leave and threatening to call the sheriff."

"Good for her! Did it work?"

He took a sip of his wine. "Not really."

That reminded Kenzie. "Wendy Hall from the Scarlet Gazette stopped by and said she wanted to interview me about my SAR and HRD work in the wake of yesterday's search. I agreed when she promised to include a fund-raising pitch for the Team. Afterward, she told me what was going on at your place and then asked me to pass a business card on to you."

Harrison's expression went black. "She manipulated you to try to reach me."

"That's what I thought, too, and I called her on it. She looked completely taken aback by that suggestion, almost hurt, and swore that wasn't her intention. She said to call her if you want to talk to a reporter who won't cross your boundaries."

"She already crossed my boundaries by bothering you with this."

Kenzie wiped her lips, set her napkin aside, and went to sit on his lap. She cupped his cheek, kissed him. "I'm sorry. I didn't mean to rain on your evening."

The anger on his face faded, replaced by an altogether different emotion. "Why don't you come upstairs and let me get you out of that dress?"

Anticipation shivered through her. "I thought you liked this dress."

He nuzzled the sensitive skin beneath her ear. "Oh, honey, I do. I like everything beneath it, too."

"How do you know? You haven't even seen my red silk panties or my bra."

He moaned, his brow furrowing. "Layers of sexy—is that it?"

"And all for you."

———

CONRAD NIPPED HER, tasted her, one hand on the curve of her hip, the other cupping her cheek. "I'd carry you upstairs, but I'd rather watch your sweet ass as you walk up the stairs in front of me."

"Seriously?" She seemed to find this funny.

"All those sweet curves in motion in a skin-tight dress? Hell, yes, I'm serious."

"Okay, then." She slipped off his lap, walked toward the stairs, looking back at him over a soft, bare shoulder. "This way, stud."

She was too damned good to be real.

He was on his feet in an instant, following her, his gaze fixed on the lush wonder of her ass, the sway of her hips, her narrow waist. By the time she reached the top of the stairs, he was hard—and horny as hell.

He took the top two stairs in a single stride, backed her up against the wall just outside her bedroom, his mouth coming down on hers in a rough kiss. She threw her arms around his neck and stood on her tiptoes, kissing him back with an intensity that matched his own, challenging him for control.

Without breaking the kiss, he reached down, dragged up her gown in fistfuls, until she was exposed to her hips. Without a word, she parted her thighs for him, and his fingers found their way inside her panties.

Oh, fuck, yes.

She was already wet.

"I've got a condom." She reached inside her bra, drew out a packet.

"God, you're amazing."

He jerked down his fly, rolled the condom onto his cock, and lifted her off her feet, pinning her against the wall with his weight. Then he reached down with one hand, moved aside the crotch of her panties, and guided himself inside her.

Their gazes met and held as he started to move, fucking her fast and deep and hard, the pleasure he felt reflected in her blue eyes. Being inside her, seeing the effect he had on her, letting her see what she was doing to him—the erotic intimacy of it sent a jolt to his chest.

"*Kenzie.*" His sweet Kenzie.

Her eyes drifted shut, her next exhale becoming a moan.

She felt so good, so unbelievably good, and he worried he would come before she did. Then she reached down with one hand to stroke herself, turning him on so much that his mouth started talking without any help from his brain. "Stroke that sweet clit. God, Kenzie. Come for me. Come around my cock."

His control in shreds, he drove into her now, rough and reckless. He wanted her, wanted all of her, wanted to please her.

She gasped, arched, cried out, bliss golden on her face.

Almost beyond conscious thought, Conrad fucked her with the full force of his desire, climax overtaking him in a rush of ecstasy.

Caught somewhere between heaven and earth, he stayed as he was, deep inside her, his body still pinning her to the wall, their heartbeats slowly returning to normal. It was Kenzie who spoke first.

"That was … *amazing*." She kissed him. "I love the way you overwhelm me."

"Yeah?" Conrad's surge of masculine pride was cut short by a puppy whine. He looked down to see Gabby and Gizmo on the stairs, watching them. "Is it okay for them to see this?"

Kenzie laughed. "Are you embarrassed?"

"Maybe." He reached down, took hold of the condom, and withdrew from her, lowering her gently to her feet. "I'm not used to an audience."

She smoothed her gown back into place. "I'll put them to bed—provided I can walk. Come on, Gizmo. Come, Gabby. It's bedtime."

While she settled the dogs for the night, Conrad washed up in the bathroom, still in a post-orgasmic stupor. He didn't know what it was about Kenzie that got to him. He'd had lots of women in his life, beautiful women, athletic women, and none of them had touched him the way Kenzie did.

She was waiting for him in the bedroom, lying in a seductive pose on her side, a dream in red beaded silk. "Undress."

Much to Conrad's surprise, he felt the first stirrings of renewed desire.

The woman was living Viagra.

He indulged her, holding her gaze while he shed his sports jacket, tugged his turtleneck over his head, slowly unzipped his jeans, and tossed them aside with his boxer briefs. "Is this better?"

"You're ticking my fantasies off pretty quickly. I'm going to have to come up with some new ones."

He wanted to hear more.

He sat on the edge of the bed behind her, his fingers seeking her zipper. "Tell me about these fantasies."

"We just fulfilled one of them. And when you carried me into the bedroom—that was a big one."

"What's left?" He pulled down the zipper, slid his hand inside the gown to cup her breast through the silk and lace of her bra.

She seemed to hesitate.

"Come on, now." He peeled the gown from her body, tossed it onto a nearby chair, and took in the sight of her in her red bra and panties. "Don't get all shy. Five minutes ago, I was inside you."

"You could tie me to the bed."

Holy hell.

Her words hit Conrad in the solar plexus. "You would like that?"

"I've never tried it. But no real pain or anything."

"I can get on board with that." He leaned down, kissed a path along her shoulder to her neck. "What else?"

"We could do it in front of a mirror so I can see your cock sliding inside me."

Another shock to the solar plexus—and blood rushed to his groin.

"We can do that—someday." He pushed her onto her back, straddled her, and jerked down her bra to expose those beautiful breasts, his cock half-hard already. "Tonight, we're fulfilling my fantasy—the one where I go down on you until I've memorized your taste and you're so exhausted from coming again and again that you fall asleep with my mouth still on you."

Her body tensed, her pupils dilating, the breath leaving her lungs in a slow exhale. "I like that fantasy."

He grinned. "Well, hold on, honey, because here it comes."

AN HOUR LATER, Kenzie lay exhausted against Harrison's chest, her heartbeat slowing, her body languid. She had always loved sex, but this felt new to her—the intensity of it, the intimacy, the happiness she felt afterward.

It took some effort, but she managed to say what she was thinking. "I didn't know it could be this good."

"Yeah," he said sleepily. "Me, neither."

———

KENZIE SNUGGLED CLOSER TO HARRISON, the sound of a puppy's whining penetrating her sleep. She opened her eyes, saw daylight, sat bolt upright.

Ten minutes past seven.

Had she forgotten to set her alarm?

"Damn." She jumped out of bed, grabbed her bathrobe, and hurried down the stairs to let the pups out. "Sorry, Gabby. I didn't mean to make you hold it so long."

She watched while they did their thing, sending Quinn a message telling her that she would be late—again. Then she called the dogs back inside to get their breakfast.

Conrad appeared at the bottom of the stairs looking incredibly hot in butter-soft jeans and no shirt, his short hair sticking up in every direction. "Did you forget to set your alarm?"

She set two bowls of kibble on the floor. "I blame you —and your tongue."

He came up behind her, drew her back against the hard wall of his chest. "It's not the tongue, honey. It's the lips. You can't do much with a tongue. Sure, you can stroke and lick and penetrate, but it gets tired fast. If you want to make a woman scream, you've got to use your lips—catch that clit, pull it into your mouth, suck on it."

Holy God.

Kenzie's knees turned to jelly. "Don't do this to me. I have to go to work. I'll be horny all day, and I have a class tonight. That makes for a very long day."

He chuckled, a deep, husky sound. "Call in sick."

Oh, the idea was tempting. "I *do* come home for lunch."

"You're thinking about a nooner?"

"Are you up for that?"

"Hell, I'm up whenever I'm with you." He nudged her with his hips, revealing his erection. "You name the time and the place."

"How about here at noon?" No, that wouldn't work. "That's when you meditate with Esri, isn't it?"

He nuzzled her ear. "I'd rather be inside you."

Again with the knees turning to jelly.

She sank back against him, her body singing for him. "I need to get into the shower and get to work."

A big hand cupped her breast, his thumb teasing a nipple through her robe. "I'm not stopping you."

"Like hell, you're not, mister." With supreme effort—she deserved a medal for this—she pulled away from him, turning to plant a kiss on his lips. "But hold onto the thought, okay?"

Before he could say another word, she darted upstairs to take a shower.

Forty-five minutes later, she entered the kennel, where Quinn was playing with the dogs in the play yard. "Sorry."

Quinn smiled, her gaze on Kenzie's backyard. "Don't apologize. If I had a hunk like that in my bed, I'd be late, too."

Kenzie looked over to see Harrison standing on her back porch, still shirtless, playing with Gabby. The sight put a flutter in her belly. "Yeah."

As much as her ovaries wanted her to go home and

jump Harrison's bones, there was work to be done. She picked up dog poo in the play yard and was in the middle of cleaning dog bowls when Quinn appeared, a big smile on her face, a copy of the *Scarlet Gazette* in her hands.

"Look at this. You made the front page." Quinn held out the paper.

"This is Scarlet Springs. The weather makes the front page." Kenzie took the paper and saw a photo of herself and Gizmo beneath a big headline.

Scentsational: Local woman trains dogs for search & rescue work.

She sat with a cup of coffee and glanced through it, pleased to see that Wendy had quoted her correctly and hadn't sensationalized her job or mentioned her relationship with Harrison. As far as Kenzie was concerned, this was proof that Wendy hadn't done this story to get to him.

Quinn had managed to find another copy and sat nearby reading it. "This is fantastic. This is going to bring you lots of business."

"That would be nice." In the meantime, there were kennels to clean.

Kenzie set the paper aside and got back to work. But by ten, five people had stopped by the kennel and the store with copies of the paper just to make sure she'd seen it, including Rose, who asked about Harrison.

"I hear the two of you are serious."

Kenzie didn't take the bait. "Well, you can't believe all the gossip."

Rose had just turned to go when there came the sound of sirens, several sheriff's vehicles racing, one after the other, through the roundabout and speeding up the canyon. "That looks like every deputy in the county—and Boulder police, too."

But Kenzie wasn't thinking about that.

In the center of the roundabout, Bear was hunched over, hands covering his ears. She couldn't see his face from here, but she could tell he was afraid.

"I'll be back in a minute." She jogged over to the roundabout, where Bear still held his hands over his ears. "Hey, Bear, are you okay?"

Most of his face was covered with a shaggy gray beard, but she could see the fear in his eyes. "The sirens are loud."

"Yes, they are, but they can't hurt you. It's just noise. Those deputies are rushing somewhere to try to help someone."

Bear took this in, but she could see he wasn't convinced.

"Why don't you come with me to the kennel and play with the dogs?" She'd brought him there before when it was cold or raining.

Winona Belcourt, whose animal sanctuary was a block away from the kennel, did the same thing. Between the two of them—and Eric Hawke's crew at Scarlet FD—they made sure Bear had shelter.

Bear smiled, lowering his hands, the sirens now distant. "I like dogs."

"I know. Come."

Chapter 16

CONRAD'S MORNING went to shit not long after Kenzie left for work. He had just come back inside from letting Gabby romp in the backyard when Candace called.

"You're making it hard for me to help you. Have you been online?"

"Hey, Candace." Why did the woman never start with *hello*? "No, I haven't."

"Let me read you some of the trending headlines from the climbing world." This was obviously the reason she'd called. "'What is Harrison Conrad hiding?' 'Conrad calls sheriff on editor of climbing webzine.' 'World's greatest alpinists loses his nerve, quits.'"

"Oh, for fuck's sake."

"This is what happens when you let them make up the news."

"You're blaming *me* because people are posting bullshit about me online?"

"You need to do those interviews. You'll put the lies to rest and get the media people off your back. If you don't want the money, put up a memorial for your friend."

Everest was Bruce's memorial—and Felix and Luka's, too.

"Or you could donate it to that monastery where you hid for all of those months."

"I wasn't hiding."

"Yes, you were. You didn't want to face what had happened, so you holed up at the monastery. I don't blame you. I know you and Bruce were close." The very way she said it seemed dismissive to Conrad. "But he's gone, and he wouldn't want you to implode like this."

Conrad bit back an angry reply. "You know *nothing* about him."

"You hired me to manage your career, and I'm telling you that it is *essential* for you to do those interviews and appease your sponsors—unless you really are committed to destroying yourself."

Was that what he was doing? Was he destroying himself?

Candace went back to reading headlines. "Oh, here's another one. This is rich. 'Harrison Conrad leaves climbing, takes ski patrol job.'"

How had that news gotten out already?

"I did take a ski patrol job. I start training next month."

Silence.

"So, you've truly given up climbing?"

"I don't know. I need an income while I figure things out."

"See a shrink, for God's sake. Get help."

Conrad's jaw went tight. "Now you've crossed a line. I pay you a lot of money to look out for my career interests, not to get involved in my personal life."

"Okay. Well, here's my career advice: Do the damned interviews!" She all but shouted at him. "You'll earn more in two hours of doing that than an entire season of babysitting people on the slopes—and you'll get these bastards off your back."

"You're sure about that?"

"As sure as I can be." She paused for a moment. "I'm not your enemy, Conrad. I am trying to do what's best for your career."

"Fine. I'll do an interview, but *I* will choose the publication—not my sponsors and not you."

"Okay, well, that's progress." At least somewhat placated, Candace changed the subject. "By the way, who is that woman—the one with the long, dark hair who keeps showing up on all the websites?"

"She's none of anyone's business." Damned if he was going to let Kenzie get caught up in his shit.

"When I signed you, we talked about how it would be beneficial for you to date, or to at least be seen with, other high-profile climbers or models and actresses—women who could draw attention to you."

"My love life isn't part of your contract." Conrad was done. "It's been great talking with you. Let's do it again soon."

He ended the call, jammed his phone back into his jeans pocket, the relaxed feeling he'd carried inside him since last night gone.

Well, fuck.

He cleaned up the breakfast dishes and showered, willing his frustration to wash away. He had a list of things to get through—and a noon sex date with Kenzie.

That, at least, was something he was looking forward to.

He registered online for the EMT refresher course that Hawke taught at the firehouse, then filled out all the paperwork for Ski Scarlet—a W-4, an I-9, emergency contacts, a form stating he'd read the resort's rules regarding discrimination and sexual harassment. It all felt surreal.

What the hell are you doing?

He didn't have anything against working for Ski Patrol, but it wasn't what he'd thought he'd be doing at the age of thirty-five.

What do you want now?

Hell, he didn't know—and that's why he'd taken the job. Working at Ski Scarlet would give him time to figure the rest of it out while ensuring he spent a lot of time outdoors and had an income to pay the bills without dipping into his savings.

Fuck anyone who couldn't understand that.

He did his best to push Candace and the bullshit headlines out of his mind. He sent Esri a text and told her that he wasn't going to make it today, either. Then Herrera called to find out if he wanted to meet up for a workout at the rock gym.

"It's been ages since you got vertical, man."

"Thanks for thinking of me, but I've got lunch plans."

"Do those plans have anything to do with Kenzie?"

"No comment."

It was getting close to noon, and Conrad had much more interesting things to do than climbing at the rock gym, but, like climbing, this would require some rope.

LEAVING GIZMO AT THE KENNEL, Kenzie drove Bear to Knockers and bought him lunch. Then she set out for home, anticipation curling through her belly. She'd never ditched work to have sex before.

She stepped through the back door into a quiet house,

a copy of the *Scarlet Gazette* in her hand. Gabby was napping in her crate. "Harrison?"

"In the bedroom."

She put the newspaper down on the table and hurried up the stairs to find the bedroom empty. "Where—"

He came up behind her, a big hand covering her mouth. "Don't scream."

Her heart gave a hard kick—not from fear, but excitement.

She nodded.

Harrison took his hand off her mouth, forced her into her bedroom.

She resisted just enough to make him work for it, putting a note of fear into her voice. "What are you going to do to me?"

He answered gruffly. "Any damned thing I want."

Her pulse skipped.

Then she saw ropes tied to the four corners of her bed —and her mouth went dry. "*Oh, God.*"

"Undress."

Under his cold gaze, she did as he asked, her hands trembling with anticipation. "Please don't hurt me."

"Then don't fight me." He reached out, palmed her breast, his touch making her burn. "Get on the bed."

On impulse, she made a dash for the door, making it only a step or two before he caught her around the waist with strong arms, scooped her off her feet, and dropped her, naked, into the center of the bed. He drew her arms over her head with one hand and began to bind her wrists.

But Kenzie didn't make it easy for him. She writhed and twisted and tried to pull away, forcing him to use his strength to hold her down.

He pressed his forehead to hers, looked straight into

her eyes. "Do you think you stand a chance? You're nowhere as strong as I am."

She tested her bonds, savoring the delicious sense of helplessness. The man certainly knew his knots. Of course, he did. "Why are you doing this?"

"I've been watching you, watching that sweet ass while you walk around in your jeans." He caught her right ankle, bound it fast, drawing the rope tight and forcing her legs wide apart, his gaze settling on her most private flesh. He reached out, stroked her. "I want you, and I take what I want. Your body is mine."

Okay, that was too perfect.

After that, it made no sense to struggle, in part because she was so desperately turned on that she wanted him inside her—now.

But he took his sweet time.

He slowly stripped out of his jeans and T-shirt, turning to give her a view of his world-class ass.

God, she wanted him.

He turned to face her, stroking his erect cock, the erotic sight of it making her womb clench. "I'm going to fuck you until you can't walk."

Promises, promises.

She thought he was going to get between her legs, but instead, he straddled her chest, his muscular thighs on either side of her, his cock above her mouth.

He rubbed himself against her lips. "Taste it."

Oh, yes.

She parted her lips, lifted her head off the pillow, and licked the engorged head, swirling her tongue over him again and again, hungry for him.

The muscles of his abdomen jerked, his gaze fixed on what she was doing to him. He fisted a hand in her hair, lifting her head, making it easier for her to take him into her mouth. "Make me good and wet. It will make things easier for you."

A thrill shivered through her.

It wasn't easy to go down on him in this position, but it was such a turn-on that Kenzie gave it all she had. She watched his eyes drift shut, saw his muscles tighten.

He drew away from her, settled himself between her thighs, his gaze betraying warmth before his eyes went hard as slate. But rather than entering her, he lowered his mouth to her breasts and began to kiss and nip his way down her body, lips and the sharp edges of his teeth making her shiver.

She ached for him now, her body longing for release.

But he had other plans.

He pulled the pillow out from beneath her head and tucked it under her hips, canting them upward. "That's better."

Then he went to work on her with his mouth, those talented lips of his caressing her, teasing her, driving her crazy.

Forgetting she was tied to the bed, she tried to reach down and slide her hands in his hair only to find herself powerless to do anything except submit.

The sweet tug of his lips. The heat of his mouth. The deep glide of his fingers.

She came with a strangled cry, gasping out her pleasure as he finished her, the intensity of her climax almost too much for her body to contain.

And then she was floating somewhere beyond this world.

"I guess I don't need these any longer."

She heard a click—a pocket knife?—and felt a tug on the ropes, her wrists and ankles free. But he wasn't finished with her.

In a blink, he turned her onto her belly, the pillow now beneath her pelvis. The crumple of a condom packet. The hard tip of his cock nudging her from behind. The sweet stretch as he penetrated her.

He fucked her hard and fast, sliding one hand beneath her to stroke her clit, his powerful thrusts carrying her once more over that radiant edge. This time, he went with her, his breath hot on her shoulder as he came.

He rolled off her, tossed the condom in the trash, and drew her against him, holding her and kissing her with such tenderness that it put an ache in her chest. "You're safe with me. You know that, right?"

"Of course. Like I said, I love the way you overwhelm me."

━━

CONRAD HELD KENZIE, his mind blissfully empty, his body content. He'd never tied a woman up before or pretended to overpower them, and he hadn't felt completely comfortable with the idea. His father had drummed respect for women into his head before he'd reached puberty.

"If you ever violate or hurt a woman, you'll have to face me," he'd said.

But Conrad had seen how aroused Kenzie had become when he'd used a little force on her, and he'd been touched by her unconditional trust. He hadn't truly forced her to do anything, of course, and, once he'd gotten past the strangeness of it, he'd found their game to be an incredible turn-on.

Who knew that Kenzie had a kinky side?

She lay with her head on his shoulder, her fingers tracing idle lines on his bare chest. She told him about her morning, about Bear and the sirens. "I brought him inside to play with the dogs for a while. They love him as much as he loves them. Then I took him to Knockers, bought him lunch, and left him in Joe's hands."

"You have a big heart." Conrad loved that about her.

"Rose came in with a copy of the paper. I think she was fishing for fresh gossip."

"Oh, undoubtedly."

Kenzie snuggled closer. "I wish I could stay in bed with you all day."

"I need some time to recover, but, hey, I'd be happy to push the limits of my sexual endurance just for you."

"What a beautiful thought." Kenzie sat up, regret on her face. "But I have to eat something and get back over there."

Conrad reached up, tucked a strand of dark hair behind her ear. "One of these days, you are going to take some serious time off."

"That would be nice." She climbed out of bed and bent over to pick up her clothes, giving him a view of heaven. "Are you hungry?"

Now that she mentioned it… "Starving."

She put on her panties, tiny blue things that barely covered her butt. "I can make you a sandwich."

"Where do you get the energy?" He was as close to a true sex coma as he'd ever been. "Maybe I didn't do my job as well as I thought I did."

"Are you kidding? You made me scream. If I didn't have to be back at the kennel, I'd be asleep."

"I'll help." He willed himself to get up.

He put on his jeans and T-shirt and walked downstairs after her, her scent all over him. While she made sandwiches, he took Gabby, who was awake, out for a quick potty trip. "Come on, Gabby, girl."

The day was sunny and warm, one of those September days that felt like summer, clouds dotting a wide, blue sky. This time last year, he'd been at the monastery, where it had rained every day as monsoons chased away summer. Nothing against the monks or Tengboche, but he preferred Kenzie's company—and Colorado's weather.

When he came back inside, two turkey sandwiches sat on plates with cans of blackberry Izze soda and vinegar and sea salt chips. He washed his hands, sat—and saw Kenzie and Gizmo on the front page of the newspaper.

"That's a great photograph."

"Thanks." Kenzie took a sip of her soda. "She did a good job with the article. She didn't misquote me or mention anything about you."

Conrad read through the first few paragraphs and thought they were pretty good. Then he remembered what Wendy had told Kenzie. Maybe she was the right person to handle this interview after all.

"Did you finish all your paperwork for Ski Scarlet?" Kenzie asked.

He nodded. "I'm driving up there this afternoon to turn it in."

"How do you feel about taking the job. I mean, really, are you happy?"

Leave it to Kenzie to ask the tough questions. Then again, she now knew him better than most people.

"It's not what I thought I'd be doing at this point in my life." That was an understatement. "But I love to ski. Spending my days outside this winter sounds pretty good. At least I'll have an income while I figure out what's next."

"That makes a lot of sense. If you don't like it, you're done by April and free to try something else." She glanced at her watch, picked up what was left of her sandwich, soda, and chips. "I need to go."

She circled the table, kissed him on the cheek. "Thanks for the best lunch break in my entire life. See you tonight after class. Bye, Gabby."

The puppy stood at the back door, watching Kenzie walk away and whimpering.

"I know just how you feel."

After he'd finished his lunch and cleared the dishes away, Conrad put Gabby in her crate in the back of his SUV and headed up the canyon to Ski Scarlet. He and Gabby had to cover some ground to find Matt, who was overseeing trail work on the slopes.

He stopped when he saw Conrad. "Let's head to my office."

Once inside, Conrad handed him the signed documents. He was about to ask Matt how word of his new job had spread to the media, but Matt beat him to it.

"I'm sorry about the leak. It wasn't me, and it wasn't human resources. It seems one of our Ski Patrol members had heard you were joining us and didn't know she wasn't supposed to say anything. She posted it online, and, well…"

"I appreciate you being above board on this and checking it out."

"I made you a deal, and I'll keep my word."

"Good enough." Conrad handed him the receipt for his EMT refresher class. "I'll be starting next week."

"Hawke teaches a good class."

"He's one of the best." Conrad got to his feet to go when an older woman he recognized from HR walked into Matt's office.

"Those sheriff's deputies are here again."

"Thanks." Matt stood, explained the situation to Conrad. "Some jackasses robbed an armored vehicle at gunpoint in Boulder this morning and made off with a few hundred grand. The cops lost them up the canyon. They think the two might be hiding in the forest around Scarlet, perhaps here on our mountain."

"Shit." The mountains around Scarlet were full of tourists who'd come to look at the aspen leaves, not to mention hunters, mountain bikers, and hikers. "I hope they catch them quickly."

"You and me both."

Conrad ran into Deputy Marcs on his way out. "Hey."

"Lock your doors if you're driving in the canyon. One of our snipers fired a fifty-caliber round through their engine block, forcing them out of their car. They may be looking to steal a vehicle, even with a driver inside."

"Got it. Thanks." He walked out to the parking lot, settled Gabby in her crate, and sent Kenzie a text message to warn her about the armed robbers. Then he checked the pistol he kept in his glove box—his dad's old Colt Python. There were six bullets in the cylinder. Satisfied, he put the firearm back in the glove box and drove back down the canyon to the office of the *Scarlet Gazette* to set up an interview.

Chapter 17

KENZIE'S behavioral training class hadn't even started when Tom, the basset hound puppy, went after Dixie, a young Miniature pinscher. She told the owners to pull them apart—both dogs were on leashes—but Tom had Dixie by the collar and didn't want to let go. The owners' panic didn't help.

Dixie's owner kicked at Tom. "Get that damned dog off her!"

"Don't kick my puppy!"

Kenzie reached down to detach the frightened Miniature pinscher's collar when Tom turned on her and bit her hard on her left wrist, his jaws clamped tight. "Shit!"

It hurt like hell.

She managed to pry the dog's jaws open to free herself, then grabbed Tom by the collar and pulled him away from the other dogs. She did her best to keep her cool, despite the pain and adrenaline. "You need to take Tom home. I work privately with dogs who have aggression problems, but he can't be here with other dogs."

"That damned dog could have bitten Dixie!" the Miniature pinscher's owner yelled.

But Tom's owner was staring at her wrist. "You're bleeding."

Well, of course, she was bleeding. She'd just been bitten.

She glanced down, saw blood spatter across the floor, then looked at her wrist. There were two puncture marks from the puppy's canines, and one of them was spurting blood in time to her pulse. "Class is canceled for tonight. We'll deal with refunds later."

While her clients filed out, she grabbed several paper towels from the dispenser and pressed them hard against the bite, but they soaked through almost immediately. She grabbed more, pressed down harder.

"You're not going to sue, are you?" Tom's owner asked.

"I'm going to have to report him to animal control. Expect to hear from them."

"He didn't mean—"

"Please, just go." She needed to get to the ER.

Even as that thought gelled, she realized she couldn't drive herself. She wouldn't be able to hold pressure on the bite and steer her truck at the same time, and she wasn't sure how many spurts it would take before she passed out. Besides, she'd make an awful mess of her vehicle.

She let go of her wrist long enough to send Conrad a text with bloody fingers, blood spurting onto her jeans, the countertop, the floor.

Bitten by dog. Got an artery. Need help!

She set the phone down, grabbed more paper towels, and applied as much pressure as she could. Her phone buzzed, but she didn't dare look at it. Then she heard a siren begin to wail at the firehouse.

There was a definite upside to knowing the fire chief—and having friends who were all EMTs and paramedics.

A few minutes later, Conrad burst through the door. He glanced at the blood on the floor and was there at her side in an instant. He pulled down more paper towels, folding them over and handing them to her. "Do you have a first-aid kit somewhere?"

She pointed toward the bathroom. "It's in the cupboard there."

"Keep up the pressure." He disappeared into the bathroom, then returned with a stack of sterile gauze squares. "I called Hawke. They're almost here."

The sirens were on top of them now.

He returned to her side, pressed the gauze on top of the paper towels. "I've got it."

She winced as he pushed down on the bite—hard. "That really hurts."

"Sorry." He reached out with one long leg, dragged a chair over to her. "Sit. You're pale as a ghost."

"I'm fine." Okay, so she was a little dizzy, whether from blood loss or adrenaline, she couldn't say.

"It looks like the dog got your radial artery. What kind of dog was it?"

"A basset hound puppy."

"Seriously? I hope you're going to hold the owner responsible."

"This was my behavioral class. We work on behavioral problems. I do my best to weed out aggressive dogs, and offer their owners private classes or refer them to someone else. I guess this pup slipped through the cracks. It's not the first time I've been bitten."

It was a hazard of the job.

The bleeding had slowed, but the pain was worse.

How could a simple bite hurt like this?

Hawke hurried through the front door in his turnout pants, carrying an orange trauma kit. Jenny Miller, a member of his crew, following behind him, pushing a gurney. Hawke saw the blood on the floor, too. "Looks like Fido got an artery."

"Easy does it." Harrison helped Kenzie up onto the gurney, keeping up the pressure until Hawke took over.

"We need to get you to the ER. They'll take care of this in no time." Hawke turned to Jenny, his voice calm and professional. It was the same voice Kenzie had heard him use on dozens of rescues. "Get an IV going in her other arm."

"An IV? Really?" Kenzie wasn't a fan of needles.

"Just in case." He gave her a reassuring smile. "They're probably going to want to give you antibiotics, too. The IV will save you another stick."

She turned her head, pressed her face into Harrison's belly, while Jenny jabbed her in the arm with what must have been an awl. "Ouch!"

"I'm just going to flush this out with some saline and tape it in place." Jenny worked quickly. "How are you doing, Kenzie?"

"I'm pissed." Had this been her fault?

"I bet."

"I need to lock the place up, and Gizmo and Gabby—"

"Where are your keys?" Harrison asked.

"In my handbag." She glanced at the floor. "I'll clean this up later."

"Don't worry about that now." Harrison set the handbag on the gurney beside her and pulled out her keys.

When they wheeled her outside, a small crowd of locals was standing on the sidewalk—Frank from the gas station,

Rose, Kendra and Bob Jewell, Bear, and Hank, a local barfly who was best known for blowing up his own home.

Kenzie couldn't see all the faces.

"What happened?" That was Hank. "Was it them robbers who got her?"

Kenzie didn't want Bear to be frightened. "Just a bad dog bite. I'm okay."

"What did she say?" Rose asked.

"A bad dog bite," Bob answered. "Turn up your hearing aids."

"I don't wear hearing aids." Rose sounded angry.

"Maybe you should get some," Bob said.

Hawke and Jenny lifted the gurney into the back of the ambulance.

Harrison locked the kennel's front entrance, climbed in beside her, and took her right hand in his. "I'm going with her."

Eric held steady pressure on her wrist, his gaze meeting Harrison's, a hint of a smile on his face. "I see that."

Then Kenzie remembered. "Please don't use the sirens. They scare Bear."

"You got it."

———

CONRAD SAT in the surgery waiting room. They'd taken Kenzie back to the OR to stitch up her artery and repair a tendon that the dog's canine had damaged. They'd said it would take a half hour at most—and that had been an hour ago.

Ellie, a registered nurse and Moretti's better half, walked up to him. "She's out of surgery and doing great. They did a nerve block with sedation, so she won't have to recover from anesthesia. They'll make sure she's comfortable, and then we can discharge her. Can I get you something to drink?"

"No, thanks." He just wanted to know that Kenzie was okay. "Is her hand …?"

"Dr. Warren is in with her now, but he should be out in a few minutes."

"Thanks." Conrad's phone buzzed for the hundredth time.

This time it was Megs.

The place is cleaned up and locked tight. That was a lot of blood. Sasha has dogs and will bring them by when you call. I will drop off keys tomorrow. Tell Kenzie to take it easy.

Conrad had known that Kenzie would worry about the dogs and the mess in her classroom and had called Megs, who had paged Team members to help. They weren't grossed out by blood, after all, and every member of the Team cared about Kenzie and her dogs. It was one of the things about the Team that meant a lot to Conrad.

They always had one another's back.

He'd been in the middle of his interview with Wendy when he'd gotten Kenzie's text message. As independent as she was, she wouldn't ask for help unless she truly needed it. He'd called Hawke and rushed Wendy out of his house, where a few stubborn journalists were still camped out, with a promise to call her later to set up a new time.

He glanced up at the clock, got to his feet, walked over to the window to look out at the darkness. Behind him, a door opened. He turned to see a man in blue scrubs.

"I'm Dr. Warren. You're Harrison Conrad, right?" He held out his hand, a smile on his face. "It's a pleasure to meet you. I'm a bit of a fan."

"Thanks—and thanks for helping Kenzie."

"My pleasure. I like working on wrists."

Okay, *that* was a little weird. "How is she?"

"She's fine. The surgery went well. She'll need to elevate and ice her wrist to prevent swelling. We've splinted it for now. We've given her antibiotics and pain meds, as well as a prescription to take home that she can fill at our pharmacy. She should be ready to leave in about an hour. You're welcome to go back to our day-surgery area if you'd like. She's been asking for you."

"Thanks."

Conrad found Kenzie sitting up in a hospital gown, her wrist splinted and resting on a couple of ice bags on a pillow. She looked worried. "Hey."

"Hey." He kissed her cheek, sat in the chair beside her. "How are you feeling?"

"Better. Thanks. They gave me some pain pills, so I'm kind of loopy." Her eyes went wide. "Have you checked on the dogs?"

"Relax." He brushed a strand of hair off her cheek. "Sasha has them. Megs and the Team cleaned up your classroom, and Sasha took both dogs to her place. She'll drop them by when we get home."

Kenzie seemed surprised by this. "Oh. Wow. That's kind of them. Thanks for being there. I probably ought to have called 911, but…"

"Hey, I'm better than 911." He took her uninjured hand in his.

"You got there fast."

He'd raced the few blocks to the kennel. "I was at my place doing an interview with Wendy."

"You called her?"

"I stopped by the newspaper this afternoon on my way

home from Ski Scarlet to set it up. I thought it might get the media off my back."

"How did it go?"

"We hadn't gotten very far into it before I got your text. I'm supposed to call her to set up another time." He had to ask. "What happened?"

"Tom, a four-month-old basset hound, went after a young miniature pinscher, Dixie, and managed to get his teeth on her collar. When I tried to release the collar, Tom bit me. I had a hard time prying his jaws open to free my wrist."

"Did no one help you?"

She shook her head. "I'm the expert. I'm sure they thought I'd handle it."

"But what about after you'd been bitten? Did anyone help?"

She shook her head. "I sent everyone home. I don't think I realized right away how bad the bite was."

"What about the basset hound's owner? Why didn't he do something?"

"He stood there watching me bleed and asking me whether I was going to sue. I just wanted him and his dog out of my space."

Conrad wanted to punch the guy in the face. "Some people are useless."

She leaned her head back on her pillow, and Conrad could see the fatigue and strain on her face. She seemed pale to him—but maybe he was imagining things. "I want to go home."

It seemed to take forever for the nurse to bring her discharge instructions and remove her IV. Conrad helped her to dress, then walked with her down to the pharmacy to fill her prescription. It was almost midnight when they got to her house. He helped her out of the vehicle and took her indoors. Then he texted Sasha to tell her they were home.

Kenzie needed help getting undressed, putting on her pajamas, and getting situated in bed. He put a pillow beneath her arm and set her pain pills and a glass of water on her nightstand.

"There must have been something I could have done to avoid this."

"This wasn't your fault. Just rest." A text and a knock told him Sasha was there. "I'll be right back."

Sasha breezed through the door, dogs at her heel. "How is she?"

"She's in a bit of pain but doing okay. She's upstairs in bed."

"Thanks for letting me help. I had the greatest time with these two. If I didn't travel so much, I'd get a golden retriever puppy just like Gabby." Sasha knelt down, removed the leashes, and gave each dog a hug. "You be good for Kenzie now. Come play with your Auntie Sasha again soon."

When Sasha had gone, Conrad settled the dogs for the night and then made his way upstairs to check on Kenzie.

"Are Gizmo and Gabby here?" she asked in a sleepy, drugged voice.

"They're curled up asleep downstairs."

"Good." She reached for him. "Come to bed."

"I'm afraid I'll hurt you."

"No, you won't."

And because he wanted nothing more than to be there beside her, he undressed and climbed into her bed.

⎯⎯

PAIN WOKE Kenzie up a few times during the night, and

both times Harrison was there to give her a pain pill or help her get into a comfortable position. Once she woke to find him sitting on the edge of the bed, face in his hands.

"What is it?"

"Nothing. Bad dream. It's okay."

"You had another nightmare."

He lay back down beside her, kissed her forehead. "It's nothing, really. Sleep."

But even in the dark, she could see in his eyes that it was far from nothing.

―――

KENZIE WOKE the next morning to a knock on the front door.

"I've got it." Conrad rolled out of bed, slipped into his jeans.

He left the room, his footfalls disappearing down the stairs.

She heard men's voices, and then Conrad returned.

"Animal control."

"Right."

The hospital had reported the dog bite to animal control, so the officer was there—at eight in the morning, for God's sake—for information.

Harrison helped her dress then disappeared into the kitchen while she answered the officer's questions. Who owned the dog and what kind of dog was it? Where and how did the bite happen? Did she want to press charges?

Kenzie had no intention of pressing charges. "The basset hound is only four months old and would probably do well with some behavioral training."

In the middle of this, her keys fell through the mail slot in her door to the floor.

Megs.

The officer finished jotting down notes. "I hope you feel better soon."

The moment he'd left, Kenzie remembered that she hadn't checked in with Quinn or Dree. While Harrison finished making breakfast, she called the kennel first and then the store and told them what had happened, arranging to take the rest of the week off and promising to be available by text if they needed her.

Harrison didn't say much during breakfast, a troubled expression never far from his face. "I need to call Wendy. Do you mind if we do the interview here?"

"Not at all—but are you sure you want to do this interview in the first place?"

He sipped his coffee. "No, but I don't see that I have a choice. My agent is on my case, and my sponsors, too. I can't decide if I even want sponsors at this point—or an agent, for that matter. I don't know anything anymore. My agent says I'm trying to destroy myself."

"How can she say that? You're dealing with a tragedy as best you can. You almost died up there." She reached across the table with her good hand. "Forgive me for saying this, but your agent sounds like a bitch."

That made him smile. "She's just trying to hold onto my sponsors. I've lost a few. They can't pay me for sitting on my ass."

"I suppose not." She'd heard of athletes having sponsors, but she didn't understand how that worked. "What are sponsors? What do they do?"

"Companies that make stuff climbers want to buy—gear, clothes, energy drinks—ask for the endorsements of well-known climbers in exchange for an annual salary with bonuses for stuff like interviews and posts on social media."

"Endorsements? So, you do an ad and say, 'I'm Harrison Conrad, and I climbed all of the world's eight-thousand-meter peaks wearing this awesome underwear.'"

He chuckled. "Yeah, kind of. There are ads, but that's only part of it. When I do an on-camera interview or photo shoot, I wear their gear with the logo showing. I used to get paid almost a grand per tweet, but I haven't been on Twitter since…"

The grin faded.

Now Kenzie understood. Her heart ached for him.

His sponsors wanted him to get back in the game and do some interviews or else. Meanwhile, he was trying to decide whether sharing his pain with the world was worth what they wanted to pay him—and whether he was truly done with climbing.

There was nothing small about any of this—and all of it came on top a near-death experience and the loss of his friends.

She got to her feet, walked around the table to stand behind him, and wrapped her right arm around him, leaning down to kiss his temple. "I can't imagine how hard all of this is. I trust you to make the best decision for yourself, and I'll be right here."

He pressed his hand over hers. "Thanks, Kenzie. I …

She waited for him to finish. "Yes?"

"I need to call Wendy."

Chapter 18

HARRISON SAT in Kenzie's kitchen across from Wendy, a digital recorder in front of him, the setting sun sending a shaft of light through the window and across the table. Kenzie sat beside him, splinted wrist resting on an ice bag.

"It was the Stenger twins' first ascent of an eight-thousand-meter peak. Bruce and I gave up his plan of going for the so-called Khumbu Triple Crown—Nuptse, Everest, and Lhotse in a single push."

Wendy gaped at him. "All three peaks in a single day?"

"God, no." He couldn't help but laugh. "The last climber to do that did it in six days. Bruce was hoping to do it in four or five. But, as I said, we gave up that idea. We wanted to get Felix and Luka to the summit of Everest and down again. It would be a huge boost to their careers and fun for us."

Conrad steeled himself and went on. "We'd been at Base Camp for a few weeks, acclimating, waiting for a break in the weather. Luka and Felix—the scene at Base Camp was new to them. They were having a great time, hanging with the different climbing teams, taking photos, drinking, checking out the women, getting into snowball fights, trying to scam the cooks into feeding them extra."

He told Wendy how they'd gotten a thumbs-up from the weather guys on May 9 and had climbed up Khumbu Icefall to Camp I the next morning.

"It went off without a hitch. The twins were in great form. Luka was a little uncomfortable crossing the ladders on the Icefall, but that's not unusual when a person is new to it."

"Were you afraid of the ladders on your first climb?"

Conrad shook his head. "I kind of like that part."

Wendy's expression told him how crazy she thought that was.

"We ascended to Camp I, put up a tent, ditched some gear, and made our way back to Base Camp." A knot formed in his belly. He ignored it. "The next morning, we were up early for the puja—that's a Buddhist prayer ceremony—and then hit the Icefall at about four in the morning."

"Can you describe the Khumbu Icefall for me?"

"The Khumbu Icefall is a big-ass glacier that hangs between Base Camp and Camp I. It's always moving, always changing. New crevasses open up. There are avalanches. There are also seracs—big pillars or walls of ice that can collapse without warning. In the climbing world, we joke that no climber in his or her right mind would set foot on the Icefall if it weren't the path to the summit of Everest."

Except that it wasn't a joke. It was the truth.

"We were out on the glacier. Bruce was leading. The twins were in the middle—first Felix and then Luka. I was bringing up the rear."

"Was there a strategy to that?"

Conrad nodded. "It's good to have your most experienced climber leading. Bruce and I had planned to switch off, keeping the twins sandwiched between us."

"That makes sense." Wendy waited for him to say more.

Shit. Shit. Shit.

The knot in Conrad's gut tightened.

Why had he set this up?

"Bruce had already crossed the crevasse. Felix went next. I was on belay as Luka walked across the ladder. When Luka hesitated again, Bruce shouted, 'Don't worry, mate. If you fall and your harness fails, it will only kill you.' That was Bruce—he had a dark sense of humor. But those were his last words."

"How long had you two climbed together?"

"Twenty years, I think." He tried to do the math, but his adrenaline had kicked in. "Around twenty years."

"That's a long time."

"Yeah." Conrad willed himself to go numb. "Luka made it to the other side and belayed me. I was halfway across the ladder when I heard a crack and a rumble and looked up to see a serac collapsing on top of us. The ice beneath the ladder shifted, and I fell to my knees. I had just a minute to think that this might be the end before something hit me on my helmet—and then everything went black."

KENZIE FOUGHT to rein in her own emotions, not wanting to make this harder for Harrison. He seemed outwardly calm, cool, professional. But she could tell how much it hurt him to talk about this—the hard set of his jaw, the ice in his voice, the shadows in those gray eyes.

"Did you actually see the serac bury your friends?"

Harrison shook his head. "It all happened so fast. The rumble. Bruce and the others shouting. Then … nothing."

Wendy waited for him to go on.

"I came to hanging upside down in my harness. I had no idea where I was or what had happened. I hung there, swinging in a slow circle a few feet away from the ice wall of the crevasse."

His nightmares. This was how they always started.

"Were you afraid?"

Oh, for God's sake! Why did journalists ask stupid questions like this? Who wouldn't be afraid in that situation?

Harrison nodded. "Afraid, confused. My head hurt like hell."

"You didn't remember you were on Everest?"

"It took a few minutes for me to make sense of things. When I realized where I was, my first thought was that I'd fallen. I wondered why Bruce and the others weren't looking for me. I called for them, righted myself. Then some big blocks of ice fell into the crevasse, crashing past me, and I remembered."

For a long moment, Harrison was silent, the fingers of one hand curling into a fist. Kenzie found herself holding her breath, the nails of her right hand digging into her palm. She'd been in the Ops Room, listening in to the climbing website while he'd been fighting for his life.

"I shouted for them. No response. Then I understood. They were gone—all of them. I was in the crevasse and alone."

The desolation in his voice put a lump in Kenzie's throat. Not caring what Wendy might think, Kenzie reached over and took his hand in hers to find his fingers cold.

"How did you get out? What about the ladder?"

"The ladder had disappeared. I had to climb the ice."

His fingers threaded through hers while he described a harrowing hour or more of using his crampons and ice tools to climb unstable ice.

"I had some broken ribs—I think I took a whipper into the wall of the crevasse when I fell—and that made it harder. I would climb a few feet, and the ice would break off and fall, taking me with it. I would have to start again."

"How far did you have to climb?"

"It wasn't that far—maybe thirty feet."

That sounded pretty damned far to Kenzie.

"What were you thinking during that time?" Wendy asked.

"I kept telling myself to hurry because they might still be alive. That hope, that sense of urgency—it kept me going."

"Did you truly think they might have survived?"

Harrison's brows drew together in an irritated frown. "I didn't stop to logic it out. I was running on adrenaline with a concussion and broken ribs."

"You kept going."

He nodded, his hold on Kenzie's hand growing tighter. "I reached the top to find a jumble of ice—blocks as big as buses, as big as houses, piled on top of each other. The rope that had saved my life disappeared beneath that mess, Luka somewhere at the other end. I slashed at the ice with my ice tools, but there was no way I could get to them."

"What did you do then?"

"I sat down. I just sat there. Was I in shock? I don't know."

"It was a rescue team of Sherpas that helped you back to Base Camp, right?"

He nodded. "They put up new ladders, sent a rope

over, and belayed me back. I made my way with them down to Base Camp."

In a voice almost devoid of emotion, Harrison told Wendy how he'd contacted Bruce's wife and the twins' parents the moment he'd gotten back to Base Camp. He told her how all climbing had stopped until monks performed a puja in memory of the three men. He told her how the camp doctor had tried to examine him, but he had refused.

"How was it to tell their relatives that they were gone? Bruce had a wife and kids. Luka and Felix were their parents' only children."

Okay, *that* was going too far. Was she trying to twist the knife?

A muscle clenched in Harrison's jaw. "That's none of anyone's business. Those conversations were private."

Kenzie gave his fingers a supportive squeeze.

Wendy changed the subject. "How did you end up at the Tengboche Monastery? Have you always had an interest in Buddhism?"

He shook his head. "I took what I could carry in my pack and started the trek back to Kathmandu. When I reached Tengboche, I just stopped. We had camped there on our way to Base Camp, admired the view of Everest, talked about the climb. Somehow, as long as I could see the mountain, it didn't feel real to me that they were gone."

Kenzie blinked back tears.

———

THE ONLY WAY TO finish this was to finish it.

Conrad answered Wendy's questions about his time at the monastery, describing his daily life, telling her about the work he'd done to help the monks, how meditation had helped him cope with survival guilt.

"Do you feel guilty for making it back alive?"

"In my mind, I know I shouldn't, but in my heart…" How could he explain? "I know I couldn't have done anything to save them, but if I had led that morning and died instead of Bruce, there wouldn't have been anyone left behind to grieve besides my mother."

Kenzie shot to her feet. "That's not true! It's not true."

Were those tears on her face?

Shit.

Looking surprised at her own outburst, she walked to the kitchen counter, grabbed a tissue, wiped her tears away. "I'm sorry. I didn't mean to interrupt."

"Is this hard for you to hear?" Wendy asked her.

Kenzie wiped the tears from her cheeks. "Of course, it is. I was at The Cave at the time. Most of the Team was there. We all felt helpless. No one spoke. All we could do was listen, hold our breath, and pray that Harrison had survived."

"How did you feel when you heard the news that he was okay?"

"The whole room exploded in cheers." Kenzie gave Harrison a wobbly smile. "I was *so* relieved."

Conrad had thought of Kenzie during those long months at the monastery, but he'd never thought about how his brush with death might have affected her or the rest of the Team. Her obvious concern for him, the intensity of her emotions—he'd be a liar if he said it didn't touch him. Still, if he'd been leading instead of Bruce, she and the others would have gotten over his death. Bruce's wife and kids would miss their husband and father for the rest of their lives.

He knew what it was to lose a father.

Wendy turned her gaze back to Conrad. "I guess you would have had plenty of people grieving for you."

"Not a wife. Not children."

"I hear you've joined the Ski Patrol at Ski Scarlet for the winter. Have you given up climbing?"

"I'm not sure."

"You're a hero to a lot of people out there. They'd be disappointed if you—"

"I'm not a hero." Why did people say that? "I'm just an athlete. Whether I'll continue with this sport or move on to something else, I can't say. I haven't decided."

Wendy ran through the rest of her questions, mostly basic stuff like what had gotten him into climbing, where he'd grown up, and some technical climbing stuff. Then she turned off the recorder and stood. "I know it couldn't have been easy to talk about this, but I'm grateful that you trusted me. I'll have a photographer get in touch with you for a photo."

Oh, great.

Wasn't that just what he wanted?

"There are climbing photos in the press section of my website if you need those."

"Thanks." Wendy slipped her recorder into an over-sized handbag. "I'll do my best to do justice to your story. It's scheduled to run on the front page. Not this Sunday, but the next. Have a good night. You, too, Kenzie."

When the door closed behind her, Conrad locked it—and let out a breath.

Then Kenzie was there, sweet Kenzie. She slid her arms around him. "That was incredibly brave. Are you okay?"

Was he okay?

Hell, he didn't know. He'd ripped his chest open, torn

out his heart, and thrown it on the floor. But he was alive, and he was with Kenzie.

He kissed the top of her head. "Yeah. I'm okay. How about you?"

"I'm good. Sorry that I got emotional."

"Hey, don't apologize. I'm touched to think that you were all at The Cave together, pulling for me."

She smiled up at him. "This may come as a surprise, but I had a thing for you even back then."

Her words slid, warm and soothing, into the empty space behind his sternum. He held her close. "I don't know what I'd do without you right now."

He'd never said anything like that to a woman before, but it was the truth.

———

IT HAD BEEN a long time since Kenzie had enjoyed a three-day weekend and even longer since she'd spent three entire days alone with a man. They made love whenever they felt like it, stayed up late watching Netflix, and slept in—at least until the dogs woke them. What a luxury it was to wake up in Harrison's arms, spend the day with him, and then slide into bed with him at night. He made the meals, helped Kenzie wash her hair when she was free to shower again, and carried in groceries, handling anything she couldn't easily do herself.

He was everything she'd ever wanted in a man. That ought to have made her happy, but it didn't. Instead, she was terrified. Somewhere along the way, she had fallen in love with him.

Could she possibly be more of an idiot?

She'd tried to stop this from happening. She'd told her heart that he would soon get bored with her and leave her for a mountain—or a woman who loved to climb like he did. But her heart didn't want to hear it. It didn't care about experience or consequences.

It wanted him.

Kenzie pushed aside her worries as best she could and focused on the moment. The light in his gray eyes. His smile. The gentleness of his touch. The deep timbre of his voice. The way he felt inside her.

As special as these days were, she knew that doing the interview with Wendy had made things worse for him. He had nightmares every night. Twice, she'd woken to find him sitting up in bed, his body tense, his skin covered in cold sweat. Both times, she'd asked him if he wanted to talk, but he'd shaken his head and told her not to worry.

By Sunday, there were serious dark circles beneath his eyes. A few times when he didn't know she was watching, she'd caught him staring into nothingness, a troubled expression on his face. If he was emotionally distant at times, he made up for it when they made love. He fucked with the intensity of a condemned man, seeming to find a measure of forgetfulness and peace with her. If sex could be an escape from grief for him, well, she was more than willing to do her part.

She was just selfless like that.

On Monday, she went back to work, and they fell into an easy routine. Every morning, he dealt with the dogs and made breakfast while she showered. While she was at work, he did his own thing, taking Gabby with him and sometimes joining her for lunch. Except for Tuesday when he had his EMT refresher course, he made dinner.

"You'd make a good househusband," she teased.

He chuckled. "Are you proposing?"

She could tell he was joking. Still, his words made her pulse skip.

On Saturday, he came to her puppy kindergarten class, where Gabby and shy little Snickerdoodle were now best buddies. At one point, he slipped his arm around Kenzie's waist, putting a frown on Hannah's face.

"I think I disappointed someone," he whispered to Kenzie.

That afternoon, the Team was toned out to help a woman who had taken one too many steps backward while snapping photos and had fallen a good twenty feet down a rocky embankment. No canine help was needed, so Kenzie sat that one out. Megs didn't want her up there anyway out of concern she might trip and hurt her wrist. But Harrison went and helped evacuate the woman to a waiting ambulance.

They made love that night, then lay in the dark afterward, climax fading into sleep, Harrison's fingers tracing lines over the skin of her arm. "I want you to know how much you mean to me. I don't ever want to hurt you."

She didn't want that either. "You mean a lot to me, too. I'm here for you, Harrison. I'm here if you need someone to listen."

"I don't want to bother you with my bullshit."

"Nothing about you or your feelings is bullshit—not to me." She could feel the tension in him, as if he were dreading something.

And then she remembered.

Tomorrow was Sunday. The interview he'd done with Wendy last week would be on the front page of the *Scarlet Gazette* in the morning.

Chapter 19

CONRAD TOOK the dogs out while Kenzie started coffee, his heart full, his mind empty. Mornings with Kenzie gave new meaning to the phrase "bed head." He grinned at the thought, amazed by the sense of peace he found in her arms. It was better than meditation. It was better than sex with any other woman. It was even better than the high he got standing on the summits of mountains.

Are you out of your mind?

He must be, but he didn't care.

He looked up at the bright blue sky then west to the bank of gray clouds that was just visible over the mountains. A chilly wind was pushing those clouds their way, bringing snow for the high country and rain for Denver.

When he came back inside, dogs at his heels, he found the Sunday paper sitting on the kitchen table. On the front page was a large photo of him beneath a big headline: *Local hero—Conrad recounts Everest tragedy*.

And that *right there* trashed his good mood.

Kenzie poured cups of coffee and held one out to him.

"I read it. I think she did a good job. All the quotes seem accurate."

"Thanks." He took the coffee. "The headline is bullshit."

He wasn't a hero.

He took a sip of coffee, watched her drown hers in half-and-half. "If you hate coffee that much, just drink milk."

She laughed. "I *love* coffee—with enough half-and-half and sugar."

He tried to forget the article and focus on breakfast, throwing together pancakes using his father's recipe. But that headline stayed in his mind, niggling at him while they ate, did dishes, talked about the day ahead.

"We could take the dogs on a walk at Moose Lake." Kenzie wiped the stove top. "Gabby hasn't been up in the mountains before. We could do some puppy runaways. She's gotten good at that, so it's time to move to the next step."

What was wrong with him that he couldn't focus on the joys of the moment? Why couldn't he lose the feeling that his world was about to come crashing down?

"That sounds good." He hadn't been to Moose Lake since he'd come home.

They packed the dogs in Kenzie's truck and drove the short distance to the lake, where Taylor, in his uniform and Smokey the Bear hat, was busy writing out parking tickets for people who somehow managed to drive but couldn't read the NO PARKING signs posted along the rescue vehicle lane.

He tucked another ticket beneath a windshield wiper then walked over to say hello. "Hey. I saw the article today. Great interview, man."

"I haven't read it." And Conrad didn't plan to.

Taylor glanced down at Kenzie's splint. "How's the wrist?"

"I got the stitches out Friday," Kenzie answered. "The doctor said it's healing well. I have to wear the splint for a couple more weeks. Thanks for asking."

Gizmo recognized Taylor, wagging his tail and barking out a greeting.

Taylor knelt down on the gravel. "How are you, buddy? What's your little friend's name?"

"Gabby," Conrad and Kenzie answered together.

"Hey, Gabby. Aren't you cute?"

Conrad was surprised to find himself feeling pride. Yes, Gabby *was* cute, and it was good and right that everyone should recognize that.

Kenzie leashed both dogs, handing Gabby's leash to Conrad. "We're going to step up her training a little bit. I thought it would be good to get her into the mountains."

"Just keep your eyes open." Taylor stood again. "They still haven't found those two guys who robbed the armored vehicle. Some people think they've moved on, but a camper thought she spotted one of them a few days ago. He started to approach her, and when he saw she was with friends, he took off."

Conrad wished he'd brought his revolver. "Is anyone actively hunting for them?"

Before Taylor could answer, a woman's angry voice cut him off.

"What the hell? I didn't see any 'No Parking' signs." A woman in leggings and a fleece jacket stared at her ticket in indignation.

"Have a good hike." Taylor walked over to the woman. "There's a sign right next to your vehicle, ma'am. In fact, to get out of your car, you would have almost hit it with your driver's side door."

"Well, I didn't see it, and I'm *not* going to pay this."

Conrad wasn't sure how Taylor could stand dealing with these idiots.

He followed Kenzie up the trail, Gabby running along beside him, stopping every few feet to sniff. His cellphone buzzed, but he ignored it.

They hiked until they came to the trail that circled the lake. Then Kenzie put Gabby in her tiny little harness.

"I'm going to run pretty far this time—far out of sight. Hopefully, she'll follow her nose this time. If she gets distracted by something, say 'Leave it,' and praise her when she gets back on track."

"Got it." Conrad stroked the puppy's fur. "You can do it, Gabby."

"Sweet, sweet doggy." Kenzie hugged the puppy, tousled her ears, kissed her—then stood and hurried away with Gizmo.

When she had disappeared from view, Conrad let Gabby go. "Gabby, go find!"

The creamy furball took off running down the trail, still on leash, with Conrad walking behind her. She seemed to know she was looking for Kenzie, but there were so many new and fun things to distract her—a patch of kinnikinnick, a bird, a tree root. "Leave it. Good girl! Gabby, go find!"

It took almost ten minutes, but Gabby eventually veered off the trail and ran behind a large boulder—and into Kenzie's arms.

"Good girl! Good girl!" Kenzie let her play with her favorite toy.

Conrad praised her, too, and gave her a few treats. "Who's the smartest puppy ever? No offense, Gizmo."

But Gizmo seemed to be excited by Gabby's triumph,

too, his tail wagging as he walked circles around her, tangling all of them in his leash.

Conrad gave him a treat, too. "Way to be a good big brother."

His cellphone buzzed again. He drew it out of his pocket, checked the caller ID. It was his agent. She was probably pissed off about the article. Well, let her stew.

Kenzie looked over at him. "Is something wrong?"

"No." He shoved the phone back into his pocket.

Candace would have to wait.

———

KENZIE STOPPED by the kennel to welcome a new boarder—a St. Bernard named Tiny—whose people were heading to Wyoming for their annual elk hunting trip. Tiny was a gentle giant who quickly warmed up to the other dogs and Inéz.

While Inéz played with Tiny and got him settled, Kenzie took care of Tiny's paperwork, still unable to do some of the physical work because of her wrist.

"I know you must miss poop-scooping the play yard," Inéz joked.

Kenzie held up her splinted wrist. "I'll trade if you want."

"No thanks. I'll take dog poop over a dog bite any day."

When Kenzie stepped through her back door, she heard Harrison shouting.

"You had no right to do that! I don't give a goddamn what the contract says!"

His agent.

It had to be.

Kenzie already despised the woman. Maybe that

wasn't fair, but it seemed to her that this Candace person had no compassion for what Harrison had gone through and was only interested in money.

"I told you I would pick the publication. It's not just *some* small town. It's my home! It's where I've lived for the past ten years."

Kenzie tried not to overhear, taking the dogs out for a break, sitting on the back deck to give Harrison privacy.

After ten minutes, he stepped outside, anger rolling off him. He stood near the door, arms crossed over his chest. "My agent has arranged for me to be interviewed on the Good Day Show. I don't seem to have a choice."

"How can she force you to go on television?"

"Doing the interview with the Scarlet Gazette just pissed off Extreme Exposure, my major sponsor, who sees it as a potential breach of contract. As long as I wasn't doing interviews, they were willing to wait. But now they're insisting I do the TV interview, wear their logo, and smile."

Okay, that *sucked*.

"Can't you walk away from the contract?

He shook his head, looking beaten down and weary. "They stood by me the whole time I was away. I owe them. Besides, if I ever climb again and need sponsors, I'd be screwed."

So, he truly hadn't made up his mind about whether he was done with climbing. Was she surprised? Climbing had been his passion and his livelihood. How could she have expected he would give it up entirely?

"I guess you don't have a choice, do you? When do you leave?"

"I fly out tomorrow. I'll be home the day after." He sat down in the chair beside hers, took her right hand, kissed it. "Do you want to come with me, see a little of New York City? We can fly out tomorrow morning and be home late the day after. You'd be gone two days total."

Her first impulse was to tell him that she couldn't go. She'd already missed too many days at the kennel. She would have to cancel her private lesson with little Prince. She'd also have to find someone to take her class on Tuesday evening.

But then she saw the hope in his eyes. "That could be fun."

Some of the weariness left his face. "Pack that dress— the shiny red one."

"We won't make it out of the hotel room if I bring that dress."

He grinned. "Exactly."

He handled the plane tickets, ground transportation, and hotel, leaving her time to pack and to arrange for Sasha to watch Gizmo and Gabby.

Early the next morning, they handed the dogs over to a very excited Sasha, who kissed them each on the cheek. "Don't worry about the dogs. We're going to have so much fun. And don't worry about the interview. You'll crush it."

Harrison drove them to the airport, parked in the valet parking, and carried her bag and his duffel to the check-in counter. It was the first time Kenzie had traveled without a carry-on, and that made getting through security a breeze.

"You do realize this is the line for first class?" she whispered.

"We're flying first class."

"Really?" This was going to be an adventure.

He chuckled. "When you're my height, traveling economy is hell."

Kenzie hadn't traveled a lot, and when she had, it had always been economy. She'd stood there while people with first-class tickets had boarded ahead of everyone else. Now, she was one of those people—and she was boarding with a man who was so good looking that women stared.

Enjoy it while you can.

They found their first-class seats, Kenzie buckling her seatbelt just as a pretty flight attendant offered them glasses of champagne.

"How much did you earn from these sponsorships?" Kenzie meant the question as a joke, so she wasn't ready for the answer.

"Before my last climb, I was making a combined total of about a million a year pre-tax, not including gear and travel. I set a lot of it aside for retirement—or to help in case I had a catastrophic accident."

She stared at Harrison, speechless.

An announcement came over the PA system. "Ladies and gentlemen, please stow your carry-on bags in the overhead compartment wheels first. If you're having trouble finding space, please ask a flight attendant for help."

Harrison took her hand, caressed it with his thumb. "You seriously had no idea that I made good money?"

"How could I? You live in a small rental house with mint-green appliances that date to the Fifties."

For the first time since his agent's call yesterday, Harrison laughed. "I can't wait to see what you think of our hotel."

Kenzie couldn't wait either. "What's the name of it?"

"The Conrad New York." He shrugged. "I figured it had my name on it."

———

CONRAD HAD NEVER CARED MUCH for big cities. Maybe it was the homesteader in him, but he didn't see the point of living crowded together with so many other people. There was too much noise, too much trash and pollution, too many assholes. But seeing the city through Kenzie's eyes made it fun.

She squealed at the hotel room with its view of the Hudson River, gaped wide-eyed up at the skyscrapers, moaned at the taste of the New York-style pizza slices they had for lunch sitting on a bench in Central Park, and wept as her fingers traced the names of the dead at the 9/11 memorial.

Conrad wondered what it must be like to live with such an open heart. Had he ever been that untouched, that innocent?

They went back to the hotel and changed for dinner, he into his old, wrinkled tux, which the hotel staff had pressed into a respectable state, and she into that sexy red dress.

"Where are we going?"

"You'll see." He'd bought VIP passes for dinner with a view at the State Bar and Grill in the Empire State Building so that she could see the sunset.

She stared down from the observation deck. "It's beautiful—like a forest of buildings and fairy lights."

He'd never thought of it that way before. He'd only ever seen the steel and concrete, the asphalt, the traffic, the crowds.

"Have you ever climbed anything this tall from bottom to top?"

"El Capitan is more than twice this height. So is the Dawn Wall."

"No way!"

"Way."

The food was fantastic, but Conrad could barely taste it, his senses focus on the beautiful woman who sat across from him—the sparkle in her blue eyes, her luminous skin, the sweetness of her laugh. He wasn't the only one staring. The server was so fixed on her cleavage that Conrad was afraid he'd miss their champagne glasses altogether.

Yeah. Been there. Done that.

They took a cab back to their hotel, Conrad's fingers twined with hers, champagne warming his blood. Back in their room, he undressed her, kissed every inch of her, lost himself inside her.

She fell asleep in his arms, but Conrad couldn't sleep at all.

━━

HER STOMACH SWARMING WITH BUTTERFLIES, Kenzie sat in a chair just off the set, watching while the hosts of the Good Day Show talked about the weather. They had taken Harrison backstage the moment they arrived and given Kenzie a tour of the studio before offering her a cup of coffee and seat where she'd be able to watch Harrison's interview.

Kenzie was afraid for him. She knew him well enough now to see what a strain this was on him emotionally. He hadn't said a word in the cab all the way here, his body radiating tension, lines of fatigue on his face. He was going to have to tell the entire story again, which meant he would have to relive all of it—the horror, the grief, the guilt.

God, how she wished he had opened up to Esri and let her help. His nightmares had gotten worse after the interview with Wendy. What would this interview do to him?

Even the strongest person could take only so much.

"Coming up next, a story of courage, loss, and heroism on Mount Everest. Celebrated mountain climber Harrison Conrad is here to talk about the catastrophe that claimed the lives of his friends and almost killed him."

Pablo, the young man who'd given her a tour of the studio, hurried over to her. "Can I get you more coffee?"

"That would be great. Thanks." She handed him her empty cup.

"If there's one thing we never run out of in this studio, it's coffee."

She could believe that. She and Harrison had gotten up at five a.m.—three in the morning Colorado time—to get here by seven. For the staff, getting up early was just part of their job.

The hosts bantered with each other through the commercial break, amusing the live studio audience. And then they were back.

"Harrison Conrad has been called the world's greatest alpine climber," said Corinne Roberts, the only host Kenzie recognized. "He's part of an elite group of climbers who have conquered all fourteen of the world's eight-thousand-meter peaks, including Mount Everest, which he has summited twice.

"But a year and a half ago, a tragic accident killed his climbing team and almost ended his life. He's here today to share his story for the first time with a national audience. Please welcome Harrison Conrad."

The audience applauded, and Kenzie clapped with them, the butterflies in her stomach fluttering with renewed vigor.

Conrad walked out onto the set wearing a fleece jacket with the Extreme Exposure logo, a forced smile on his face. He acknowledged the studio audience with a wave and sat beside Ms. Roberts.

Kenzie found it hard to breathe while Ms. Roberts asked question after question. What drew you into climbing? What qualities does it take to be a world-class mountaineer? Aren't you afraid when you're up there? What happened on Everest?

Harrison stayed outwardly calm and professional, his gaze seeking Kenzie out as he repeated the story he'd told Wendy. Being on belay while Luka Stenger crossed the ladder. Bruce joking about death. Stepping onto the ladder himself. The crack. The rumble. Falling. Coming back to consciousness hanging over an abyss, not knowing where he was. Climbing with injuries. Trying to dig out his friends with ice tools. The climb down to Base Camp. Fifteen months of at the monastery.

Kenzie stood, moved to where he could see her more clearly—still off the set and out of sight of the studio audience. If it helped him to know she was here, then she would do all she could to support him.

Ms. Roberts listened, offering a sympathetic word or two. "Now, I have to ask you what people at home are probably wondering. Why risk your life over and over again just to conquer a mountain?"

"That's just it—we're not trying to conquer the mountains. When I climb, I'm trying to conquer myself, my human weakness. You fight the cold, exhaustion, pain, hunger, even despair. There are times you want to give up, go back to your tent, sleep, but you can't. If I overcome myself, I've done what I set out to do."

"So it's not man versus mountain," Ms. Roberts said. "It's man versus himself."

"Exactly."

"This morning backstage, you asked me not to call you a hero. You told me you don't like it when people use that word to describe what you do. Why is that?"

Harrison's gaze shot to Kenzie's, and she could see he was furious. Kenzie couldn't blame him. By phrasing her question like that, Ms. Roberts was pretending to respect his boundaries while still forcing him onto a topic he'd hoped to avoid.

Kenzie wanted to smack her.

Still, Harrison kept his cool. "The word 'hero' should be used to describe the men and women who risk their lives in the service of others. I have friends who are heroes —firefighters, EMTs, law enforcement, combat veterans. They don't run into burning buildings just to see whether they can. They do it to save lives."

"I know the women in the audience want to hear the answer to this question: Is there someone special in your life?"

Harrison's gaze met Kenzie's again. "My private life is private."

And the interview was over.

Chapter 20

CONRAD WAS SO angry he could barely speak. He walked in silence with Kenzie toward the exit to meet their driver, ignoring the cheers and comments of people they passed along the way.

"Well done, Conrad."

"I don't care what you say. You're my hero."

"Great interview."

Outside, a light rain fell, the sky overcast, a cold wind blowing through the urban canyons. He opened the rear driver's side door for Kenzie, shut it behind her, and then walked around to the rear passenger door and climbed in beside her.

"I'm sorry." She looked up at him through blue eyes filled with worry. "She was out of line."

"She gave me her word." He leaned forward, spoke to their driver. "The Conrad New York, please."

He stared out the window unseeing, his gaze sliding over the blurred mass of humanity that made its way down wet sidewalks, crossed streets, dodged cars, cabs, and buses, street noises barely penetrating his thoughts.

Kenzie's small, cold fingers grasped his—a lifeline.

Was he really so broken, so damned weak that he needed her like this?

Back at the hotel, people now recognized him. Some applauded as he passed. Others simply stared. One kid hurried over and asked for his autograph, handing Conrad a notepad which he signed, teeth grinding.

None of this is his fault.

"Thanks, man. You've been my hero since I was a kid."

"Do you climb?" Kenzie asked the kid.

"A little. I've done some bouldering, mostly in the gym."

"Keep it up." Conrad took Kenzie's hand and walked over to the elevator, turning his back on all of them.

Kenzie waited until the door to their room closed behind them to speak. "They don't mean to get on your nerves. I agree with what you told Ms. Roberts. But to that kid in the lobby, you're a hero because you do things he can only dream of doing."

Conrad lifted his duffel onto the bed and started shoving things into it, anger like pressure in his chest. "You know who's a hero? Hawke. He saves lives every day."

"You're a hero, too, not because you climb, but because of your service on the Team. You've helped to save lives, too, and no one pays you a penny for it. You're the only one on the Team who can—"

"Stop. Just stop." He closed his eyes, drew a breath. "I know you're trying to help, but it's not working."

She stood across from him, her bag on the bed. "If this upsets you that much, maybe you should call Esri. She can help—"

"Are you saying you think I'm fucked up?"

She flinched. "No! But this and your nightmares—it's tearing you apart. You haven't had a full night's sleep since doing that interview with Wendy. It breaks my heart to see you hurting so much. I know it's hard for you to reach out but—"

"You don't know a damned thing about it!" He shouted the words at the top of his lungs. "Do you climb?"

She jerked as if she'd been struck, her face going pale. Then she turned and walked into the bathroom, shutting the door behind her.

Fuck, fuck, fuck!

Crushed by a sense of guilt, his emotions threadbare, he stared after her. Hadn't he promised her he would never deliberately hurt her?

You're a fucking wreck, man, and she called you on it.

When she emerged from the bathroom, he could see she'd been crying.

Yeah, that's your fault, asshole.

He should never have gotten involved with her. He'd known it was a bad idea, but he'd been too damned selfish, too damned broken to keep himself away from her. But he could fix that now.

He could end it before he truly *did* hurt her.

———

KENZIE HAD LOST HIM.

Harrison had shut down. He'd shut her out, barely speaking a word to her since leaving their hotel. He sat in the aisle seat beside her, eyes closed, but she knew from the hard set of his jaw that he wasn't asleep. He simply didn't want to interact with her.

If only she'd kept her mouth shut…

Would that have helped him?

No. Maybe. She didn't know.

She couldn't just sit by while he was suffering and say

nothing. She'd said what she believed was true. He needed trauma therapy. If he wanted to end their relationship because she'd tried to help him, then maybe he was doing them both a favor.

That's what she told herself, but that's not how she felt.

Inside, her heart was breaking.

Maybe this wasn't what it seemed. Maybe they'd get home, and he'd get some sleep and apologize to her for shouting. Maybe things would go back to the way they'd been before this trip. Breakfasts for two. Watching Netflix on the sofa at night with Gizmo and Gabby. Mind-blowing sex.

God, she hoped so, because she couldn't imagine her life without him. She loved him. With everything she was, she loved him.

The flight seemed to go on forever, Harrison finally giving up the charade of sleep to stare resolutely at the little TV screen in the seatback in front of him. Afraid he would reject her outright, Kenzie didn't reach for his hand or rest her head against his shoulder. By the time they landed, she was fighting tears.

He carried her bag to his car despite her insistence that she could handle it. She did have one good hand, after all. She tried to see some hope in this little act of chivalry, but it was dashed when they climbed into his vehicle.

"I'm sorry I raised my voice at you, Kenzie. When we get back to your place, I'm going to get my stuff and get out of your hair. Back when this first started, I told you I wasn't in a good space. You don't deserve this."

She blinked back tears. "Don't use me as your excuse. If you don't want to be with me, if you don't care about me, just say it."

"I *do* care about you. That's the whole point."

The drive back to Scarlet was excruciating, the pain

behind Kenzie's breastbone almost unbearable. He carried their bags inside and disappeared upstairs, where he grabbed his things out of the bathroom, her closet, and the laundry, and shoved it all in his duffel. He stopped at the front door, turned to face her.

"You're the most amazing woman I've ever known. Thank you for everything. I'm sorry. I'm sorry for all of this. If I could… " He stopped, cleared his throat, a muscle clenching in his jaw. "Tell Gabby… Tell the little scamp I will miss her."

So he would miss the puppy, but he wouldn't miss Kenzie.

She wanted to scream at him, to shout in his face, to tell him she loved him, but there was no point in doing that now. She mustered every shred of dignity she had left. "Take care, Harrison. I will miss you."

Then he turned and walked out of her life.

THERE WERE BREAK-UPS. There were broken hearts. And then there were nuclear winter heartbreaks.

Kenzie didn't know it was possible to hurt this much and still breathe. The dogs got her out of bed every morning, and her job forced her to leave the house. But she was only going through the motions, habit holding her hollow life together when she had shattered into a million pieces.

Every time her phone buzzed, she hoped it was him, but it never was. Every reminder of him made her cry— the few leftover condoms, the pair of socks Gabby had found under her bed, the lingering scent of his skin on her pillow. Every time she went to Food Mart, she thought she would run into him, but she never did.

She couldn't quit thinking about him, couldn't quit missing him, couldn't stand the nights without him.

There was no one she could talk to. She didn't want to bare her feelings to her friends on the Team, because they were also Harrison's friends. She couldn't confide in her employees. She didn't pay them to give her emotional CPR. After a week of this, she called Esri and made an appointment for the afternoon.

She burst into tears the moment she sat down in Esri's office. "It's over. He broke up with me. I suggested he call you, and it all fell apart. Why do I always fall in love with men who don't want me?"

Esri handed her a tissue. "Let's start at the beginning, okay?"

Kenzie told Esri the whole story—how the two of them had become lovers, how he'd warned her, how the interview with Wendy had made his nightmares worse, how the trip to New York City had turned into a disaster.

"If there were any man in my life that I thought one hundred percent for sure I could love for the rest of my life, it would be Harrison." She blew her nose. "But just like the others, he walked out the door and didn't look back."

"Why don't you tell me about them?"

Kenzie spent the next ten minutes giving Esri the condensed version of her love life. "Basically, I'm drawn to climbers, outdoorsy kinds of men, but they prefer rocks and mountains and piles of snow to me. Story of my life right there."

"What attracts you to them?"

"Well, they're strong and ripped and good looking. God, that sounds shallow."

Esri smiled. "I won't judge. What else?"

"They're adventurous, driven, exciting. There's an air

of—I don't know—danger and daring about them. They're not like me at all. I'm boring."

"Why do you say that?"

"I don't climb. I don't like to ski. I haven't traveled. I spend my life doing paperwork and picking up dog poop."

"You train SAR and HRD dogs, and you volunteer for the most respected search-and-rescue team in the country. Your work has saved lives. Some people would say that's pretty exciting."

"Okay. That's probably true."

"What do you think drew Harrison to you?"

"Gabby." That was the truth. "He adores her. When he left, he told me to tell Gabby he'd miss her, but he didn't say anything about missing me."

This brought a fresh rush of tears.

"I'm betting there was more to his attraction than your puppy."

"We had an incredible sex life—I mean, off-the-charts incredible."

"That tells me there was some real connection there. People who don't have a true emotional connection rarely have sex lives that are off the charts."

"Really?"

"Really." Esri handed her another tissue. "Let's talk about what happened in New York again."

Kenzie told the story once more. "Then he said, 'I do care about you. That's the point.' Does he really think that dumping me and leaving me out of his life helps me?"

"Let me ask you this: Do you think you did the right thing?"

Kenzie nodded. "He needs to talk to someone. I bit my tongue for a long time, afraid that pushing him to get counseling would drive him away. That day I didn't feel like I had a choice. If you could have seen him and how on edge he was… "

"For what it's worth, I think what you did was completely valid. The two of you were intimate, and you had every reason to be worried about him."

"But what good did it do if I alienated him? I don't think anyone has seen him. He didn't show up when the Team was toned out yesterday to help the guy with the asthma attack. Maybe what I did just made things worse."

Esri reached out, took her hand. "What Conrad does is his responsibility, not yours. When he decides he needs help, I'll be here."

"So what can I do? I can't stand feeling like this. It hurts so much that I can barely breathe. Are there some meditations or exercises I can do to make it better?"

"I wish I had the cure for a broken heart, but I don't." Esri squeezed her fingers. "It will get better with time, I promise you."

But Kenzie wasn't so sure about that.

———

CONRAD WAS PASSED out drunk on the sofa when a *thunk thunk thunk* woke him. Had Gabby gotten into something?

He lurched to his feet—and remembered Gabby didn't live there anymore. "Shit."

He was about to flop back onto the couch when the noise came again.

Thunk thunk thunk.

Was someone knocking on his door?

Kenzie.

God, he missed her. He missed her so fucking much.

Heart slamming, he threaded his way through empty

bottles and pizza boxes to the front door, too unsteady on his feet to make use of the peephole.

He opened the door. "Megs."

She must have heard the disappointment in his voice.

"I'm happy to see you, too." She pushed past him, glanced around at his mess. "You've redecorated—a little less nineteen-fifties, a little more Jim Beam. I'm not sure I like it, but I guess it's the new you."

Something about that seemed like an insult, but before he could work it out, she started picking up his trash.

He shook his head. "You don't have to do that."

"I know, but I don't want to trip and break my damned neck."

He tried to bend down to pick up a beer bottle but came close to falling.

"Sit down. You got coffee in that kitchen?"

"Yep." His ass landed on the sofa where it had been these past two weeks.

In a few minutes, Megs returned with a cup. "You drink yours black, right?"

He took the cup from her. "Thanks."

She went back to picking up empty bottles and pizza boxes, carrying them out to his recycling bins. Then she opened his curtains, flooding the room with daylight that made his head ache. "That's better."

"You came here to clean my house?"

"I came here to tell you a story." She sat on the other end of the sofa, crossed her legs. "Back when God was still a child, Ahearn and I came to Colorado to tackle the famous fourteeners."

"You really *are* telling me a story."

"A true story. Drink your coffee and listen." Megs went on. "We were on our way down from the summit of El Diente—that's in the San Miguels—when our good buddy

Dean slipped on talus, fell, and broke his ankle. Have you ever climbed El Diente?"

Conrad nodded. "It's steep, lots of loose talus, and some drop-offs—big cliffs."

It was an easy place to kill yourself if you didn't know what you were doing.

"We tried to get Dean on his feet. We thought maybe he could hop down the mountain with the two of us for support, but, as you say, it's steep. After some slipping and a near fall, the three of us decided that it would be best to leave Dean behind with some food and water and head down the mountain to get help."

Conrad nodded. "That makes sense. If you're all injured, no one gets out."

Climbing sometimes involved making tough choices.

"That's how we saw it. We made it back to our truck and drove to the nearest town, but no one there was willing to head out that late in the afternoon to rescue a climber. There were no rescue teams at that time. Climbing was a young sport. The sheriff's department promised to head up to get him the next morning."

Wait. Had she told Conrad this story before? It sounded familiar.

"That night, the San Miguels were hit by a freak snow-storm—whiteout conditions, freezing temps."

"I guess it's lucky you got down."

"Lucky for us. Not so lucky for Dean."

Conrad had forgotten about him. "Shit."

"We headed up the next morning through deep snow, but it was too late. Dean had frozen to death right where we'd left him, the food and water we'd left behind with him frozen solid."

"God. I'm sorry."

"I grieved for a long time afterward, and I blamed

myself. I ran different scenarios through my mind. If only we'd done this or that, Dean might be alive."

Conrad shook his head. "You can't know that. Maybe you would have all died up there in that snowstorm."

Megs nodded. "Ahearn held me together after that. He got me through it. He came up with the idea for the Team, gave me a new focus, a new passion."

That is where Conrad had heard this story. Dean's death had inspired Megs and Ahearn to found the Team.

Megs went on. "But none of that changes the fact that Ahearn and I left Dean behind. We left him there, alive and breathing, and when we came back, he was a corpse. We left him because it was easier for us. For the rest of my life, I will regret that we didn't push on and try harder to get him down. And do you know what makes it tougher to live with?"

Conrad shook his head. "No."

Fuck, he was drunk.

"All these years of doing rescue work have proved to me that we *could* have gotten him down. Dean died because we didn't try hard enough."

"You're too hard on yourself."

"Pot meet kettle." Megs pointed straight at him.

Wait. "What?"

"I read your interview in the Scarlet Gazette. I watched the Good Day Show with Corrine Roberts in her very fine makeup. If anyone knows what you're going through, I do —and Ahearn. You're not the only climber to lose a close friend."

"I know that." Conrad didn't like where this was headed.

"You feel guilty that you survived and they didn't. You wonder if the sport you dedicated your life to is even justifiable in the face of their deaths. You swear you'll never climb again. You ask yourself what you should have done differently. Would they still be alive if you had done X instead of Y?"

"Stop! I don't want to talk—"

"Here's the thing—Bruce and the Stenger twins were killed by tons of falling ice. They died instantly, and no force on earth could have saved them. They were in the wrong place at the wrong time. You didn't walk away like we did and leave them there to die. There was *nothing* you could have done to help them. You were almost killed, too."

Something inside Conrad cracked, a fissure opening in his chest, the nearly empty coffee mug falling from his hand to the floor. "I *did* leave them there. I tried to dig them out, but I couldn't. I tried. God, I tried. But when the rescue team came, I turned my back on them, and I walked away. I walked away, and I left them."

Megs was there beside him, drawing him into her embrace, holding him like a mother holds a child. "I know how it is. I know."

For the first time since his father's death, Conrad wept.

Chapter 21

CONRAD WOKE THE NEXT MORNING, feeling lighter despite intense thirst and a raging headache. He sat up, reached for the glass of water on his nightstand, and drank. When he set it down, empty, he remembered who'd put it there for him.

Megs.

He groaned as memories of last night flooded back.

I walked away, and I left them.

I know how it is. I know.

Shit.

He'd made a complete ass of himself. Not only had Megs seen him stupid-drunk, his home a garbage dump, but he'd lost it in front of her and cried like a fucking baby on her shoulder.

No, he hadn't.

Oh, yes, he had.

Do you like how this feels? Welcome to rock bottom, buddy.

God in heaven.

How was he going to face Megs again?

Even as the question ran through his mind, he knew

she wouldn't say a word about it to anyone, except maybe Ahearn. She wouldn't even bring it up with Conrad. His secret was safe with her.

Megs had understood.

He owed her—big-time.

He got out of bed and walked naked into the bathroom to take a leak. There on the mirror was a sticky note in Megs' handwriting.

You promised me you'd call Esri.

Meg had understood, but she was still a hard-ass.

He washed his hands and face and brushed the disgusting taste of cheap beer out of his mouth. Then he put on a clean pair of boxer briefs and walked out to the kitchen, checking out of habit to make sure Gabby wasn't underfoot, more of his conversation with Megs coming back to him.

God, I miss Kenzie. I don't know how I'm going to face this without her. She's the most amazing, beautiful, sweet, adorable woman I've ever known. I think I love her.

Had he said that? Had he truly said he loved Kenzie?

In vino veritas.

"Don't tell me that," Megs had said. "Talk to Kenzie. That girl has been crazy about you for years, and you're an idiot if you don't fight to hold onto her."

Fuck.

Well, he *was* an idiot.

The last thing he'd said to Kenzie, words he regretted, came rushing back.

Tell Gabby… Tell the little scamp I will miss her.

Conrad stopped in his tracks and squeezed his eyes shut, trying to shut out the memory of the pain that had filled Kenzie's blue eyes. He'd give anything to go back in time and shut his own damned mouth. He'd hurt her. Dear

God, he'd told her he would miss her puppy—but hadn't said a word about missing her.

What the fuck is wrong with you?

His mother's words came back to him.

If you find someone you love, don't walk away from her. Don't turn your back on her. Fight for her. Don't make my mistake.

He needed to call Kenzie right now. No, he needed to apologize to her face. He needed to ask her if she could forgive him and give him a second chance.

It was true. He was in love with her—headfirst in love.

But would she take him back?

If she didn't, he'd have no one but himself to blame.

He made himself an omelet of four egg whites and one egg and sat down with a cup of coffee, hoping the protein and caffeine would help him pull his head out of his ass— or at least take the edge off his hangover. Then he took a long, hot shower and shaved off two weeks of stubble, Megs' note there in front of him.

You promised me you'd call Esri.

When he was dressed, he sat on the sofa and picked up his cellphone.

He had a promise to keep.

━━━

KENZIE GOT BACK to the kennel from her depressing private lesson with poor little Prince. Mari, the puppy's owner, had hinted that Kenzie should take the dog. When Kenzie had asked her what she'd tell her children, Mari had said she'd tell them that the dog had run away. Kenzie wanted to help little Prince, but she couldn't be a part of that.

"Can I take my lunch now?" Quinn asked. "It's supposed to snow, and I'd like to get a jog in before the paths get icy."

"Sure." Kenzie had gotten her splint off last week and could manage now. Besides, she had nothing going on these days, no crazy lunchtime sex that made the rest of the afternoon float by. "How much accumulation are we expecting?"

"Up to six inches."

It would be their first major snowstorm of the season. Colorado needed the moisture, and the ski resorts needed the snow.

Kenzie cleaned up the play yard, washed her hands, then played with the dogs—all except for Gabby, who sat by the door.

"You miss him, too, don't you, Gabby girl?"

Gabby looked over at Kenzie with big brown eyes, her tail thumping against the floor at the mention of her name.

Kenzie let the other dogs out into the play yard, taking a few minutes to sit with Gabby, petting her, playing with her. Then she settled the puppy in her crate for a nap and started sweeping out kennels.

The door behind her opened, and she thought for a split second that Quinn was already back from her run.

The sound of a man's voice made her jump.

"Are you Kenzie Morgan—the woman who trains search dogs?" A man with a baseball cap stood just inside the door, wearing a black down jacket and jeans. His jaw was covered with stubble, and there was the faint scent of wood smoke about him.

He held up a copy of the newspaper with her photo on it, his gaze moving around the room. "I read about you."

"Yes, I'm Kenzie. Can I help you with something?"

"How good are dogs when it comes to finding people?" He glanced over his shoulder out the door.

"It depends on the…" Her heart gave a hard kick.

He had a gun—and he was pointing it straight at her. Where had that come from? "Which one of these dogs is yours? Which one found that dead woman?"

Oh, God! Oh, God!

She swallowed hard, willing herself to look calm. "You can aim that gun at me, but that won't get you an answer. Why are you asking?"

He glanced over his shoulder again, clearly nervous. "I need your help finding someone, and if you don't help me, I'll shoot every damned dog in this place and you along with them."

He aimed his gun at Gabby inside her crate.

Kenzie's mouth went dry.

"I'll help you." She moved to stand between Gabby and the barrel of his gun, hands raised, heart slamming in her chest. "But only if you leave the dogs alone. Hurt even one of them, and you'll have to kill me, and then who will help you? No one else around here does what I do."

A part of her couldn't believe what she'd just said, but she meant it. She would die before she'd let him hurt these dogs.

His eyes narrowed. "You've got a smart mouth for such a little lady."

She glared at him. "And you've got despicable manners."

He grinned. "Okay. I promise I won't hurt you or the dogs. Now, which one found that dead chick? I need you and it to come with me."

She didn't want Gizmo anywhere near this son of a bitch, but what choice did she have? "Lower the gun, and

I'll call him in. You don't need to point it at me. We both know you have it."

Slowly, the bastard lowered the gun.

Kenzie walked over to the door that led to the play yard and called the dogs in. "Come here, Gizmo. Come here, boy."

He whimpered, surely sensing her fear.

"I need to put the other dogs in their kennels." Her mind raced, trying to figure out how she could pull out her cellphone and call 911.

But he watched her like a hawk. "Don't try anything."

The security cameras.

He hadn't noticed them. They had a view of this entire room. Surely, they'd gotten a clear image of him. Or did his baseball cap hide his face?

Regardless, she needed to get him out of here before he hurt the dogs—and before Quinn got back from her run with Sheba or Dree walked in.

When Tiny was in his kennel, she turned to face the man who was about to become her abductor. "My search-and-rescue gear is in the back of my truck."

"We'll take your truck then."

She leashed Gizmo, fear leaving her queasy. If anything happened to him, she would never forgive herself. "Let's go, boy."

As she led Gizmo out to her truck, the jerk walking close behind her, she held onto one thought.

She still had her cellphone.

DREE HELD her breath and tiptoed back up the hallway to the store, her pulse like thunder in her ears. She hurried toward the shop's front door, but there was a bell on it. If she opened it, he would hear. Instead, she ran into the stock room and hid behind the shelves, fumbling to get her cellphone out of her pocket.

She dialed 911, whispering to the dispatcher. "I-I'm at the Scarlet Canine Care. You have to hurry! A man with a gun is kidnapping my boss and her dog."

CONRAD PUT on his best pair of jeans and his black cable-knit sweater and then grabbed his parka and the keys to his 4Runner. He drove to Food Mart to pick up a dozen red roses from the floral department, pulling over along the way to let a sheriff's vehicle go by. It was running silent, lights flashing.

Something was up.

By the time he got to the store, doubt assailed him. Did Kenzie even like roses? Maybe he should get ice cream instead. He knew she liked ice cream.

But what would ice cream or roses matter if she told him to get lost?

He wouldn't blame her. He'd told her that he was ending things because he cared about her, but that was bullshit. He'd been running—from himself, from the nightmares, from the truth that she'd laid out for him that day.

She'd been right. He *did* need help.

He'd kept his promise to Megs and called Esri. She had offered to see him today during her noon meditation time. But he hadn't been able to wait to see Kenzie, so he'd scheduled an appointment for tomorrow.

Truth be told, the idea of talking with a therapist— even Esri—terrified him. But what scared him more was the prospect of a life without Kenzie. He needed to unfuck himself so he could be the man she deserved.

In the end, he picked up a pint of cookie dough ice cream to go with the roses, paid, and drove straight toward her place. He'd just neared Bear's roundabout when he saw several sheriff's vehicles converged in front of Kenzie's store.

Probably some traffic stop. Drugs. Maybe poachers.

He yielded to traffic, which was backed up thanks to everyone slowing down to stare, then turned onto her street and parked out front.

Her truck was gone.

Damn it.

He let out a frustrated breath. He would just have to come back tonight when she was home.

Maybe you should call first.

He had just restarted his engine when Deputy Marcs stepped out of Kenzie's house wearing blue nitrile gloves.

What the fuck?

Forgetting the ice cream and roses, he turned off his engine and strode up Kenzie's front walk. "What's going on?"

The expression on Deputy Marcs' face made his pulse skip.

"A man abducted Kenzie and Gizmo at gunpoint about fifteen minutes ago. From the description given by a witness, I think it was one of the two men who robbed the armored vehicle last month."

Conrad's heart hit the back of his sternum, adrenaline flooding his bloodstream, turning his blood to ice. "What the hell are you doing here? Shouldn't you go after them?"

Deputy Marcs put her hand on his arm. "We've got deputies in pursuit and a call into SWAT, but we don't want this to turn into a hostage situation. We've got a few things on our side. We just got a ping on her cellphone, so we know exactly where they are and which direction they're headed. Also, we know the make, model, and license plate number of the vehicle."

Conrad looked over at the empty driveway. "Her truck."

"Yes."

His gaze snapped back to Marcs. "Where's Gabby? Where's the puppy?"

"The little golden retriever? She's safe with the rest of the dogs at the kennel."

Thank God for that at least.

"You said there were a few things on our side. You named two."

"The witness overheard the suspect tell Kenzie that he needed her to find someone for him. He wants her and Gizmo to track someone. That means he needs the two of them whole and alive—at least until he finds whoever he's looking for."

Conrad wasn't reassured by that. A man could do a lot of things to a woman without killing her. "I want to ride along."

"I can't let you do that."

"She needs me."

"If you want to help her, you need to let us do our job."

But Conrad couldn't just sit on his ass, not when Kenzie's life was on the line. "Just tell me which way they went. Did they head up the canyon?"

Deputy Marcs shook her head. "I'm not authorized to share that information."

Conrad nodded, pretending to understand. "I know you'll do your best."

An idea half-formed in his mind, he started through Kenzie's front door.

"Hey, what are you doing?" Deputy Marcs moved to stop him.

"I live here most of the time now. I'm coming home." He walked around her and stepped into the familiar warmth of Kenzie's house, locking the door behind him.

For a moment, he stood there, breathing deeply, trying to clear his mind and get control of his fear. If anything happened to Kenzie...

He banished that possibility from his thoughts and set off in search of her laptop. If the sheriff was using her cellphone to track her, he could, too.

———

"PULL OFF THE ROAD HERE."

Kenzie did what her captor, who said his name was Don, told her to do, signaling and pulling off the main highway onto a dirt road. So far, he hadn't done more than reach over and touch her thigh. She had smacked his hand away and told him that if he touched her again, she would refuse to help him.

Since then, he'd kept his hands to himself.

"Keep driving."

By now someone must have noticed she was missing. Quinn would have come back, found the dogs in their kennels. She would wonder why Kenzie wasn't there. But would she tell the police? If Quinn didn't report it...

Kenzie didn't have any classes tonight. No one was expecting her. If Quinn didn't think anything was wrong, if she didn't call the police, then it would be sometime tomorrow before anyone would start looking for her.

She was on her own.

Fighting despair, she headed up a narrow, steep road

until it came to an end. She knew the mountains well, but she wasn't familiar with this area. "What now?"

"We find my buddy."

"I'll need a scent article."

"A what?"

"A scent article—something that he wore, something of his that carries his scent. Gizmo can't track a scent he can't identify." In her back pocket, her cellphone buzzed again, but the sound was muted by the bounty of her butt.

Another reason to eat more ice cream.

"Get out."

But her cellphone was still buzzing. "Hang on."

She put on her emergency brake, checked herself in her mirror, put on lip balm, waiting for the call to end.

"Hurry the fuck up!"

"Fine." She climbed out, quickly pulling her phone out of her jeans, lowering the volume to silent to mute the buzz, and concealing it in her bra, certain he'd see the outline of it against the denim fabric of her pocket.

A frigid wind was blowing from the northwest, dark clouds moving in, bringing snow. She didn't want to get caught in the storm. She wasn't dressed for freezing temps, and the bastard who'd abducted her hadn't let her change her clothes.

She met Don—if that truly was his name—at the back of the truck, opened the tailgate and topper, and got Gizmo out of his crate. "Hey, there buddy. Are you ready to go to work?"

Gizmo whined, licked her hand, his ears down.

He knew something was wrong.

It broke her heart to bring him out here, to expose him to danger. If anything were to happen to Gizmo…

Feeling like she was betraying his trust, she slipped him

into his vest, leashed him, and took out her backpack, slinging it over one shoulder.

"What's that?" Don started to yank the pack away from her.

She held on tight. "It's the backpack I carry when I work. It's got first aid supplies, food, water, an emergency blanket, and stuff for Gizmo—dog food, treats, his favorite toy. That's how I get him to search. To him, it's a game."

"You got a cellphone in there?"

"A cellphone? I wish!" She jerked it away from him. "Do you want my help or not? I won't take my dog out without this. He can't work without food and water."

"I'm going to search it, and if I find a cellphone, you're in deep shit."

"Search it if you want, but I'm holding onto it." She held one of the straps while he dug through the pockets.

"Nice." He took out a granola bar, tore open the wrapper, and shoved in his mouth. "Okay. This shit could be useful. Get going. This way."

She settled the backpack on her shoulders and followed Don uphill through stands of spruce and Douglas fir. After maybe ten minutes, they came to what looked like a makeshift campsite. A plastic tarp was slung over some low-lying branches to make a tent, a sleeping bag beneath it on top another tarp, soot-blackened rocks surrounding a recently dug fire pit. A short distance away lay several empty money bags, the kind used by banks—or armored car services.

Chills skittered down her spine.

The men who robbed the armored vehicle.

Don must be one of them. Where was the other?

"What kind of scent thing do you need?"

"I need something that belonged to your partner in crime, something that was close to his skin."

Don grinned. "So you know who I am?"

"I know what you are."

His grin disappeared behind a scowl. "For a prisoner, you sure are a mouthy bitch. My *partner* took off in the middle of the night with the money. You're going to help me find him so I can get my share back—and make him pay."

"I won't help you if you're planning to kill…"

The gun was out before she had finished speaking. "You'll help me, or I'll put you down right now and take your fucking dog to find him myself."

Staring down the barrel of that gun, her pulse thrumming in her ears, Kenzie fought to find her courage. Like an aggressive dog, this asshole would become more dangerous if he sensed her fear. But, *damn*, she *was* scared.

She made herself laugh. "You know nothing about search dogs. You wouldn't succeed without me. Lower that damned gun, or fuck off."

Slowly, he lowered the weapon. "You better be worth all this trouble."

Kenzie would find a way out of this. She had no choice. But for now, she had to play along. "Do you have a scent article or not?"

Chapter 22

CONRAD STOOD WITH MEGS, Hawke, Herrera, Belcourt, and Acharya, looking from Kenzie's Find My Phone app on her computer to the big topographical map of the Indian Peaks Wilderness that hung on the wall. "It looks like they're headed toward the old Hastings mine."

Hawke tapped the site of the old mine with his finger. "That's the only thing up there. If this asshole is forcing her to track someone, it could be that the person she's tracking is hiding there."

A knot of dread formed in Conrad's chest, dropping like a rock into his stomach.

Son of a bitch.

"That's a long damned climb for someone who isn't used to it." Conrad pointed to a dark line on the map. "There's an exposed ridge here—a knife's edge with a thousand-foot drop on either side. When it's windy, it's hard for me at six-five and two-ten to make it across. Kenzie is one-ten at the most. If he forces her to cross, she could get blown off the mountain—and Gizmo with her."

When it was icy, it was a full-on technical climb. No

inexperienced person could possibly make it across.

"The miner's cabin is still there, isn't it?" Herrera asked.

Conrad nodded. "Last time I was up there, it was still standing, but they're going to have to cross that razor's edge to reach it."

Megs relayed this information to Dispatch, describing the Hastings mine and giving them its GPS coordinates, so they could pass it on to Incident Command.

Sheriff's deputies had called in SWAT to help them apprehend this fucker. They had located her vehicle and were moving up the mountain after her, but not fast enough for Conrad. He had planned to beat them there, but Taylor had stopped him with a palm to the sternum.

"When is the last time you got into a firefight with outlaws?"

Well, the last time was … "Never. But I grew up hunting. I can shoot."

"I know you can, but you don't want to force this guy into using Kenzie as a hostage—or get shot and killed when you find them. That won't help her."

"I can't just sit here!"

"I'm off duty, but I'll volunteer to be part of the search and go up with them to be your eyes and ears," Taylor had offered.

The Hastings mine was located on county land, and Taylor, a ranger, was county law enforcement. He had a right to be there, while Conrad did not.

Conrad hated feeling helpless. "You would do that?"

"If it keeps your ass out of trouble, hell, yes, I'll do it. I care about Kenzie, too, you know. We all do."

Taylor was now sending Conrad texts periodically to keep him updated.

It was something.

Wind strong. Temps dropping. Flakes starting to fall.

Conrad glanced outside, where street lights had come on, the sky darkened by storm clouds. If they didn't hurry up and rescue her, Kenzie and Gizmo were going to be trapped on a mountainside in a blizzard.

———

OUT OF BREATH and cold to the bone, Kenzie leaned into the frigid wind, fighting her way up the steep slope, icy snowflakes blowing into her face, snow making each step treacherous. Gizmo had found the scent trail and was leading them upward, doing what he asked her to do even though he must be cold and tired.

She glanced down, saw that he was favoring his left front paw.

"We have to stop!" She had to shout to be heard above the wind.

She slipped out of her backpack, opened up the center side pocket, and took out the packet that held Gizmo's protective booties. Close to tears, she slipped a warm bootie onto that sore front paw first. "I'm sorry, buddy. I'm so sorry."

"What the hell are you doing?" Don bent down, shouting in her face. "We have to keep going!"

"He can't! The snow and rock are hurting his paws!"

Don threw up his hands. "Fuck! Fuck!"

Kenzie finished covering Gizmo's paws then poured a drink of water into a collapsible dog bowl. He lapped thirstily, then took a few treats from her hand.

She petted him, praised him, swallowing the lump in her throat. "You're such a good boy, Gizmo. I love you."

No matter how this ended, he had always been the best

dog. He would follow her anywhere, even if it killed him. But she couldn't let that happen.

"Come on! Move it!"

Kenzie put the treats and collapsible bowl back into her pack, slipped it onto her shoulders, and stood on tired legs. "We need to find shelter, ride out the storm! We'll freeze to death out here!"

In the past few minutes, the storm had gotten worse, making it hard to see.

"No! You want to keep warm? Keep moving!"

Kenzie had no choice but to urge Gizmo onward.

Up they went, but soon the snow was falling so hard that she could barely see Don just a few feet ahead of her.

White-out conditions. A true blizzard.

She could turn and run downhill. If she could get far enough away, he wouldn't be able to see to shoot her. But if she didn't—if she slipped and broke her ankle—he would probably kill her outright.

She needed to get him to stop before they went much higher. There was no shelter above timberline and no dried wood for a fire. "We have to stop! We could walk off a cliff! Gizmo can't track in this anyway!"

Don turned on her, gun drawn, his face pinched from cold. "If you stop again, I'll kill you and take the dog!"

"You're going to get us all killed anyway!"

Kenzie trudged after him, the trees thinning, the storm getting worse.

━━━

CONRAD STOOD in the kitchen at The Cave, wolfing down a microwaved burrito that Sasha had brought for him when she'd heard he hadn't eaten lunch. Most everyone was here now, listening in on the radio, waiting this out.

Everyone loved Kenzie, but no one loved her the way he did.

A collective groan went up from the group in the Ops Room.

Hawke's voice rose above the rest. "That's bullshit!"

"What the hell?" That was Herrera.

Conrad ran back to the Ops Room, the last bite of burrito sticking in his throat. "What's going on?"

Megs stood, turned to face him. "SWAT is calling off the search until the snow lets up. They say they've got whiteout conditions up there. They're just not equipped to handle it."

"Goddamn it!" Conrad set out for the bays where the Team's gear was stored and began throwing together a backpack.

He wasn't going to let Kenzie freeze to death out there.

Crampons. Snowshoes. Ice axes. Two fifty-foot lengths of rope. Rack of climbing gear. Advanced first-aid kit. Hand-warmers. Fire starters. Emergency blankets. Two sleeping bags. Propane stove kit. Summit pants.

Megs followed him. "If you go up there, you could end up in trouble, too."

"You think I don't know that?" He'd done his share of climbing in bad conditions, but usually, he hunkered down and rode out the storm. "She'll die if someone doesn't get to her."

Megs nodded. "If I can't stop you…"

"You can't."

Hawke strode in from the Ops Room. "Are you heading out in this blizzard on some insane rescue mission? Because if you are, I'm going with you. You'll need a paramedic."

"Count me in." Moretti hurried out the bay doors toward his vehicle, calling to them over his shoulder. "I'll be right back. I'm going to grab my rifle and ammo and winter gear. You're going to need someone who can shoot."

Conrad started to say that he was a good shot—but he wasn't a combat veteran. He'd be grateful to have Moretti with him

"I'm going." Belcourt, too? "Everyone needs an engineer."

"Well, if you're all going, then I'm going, too." Megs took a backpack down from the wall. "Someone has to make sure you know what you're doing."

It seemed to take an eternity to gear up. In the process, they came up with a plan. They would park behind Kenzie's vehicle and go in hard and fast, double-timing it up the mountain. Ahearn would stay in touch via sat phone to let them know the GPS coordinates of Kenzie's phone. If they encountered live fire, Moretti would take control of the operation until the threat was neutralized. When Kenzie was freed, they would get her down and off the mountain—alive.

There were a thousand things that could go wrong, but, damn, it felt good to be taking action and not just sitting around.

When everyone was geared up, they stowed their packs in Rescue 1, Belcourt sliding behind the wheel.

"Good luck, everyone." For once, Sasha wasn't smiling. "We'll be listening in."

Herrera pushed the button that opened the big bay door, snow swirling in. "We'll have a backup team ready if you need us."

Ahearn drew Megs into a hug. "Be careful up there."

A wool hat on her head, Megs kissed him. "You know I

will be."

Belcourt nosed the vehicle out the bay door and into the blizzard.

Conrad had only one thought in his mind.

I'm coming for you, honey. Stay alive.

━━━

EXHAUSTED, out of breath, and colder than she'd ever been, Kenzie struggled for every step, the wind threatening to blow her onto her face. Gizmo had led them far above timberline now, nothing around them but swirling white. There was no shelter here, nowhere to get out of the frigid wind or biting snow.

Don, the evil bastard, had taken her spare pair of gloves, her extra hat, and her hand warmers, leaving her nothing. He'd eaten most of the food and drunk her water, too, sparing only the dog treats.

You're going to die out here. He's going to kill you—or let you die.

No. No, she would find a way.

Fighting despair, she put one foot in front of the other, sliding on snow and talus. Her toes ached, her fingers, too. But she had no choice to keep going. She thought of Harrison coming to while hanging upside down in that crevasse, thought of how hard it had been for him to climb out. If only she had his strength…

The minutes dragged on in misery, her mind growing dull.

Then, abruptly, Gizmo stopped, lay down, barked.

Kenzie sank to her knees beside him. "Did you find him, boy?"

She looked into the snow, expecting to see a corpse. Then a gust of wind blew the snow aside for a moment, knocking her onto her belly, and she saw.

They stood on the brink of an abyss, ground giving away to nothingness, the air divided by a thin razor's edge of rock.

She shrieked, scooted backward, pulling Gizmo with her. If Gizmo hadn't stopped her, she would have gone right over that edge.

She looked over her shoulder at Don, speaking through chattering teeth. "I-I th-think he's d-down there."

Another gust of wind came, knocking her to the ground.

"He's not down there!" Don shouted, bent low against the gale. "He's over there."

Kenzie squinted and was just able to make out the ghostly shape of a cabin on the other side of the ridge. Well, that was it then. If he was over there, they couldn't reach him. Even in good weather, they would need technical gear to cross the rock, and she wasn't a climber.

"What are you waiting for? Move!"

Kenzie crawled back from the edge. "We c-can't cross th-that in this s-storm. We'll g-get blown off or f-fall. We need t-technical gear, ropes—"

"I want my goddamn money!"

"You don't need us anymore. We've f-found him for you." She saw on his face that she'd made a fatal mistake.

Still bent low, he drew the gun. "You're right! I don't need you."

Kenzie knew she was going to die. Up here. In the cold.

He stood upright, aimed the barrel at her, then pointed the gun at Gizmo.

"No!" Kenzie threw herself at him.

The *crack* of the gun.

Don shrieking, arms flailing, as he toppled backward into the abyss.

Stunned, Kenzie lay in the snow, staring in horror at the empty space where Don had stood, no sound now but the wind.

He was gone. The bastard was gone.

She had knocked him over the edge.

Gizmo whined, licked her face.

Then she noticed it. Blood. Scarlet drops on the snow.

Frantic, she searched Gizmo to find where he'd been hit. Only when she saw the blood on her jeans did she realize that she, not Gizmo, had been shot.

"Shit."

Then the pain kicked in, knife-sharp, sheering through her left thigh. If the bullet had hit her femoral artery, she was dead.

Fueled by adrenaline, she crawled farther away from the edge, pulled off of her backpack, and searched with aching fingers for her first-aid kit. Inside, she had Quikclot bandages and a tourniquet. She found the kit, pulled it out, then checked the wound.

Relief flooded her.

The wound was low on the outside of her thigh. Though it bled heavily and hurt like hell, it wasn't an arterial bleed.

Gizmo whimpered, snuggling against her, cold, exhausted, afraid.

"It's g-going to b-be okay." She packed the clotting bandages inside her jeans and used the tourniquet to bind them into place. She couldn't do more than that, or she would freeze to death right here.

She tried to stand, but the pain was too much. Instead, she crawled again. "H-help me find the w-way back, buddy."

She tried to follow their tracks, but wind and snow quickly erased them. Soon, there was no trail to follow, nothing but Gizmo's senses to lead them through the land-scape of white.

Keep going. Keep. Going.

Soon, it was too much even to crawl. She stopped to check the bandages and saw that they had bled through. She needed to apply more, needed to stop the blood loss.

But cold enfolded her like a tomb, pinning her down, dulling her mind.

"I-I'm sorry. I'm s-so sorry. Good … b-boy, Gizmo. Run h-home. G-go."

He licked her cheeks, whimpering for her.

Her last thought as she lapsed into unconsciousness was of Harrison.

———

"YOU'RE ALMOST DIRECTLY DOWNHILL from her signal. The blip quit moving a few minutes ago."

"Copy that." Conrad jammed the satellite phone back into his pocket, his sense of dread growing into the fear that they were already too late. "He says we're just downhill from her signal. He says she isn't moving."

That meant that the phone had been abandoned—or that Kenzie had stopped. In this cold, that would be fatal.

Hold on, honey. We're almost there.

The five of them started up the mountain at a jog again. They practiced for situations like this. Anyone who couldn't complete a four-mile uphill trail run with a full pack in thirty-five minutes didn't make the Team. It kept a person warm in the cold, but running on talus at altitude in snow came with risks. One slip, one stone flipping beneath your feet, and you'd have a broken ankle and be in need of a rescue yourself.

Conrad was faster than the others. He had also

climbed at more than twice this altitude. Running up a talus slope in a blizzard at eleven thousand feet was a helluva lot easier than slogging up a snowfield at twenty-eight-thousand feet. But none of this would matter if he didn't reach Kenzie soon.

With every step, his last words to her haunted him. He couldn't let those words be the last thing she'd heard from him. He couldn't.

From somewhere in the distance, Conrad thought he heard a dog bark.

He stopped, listened, heard only wind.

He started forward once more—and he heard it again. He looked around but saw nothing. He whistled. "Gizmo! Gizmo, come here, boy!"

Hawke stopped beside Conrad, breathing hard. "I don't see him."

"I don't see him either, but I thought I heard... There!"

Up above them and a little to their right, Gizmo bounded toward them, snow in his golden fur.

"Come here, boy! Come here!" Conrad knelt down, took the dog into his arms. There were booties on his feet —proof of Kenzie's love for him. "God, am I happy to see you. What a good boy you are."

Belcourt, Megs, and Moretti caught up with them.

"I brought some treats." AR slung over his shoulder, Moretti fished a few pieces of kibble out of his pack and held them out for Gizmo, who gobbled them.

But where was Kenzie?

Conrad stood, tried to see through the storm, looking for her dark hair, her blue parka, any color at all.

Nothing.

Fear closed around his heart like a fist.

He knelt down beside Gizmo again, drew the pink

bandana he'd taken from Kenzie's truck out of his pocket, and let the dog sniff it. "Where is Kenzie, buddy? Where is she? Gizmo, go find!"

Gizmo turned and plodded his way back up the slope, head down against the blowing snow. They'd gone on for about five minutes when Conrad saw a hint of dark hair and blue parka against the white.

He ran, shouting for her, fear constricting his chest. "Kenzie!"

She didn't move.

Gizmo reached her side and sat.

Conrad was a few steps behind him. "Good job, Gizmo! You're my hero."

He dropped to the ground beside Kenzie, shed his pack, and lifted her into his arms. "Kenzie, it's Conrad."

She was deathly pale.

Then he saw the blood on her jeans and her attempt at a tourniquet.

"Jesus." She couldn't be dead. "Kenzie! Can you hear me?"

Hawke knelt down beside him, spread an emergency blanket on the snow, Megs helping him to hold it in place against the wind. "Put her here."

Conrad laid Kenzie gently down on top of it, barely able to breathe.

Hawke yanked off a glove, pressed two fingers against her carotid artery. "She has a pulse."

Conrad exhaled, relief flooding him with warmth.

"Thank God!" Megs shared the news with Ops.

Hawke ran his hands over her injured thigh and checked beneath the make-shift tourniquet. "It looks like she has a single GSW to the thigh. I don't know how much blood she's lost, but it doesn't look like the artery was severed. The bone isn't broken."

"All good news," Moretti said.

Hawke wrapped the emergency blanket around her. "I don't think she'll make it down the mountain. It's not the gunshot wound that is going to kill her. It's the cold. We need to warm her up—and fast."

"What other choice do we have?" Megs asked. "No pilot can get a chopper up here. Visibility is zero, and the wind … "

Belcourt pointed. "The cabin. We can ride this out there."

Conrad had been there once a long damned time ago. "We'd have to cross that knife's edge in this wind to get there."

Belcourt glanced from Kenzie to Conrad to the cabin, probably doing the math in his head. "We can do it."

"You're as crazy as I am." Conrad took hand warmers out of his pack to put inside the emergency blanket with Kenzie.

"Get ready for a welcoming committee," Megs said. "Those bastards are probably holed up in there."

Moretti checked his AR. "Oh, I'm ready."

They talked through their options and quickly realized they had none. It was at least a two-hour descent to the vehicle with rapidly falling temps, and Kenzie might not have two hours. Even if they bundled her up in a sleeping bag and emergency blankets, she might be dead before they reached Rescue 1. If anything happened to slow them down—if they got lost or someone got hurt—they would lose her.

They had no choice. They would have to cross the knife's edge in high winds with Kenzie unconscious on the litter if they wanted to save her life. If they pulled it off, it would be a world-class bit of rescue work. If they didn't…

Kenzie wouldn't be the only one to die.

Chapter 23

THERE WAS nothing they could use to build an anchor up here—no trees or boulders, no human structures except for the cabin they hoped to reach. A Tyrolean traverse was impossible. So Megs and Belcourt became the anchors, staying far from the edge and setting up belays while Conrad, Hawke, and Moretti made Kenzie as warm as they could, secured her to the litter, and stepped into their climbing harnesses.

Moretti, armed with his rifle, went first, crawling through wind and snow to the razor's edge.

Lying flat, he moved forward until he was straddling the rock. "Fuck. I think I just castrated myself."

Slowly, inch by inch, he made his way to the other side. Once across, he hunched low so as not to catch the wind and moved toward the cabin, rifle now in his hands.

But Conrad's focus was on Kenzie. He tied the litter into the ropes, double-checking every knot, every connection. "Hold on, honey."

She hadn't moved or opened her eyes, and it scared the hell out of him.

Beside him, Gizmo whimpered, leaning over Kenzie, licking her face.

It put an ache in Conrad's chest. "I'm going to take good care of her, and Megs is going to take good care of you. When we all get home, I'm going to treat you to a steak dinner. Do you like rib eyes?"

At that moment, Moretti kicked open the cabin door and moved inside. He stepped out, shook his head, shouted back across the abyss. "Clear!"

Conrad went next, his upper body on top of the litter, inching it and himself along. The wind was unreal, forcing Conrad to grip the rock with his thighs. If he let himself be blown off this ridge, Kenzie would fall with him. Though he wouldn't fall far—Megs and Belcourt were taking up the slack—it still wouldn't be fun or safe for either of them.

Behind him, Gizmo barked in distress. Megs had attached his leash to her harness. Gizmo was so loyal to Kenzie that they'd been afraid he'd try to follow and end up falling or being blown away.

Lying on his belly and still roped in, Moretti met him halfway, helping Conrad to guide the litter off the sharp rock's edge and into the snow.

Kenzie was safely across.

Thank God.

Conrad reached the other side a moment later, crawling forward beneath a battering wind. He untied the rope, let Megs and Belcourt pull it back.

Hawke roped in and started across, a gear bag dangling over each side on cords—a safer option in this wind than a backpack.

But Conrad's concern now was for Kenzie. He and Moretti lifted the litter and carried it up wooden steps to the cabin door. Moretti shouldered the door open, and at last Kenzie was inside. Though it was still below freezing in the cabin, it was much warmer, the bitter wind held at bay by sturdy log walls and a thick stone foundation.

Conrad glanced around the dim interior. There was an old bed frame in one corner, an empty sleeping bag beside it. There were a few large ammo boxes next to the sleeping bag. A pot sat next to the fireplace and beside that a stack of firewood. "Someone has been living here."

He didn't have to wonder who it might have been.

"I'm going to check around the back, make sure no one's walking up behind us." Moretti grabbed his rifle and headed back out into the storm.

Conrad got a fire going, warmth spilling through the small space. He returned to Kenzie, drew her closer to the fire, stroked her face. "Kenzie, honey, can you hear me?"

He'd been an EMT for most of a decade, but this was somehow different. Everything he knew seemed to vanish from his mind, chased away by adrenaline. "Snap out of it, goddamn it."

Behind him, the door opened, and Hawke walked inside, dragging the gear bags with him. He bent down, hands on his knees, to catch his breath, then walked over to Conrad, gear bags and all.

"You've done your part. Let me take care of her."

Conrad nodded, moving aside for Hawke who ripped into one of the gear bags and pulled out an advanced first-aid kit.

In his earpiece, Conrad heard Megs tell Ahearn back in Ops that they were heading back down to Rescue 1. Belcourt asked Ahearn to tone out a vet and said he was carrying Gizmo down wrapped in an emergency blanket.

It would be a long, cold descent.

Hawke knelt at Kenzie's side. "Help me get her out of the sleeping bag. I need to check that bullet wound and make sure it's not bleeding. Then we can warm her up."

Conrad gently lifted Kenzie while Hawke got her out of the sleeping bag and then laid her gently back into the litter. "Kenzie, we're going to take care of you now."

She didn't move, didn't make a sound.

Hawke carefully removed the tourniquet then cut off her jeans to expose several blood-soaked bandages that had frozen together. "The cold probably helped slow the bleeding. As she warms up, it might be a bigger problem."

Hawke tossed the frozen Quikclot bandages aside, pressed fresh ones against the wound, and bound them in place with gauze. "Okay, buddy, time to strip down to your skivvies."

While Conrad shed his parka, summit pants, and jeans, Hawke undressed Kenzie down to her bra and panties—a strange thing to watch.

"Look at this." Hawke reached for something that was sticking out of her bra—and pulled out her cellphone.

You sweet, beautiful, smart woman.

If not for that cellphone…

Conrad didn't want to think about that.

Half-naked now, he discovered the cabin wasn't as warm as it had seemed at first. They worked quickly, zipping Kenzie back inside the sleeping bag and moving it closer to the fire. Hawke put a dry woolen hat on her head. Then Conrad crawled inside with her, holding her against him, trying to warm her with his body heat.

"Come on, Kenzie. Wake up."

The door opened, and Moretti strode inside. "I didn't see anyone.

He leaned his AR-15 against the wall and took off his parka. "I guess they must still be armed if they have all this ammo."

Moretti walked over to the ammo cans and opened one. "Jesus H Christ on a fucking crutch."

He reached in—and pulled out a fat stack of bills.

Conrad stared. "Holy fuck."

So that bastard who'd abducted her *had* been one of the robbers.

Moretti opened all of the ammo cans and found cash in each.

Hawke gave a low whistle. "There's no way those guys just walked off into the sunset and left all that loot here."

"Yeah." Moretti crossed the room, grabbed his weapon. "I'll stay alert."

"You better call that in." Hawke said. "Let dispatch know we found the money."

"Right."

Now they could do nothing but hope that the others made it back safely and wait for a rescue in the morning.

———

KENZIE HEARD HERSELF MOAN, pain driving her from sleep.

"I think she's coming around."

A warm hand stroked her cheek. "Kenzie, I'm right here."

Harrison.

"See if you can get her to drink."

Someone lifted her head.

"You need to drink, honey. Come on."

She felt the edge of a cup press against her lips and sipped, something warm and wonderful sliding down her throat.

Conrad coaxed her into drinking more. "That's it. We need to warm you up and get you hydrated."

She drank again, the warmth soothing.

"How do you feel?"

She managed one word. "Hurts."

"I'm going to give you some morphine, okay?" That sounded like Hawke.

She felt a prick—and everything faded.

She had no idea how much time had passed when Harrison's voice urged her awake again. "Drink."

She sipped.

"There you go. Good job."

She opened her eyes, found herself in his arms in a sleeping bag, the crackling of a fire somewhere nearby. But this wasn't her home. "Where are we?"

"We're in the old cabin at Hasting's mine."

It took a moment for his words to sink in, but when they did, it all came rushing back to her. Don. His gun. His arms flailing as she knocked him over the edge. Gizmo licking her face.

Her eyes flew wide on a jolt of panic. "Gizmo! Where—?"

"He's safe back in Scarlet. Megs has him."

"He's okay?"

"She took him to see a vet. Apart from exhaustion and some sore paws, he's okay." He kissed her forehead. "I've promised him a steak. That dog is a hero."

Hot tears blurred her vision, her emotions threadbare. "I was so afraid he'd be hurt. That bastard tried to shoot him. I threw myself at him, tried to stop him. I didn't mean to knock him over the edge."

Harrison's brows drew together in a frown. "Rest. Don't think about that now. You defended yourself and Gizmo. You're safe. Hawke and Moretti are here, too."

"Hey, Kenzie." Eric sat right beside her to her left.

Jesse stood behind him. "Glad to see you feeling better."

"Hi, guys." Then it dawned on her that she was all but

naked—and stuffed inside a sleeping bag with Harrison, who was all but naked, too. Well, this was different. "I never thought you'd be rescuing me."

Exhaustion pulled her back into sleep.

———

CONRAD WOKE to the sound of Moretti putting wood on the fire. He raised his head, watched the peaceful rise and fall of Kenzie's breathing.

She'd almost been killed trying to save Gizmo's life. She'd taken a bullet for him. And Gizmo would have died to stay by her side.

The thought put an ache in Conrad's chest.

Hawke met Conrad's gaze. "She's going to be okay."

"I almost lost her. If we had waited…" The thought put a knot in Conrad's gut.

"We didn't." Moretti stretched out on his sleeping bag, rifle at his side.

Conrad looked from Moretti to Hawke. "Thanks. I couldn't have gotten to her in time without you."

Hawke chuckled. "Bullshit."

"If anyone could have done this on his own, it's you. You kicked my ass running up the mountain." Moretti turned onto his back. "You're a fucking hero, man. Now shut up and let me get some shut-eye."

Hero.

This time the word didn't bother Conrad.

He drew the sleeping bag up to Kenzie's chin, doing his best to hold in every bit of warmth. He didn't know what tomorrow would bring, whether she would want him in her life again, but she was alive.

In this moment, that was everything.

———

BUNDLED UP AGAINST THE COLD, Kenzie watched the sky pass by overhead as Harrison, Eric, and Jesse carried her litter down the steep, snowy slope behind the cabin toward the waiting chopper. For some reason—probably the morphine—she found this all rather wonderful.

"You guys are doing a great job."

Harrison grinned down at her. "Hey, we're professionals, remember?"

Some of the crew from the helicopter joined them, helping to carry the litter the rest of the way. They lifted her into the bird, the rotors unmoving overhead, Harrison, Eric, and Jesse climbing in behind her.

"I've never been in a helicopter before."

Brandon Silver, one of Hawke's crew, stuck something on her finger. "Hey, Kenzie. I'm going to take good care of you till we get you to the hospital."

He put an oxygen mask on her face and started an IV. "This is just heated fluids. The oxygen is warm as well. They'll help bring up your core temp. I've got some heated blankets here, too."

The warmth felt wonderful.

"Harrison?"

A big hand took hers. "I'm right here."

"Stay."

"I promise."

The journey to the hospital lasted perhaps fifteen minutes—Kenzie was so out of it that she couldn't tell. She was lifted onto a gurney and hurried inside to the ER, where Malachi O'Brien took over her care, putting her on a bed with a body-length heating pad, giving her IV antibiotics and pain medication, examining the wound in her leg, and sending her off for an X-ray.

"You're incredibly lucky," he told her. "There's no damage to the bone or your artery. But you are going to need surgery to get that ball out. I'm going to page Dr. Warren. In the meantime, you rest. We want to stabilize your core temp first."

And for the first time since Harrison had walked out of her house, Kenzie and Harrison were alone.

"Thank you for—"

"Kenzie, I—"

They spoke at the same time, laughed.

"Please, Kenzie, there's something I need to say." He drew a breath. "I am so sorry for what I said to you. Yes, I *do* miss Gabby, but I miss you more."

He got a troubled expression on his face. "That's not coming out right."

Kenzie wasn't all that clear-headed, but she thought she knew what he was trying to say. Hope blossomed behind her breastbone. "I'm listening."

"You were right. I need help. I called Esri."

That was good news—but it wasn't what she'd been hoping for. "I'm so glad."

"I'm blowing this." He leaned back, let out a breath, ran a hand over the stubble on his chin. "Shit. I had no idea it would be this hard."

"Just say it."

His gaze met hers, a muscle clenching in his jaw. "I love you, Kenzie. I'm so sorry about what I said and how I walked out on you. I want to be a part of your life—if you'll have me back."

Kenzie's eyes filled with tears, her spirit soaring beyond the pain and fatigue in her body. "In my heart, you never left."

His relief was palpable. "I was on my way to your place with flowers and ice cream to apologize when I heard you'd been abducted. I was so afraid."

"Thank you for coming after me." More tears. "If you hadn't found me…"

"There is nothing in this world that could have kept me away from you."

Kenzie told him what had happened from the moment Don had walked in until she'd begun to lose consciousness. "I tried, Harrison, really I did. I tried to keep going, but I had to crawl, and it was so cold."

"You did enough. You hid that cellphone. You stood up to that son of a bitch, kept him off-balance. You stayed alive until we could reach you."

"I thought I was dead. All I could think was that Gizmo would die because of me—and that I would never see you again."

Harrison wiped a tear from her cheek. "That's not how our story ends."

He took over from there, telling her how Dree had seen and called the police and how he'd used the Find My Phone app on her laptop to find her. He told her how SWAT had called off the search and how he and the others had pulled together to go after her. He told her how Gizmo had found them and led them to her. He told her how they'd gotten her across the knife's edge to the cabin and done what they could to stabilize her.

"I'm so glad I was unconscious." Good freaking heaven! "I would have been terrified."

"I wasn't going to let anything happen to you."

"What about the other guy—Don's partner? That's who Don made me track. He stole Don's share of their money."

"No honor among thieves, I guess. We didn't find that bastard's partner—but we did find the money they stole."

"What?"

"It was there in the cabin stashed in ammo cans. We brought it back on the helicopter. Hawke turned it into the sheriff."

A new fear niggled at her. "What if this guy comes after Gizmo or me? What if he shows up—"

Then Dr. Warren walked in. "Young lady, don't take this the wrong way, but I'd like to see a lot less of you in the ER."

Kenzie smiled. "Me, too."

Harrison stayed with her, walking beside her as she was wheeled off to the operating room. "I'll be right here when you get out."

"Thanks." Then she remembered.

How could she have forgotten?

She squeezed his hand. "I love you, too."

———

CONRAD FOUND most of the Team in the surgery waiting area.

"How is she?" Megs sat with Gizmo on a leash beside her, his two front paws in protective bandages.

"She's sore and in some pain, but they say she's going to be okay." He knelt down. "How's the bravest dog ever?"

Gizmo wagged his tail and slathered Conrad's face with kisses.

"Are you going to tell us what happened up there?" Sasha had Gabby, who whined and pranced, tail wagging.

Conrad scooped the puppy up, held her. "I've missed you so much."

He sat, Gabby on his lap, Gizmo at his feet, and shared what Kenzie had told him about her ordeal, the horror of it hitting him hard.

He had come so damned close to losing her.

"She threw herself at the bastard to stop him from killing Gizmo. He fell backward over the edge. The round hit her in the thigh."

When Conrad reached the part where Kenzie realized she was lapsing into unconsciousness, he had to stop, his throat too tight to continue.

He swallowed, drew a breath. "Gizmo stayed with her, right beside her, until he heard us. He barked. I heard him and called for him. He led us to her."

He didn't have to tell them about the rescue. The entire Team had stood together in the Ops Room, listening.

Sasha wiped tears from her face then knelt down and hugged Gizmo. "You're just about the best dog ever. Yes, you, too, Gabby."

Then everyone had to pet Gizmo and praise him, which didn't bother him at all. He soaked up the attention —and deserved all of it.

"That was some epic climbing, seriously risky shit," Herrera said. "It had to be hairy crossing that ridge. I've been up there and seen it."

Moretti shook his head. "I've never experienced wind like that."

Hawke grinned. "How are the family jewels?"

"Fine." Moretti cleared his throat. "We had to straddle the rock."

A chorus of "Ohs" went up as understanding dawned.

This was followed by snorts and guffaws.

"I wonder what happened to the other guy—the partner who took off with the money." Ahearn stood, went to pour himself another cup of coffee. "He wouldn't just leave it there."

"No way," Moretti agreed. "I've never seen so much cash."

"I'm so glad you all made it back safely." Nicole sat on the floor next to Conrad and petted Gizmo. "I can't imagine how scary that must have been for Kenzie to be up there alone with that son of a bitch."

Belcourt, who'd sat quietly off to one side with Naomi and Winona, finally spoke. "She was never alone. We were with her the entire time."

"Mr. Conrad?"

Conrad looked over his shoulder to see Wendy from the newspaper standing there with a camera and notepad.

Ah, hell.

"I was just sitting over there and heard what you shared with everyone. Can I ask you a few questions? About the rescue, I mean. I thought SWAT called it off."

"They did, so the Team took over." Megs stood. "I'd be happy to answer your questions. Is there somewhere we can go where we won't disturb everyone?"

Conrad knew that Megs had already spent hours this morning being debriefed by the sheriff and SWAT. They had chewed her out for interfering with a law enforcement operation. To hear her tell it, she had laughed in their faces.

"As I recall, you all tucked tail and ran when the snow started to fall," she'd said. "I think the right words are, 'You're welcome.' This is why the Team exists—to save lives. If we had done this on your timetable, Kenzie would be dead."

Law enforcement would want to talk to him and Kenzie when she was up to it.

Conrad waited with his fellow Team members for almost an hour before Dr. Warren reappeared, a grin on his face.

"Good news. We got the bullet, and she's going to be fine. She'll be sore for a while, but she should have no permanent damage." The doctor rested a hand on Conrad's shoulder. "She's asking for you."

"Can I bring the dogs? It will mean so much to her."

Dr. Warren didn't look thrilled with the idea. "That's fine—but one at a time."

Conrad followed Dr. Warren back to recovery, Gizmo at his heel.

"She's in here."

Conrad found her dozing and sat in the chair beside her bed, waiting for her to wake up. Gizmo whined and strained at his leash, excited to see her.

"Hold on, buddy."

Kenzie's eyes fluttered open. "Harrison?"

"I'm right here." He got to his feet, holding tightly to Gizmo's leash. "Someone else is here, too."

Gizmo whimpered and would have jumped onto her bed if Conrad hadn't restrained him. In the end, Conrad let him stand with his front paws next to her.

"Gizmo!" Kenzie's face lit up. "I'm so happy to see you. How's my sweet boy?"

Clearly out of his doggy mind to be reunited with her, Gizmo whined and licked her, his entire back end wagging.

"I'm so sorry, Gizmo." Her eyes filled with tears. "You were very brave. You would have stayed with me until you died. I know you would have."

"He loves you." Conrad kissed her cheek. "So do I."

Chapter 24

KENZIE WAS DISCHARGED the next afternoon and went home to recover. Every muscle in her body was sore from adrenaline and exertion, and her thigh hurt like hell. Although she was dressed warmly, she couldn't seem to *feel* warm.

Harrison helped her up her front stairs, opening the door and standing back while she made her way inside on crutches. She stopped in the doorway and stared.

There were bouquets sitting on every visible surface—the kitchen counter, the table, window sills, her coffee table.

"Oh!" She looked up at Harrison. "Who sent these?"

He chuckled. "I think literally everyone. There are bouquets upstairs, too. I'm running out of places to put them."

"That's so sweet. My house looks like a flower shop." It smelled like one, too, the soft scents of roses, lilies, and freesia infusing the air.

"People in this town love you." He helped her get out

of her coat and settled her on the sofa, her leg elevated, a warm fleece throw tucked in around her.

The bouquet on the coffee table was enormous with three dozen red roses in a lovely crystal vase.

"Who sent that? It's beautiful."

"That's from me." He sat beside her, took her hand. "I love you most of all."

"That's so sweet of you."

He raised her hand to his lips. "Welcome home."

The next few days were a mix of wonderful and terrible. Wonderful because Harrison was right there, telling her he loved her, watching over her. Terrible because her ordeal seemed to have left its mark on her.

He took care of the dogs, kept a warm fire going, made meals, answered the door, took calls, brought her water and pain pills, did the grocery shopping and all the household chores. He also found creative ways the two of them could have sex without hurting her injured leg.

"You're spoiling me." She snuggled against his bare chest.

He stroked her hair. "Damn straight, I am."

But, although it was good to be home, she couldn't lose the feeling that something terrible was going to happen at any minute. Her second night home, she started having nightmares about Don shooting Gizmo and leaving him to die in the snow. It had seemed so real, and she'd woken up sobbing.

Conrad had held her, stroked her hair. "It's over. Gizmo is fine. Because of you, he's okay. Do you want to see him?"

She sniffed, nodded. "But it's against the rules to let him sleep in the bed."

"Screw the rules." Harrison got up, walked downstairs,

and returned with Gizmo and Gabby, both of whom glee-
fully jumped onto the bed, tails wagging.

"Hey, you two, leave room for me." Harrison nudged
Gizmo over. "Come on, buddy. That's my spot. She's
my woman."

That made Kenzie laugh.

It might have been silly, but it made a real difference to
be able to reach out in the middle of the night and feel
Gizmo safe and alive nearby.

Conrad had his troubles to face, too. He'd begun
having sessions with Esri once a week. She had diagnosed
him with post-traumatic stress, which was hard for him to
accept, not because he didn't see himself as human, but
because he had always associated PTSD with those who'd
served in the military—true heroes, he called them.
Though he often came home from his sessions drained, his
nightmares had stopped.

He seemed to find some peace, too, in donating all the
money from the two interviews he'd done to the fund that
the climbing community had set up for Bruce's widow and
children.

"Bruce would have liked that," Kenzie told him.

"Bruce would think I was nuts." Harrison laughed,
then took on an Aussie accent. "You're crackers, mate,
completely mental."

Halloween came and went, but Kenzie felt strangely
detached from it all—the fall fun, the change of seasons.
She got her stitches out, and she was able to ditch the
crutches, though walking was still painful.

That following Monday, she felt strong enough to go
back to work. Though she knew Don was dead—the Team
had been toned out the afternoon after her surgery to
retrieve his body—she felt ill at ease at the kennel. It was

her property, her business, a place she had always felt safe. Now, her sense of safety was shattered.

Worse than that, Don the Dickhead's partner still hadn't been found. Harrison and Hawke believed he was dead up there somewhere and would melt out in the spring, but no one knew for certain.

"I can't shake the feeling that he's going to come after Gizmo and me," she told Harrison over dinner one night. "Because of us, he lost the money he stole."

Harrison reached across the table, took her hand. "I've been talking with Herrera. We're going to install some security upgrades at the kennel."

"I can't afford that right now." She had lots of holiday reservations on the books, but she needed that money to ease the cash-flow crunch of slower months.

"Who said anything about you paying for it? You don't have to worry about money now."

"But you can't—"

He pressed his fingers to her lips, stilling her. "It's my money. I risked my neck to earn it. If I want to spend it on you, let me."

The weekend following Halloween, Harrison and Creed put in bullet-resistant glass doors and windows and a new lock system that required a key card to enter the kennel. They also installed a security door between the store and the kennel that also required a key card. The store was still open to the public, but the rest of the facility, including the classroom, was effectively on lockdown.

They also made some improvements to her house, installing deadbolts and a new security system.

"Thanks, guys. I feel safer."

But when the nightmares and anxiety didn't abate, Kenzie knew there was only one thing she could do. Call Esri and ask for help.

CONRAD STOOD on the summit of Eagle Ridge looking down at the resort's double-black runs and glades, ready for his ski test. It was his fifth day of training. So far this day was much better than the others, which had been spent indoors in meetings.

Conrad adjusted his goggles and his hold on his poles, waiting for Matt to give him the go-ahead.

"Sorry about this." Matt gave a helpless shrug. "I know you can ski well, but the insurance company demands that we test everyone."

"Hey, I don't mind. I'm getting paid to ski."

Matt chuckled then pressed a finger to his earpiece. "They're set, so whenever you're ready…"

Other patrollers and staff were spread out on the mountain, some to evaluate him and some because they just wanted to watch him ski.

That was fine by him.

"See you at the bottom." Conrad pushed off with his poles, shot out over the edge, and was off.

Sunshine. Wind and powder in his face. Fresh air.

This did *not* suck.

He tore down Silver Bullet, a double-black diamond, traversed to Snow in Summer, and flew through the glades, taking face shots all the way. He emerged from the trees, connected with Silver Bullet again, catching air on the moguls.

Sweet.

Hell, yeah, he could do this job—at least for a while.

All too soon it was over.

He edged to a stop, the sound of cheers and applause drifting down from above.

Moretti, who had already finished his test, walked over to him. "Show-off."

"Are they always like this—cheering and shit?"

"Nah, man. I think they all have a crush on you, even the guys. You ought to tell them all you're taken, or you're going to spend the season fending off women."

Conrad snorted. "Give me a break."

Then again, he had been asked to sign a lot of autographs this week.

Jesse turned his tips toward the lodge. "Let's grab some lunch while we can."

Over sandwiches and coffee, Moretti talked about the different runs and shared Ski Patrol traditions. "At the end of the day, we all stay in our gear until everyone is off the mountain. When the last patroller is in, we all crack a brew and celebrate."

"I like it."

The other patrollers joined them one by one as they finished their tests. Conrad was still learning their names.

"Great run, Conrad. You've really skied Everest?" This was Amanda.

Conrad nodded.

"Sick, dude." That was Travis.

"Where did you learn to ski?" Christa sat beside him, leaning a little too close.

"Alaska. I grew up on a homestead in the Brooks Range."

"That's hardcore." That guy was Doug.

No, Doug was digging through the fridge. That was Steve.

Moretti got up from the table and walked out of the room.

"I would love to ski Alaska." Christa touched Conrad's arm. "If you take a trip there, count me in."

Maybe Moretti was right about this crush thing.

Conrad didn't know how to answer. "Well…"

Matt stepped into the room, interrupting Conrad. "It won't surprise you all to know you passed. Insurance requirements have now been met."

Then Moretti's voice came over the PA system. "Attention all staff, Conrad has a serious girlfriend. I repeat, Conrad has a serious girlfriend."

Conrad froze, coffee cup in hand.

Moretti, I'm going to kick your ass.

Christa flushed pink and scooted away. "Why did he do that? We're just talking."

Conrad took a sip of coffee to hide his grin.

━━━

"SO THEN MORETTI gets on the PA system and says, 'Attention all staff, Conrad has a serious girlfriend. I repeat, Conrad has a serious girlfriend.'"

Kenzie had just taken a drink and almost choked laughing. "No way!"

"Then she scooted away from me and pretended like she hadn't been trying to flirt. I was going to kick Moretti's butt, but I think maybe I owe him."

Kenzie caught her breath. "Or maybe *I* owe him."

Conrad leaned forward, a teasing glint in his eyes. "Are you jealous?"

"Not at all." She dabbed her lips, set her napkin aside. "You didn't cross the Knife Blade of Death in a blizzard to save her life. You did that for me."

That's true." His lips curved in a lopsided grin. "How was your day? How did your session with Esri go?"

"Pretty well. She's given me some ways of coping when

I feel anxious and afraid." It was good just to know that Kenzie didn't have to deal with this alone.

But she had more important news to share.

"I have something to tell you. I hope it will make you happy." She put on a straight face. "I went to my OB-GYN last week."

His brow furrowed—then his eyes went wide. "You're not ... are you? I mean ... you can't be ... But if you are, that's okay. I'll be here with you."

God, he was sweet.

"I got an IUD." Just in case he didn't understand what that meant, she leaned forward and whispered. "*No more condoms.*"

He grinned. "Oh, you little scamp."

She picked up her napkin, threw it at him, and ran for the stairs. Her leg was still sore, making her limp, slowing her down. But speed wasn't the point.

She heard his chair scoot from the table, heard his heavy footfalls on the floor, and was swept up in his arms, laughing.

He swung her over his shoulder, gave her a smack on the butt. "You know just what to say to make me hard."

He carried her to the bedroom, set her on her feet, the two of them shedding their clothes as quickly as they could. They fell to the bed together, rolling, lips finding lips, hands seeking sensitive skin, looking for ways to please. He knew her so well, knew what she loved, what drove her crazy. Licking and sucking her nipples. Stroking her clit *right there*. Sliding his fingers deep inside her.

"*Now.*"

He raised himself up, his gaze meeting hers as he settled himself between her thighs. She reached down, guiding him as he buried his cock inside her.

He groaned, his big body covering hers. "Fuck. You feel ... *so* good."

There was no latex now, no chemicals, no artificial lubrication, nothing to separate the two of them as he moved in and out of her, driving deep.

Kenzie wrapped her legs around him, pressed her heels into the shifting muscles of his ass, opening herself fully to him, urging him on. "God, *yes.*"

It felt so good. *He* felt so good, thick and hard inside her.

He shifted his hips to ride her high, stroking her clit with his cock, stretching her, filling her. She moaned his name, her nails digging into his back. Every thrust brought her closer to climax, leaving her desperate.

She cried out, pleasure washing over her, a tide of luminous bliss.

But he was right there with her. "I love you, Kenzie. God, I love you."

He groaned, coming apart in her arms, spilling himself inside her.

———

CONRAD SHOVED the last box of his shit into Kenzie's truck. "That's it."

Mrs. Beech's house had finally sold. He and Kenzie had talked about it, and they had agreed that it was time they quit pretending that he had his own place. He was always at her house, so why not make it official? Most of his stuff was already there. Though he had more than enough money in savings to buy some showy mountain home for the two of them and the dogs, he knew it was important to her to live next to her business.

Besides, he liked her house. There were a few things

that needed fixing—the Victorian trim, the roof, back steps —but he liked projects. It was homey and charming and had room for his gear and a couple of spare rooms for guests—or maybe kids one day. Not that he was making plans or anything.

He shut the tailgate and closed the topper.

"Are you leaving?" His neighbor stood on her front lawn in a bright yellow housedress and pink frilly apron. "I was just getting used to having you here."

Conrad chuckled. "The house sold. It's time for me to move on."

"Well, that's too bad," the woman said. "You're the most interesting neighbor I've had. Take care of Miss Morgan. Yes, I know you're moving in with her. The two of you are all kissy-kissy. I might be eighty-two, but I still remember what it was like to be young and horny and in love."

Conrad and Kenzie exchanged a glance, both trying not to laugh.

Conrad grabbed the box of chocolates from the front seat of Kenzie's truck and carried them to the old woman. "These are for you. Take care, ma'am. If you ever need help around your place, give Kenzie's kennel a call. I'd be happy to help."

She took the box from him. "Aren't you a sweet thing? You're a handsome fellow up close—big, too. All the best to you."

Then she turned and went inside.

They were almost back to the house, Conrad behind the wheel, when Kenzie's cellphone rang.

"This is Kenzie. Yes, now's a fine time, Sheriff."

Sheriff Pella? Something must be up.

"Are you serious?" She turned to Harrison. "They found the other guy's body. Some hikers spotted a leg sticking out of the snow at the base of the razor's edge. He fell off the other side from his buddy."

That was a relief.

Kenzie went back to her phone call. "Thanks, Sheriff. What? Really? I'm honored, but I didn't do anything. Seriously you don't have to... Really? You're kidding. But I ... Yes, sir. November twentieth. Six p.m. Yes, sir. Thank you."

She ended the call, looked over at Conrad, a strange expression on her face.

"What did Pella want?"

"He said his department and the Scarlet Springs Town Council want to give Gizmo and me Distinguished Citizen medals. That's bananas."

"It doesn't seem bananas to me. You kept your head during a terrifying ordeal and helped investigators recover the money."

"I was unconscious when the money was found. I didn't do anything. You, Eric, and Jesse found the money. You should get the medals—and the reward."

"Reward?"

"The company of the armored vehicle that was robbed is giving me a reward of thirty-five grand. That's bananas."

Conrad was so surprised by this that he almost missed their turn. "Thirty-five large. That's sweet."

"I only did what the man with the gun told me to do."

"You trained Gizmo, and Gizmo found the robber's hideout. That seems like something to me."

"Well, Gizmo deserves the medal, not I."

"I guess you'll have to take that up with the sheriff and Town Council."

KENZIE STOOD at the front of the Town Council meeting room in Town Hall holding Gizmo's leash, her gaze moving over the audience. Everyone was there—or almost everyone. Her friends on the Team. Rain and Joe. Ellie and the twins. The Belcourts—Winona, Chaska, and Naomi. Dr. Warren. Cheyenne and her parents. Conrad's former neighbor wearing a fine little hat. Even Bear, who had found the table with the cupcakes and had pink frosting on his beard.

She drew a breath, tried not to be nervous.

"For bravery in the face of danger, for unfailing loyalty, and for countless hours of selfless service to this community, I am pleased to present you, Gizmo, with the Sheriff's Distinguished Service Medal."

Sheriff Pella bent down and slipped the medal around Gizmo's neck.

The room exploded with cheers and applause.

Kenzie knelt down, petted Gizmo's chest. "Shake the sheriff's hand, Gizmo."

Gizmo shook.

"Good boy!"

Laughter.

Sheriff Pella reached for another medal and came to stand before Kenzie. "For unshakable courage in the face of terrible danger and for years of service to your community, I am pleased to present you, Kenzie Morgan, with the Sheriff's Distinguished Service Medal. Congratulations."

The room burst into cheers and applause again as Sheriff Pella slipped the medal over her head and then shook her hand.

"Thank you, sir." Kenzie met Harrison's gaze.

His smile almost took her breath away.

Then Mr. Winslow, the district manager of the armored car company, stepped forward in his suit and tie, a piece of paper in his hands. He introduced himself, talked about the important role armored vehicles played in society, then shared the history of the company until even Kenzie had forgotten why they were all here.

Megs, who was a member of the Town Council, cleared her throat. "Maybe it's time to move on."

Mr. Winslow seemed to catch himself. "We are so grateful to Ms. Morgan and to Gizmo for enabling the authorities to recover the money stolen from us in September. As a sign of our gratitude, here is a check for thirty-five-thousand dollars."

More cheers and applause.

Kenzie took the check, shook his hand.

She'd thought long and hard about this and knew what she had to do. "Thank you, sir, but I don't deserve this. Yes, Gizmo and I tracked one of the men who stole your money, but only because the other one pointed a gun at me. It was the Team that recovered your money. They risked their lives in a blizzard to save mine. Without them, neither Gizmo nor I would be here tonight."

She swallowed the lump in her throat. "Thank you for this, but I am signing the check over to the Rocky Mountain Search and Rescue Team."

People leaped to their feet, cheering, whistling, the applause deafening.

Megs gaped at Kenzie for a moment, looking utterly astonished. She walked over to Kenzie, hugged her. "On behalf of the Team, which you have served many years, I accept your insanely generous donation. Thank you, Kenzie. You are an angel."

CONRAD DRANK the last of his beer. "Come dance with me."

The Timberline Mudbugs were playing tonight, a pre-Thanksgiving show. They had just slipped into a slow dance, a Zydeco rendition of *When A Man Loves A Woman*.

"Dance?" Kenzie's face was flushed from a little too much alcohol. Joe and Rain had told her to order anything she wanted tonight on the house. That had included one two many Sex in the Spotlights. "I was shot in the leg. I don't know if I can dance."

Conrad slid a hand up her thigh. "The last time you wrapped your thighs around my waist, your leg seemed pretty strong to me."

Her cheeks got pinker. "Sasha, can you watch Gizmo and Gabby for me?"

Conrad had made good on his promise to Gizmo and ordered him a rib eye, cutting bits and pieces of it off for little Gabby. The dogs were now curled up at Kenzie's feet in a protein coma, Gizmo still wearing his medal.

Sasha reached down to pet Gabby. "I would love to."

Conrad led Kenzie through the restaurant to the dance floor, waving to Christa and Amanda, who were listening to the band, drinks in their hands.

They waved back, but their gazes were fixed on Kenzie.

He took her into his arms, the two of them moving to the slow, sensual rhythm of the music, the feel of her sweet in his arms. She followed easily despite her leg and the booze, one of her hands in his, the other on his hip, a tipsy-happy smile on her face.

"You blew us all away tonight. I was surprised, but I shouldn't have been. You're an amazingly generous person."

"I couldn't take a reward for something I didn't do."

"I thought Megs was going to faint."

Kenzie laughed. "She looked shocked, didn't she?"

"Completely gobsmacked."

Kenzie looked up at him, her smile gone. "Now I understand how you felt when you didn't want people to call you a hero."

"What do you mean?"

"At the ceremony, everyone acted like I'd done something remarkable. But the truth is, all I did was get abducted."

"All I did was not get crushed by ice."

"That's not true. You've summited mountains. You climbed out of a crevasse and saved yourself. You battled that blizzard and saved Gizmo and me."

He stopped dancing, caught her chin, lifted her gaze to his. "Don't you know that you saved me, too? A few months ago, I was barely holding on. I was dead inside. I had forgotten what it feels like to be happy, to wake up in the morning and look forward to the day. *You* brought me back to the world of the living."

Every word he'd just said was true. If not for Kenzie…

She shook her head. "I didn't do that. Gabby did. I hoped she would. That was the whole point. I'd hoped…"

Kenzie's eyes went wide as if she'd just said something she hadn't meant to say.

And the pieces came together with a *click*.

Conrad swirled her in a circle, laughing. "Gabby and Gizmo never had problems getting along, did they? Tell me the truth."

"Well, I … You … Um … No." Kenzie's cheeks flushed scarlet, a rush of words spilling from her. "But pets help reduce stress, and I knew you loved dogs. I didn't want to lie to you, but I cared about you and hated seeing you hurting so I had to find a way to get a puppy into your life so that you'd have someone at least and …"

Her words faded and she looked guiltily up at him. "I'm sorry. I shouldn't have lied to you. Are you angry with—"

He stilled her with a soft, slow kiss. "Hell, no. I'm touched that you cared so much. But you're wrong. It wasn't Gabby. It was *you*, Kenzie."

"You mean that?"

He thought of what the Lama had said to him and couldn't help but smile. "The night before I left the monastery, the Lama told me that, if I hadn't found my truth there in all that time, then I needed to move on. He was right. *You* are my truth, Kenzie. You're my truth and my peace."

Conrad took her mouth with his, kissing her deeper this time, holding her close, her arms sliding around his neck.

The music ended, and still, they stood together kissing, oblivious to everyone around them, unaware of the quiet laughter and smiles.

Up on stage, the lead singer for the Mugbugs took the mic. "This next one is for the couple making out in the middle of the dance floor. Hit it!"

In the next instant, the band broke into *Fooled Around and Fell in Love*.

But Conrad and Kenzie stayed as they were, lost in each other.

Epilogue

July 28

KENZIE'S ALARM went off at five a.m. She turned it off, sat up, found Harrison already dressed and feeding the dogs. "I can't believe I let you talk me into this."

Conrad looked over his shoulder at her, clearly amused. "You promised to have a good attitude, remember?"

"Right." She hopped naked out of bed. "Let's do this."

He chuckled. "That's better."

Climbing fourteeners was not on her bucket list. She'd climbed Mt. Evans but hadn't enjoyed it. Still, climbing was Harrison's passion. He had asked her to climb Mt. Sneffels with him, and it seemed only right to try.

They'd brought Gizmo and Gabby, who was now ten months old and almost as big as Gizmo. She would be taking her SAR exam next month and loved being in the outdoors. But they'd had to leave little Prince at the kennel. It had broken Kenzie's heart to leave him behind, but Harrison had insisted there was no way a little Cavalier King Charles spaniel could handle Mt. Sneffels.

Kenzie had brought Prince home just before Christmas after Mari had smacked him on the nose right in front of her during a lesson. She'd decided then that Mari lying to her children would be on Mari's conscience, but her leaving the poor puppy to be abused would be on hers. Kenzie hadn't regretted it. There wasn't a sweeter dog in the entire world.

She, Harrison, and the two big dogs had driven over the Continental Divide and stayed in a hotel in the mountain town of Ouray. They'd had a picnic and gone wading in the Uncompahgre River before heading to their hotel.

Yesterday had been the fun part of this trip. Today was about pain.

Harrison checked his backpack while she dressed and filled their water bottles—four each for herself and Harrison and four each for the dogs. They ate a breakfast of coffee, toast, boiled eggs, and fruit in their room and grabbed the packed lunches they'd had room service prepare last night. Then it was time to hit the road.

Ouray was beautiful, a tiny town nestled in a narrow valley surrounded by steep mountains. It was less than an hour's drive to the trailhead, which sat just above timberline. They parked, climbed out, got the dogs, then shouldered their packs.

Okay, so Kenzie was carrying a small daypack with trail mix, dog treats, and water. Harrison was the one with the heavy backpack. He had filled it with all kinds of gear they wouldn't need to help him prepare for the big expedition.

He was training again.

His climbing bug had come back the moment ski season ended, and he'd been negotiating with his sponsors about trying for the Khumbu Triple Crown—alone. No man in history had done that.

It had been Bruce's big dream to climb Nuptse, Everest, and Lhotse in one expedition, and Harrison hadn't been able to let that idea go. It wasn't about ego or achievement this time, but honoring the life and legacy of his best friend.

A part of Kenzie had wanted to rage at him when he'd brought it up with her. What was she supposed to do while he was gone—sit by the phone and wait to find out that he'd fallen or frozen to death or been buried alive in an avalanche? But she had kept her fears and her tears to herself.

She'd known he would want to climb again once his heart had healed. He'd talked about writing a book or opening a store that sold climbing gear, but that just wasn't Harrison. She loved him for the man he was. She couldn't take his dreams from him—even when they scared her to death.

More than that, he needed a kind of closure that therapy couldn't give him, the kind he could only get up there where he and Bruce had spent so much time together. She couldn't get in the way of his finding peace, even at the expense of her own.

They leashed the dogs and headed for the trailhead. The trail itself was just a skinny path that wound its way upward through talus and dark, jagged rock.

"Are you sure this isn't the trail to Mordor?" Kenzie joked.

Conrad grinned. "Hey, this is pretty easy going."

The dogs loved it, their noses in the wind, but Kenzie quickly found herself out of breath. She wasn't used to this kind of exertion. She stopped, put her hands on her knees. "I think you're going to have to jog to the summit with the dogs a few times to keep yourself from getting bored. I'm slowing you down."

He stopped beside her. "That's okay. We'll take this at your pace. This is about us being together, not about rushing to the summit."

When she'd caught her breath, they moved on.

The scenery around them was stunning, the valley below them full of wildflowers. Kenzie stopped to take it in, the sight breathtaking. She'd seen wildflowers and mountain meadows before, but she'd never seen anything like this.

"Yankee Boy Basin." Conrad drank from his water bottle. "It puts on quite a wildflower show in early summer."

She pulled out her cellphone, took a few photos that could never do justice to what her eyes were seeing.

Maybe climbing mountains wasn't all pain and misery.

━━━

CONRAD PULLED off Kenzie's boot. "You've got the start of a blister here. A little moleskin will fix this."

While she nibbled on trail mix, he fished the first-aid kit out of his pack, snipped off a piece of moleskin, and taped it to the hot spot on her left heel.

He wanted this to be fun for her. He was sure she could make it. Mt. Sneffels wasn't the toughest fourteener by any measure, but he wanted today to be a special memory, not something she wanted to forget.

It was the most important day of his life.

"You should be good now. Put your boot on and see how it feels."

Her eyes went wide, and she pointed, delight on her face. "Look."

He turned his head and spotted a fat marmot on a rock nearby. "Hey, buddy."

The dogs were curled up, napping, and didn't care.

She fumbled for her cellphone, took a few photos. "He's so cute."

"He's probably used to climbers. He's hoping we'll leave some food crumbs for him to nibble."

She slipped her phone back into her pocket, put on her boot, and stood, taking a few steps. "That's much better. I don't even feel it now."

He stood, shouldered his pack, and grabbed Gabby's leash. "Come on, girl."

Clouds rolled in from the west, threatening rain, the sun still shining in a blue sky to the east. They needed to be on and off the summit before that storm rolled in. At fourteen thousand feet elevation, lightning was a real hazard.

Kenzie glanced up at him, looking beautiful, her cheeks flushed pink from exertion. "So far, there's only one thing about mountain climbing that I don't like."

"What's that?"

"It's all uphill."

He grinned. "True that."

But as they went, it was clear to Conrad that Kenzie *was* enjoying herself. She took photos of everything they encountered along the way—wildflowers, chipmunks, marmots, pika, the little rivers, lakes, and waterfalls in the valley below.

"It's beautiful up here."

"I've always said that this is scenery you have to earn. You can't get it sitting at home on your sofa."

"Is that why you love it—the natural beauty?"

"That's part of it." How could he explain it? "I love the exertion and the physical challenge. I love the fresh air and wide-open spaces."

"I bet that reminds you of homesteading with your dad."

"Could be." He hadn't thought of that. "Up here, everything is simple like it must have been at the beginning. This is my church—all of this."

Until he'd met Kenzie, this had been his entire life.

They stopped for lunch in the shade of a large boulder at Lavender Col—roast beef sandwiches, carrot sticks, and apples for them and water for the dogs. From here, the climb got more challenging, and Conrad wanted Kenzie to be rested.

She ate with enthusiasm. "Why does food always taste better when you've been outdoors all day?"

Conrad had to laugh. "That rule doesn't apply to the freeze-dried shit we take on big expeditions."

After they'd eaten, he talked her through the rest of the climb.

"We're going to let the dogs off their leashes here. I don't want them pulling you off balance, and they'll do better on their own. We'll head up through this col and then head a little to our left over the talus. There are some big rocks. They can flip under your foot or roll on you and break bones. So watch your step, and watch for falling rock, too. We'll go through the V-Notch at the top of the talus, which takes us to another, steeper col with big cliffs on either side. If there's snow, I'll break out the ice axes and help you with that. After that, there's an area with a lot of exposure."

Kenzie looked like she wasn't sure this was a good idea after all. "Like that knife's edge leading to the Hastings mine?"

"Nothing like that, but it is exposed with some big drop-offs. I'm going to create an anchor for you so you can belay yourself up that area. I wouldn't have brought you here if I didn't know that you can handle it."

He could tell she was nervous, but she nodded.

"Before we reach the summit, we'll have to do some scrambling—climbing with your hands. The dogs might need a little help. I'll be right there to talk you through it."

She stood. "I'm ready."

It meant a lot to him that she trusted him enough to keep going.

"Hey, I'm with one of the world's greatest mountain climbers. I have nothing to be afraid of, right?"

———

KENZIE REACHED the summit of Mt. Sneffels, Gizmo at her side, just after two in the afternoon. "I did it! I can't believe I did it!"

That last part had been physically tough and more than a little scary, but Harrison had been right behind her, guiding her all the way.

Harrison grinned down at her from behind his mirrored sunglasses, Gabby beside him. "I knew you could handle it."

A handful of people, other climbers, sat around on the small summit, eating, hydrating, taking photographs. Some of them smiled and waved. Others stared.

"That's Harrison Conrad."

"The dude is a badass."

Kenzie barely heard them, her attention on the amazing view. High peaks dotted with snow reached for the sky in every direction. There were lakes and valleys below, rivers and streams, meadows and forest. It took her breath away.

"It's beautiful, truly, Harrison."

He came up beside her, took her hand. "Everest is more than twice this high in elevation. You stand there on the summit, freezing your ass off and looking down on the entire world. You can feel eternity up there."

"How about here?" She knew this posed no challenge for him.

"Here, too. These mountains were formed eighty million years ago. It's hard to wrap your mind around that. I'm going to find the summit registry."

While he did that, she took out her cellphone and took photos, wanting to remember this place. It was her first fourteener with Harrison, after all.

"Hey, come sit over here," Harrison called to her. "You need to sign the registry."

She put her phone away, carefully negotiating her way across the jumble of rock that was the mountain's highest point. "What's that?"

"All the major peaks in Colorado have registries. When you make it to the top, you write in your name, the date, and a little bit about your climbing party."

She sat on a rounded stone beside him. "Okay."

He handed her a steel canister. "Open it up. The registry's inside."

She unscrewed the top and tipped it into her palm. Out came a tattered, rolled-up paper scroll of sorts and a small velvet box. "I wonder what that is."

"Open it."

Something in the tone of his voice drew her gaze to his. "Harrison?"

"Go on."

She lifted back the top—and stared. "Oh!"

A glittering oval diamond nestled in white gold stared back at her.

She looked up, stunned, to find Harrison on one knee.

"There are probably a lot of reasons you shouldn't marry me. I go away for long periods of time. My job is really dangerous. I do my best to be safe, but you know only too well that anything can happen."

"Dude, you're not really selling it," a man's voice said.

Kenzie hadn't realized that everyone else on the summit had stopped what they were doing to watch and listen—and film this with their cellphones.

Harrison ignored the guy. "But I promise you that I'll always do everything I can to get home to you. *You* are my highest height, Kenzie. Without you, nothing I've done and nothing I will ever do even matters."

Tears blurred her vision, happiness giving her heart wings. "Of course, I'll marry you. Did you even think for a moment I might say no?"

As he slid the ring onto her finger, the summit of Mt. Sneffels at 14,150 feet above sea level, exploded into cheers.

———

Ten months later

KENZIE SAT in the Ops Room with the others, waiting for her phone to ring, Gizmo and Gabby napping near her feet. For days now, she'd barely been able to breathe. Harrison was pushing for the last summit today and far beyond the ability of anyone to help him should something go wrong.

She'd told herself to get used to this—the helplessness, the anxiety. This wasn't the only time in her life when she'd be waiting and wondering whether her husband was still alive. She'd signed on for this when she'd fallen in love with him. But that didn't make the waiting or the worrying any easier.

"This is the hardest part," said Joanie, Bruce's widow.

When she'd heard what Harrison was attempting and why he was doing it, she'd contacted Kenzie and the two had become good friends. She'd flown all the way from Perth with her two sons, Richard and James, to be here with Kenzie. The boys were outside, playing on one of Hawke's fire engines under Brandon Silver's supervision.

Laurie, Harrison's mother, glanced at her watch again. "I used to send him away with his father in a bush plane and then spend the entire summer wondering whether I'd see him again."

"That would be hard for a mum," Joanie said.

Harrison and his mother had mended their fences, and she'd come to be a support for Kenzie—and to get to know her new daughter-in-law.

Everyone else in the Ops Room was ready for a celebration. Team members stood around, talking and joking, checking gear. Fruit and veggie trays sat on the meeting table with several pizzas, while soda and beer chilled in whiskey barrels of ice. There were bottles of champagne in the fridge, too, ready to be opened at the big moment when Harrison called from the summit of Lhotse.

He'd summited Nuptse three days ago and Everest yesterday, calling Kenzie from their summits to let her know he was okay and to tell her he loved her. He had sounded strong and in good spirits, which had been a relief. But the moment she'd hung up the phone, Kenzie had gone back to worrying.

His plan had been to push himself through the night, resting below the Death Zone of 26,000 feet only long enough to eat and recover before moving on again. He'd been expected to summit Lhotse a few hours ago.

If he succeeded—and he was so close—he'd become the first man in history to climb all three 8000-meter peaks alone and the first to do it in only five days. But if anything went wrong…

Nothing could go wrong.

Megs sat at the Ops desk, listening in to one of the adventure climbing sites, just as they'd done the day when Bruce and the Stenger twins had been killed. Every once in a while, a climbing party coming back to Base Camp would say they'd passed him on their way down or spotted him through binoculars somewhere in the distance. But for a while now, there'd been nothing but silence.

Kenzie willed herself to eat a slice of pizza and some fruit, doing her best to laugh and smile with the others, time seeming to creep by.

There came a burst of static.

A woman's voice came over the Internet. "We've got a storm front moving in."

Kenzie's pulse took off, the Ops Room growing quiet as they listened to the rest of the weather report.

Joanie reached over, squeezed Kenzie's hand. "He'll be off the summit by then, love. Bruce always told me Conrad was the brains of the operation."

Kenzie hoped what Joanie said was true. Harrison had promised to come home and make a baby with her. She would hold him to that promise.

———

CONRAD PUT one foot in front of the other, his fingers aching from cold, his body near its limits. He'd spent more time in the Death Zone on this expedition than ever before, and even with supplemental oxygen, he could feel its effect on mind and body.

One step. Breathe. Another step. Breathe.

He couldn't sit. He couldn't rest. If he did, he'd

become just another frozen corpse littering the mountainside.

The summit wasn't far now. He would have been there a few hours ago if he hadn't stopped to render medical aid to a German climber who had developed high-altitude pulmonary edema. He'd given the man an injection of Nifedipine out of his own pack and helped his party get him down to a lower elevation.

Now, the summit was within sight.

Step. Breathe. Step. Breathe.

The sensation in his body went beyond fatigue, beyond cold, beyond pain. Every moment brought pure, distilled agony, his mind screaming at him to stop.

Step. Breathe. Step. Breathe.

Kenzie.

He'd promised her he'd come home. He'd promised her a baby. What the hell was he doing here? He ought to be home with her. He could turn around right now and head back to camp, make a meal, and sleep.

But Bruce had wanted this.

Harrison couldn't give up now. He was close, so close.

Step. Breathe. Step. Breathe.

Pain became an aching numbness as he shut out any thought of giving up.

Step. Breathe. Step. Breathe.

He willed himself onward, willed his mind to focus, exhaustion and extreme altitude a threat to mental clarity. Climbing without fixed ropes or a belay meant that one slip could mean death.

Step. Breathe. Step. Breathe.

Another step and another and another, and, at last, he was there.

It took a moment for that fact to penetrate his pain and exhaustion. When it did, adrenaline surged through him, boosting his energy. He turned, glanced back at the summit of Everest, where he'd been just yesterday, then looked down at the Khumbu Valley below. He was there. He'd made it.

A torrent of emotion washed through him, making his throat go tight. He ripped off the oxygen mask, took the sat phone out of his pocket, and called Kenzie, not wanting her to worry. "I made it. I'm here on the summit of Lhotse, and I'm fine."

In the background, he thought he heard pandemonium —cheers, shouts, Team members calling his name.

"Oh, thank God!" She sounded like she was in tears. "Congratulations. I'm so proud of you. We all are. Now come home to me. There's a storm headed your way."

"I see it. I'll be on my way back down in a minute." He glanced at the approaching clouds. "Tell the Team and my mom hi. And tell Joanie …"

Conrad's throat went tight. "Tell her I got it for him."

"I will. Everyone sends their congratulations. I love you. Be safe."

"I promise. I love you, too." He ended the call, tucked the phone back into his pocket, energized by the sound of her voice.

He reached into another pocket, took out a small steel cylinder. Inside, was the magazine cover of him and Bruce together on the summit of Everest. He pushed the cylinder deep into the ice and snow, stomping on it with his boot, driving it deep.

Tears filled his eyes, a choked sob rising from his chest. "We got it, Bruce. Do you hear that, buddy? We got it."

He remained just a moment longer, letting peace sink into his chest. Then he put on his oxygen, turned, and began the long descent back to camp.

CONRAD STOPPED in at the Tengboche Monastery on his way back to Kathmandu to pay his respects. It was strange to see the place again, to hear the chanted prayers, smell the incense. The days when he'd taken refuge here seemed so distant now.

The Lama received him, shared a meal and tea with him, listening to his account of the climb. "You are not the same man who left here all these months ago."

"No." Conrad couldn't help but smile. He pulled a photo of Kenzie out of his jacket. "She's the reason. My wife, Kenzie."

"I am happy for you."

"May I ask you a favor?"

"Of course."

"I have a friend at home whose father came from Tibet. Her ancestors were monks here long ago. I would like to take something back for her—a scarf perhaps, a word or blessing from you. It would mean so much to her."

The old man nodded, chuckling. "What is that song?"

At that, the Lama began singing. "It's a small world after all…"

It was either the most sublime or the craziest moment of Conrad's life.

Ten days later

KENZIE DROVE with Laurie and Joanie and her boys to DIA to welcome Conrad home. The media were there in force, thronging around International Arrivals. He was getting a hero's welcome, whether he wanted one or not.

God, she couldn't wait to see him, to hold him in her arms again.

On the screen above, it said his flight had landed ten minutes ago. He had a lot of gear, and he had to get through customs, so it would probably take a while.

She, Laurie, and Joanie sat and talked quietly, keeping clear of the reporters, while the two boys pretended to be airplanes.

"There he is!" Laurie pointed.

Kenzie looked up, hear heart swelling at the sight of him.

He stepped out of customs, pushing a cart piled high with duffel bags. Reporters and TV cameras crowded around him, everyone asking questions at once.

"How does it feel to be the first man in history to conquer all three peaks alone and in only five days?"

"After this, what's next?"

"Which peak posed the greatest challenge?"

Kenzie couldn't hold herself back. She ran into his arms, pressed her face into his chest, fighting tears. "I'm so glad you're home."

He held her tight, kissed her, ignoring the reporters. "God, I missed you."

"Your mom, Joanie, and her boys are here, too."

"Harrison!" Laurie hurried over.

"Hey, Mom."

Kenzie stepped aside, making room so Laurie and Joanie could welcome him home, the two of them hugging him tight.

Joanie blinked back tears. "He loved you like a brother."

Harrison kissed Joanie on the cheek. "I loved him, too."

Harrison answered a few questions from reporters

before they headed out to the minivan Kenzie had rented to transport both people and gear.

He looked up at the Rockies. "I can't wait to get home."

Kenzie had to warn him. "The town has gone crazy over this, so be ready. They want to have a reception for you at Knockers tomorrow. They're talking about naming a street after you."

"What?" He grinned, shook his head. "That's bananas."

They drove out of Denver and toward Scarlet Springs, the boys asking Harrison a thousand different questions, including the heartbreaking, "Did you see our dad?"

"No, I didn't see him, but I did feel him up there."

They were a couple miles outside of Scarlet when they saw their first sign.

Welcome home, Conrad, you badass!

It wasn't the only one. As mountain residents often did in the wake of big events, people had spray painted messages onto old boards, squares of plywood, or anything else they had lying around.

It warmed Kenzie's heart to see how the words touched Harrison.

Just outside Scarlet, they came to the town limits.

Scarlet Springs Town Limit, Pop. 1,458, Elevation 8,936.

But the sign had changed. Someone had tacked on a two-by-four.

Home of Harrison Conrad.

"Good grief." He shook his head again, but there was a smile on his face.

"You must be tired," Laurie said. "We should let you catch up on sleep."

Harrison nodded. "Pretty beat, yeah."

Kenzie dropped Laurie, Joanie, and the boys off at the Forest Creek Inn and headed home. "The dogs are going to go crazy when they see you."

He grinned. "I can't wait."

He stepped through the front door, arms loaded, to a welcoming committee that whined and licked and wagged tails and jumped on him. "Hey, Gabby, girl. God, I missed you. You, too, Gizmo. Hey, Prince, you loverboy. Yes, good doggies!"

Kenzie helped him carry his stuff inside, finally alone with her husband. "Do you want anything to eat before you go to sleep?"

He had to be seriously jet-lagged, not to mention depleted from the climb. He reached for her, drew her against him. "I want you."

"You have energy for that?"

"Are you kidding? I haven't seen you in two months. Besides, I promised you a baby, didn't I?"

Those words put a flutter in her belly. "Yes."

They went upstairs to the bedroom and undressed each other, Kenzie running her hands over the skin of his chest, his body precious to her. "You've lost weight."

"Up there, you can't eat enough to keep up." He palmed her breasts, teasing her nipples. "You're just as beautiful as I remember."

He made sweet, slow love to her, telling her how much he'd missed her with every touch, every kiss, every caress.

Afterward, he held her close. "On the last stretch of the climb on Lhotse, I kept wondering what the hell I was doing up there, why I wasn't home with you. You matter more to me than summits, Kenzie. I won't do anything that extreme or risky again."

"I don't know about that." Kenzie ran a hand over the muscles on his belly. "Your next adventure is pretty risky."

His brow furrowed. "What adventure?"

She tilted her head back, smiled up at him. "Parenthood."

Thanks for reading *Holding On*. I hope you enjoyed Harrison and Kenzie's story. Follow me on Facebook or on Twitter @Pamela_Clare. Join the Scarlet Springs Readers Group on Facebook to be a part of a never-ending conversation with other Scarlet Springs fans and get inside information on the series and on life in Colorado's mountains. You can also sign up to be added to my mailing list at my website to keep up to date on all my releases and to be a part of special newsletter giveaways.

Also by Pamela Clare

Contemporary Romance:

Colorado High Country Series

Romantic Suspense:

I-Team Series

About the Author

USA Today best-selling author Pamela Clare began her writing career as a columnist and investigative reporter and eventually became the first woman editor-in-chief of two different newspapers. Along the way, she and her team won numerous state and national honors, including the National Journalism Award for Public Service. In 2011, Clare was awarded the Keeper of the Flame Lifetime Achievement Award for her body of work. A single mother with two sons, she writes historical romance and contemporary romantic suspense at the foot of the beautiful Rocky Mountains. Visit her website and join her mailing list to never miss a new release!

www.pamelaclare.com

Made in the USA
San Bernardino, CA
19 July 2018